EUROPE
IN
AUTUMN

SOLARIS

EUR
N
AUT

OPE

DAVE
HUTCHINSON

UMN

First published 2014 by Solaris
an imprint of Rebellion Publishing Ltd,
Riverside House, Osney Mead,
Oxford, OX2 0ES, UK

www.solarisbooks.com

ISBN: 978 1 78108 194 5

10 9 8 7 6 5 4 3 2 1

A CIP catalogue record for this book is available from the
British Library.

Designed & typeset by Rebellion Publishing

Printed in the US

For you abide, a singing rib within
my dreaming side, you always stay

Postscript: For Gweno
Alun Lewis

PART ONE

EUROPE
IN AUTUMN

MAX'S COUSIN

1.

THE HUNGARIANS CAME into the restaurant around
nine in the evening, eight large men with gorgeously-
tailored suits and hand-stitched Italian shoes and
hundred-złoty haircuts. Michał, the maitre d', tried
to tell them that there were no tables free unless they
had a reservation, but they walked over to one of
the large tables and sat down. One of them plucked
the *Reserved* card from the middle of the tablecloth
and sailed it out across the restaurant with a snap
of the wrist and a bearish grin, causing other diners
to duck.

Max, the owner, had a protection deal with Wesoły
Ptak, but instead of calling them or the police –
either of which would have probably resulted in a
bloodbath – he seized a notepad and set off across

the restaurant to take the Hungarians' orders. This show of confidence did not prevent a number of diners signalling frantically for their bills.

The Hungarians were already boisterous, and shouted and laughed at Max while he tried to take their orders, changing their minds frequently and causing Max to start all over again. Finally, he walked back from the table to the bar, where Gosia was standing frozen with fear.

"Six bottles of Żubrówka, on the house," he murmured calmly to the girl as he went by towards the kitchen. "And try to be nimble on your feet."

Rudi, who had been standing in the kitchen doorway watching events with interest, said, "Something awful is going to happen, Max."

"Cook," Max replied, handing him the order. "Cook quickly."

By ten o'clock the Hungarians had loosened their ties and taken off their jackets and were singing and yelling at each other and laughing at impenetrable jokes. They had completed three courses of their five-course order. They were alone in the restaurant. With most of the meal completed, Rudi told the kitchen crew they could go home.

At one point, one of the Hungarians, an immense man with a face the colour of barszcz, began shouting at the others. He stood up, swaying gently, and yelled at his compatriots, who goodnaturedly yelled at him to sit down again. Sweat pouring down his face, he turned, grasped the back of a chair from the next table, and in one easy movement pivoted and flung it across the room. It crashed into the wall and smashed a sconce and brought down a mirror.

There was a moment's silence. The Hungarian stood looking at the dent in the wallpaper, frowning. Then he sat down and one of his friends poured him a drink and slapped him on the back and Max served the next course.

As the hour grew late the Hungarians became maudlin. They put their arms around each other's shoulders and began to sing songs that waxed increasingly sad as midnight approached.

Rudi, his cooking finished for the night and the kitchen tidied up and cleaned, stood in the doorway listening to their songs. The Hungarians had beautiful voices. He didn't understand the words, but the melodies were heart-achingly lonely.

One of them saw him standing there and started to beckon urgently. The others turned to see what was going on, and they too started to beckon.

"Go on," Max said from his post by the bar.

"You're joking," said Rudi.

"I am not. Go and see what they want."

"And if they want to beat me up?"

"They'll soon get bored."

"Thank you, Max," Rudi said, setting off across the restaurant.

The Hungarians' table looked as if someone had dropped a five-course meal onto it from ceiling height. The floor around it was crunchy with broken glass and smashed crockery, the carpet sticky with sauces and bits of trodden-in food.

"You cook?" said one in appalling Polish as Rudi approached.

"Yes," said Rudi, balancing his weight on the balls of his feet just in case he had to move in a hurry.

The Polish-speaker looked like a side of beef sewn into an Armani Revival suit. His face was pale and sweaty and he was wearing a shoulder-holster from which protruded the handgrip of a colossal pistol. He crooked a forefinger the size of a sausage. Rudi bent down until their faces were only a couple of centimetres apart.

"Respect!" the Hungarian bellowed. Rudi flinched at the meaty spicy alcohol-and-tobacco gale of his breath. "Everywhere we go, this fuck city, not respect!"

This statement seemed to require a reply, so Rudi said, "Oh?"

"Not respect," the Hungarian said, shaking his head sadly. His expression suddenly brightened. "Here, Restaurant Max, we got respect!"

"We always respect our customers," Max murmured, moving soundlessly up beside Rudi.

"Fuck right!" the Hungarian said loudly. "Fuck right. Restaurant Max more respect."

"And your meal?" Max inquired, smiling.

"Good fuck meal," the Hungarian said. There was a general nodding of heads around the table. He looked at Rudi and belched. "Good fuck cook. Polish food for fuck pigs, but good fuck cook."

Rudi smiled. "Thank you," he said.

The Hungarian's eyes suddenly came into focus. "Good," he said. "We gone." He snapped a few words and the others around the table stood up, all save the one who had thrown the chair, who was slumped over with his cheek pressed to the tablecloth, snoring gently. Two of his friends grasped him by the shoulders and elbows and lifted him up. Bits of food adhered to the side of his face.

"Food good," the Polish-speaker told Rudi. He took his jacket from the back of his chair and shrugged into it. He dipped a hand into his breast pocket and came up with a business card held between his first two fingers. "You need working, you call."

Rudi took the card. "Thank you," he said again.

"Okay." He put both hands to his face and swept them up and back in a movement that magically rearranged his hair and seemed to sober him up at the same time. "We gone." He looked at Max. "Clever fuck Pole." He reached into an inside jacket pocket and brought out a wallet the size and shape of a housebrick. "What is?"

"On the house," Max said. "A gift."

Rudi looked at his boss and wondered what went on underneath that shaved scalp.

The Hungarian regarded the restaurant. "We break much."

Max shrugged carelessly.

"Okay." The Hungarian removed a centimetre-thick wad of złotys from the wallet and held it out. "You take," he said. Max smiled and bowed slightly and took the money, then the Hungarians were moving towards the exit. A last burst of raucous singing, one last bar stool hurled across the restaurant, a puff of cold air through the open door, and they were gone. Rudi heard Max locking the doors behind them.

"Well," Max said, coming back down the stairs. "*That* was an interesting evening."

Rudi picked up an overturned stool, righted it, and sat at the bar. He had, he discovered, sweated entirely through his chef's whites. "I think," he said, "you should renegotiate your subscription to Wesoły Ptak."

Max went behind the bar. He bent down and started to search the shelves. "If Wesoły Ptak had turned up tonight, half of us would have wound up in the mortuary." He straightened up holding half a bottle of Starka and two glasses.

Rudi took his lighter and a tin of small cigars from his pocket. He lit one and looked at the restaurant. If he was objective about it, there was actually very little damage. Just a lot of mess for the cleaners to tackle, and they'd had wedding receptions that had been messier.

Max filled the two glasses with vodka and held one up in a toast. "Good fuck meal," he said.

Rudi looked at him for a moment. Then he picked up the other glass, returned the toast, and drained it in one go. Then they both started to laugh.

"What if they come back?" Rudi asked.

But Max was still laughing. "Good fuck meal," he repeated, shaking his head and refilling the glasses.

THE HUNGARIANS DID not come back, which seemed to bear out Max's view that they had just been out for a good time rather than intent on muscling in on Wesoły Ptak's territory.

Wesoły Ptak – the name meant *Happy Bird* – was a deeply diversified organisation. Its many divisions included prostitution, drugs, armed robbery, a soft-drink bottling factory on the outskirts of Kraków, a bus company, any number of unlicenced gambling dens, and a protection racket centred around Floriańska Street, just off the Market Square of Poland's old capital.

They were not, on the whole, known for their violent nature, preferring to apply force with surgical precision rather than in broad strokes. For instance, a restaurateur or shopkeeper who tried to organise his neighbours against the gang might find himself in hospital with anatomically-novel joints imposed on his legs. The other rebels would get the point, and the uprising would end. Another gang might be more likely to launch a massive firebombing campaign, or a wave of spectacularly bloody killings, but Happy Bird were content with a less-is-more approach.

In the wake of the Hungarians' visit to Restauracja Max, some of the other businesses began to wonder out loud just what they were paying Wesoły Ptak for. This went on for a day or so, and then the son of one of the owners suffered a minor accident at school. Nothing life-threatening, just a few bumps and scrapes, and after that the grumbling along Floriańska subsided.

A week or so later, Dariusz, Wesoły Ptak's representative, visited Restauracja Max one evening just before closing. All the staff but Rudi and Michał had gone home. Max asked Rudi to prepare two steak tartares, and he and Dariusz took a bottle of Wyborowa and a couple of glasses over to a table in the darkest corner of the deserted restaurant.

When Rudi emerged from the kitchen with the components of the steak tartares on a tray, Max and Dariusz were deep in conversation inside a cloud of cigarette smoke dimly illuminated by the little sconce on the wall above their table.

As Rudi approached with the food, Dariusz looked up and smiled. "Supper," he said.

Rudi set out on the table the trays of anchovies and chopped onions, the little bowls of pickled cucumbers, the condiments, plates of rye bread, saucers of unsalted butter, the two plates of minced beef, each with an egg yolk nestling in a hollow on top.

"We were discussing your visitors of last month," Dariusz said.

"It was an eventful evening," Rudi agreed, swapping the table's ashtray for a clean one. "Have a good meal."

"Why don't you sit and have a drink with us?" Dariusz asked.

Rudi looked at Max, sitting at the other side of the table like a smoothly prosperous Silesian Buddha, hands clasped comfortably against the broad expanse of his stomach. Max was smiling gently and looking off into some faraway vista. He nodded fractionally.

Rudi shrugged. "All right." He put the tray and the dirty ashtray on the next table, pulled up a chair, and sat.

"A busy night," Max rumbled, picking up a fork.

Rudi nodded. Takings had gone down for a couple of days after the Hungarians visited, but they were back up now. Earlier in the week, Max had murmured something about a raise, but Rudi had known him long enough not to take it seriously.

"I was wondering about Władek," Max said.

Władek was the latest of a long line of alleged cooks to arrive at Restauracja Max and then discover that they were not being paid enough for the long hours and hard work.

"He seems keen," Rudi said, watching Max use the edge of his fork to mash up the egg and beef on his plate.

"They all do, at first," Max agreed. "Then they get greedy."

"It's not greed, Max," Rudi told him.

Max shook his head. "They think they can come here and be ready to open their own restaurant after a month. They don't understand the business."

Max's philosophy of the restaurant business shared certain features with Zen Buddhism. Rudi, who was more interested in cooking than philosophy, said, "It's a common enough misconception."

"It's the same in my business," Dariusz said. Rudi had almost forgotten the little man was at the table, but there he was, mixing anchovies and chopped onion into his beef with a singleminded determination. "You should see some of our recruits, particularly these days. They think they'll be running the city in a year." He smiled sadly. "Imagine their disappointment."

"Yes," Rudi said. "The only difference is that it's easier for a sous-chef to leave a restaurant than it is for someone to leave Wesoły Ptak." Max glanced up from his plate, sighed, shook his head, and went back to mashing his meal together with his fork.

If Dariusz was offended, he gave no sign. "We're a business, like any other," he said.

"Not *quite* like any other," said Rudi. Max looked at him again. This time he frowned before returning his attention to his steak.

Dariusz also frowned, but the frown was barely discernible, and it was gone after a moment. "Well, we do less cooking, it's true," he said, and he laughed. Max smiled and shook his head.

Rudi sat back and crossed his arms. Wesoły Ptak was nothing out of the ordinary; he had encountered organisations like it in Tallinn and Riga and Vilnius, and they were all alike, and Dariusz didn't fit the demographic. He looked ordinary, a slim little middle-aged man with a cheap haircut and laugh-lines around his eyes. If he was armed, his unprepossessing off-the-peg business suit hid it wonderfully well.

"Should we worry about the Hungarians?" Rudi asked.

Dariusz looked up from his meal, his eyebrows raised in surprise. "Worry?" he asked. "Why should you worry?"

Rudi shrugged and watched Max working on his steak. Rudi hated steak tartare. The customer did all the preparation themselves, and they took up table space while they did it. Poles in particular seemed to regard it as a social occasion. They took forever about it, tasting over and over again and minutely adjusting the seasoning. When he had his own restaurant, steak tartare would not be on the menu.

Dariusz reached out and touched Rudi's forearm. Rudi noticed his fingernails were chewed. "You mustn't worry," Dariusz said.

"All right," said Rudi.

"This kind of thing happens all the time."

"Not to me it doesn't."

Dariusz smiled. "You have to think of us like nations. Poles and Hungarians are the criminal princes of Europe."

"And the Bulgarians," Max put in goodnaturedly.

Dariusz shrugged. "Yes, one must include the Bulgarians as well. We must constantly visit, check each other out, put our toes in the water," he told Rudi. "It's a matter of diplomacy."

"Do you mean what happened here the other night was a diplomatic incident?" said Rudi.

"It might well have been, if wiser heads had not prevailed." Dariusz nodded at Max.

"You haven't got a drink," Max observed. He looked across the restaurant and Michał, responding with a maitre d's telepathy, brought a clean glass over to the table for Rudi and then retreated behind the bar. Max filled the glass with vodka and said, "They were just looking for a good time, but nobody would give them one because everyone was afraid of them."

"I can't blame them," Dariusz said. He tasted his steak, winced, reached for the tabasco bottle and shook a few drops onto the meat. "A bunch of drunken Hungarians, armed to the teeth, wandering into restaurants and bars. What's one to think?"

"Indeed," Max agreed.

"It would be their own fault if someone was to over-react," Dariusz went on. He tasted his steak again, and this time it was more to his liking. This time he actually lifted a forkful into his mouth and chewed happily.

"And nobody would want that," Max said. Apparently, his steak was also prepared to his satisfaction. He started to eat.

"Well, precisely," said Dariusz. "Something like that could start a war." He looked at Rudi and cocked his head to one side. "You're from Tallinn, yes?"

"I was born in Taevaskoja," Rudi said. "But I've lived in Tallinn."

"I've never been there." Dariusz looked at his glass, but it was empty. "What's it like?"

Rudi watched Max filling Dariusz's glass. "It's all right."

"You speak very good Polish, for an Estonian."

Rudi picked up his own glass and drained it in one swallow. "Thank you."

Dariusz put down his fork and burst out laughing. He reached over and tapped Max on the shoulder. "I told you!" he said. "Didn't I tell you?"

Max smiled and nodded and went on eating. Rudi uncapped the Wyborowa and poured himself another drink. Michał had told him that Wesoły Ptak took their name from a song by Eugeniusz, one of a long line of Polish sociopolitical balladeers to rise briefly to fame before drinking themselves to death or being shot by jealous husbands or jilted lovers. The bird sings in its cage and its owners think it's happy, Michał had told him, but the bird is still in a cage. The reference had completely baffled Rudi.

"We were discussing geopolitics," Dariusz told him. "Do you think much about geopolitics?"

"I'm a cook," Rudi said. "Not a politician."

"But you must have an opinion. Everyone has an opinion."

Rudi shook his head.

Dariusz looked disbelievingly at him. He picked up his glass and took a sip of vodka. "I saw on the news last week that so far this year twelve new nations and sovereign states have come into being in Europe alone."

"And most of them won't be here this time next year," said Rudi.

"You see?" Dariusz pointed triumphantly at him. "You *do* have an opinion! I knew you would!"

Rudi sighed. "I only know what I see on the news."

"I see Europe as a glacier," Max murmured, "calving icebergs." He took a mouthful of his steak tartare and chewed happily.

Rudi and Dariusz looked at him for a long time. Then Dariusz looked at Rudi again. "Not a bad analogy," he said. "Europe is calving itself into progressively smaller and smaller nations."

"Quasi-national entities," Rudi corrected. "Polities."

Dariusz snorted. "Sanjaks. Margravates. Principalities. *Länder*. Europe sinks back into the eighteenth century."

"More territory for you," Rudi observed.

"The *same* territory," Dariusz said. "More frontiers. More red tape. More borders. More border *police*."

Rudi shrugged.

"Consider Hindenberg, for example," said Dariusz. "What must that have been like? You go to bed in Wrocław, and you wake up in Breslau. What must that have been like?"

Except that it hadn't happened overnight. What had happened to Wrocław and Opole and the little towns and villages inbetween had taken a long, bitter time, and if you followed the news it was obvious that for the Poles the matter wasn't settled yet.

"Consider the days after World War Two," Rudi said. "Churchill, Roosevelt and Stalin meet at Yalta. You go to bed in Breslau and wake up the next morning in Wrocław."

Dariusz smiled and pointed his fork at him, conceding the point.

There was a brief lull in the conversation.

"I have a cousin in Hindenberg," Max mused.

Dariusz looked at him. "For that matter," he said, "why don't you live there yourself? You're Silesian."

Max grunted.

"Do you see much of your cousin?" Dariusz asked.

Max shrugged. "Travel is difficult. Visas and so forth. I have a Polish passport, he is a citizen of Hindenberg."

"But he telephones you, yes? Emails you?"

Max shook his head. "Polish Government policy," he rumbled.

Dariusz pointed at Rudi. "You see? You see the heartache such things can cause?"

Rudi poured himself another drink, thinking that this discussion had become awfully specific all of a sudden.

"So," Dariusz said to Max. "How long is it since you were in contact with your cousin?"

"Some time," Max agreed thoughtfully, as if the subject had not occurred to him for a while. "Even the post is uncertain, these days."

"A scandal," Dariusz muttered. "A scandal."

Rudi drank his drink and stood up to go, just to see what would happen.

What happened was that Dariusz and Max continued to stare off into their respective distances, considering the unfairness of Hindenberg and Poland's attitude towards it. Rudi sat down again and looked at them.

"So here we are," he said finally. "Two men with Polish passports who would find it difficult to get a visa to enter Hindenberg. And one Estonian who can practically walk across the border unmolested."

Dariusz seemed to regain consciousness. His expression brightened. "Of course," he said. "You're Estonian, aren't you."

Rudi sucked his teeth and poured another drink.

"Rudi's an *Estonian*, Max," Dariusz said.

Rudi rubbed his eyes. "Is it," he asked, "drugs?"

Dariusz looked at him, and for a moment Rudi thought that, under the correct circumstances, the little mafioso might be quite a scary person. "No," said Dariusz.

"Fissile material?"

Dariusz shook his head.

"Espionage?"

"Best you don't know," said Max.

"A favour," Dariusz told him earnestly. "You do us a favour, we owe you a favour." He smiled. "That can't be *entirely* bad, can it?"

It could be bad in any number of unforeseen ways. Rudi silently cursed himself. He should have just served the food and gone home.

"How do I make the delivery?"

"Well," Dariusz said, scratching his head, "that's more or less up to you. And it's not a delivery."

LATER THAT NIGHT, stepping out of the shower, Rudi caught sight of himself in the mirror over the sink. He took a towel off the rail and stood looking at his reflection.

Well, there he was. A little shorter than average. Slim. Short mousy brown hair. Bland, inoffensive face; not Slavic, not Aryan, not *anything*, really. No sign of the Lapp heritage his father had always claimed for the family. Hazel eyes. The odd nick here and there, medals of his life as a chef. That scar on his forearm from an overturned wok in Vilnius, the one just above it from the time he slipped in the Turk's kitchen in Riga and the paring knife he was carrying got turned around somehow and went straight through his uniform sleeve and the skin and muscle beneath.

"Don't run in my kitchen!" the Turk had shouted at him. Then he had bandaged Rudi's arm and called for an ambulance.

Rudi lifted his right hand above his head and turned so he could see the long curving scar that started just above his hipbone and ended beside his right nipple. Not a kitchen accident, this one. Skinheads, the day he tried to find work in Warnemünde. He still didn't know whether they had meant to kill him or just scare him, and he thought that even they had not been sure. He had taken it as an omen that his wanderings along the Baltic coast were over, and he headed inland, first to Warsaw, then Kraków.

The first thing Max did after concluding his job interview was hold out a mop.

"I've done all that," Rudi protested, pointing to the envelope containing his references which Max was holding in his other hand. "Riga, Tallinn..."

"You want to work in my kitchen, first you clean it," Max told him. "Then we'll see."

Rudi really considered walking out of Restauracja Max right there and then, considered going out onto Floriańska and walking back down to the station and catching a train away from this polluted little city, but he was low on cash and the job came with a cramped little room up ten flights of stairs above the restaurant and he was just tired of travelling for the moment, so he took the mop, telling himself that this was only temporary, that as soon as he had adequate funds he'd be off again in search of a kitchen that appreciated him.

He pushed that mop for eight months before Pani Stasia, Max's fearsome chef, even allowed him to approach food. By then he was locked into a battle of wills with the wizened little woman, and the only way he was going to leave Max's kitchen was feet first.

Looking back, it seemed astounding to him that he had stood so much. He'd done this for Sergei in Tallinn, and for the Turk, and for Big Ron in that appalling kitchen in Wilno, but for Pani Stasia there was something gratingly *personal* about it, as if she had made it her life's work to break him. She yelled constantly at him. "Bring this, bring that. Clean this, clean that. So you call this *clean*, Baltic prick? Hurry, hurry. *Don't run in my kitchen!* Faster! Faster!"

He was by no means the only member of the crew to catch Pani Stasia's wrath. She treated everyone equally. One of her hip joints was deformed, and she walked with the aid of a black lacquered carbon fibre cane as thin as a pencil and as strong as a girder. Everyone, even Max, had heard the whistle of Pani Stasia's cane at some time or other as it described a swift arc towards the backs of their legs.

It was understood in the business that great chefs could be violently temperamental, and if one wanted to study under them one had to endure all kinds of invective and physical violence. The Turk, who was an outstanding chef, had once knocked Rudi unconscious with a single punch for overcooking a portion of asparagus. Pani Stasia was not an outstanding chef. She was a competent chef working in a little Polish restaurant. But something about her fury lit a slumbering resistance in him which told him that this nasty little old woman was not going to drive him from her kitchen, was not going to wear him down.

So he mopped and cleaned and washed up and the skin on his hands reddened and cracked and bled and his legs hurt so much that some nights he could barely climb up to his cubbyhole in the attic. He kept going, refused to give in.

Pani Stasia, sensing the one-man resistance movement which had sprung up in her kitchen, focused her attention on Rudi. This made him popular with the other staff, who no longer had to suffer quite so much.

One day, for some imagined slight, she chased him from the kitchen in an access of rage extraordinary even by her standards, limping after him surprisingly quickly and belabouring him about the head and shoulders with her cane. One whistling blow split his left earlobe and left him deaf in that ear for hours. One of the cooks ran out into the restaurant and told Max that Pani Stasia was killing Rudi, and when Max did nothing the cook went to the phone in the entranceway and called the police, who decided that their assets were best deployed elsewhere that evening and didn't bother to respond to the call.

Max found Rudi some time later squatting down

in the alley beside the restaurant, the shoulder and arm of his whites spotted with blood.

"You'd be better off leaving," Max told him.

Rudi looked up at the owner and shook his head.

Max watched him for a few moments, then nodded and reached down a hand to help him up.

It went on and on, until one night after closing time he was mopping the floor and she came up behind him almost soundlessly and raised her cane and he turned and caught it as it whistled towards him and for almost a minute she squeaked and struggled and swore and tried to pull the cane from his grasp. Finally, she stopped struggling and swearing and looked up at him with hot, angry eyes.

He let go of the cane and she snatched it back and stood looking at him for a few moments longer. Then she turned and stomped across the kitchen towards the exit.

The next morning, Max greeted him with the news of a pay rise and a promotion.

Not that this made much material difference. He still had to mop and clean and fetch and carry, and he still had to suffer Pani Stasia's fury. Now, however, she expected him to learn to cook as well.

She punished every mistake, no matter how small. Once, half conscious with exhaustion, he put a fresh batch of salad into a bowl with some which had been standing already prepared for some minutes, and she almost beat him black and blue.

But he did learn. The first thing he learned was that, if he wanted to remain in Pani Stasia's kitchen, he was going to have to forget his four-year drift along the Baltic coast. The things he had learned from the Turk and the other chefs he'd worked under meant nothing to the little old woman.

Fractionally, month after month, her periods of displeasure grew further and further apart, until one day, almost eighteen months after he first set foot in Restauracja Max, she allowed him to prepare one cover.

She wouldn't allow it to be served, however. She prepared a duplicate cover herself and sent it out into the restaurant instead, and then set about tasting Rudi's attempt.

As Rudi watched her he became aware that the whole kitchen had fallen silent. He looked around and found himself overwhelmed by what he thought of as a *movie moment*. Everyone in the kitchen was watching Pani Stasia. Even Max, standing just inside the swing door that led into the restaurant. It was, Rudi, thought, that moment in a film where the callow greenhorn finally gains the grudging respect of his mentor. He also knew that life wasn't like the movies, and that Pani Stasia would spit the food out onto the tiled floor and then beat him senseless.

In the event, life and the movies converged just enough for Pani Stasia to turn and lean on her cane and look at her audience. She would, she told them finally, perhaps consider feeding Rudi's service to her dog.

All the crew applauded. Rudi never heard them. He thought later that he was the only one of all of them to notice just how old Pani Stasia suddenly seemed.

She died that summer, and Rudi simply took over. There was no formal announcement from Max, no new contract, nothing at all. Not even a pay rise. He simply inherited the kitchen. He and Max were the only mourners at the funeral.

"I never found out anything about her," he said as they watched the coffin being lowered into the ground.

"She was," Max said, "my mother."

2.

It was snowing in Gliwice, fat white flakes settling gently out of a sky boiling with jaundiced clouds. He had to wait two hours for the local train to Strzelce Opolskie.

The rattling little local was full of Silesians speaking German-accented Polish and Polish-accented German. The passengers sharing his compartment were curious as to why he had chosen to visit Hindenberg, but he spoke German with a strong Estonian accent and there seemed to be a common assumption – at least among his fellow travellers – that the Baltic peoples were a law unto themselves.

"I'm on holiday," he told them. "I want to see Hindenberg." The idea of an Estonian wanting to see Hindenberg seemed such a novelty that it excused practically everything, which was what he was counting on.

A couple of kilometres outside Gliwice, some Polish kids ran alongside the track and threw stones at the train. Nobody paid them much attention; it was unusual these days to travel by train in Poland

and *not* have something thrown at you, or dropped on you from a bridge, or placed on the tracks in front of you. Rudi supposed it had something to do with Polish resentment about the Line, but Polish resentment about the Line was a complex thing, and Poles had so many other things to feel resentful about these days that it was hard to be sure. Perhaps it was just a fashion, one of those senseless neurotic fads that sometimes overtook cultures, like elevator surfing or out of town shopping malls or crush music.

The train rocked and rolled slowly through grubby little industrial towns. The Fall of the Wall was just a distant misty memory now, but Eastern Europe still needed a good scrub and a lick of paint. Some of Poland's most polluted towns had buildings of mediaeval splendour, but they were all crusted with centuries of soot. He had seen a documentary in which a Professor from the Jagiellonian University in Kraków had said that nobody *dared* clean the buildings because the dirt was the only thing standing between them and the acid rain.

Beyond the window, a snow-covered landscape of wastelands and forests and disused steelworks and rusting coking plants overlooked by monolithic Communist-era blocks of flats. A small car overturned in a ditch beside the track, its tires wearing caps of filthy ice. The sun sat low down in the sky, wan and chilly through the falling snow, too weak to cast shadows. Some of the Silesians further along the carriage started to sing. Rudi closed his eyes and dozed.

North of Strzelce Opolskie, the line ran into the border station between two ten-metre-high fences of close-woven metal mesh topped with extravagant spirals of razor ribbon. Looking through the mesh was like looking through fog. Rudi could see a bus station on the other side, people going home after work, cars orbiting a big roundabout, houses, blocks of flats, a factory chimney painted with orange and white hoops pouring purple smoke into the sky.

As the town thinned out, the train slowed down. The Silesians began to get out of their seats and put on their coats, gather their baggage from the overhead racks, settle their hats on their heads. Rudi sat where he was, looking out of the window. The borders along the Baltic were no more formal than lines on the map; this whole business was a brand new experience for him, and he was honestly interested in what the border arrangements were like here.

The train seemed to be approaching a world illuminated by a younger, bluer sun than the one that was now settling under the haze of pollution on the horizon. Lines of tall posts carried spotlights that were actually painful to look at directly. They washed out what remained of the natural daylight, and much of the natural colour outside as well. The whole frontier station sat in the middle of a great pool of this light. It was so well lit that Rudi found himself wondering if it was visible from orbit.

The border station was a compact collection of low brick buildings lining a platform patrolled by black-uniformed officers of the Polish Border Guard. More mesh and ribbon rose beyond the complex. Disembarking passengers were directed to one of the buildings, there to shuffle in four queues to passport and customs desks. When Rudi's turn came, he put his rucksack through the scanner on the desk and watched the Polish official watching its progress on a monitor.

"Passport," said the Pole.

Rudi handed over his passport, and the Pole slotted it into a reader built into the desk. He glanced at one of his screens, then at Rudi.

"Purpose of visit?"

"I'm on holiday," said Rudi.

The Pole looked at him a moment longer, then he pulled the passport from its slot and held it out. "Pass."

"Thank you," said Rudi. He took his passport, stepped past the desk, and took his rucksack from the scanner.

On the other side of the building, down a short corridor, was an identical desk. Behind this desk sat an official wearing a field grey uniform.

"Passport," the official said in German.

Rudi gave up his passport again and watched as the Hindenberger slotted it. He imagined the same farce going on in buildings on the other side of the track, where people were shuffling along an identical corridor to leave Hindenberg. Dariusz had told him that it sometimes took four hours to process each trainload, depending on how bloody-minded the respective governments were feeling that day.

"Purpose of visit?" asked the Hindenberger.

"I'm on holiday."

The official looked at him with an expression of mild astonishment. He checked his screen again. "Estonian."

"Yes."

The Hindenberger shook his head slightly.

"I only get a week's holiday a year," Rudi told him. "I'm a chef. If I take any time off my boss has to employ an agency chef."

The Hindenberger shook his head again. He unslotted Rudi's passport and held it out. "You need to get another job, mate."

"I know," Rudi said, taking his passport. He walked down the corridor and emerged on another platform, where a train was waiting to leave for Breslau.

3.

IN THE LATTER years of the twentieth century, Europe had echoed with the sound of doors opening as the borderless continent of the Schengen Agreement had, with some national caveats, come into being.

It hadn't lasted. The early years of the twenty-first century brought a symphony of slamming doors. Economic collapse, paranoia about asylum seekers – and, of course, GWOT, the ongoing Global War On Terror – had brought back passport and immigration checks of varying stringency, depending on whose frontiers you were crossing. Then the Xian Flu had brought back quarantine checks and national borders as a means of controlling the spread of the disease; it had killed, depending on whose figures you believed, somewhere between twenty and forty million people in Europe alone. It had also effectively killed Schengen and kicked the already somewhat rickety floor out from under the EU.

The Union had struggled into the twenty-first century and managed to survive in some style for a few more years of bitching and infighting and cronyism. Then it had spontaneously begun to throw off progressively smaller and crazier nation-states, like a sunburned holidaymaker shedding curls of skin.

Nobody really understood why this had happened.

What was unexpected was that the Union had continued to flake away, bit by bit, even after the Xian Flu. Officially, it still existed, but it existed in scattered bits and pieces, like Burger King franchises, mainly in England and Poland and Spain and Belgium, and it spent most of its time making loud noises in the United Nations. The big thing in Europe these days was *countries*, and there were more and more of them every year.

The Continent was alive with Romanov heirs and Habsburg heirs and Grimaldi heirs and Saxe-Coburg Gotha heirs and heirs of families nobody had ever heard of who had been dispossessed sometime back in the fifteenth century, all of them seeking to set up their own pocket nations. They found they had to compete with thousands of microethnic groups who suddenly wanted European homelands as well, and religious groups, and Communists, and Fascists, and U2 fans. There had even been, very briefly, a city-state – or more accurately a village-state – run by devotees of the works of Günther Grass. Rudi was vaguely sorry that Grassheim had been reabsorbed by the Pomeranian Republic - itself a polity of only ten or fifteen years' standing. He really liked *The Tin Drum*.

* * *

THE INDEPENDENT SILESIAN State of Hindenberg – formerly the Polish cities of Opole and Wrocław (formerly the German cities of Opeln and Breslau – formerly the Prussian towns of... etc, etc) and the areas around them – existed as a kind of Teuton island in a Slavic sea. Poland, having been forced by the EU, UN and NATO to accede to an ethnic Silesian homeland, had refused to cede more territory to give the young state a land-bridge to Greater Germany. Hindenberg had responded by imposing draconian visa requirements for Poles, to which Poland had responded by pegging the exchange rate of the złoty and the Hindenberg mark artificially low.

There had been border disputes, frontier actions, Polish war games within yards of Hindenberg's border fence. Hindenberg unofficially offered its services as a haven for some of Poland's wealthier and more powerful mafia bosses, and refused to sign an extradition treaty with its Slavic neighbour.

The latest tit-for-tat involved Hindenberg's railway authority changing the state's track gauge. The Polish response had been to embargo postal deliveries to the Silesian state.

Eventually, accepted wisdom suggested, things would settle down. Until then, Poles wishing to visit Hindenberg had to pay thousands of złotys and wait six months for a visa, Hindenbergers visiting Poland found that one H-Mark was worth about four groszy, Polish trains could not run across Hindenberg on their way to Poznań and the Greater German border, and postal deliveries into Hindenberg were in a state of chaos.

While the Poles and the Hindenbergers squabbled, telephone and data cable lines were tapped or cut altogether and radio, television and satellite frequencies were scrambled. Nobody living within five kilometres of the Polish side of the frontier could watch television or use any kind of wifi.

Rudi thought it was a ludicrous but somehow very Polish state of affairs. There was an old saying that the Poles weren't truly happy unless someone was telling them what to do. Rudi had observed that what *actually* made Poles happy was listening to someone telling them what to do, and then doing the exact opposite.

BAHNHOF BRESLAU WAS full of light, a colossal wedge of glass and tubular steel inserted into the heart of the old Polish-German city. It was awesomely clean. Rudi actually heard his footsteps echo on the marble floor as he walked from the platform to the main entrance. Just outside the automatic doors, he stopped and stared.

It wasn't just the station. The whole city was full of light.

Though Greater Germany had given up its constitutional claim to the lands in Western Poland long ago, there was a tacit understanding that Berlin was in fact quite pleased that the ethnic Silesians had finally found a home. Greater Germany was no longer quite as great as it once was, having begun to fission into ever-smaller and progressively more anarchic autonomous regions, so the prospect of extending German influence eastward seemed rather attractive. So much so that a very large amount of D-Marks had found their way into the Hindenberg National Bank, and the Hindenbergers had used them to erase Polish Wrocław and start again.

So Breslau – and Opole, and much of the land inbetween – strongly resembled Berlin; a great mass of office buildings and apartment buildings, interspersed with what mementoes of Prussian architecture had survived two world wars, fifty years of Communist occupation and six decades of Polish administration. The road in front of the station was bustling with cars and buses, and across the road rose the shining monolith of a Marriott. Rudi thought that pretty much said it all; when the hotel chains moved in you could more or less bet that a polity was there to stay.

A line of BMW taxis stood waiting outside the station. Rudi got into one and gave the driver the name of the hotel where he had booked a room for the night, and the car quietly whisked him away.

RUDI HAD READ his share of spy thrillers, so the situation he found himself in seemed familiar. More than familiar, actually; it smacked of cliché. Cloak and dagger, clandestine meetings on darkened streets in Central Europe. He didn't feel nervous, particularly. Faintly embarrassed, perhaps, but not nervous.

When the taxi turned onto Freytag Allee, not far from the hotel, Rudi leaned forward from the back seat and said, "Tell you what, mate, drop me here. I can walk the rest of the way."

The driver pulled over to the side of the road, then turned in his seat and looked at Rudi around the head-rest.

"I'm here on holiday," Rudi said. "It seems stupid to drive everywhere."

"There've been a lot of muggings around here recently," the driver said, not sounding particularly concerned.

"I heard that Hindenberg had conquered crime."

The driver laughed. "That's good," he said, taking Rudi's fare. "Conquered crime. Very good." He was still laughing as he drove off, leaving Rudi standing on the pavement. Rudi waited until the taxi turned a corner. Then he walked back up the street.

Freytag Allee was not, he was delighted to find, that darkened street in Central Europe. It was a brightly-lit shopping street, and it was still busy with pedestrians and traffic. Everyone seemed well-dressed and prosperous and happy, which was not what he was used to in Kraków. Rudi wandered along, looking in shop windows, not hurrying. He stood for five minutes in front of a Peugeot dealership, behind whose faintly-green bulletproof glass windows stood a dozen immaculately-clean cars. He looked at the prices, did the conversion from marks to złotys, and estimated that he would have to work in Max's kitchen for the next hundred and fifteen years if he wanted to buy a Peugeot in Hindenberg.

He wandered on, taking his time. A little further on, about a hundred paperscreen televisions were stuck to the inside of a huge window, all of them tuned to the same football match. From the shirts the players were wearing, Rudi gathered it was the Hungary-England international, and from the action on the pitch and on the terraces he gathered it was a spectacularly ill-tempered game.

After about five minutes, a man came along the street and stood beside him, and together they watched the match.

"That was never a goal," the man said in German after a while.

"It might have been," Rudi said. "I don't think anybody understands the offside trap any more."

"That's true," the man conceded. "*I* certainly don't."

Rudi glanced sideways, saw a stout, bulky figure well wrapped up against the cold evening. He was wearing a long overcoat with its collar turned up, and a hat with a broad brim pulled down over his brows. He also appeared to be wearing a scarf wrapped around his neck and lower face, so that all Rudi could see of him were his eyes and his body language.

"This is a very sad city," said the man.

"Many cities are," Rudi agreed, as Dariusz had told him to.

The bulky figure beside him seemed to relax. "Fifty-seven," he said.

"Fifty-seven," Rudi repeated.

The man put his hands in his pockets and started to walk away. After a few steps, he stopped, turned, and looked at Rudi.

"You're very young," he said.

Rudi tried to remember whether Dariusz had given him a response for this particular phrase. He decided that it was actually a bona fide scrap of conversation, and he found to his surprise that he was completely flatfooted by it. "I'm sorry," he said.

The bulky man looked at him for a few moments longer. Then he shrugged and turned and walked away along the street. Rudi watched him turn a corner and vanish out of sight beyond the Peugeot dealership.

And that was it. Rudi stood in front of the shop window and watched the Hungary-England game on the other side of the glass. He couldn't quite work out where the pictures were coming from. Not from terrestrial or satellite sources, certainly; the Poles would have jammed them. Ditto for cable links from Greater Germany. Maybe someone had brought the footage in on a stick earlier this evening. The cameras showed a shot of the stands. Someone had managed to smuggle a yachting flare past the metal detectors and the explosive detectors and the random security pat-downs. In a sea of heaving bodies, thick orange smoke boiled out across the crowd from a furious white-hot pinpoint.

He stood there for ten or fifteen minutes. Hungary won a penalty and scored a goal. There were no sirens. Nobody else approached him. Nobody tried to arrest him. Nobody tried to mug him. Finally, he wandered off to his hotel.

4.

KRAKÓW LOOKED DIRTY. There was no way around it; after Breslau, it looked dirty. Stately, beautiful, but filthy. Stumbling down from the train at Kraków Główny, he found himself noticing the pollution in the air for the first time in years. It was a gorgeous sunrise. Kraków had more than its share of gorgeous sunrises, because of the pollution. For the same reason, also it tended to have apocalyptic sunsets.

Rudi walked towards the centre of the city. Some of the pizza and kiełbasa stalls were already open in front of the Barbakan, and the smells of meat and hot oil on the morning breeze made his mouth water, but he walked past them. He thought that only tourists were foolish enough to risk buying a slice of pizza from one of the stalls.

Floriańska was almost deserted. Rudi let himself through Restauracja Max's front door and locked it behind him.

Downstairs, the tables and chairs were stacked along the sides of the room and one of Max's Filipina cleaning women was pushing an ancient Dyson vacuum cleaner across the carpet. Rudi waved hello to her and pushed through the swing-doors into the kitchen.

Max was standing among the tiled and stainless steel surfaces, clipboard in hand, ticking off the morning's food delivery.

"That bastard Tomek's light on his pork delivery again," he told Rudi.

"Where's Mirek?" Mirek was Rudi's sous-chef, a sometime presence in the kitchen who Rudi was working himself up to dismissing.

Max shrugged. Unlike his mother, Max was at a loss when it came to the kitchen staff. In Rudi's absence, Mirek should have been in charge of the kitchen, but Mirek was a force of nature, captious and unreliable. He was also, unfortunately, an outstanding chef, and Max's customers were going to miss him, even if Rudi didn't.

"I'll phone Tomek," said Rudi, stuffing his bag under one of the work-surfaces. Tomek had his own problems, mostly concerning suppliers and staff and kickbacks. The restaurant business had a lot in common with international relations; there was an awful lot of diplomacy, more often than not of the gunboat kind. He took off his jacket. "Have you missed me?"

"It would have been better if you had been here," Max admitted.

"Does that get me a raise?"

Max gestured with the clipboard.

Rudi hung his jacket in a cupboard and rubbed his eyes. It seemed absurd to feel jetlagged after having travelled such a small distance. "I'll sort out Mirek."

"I had to get an agency chef in last night," Max told him.

Which, in Rudi and Max's world, was about the worst thing that could happen to a restaurant. Rudi thought of the smoothing of feathers he was going to have to do with his crew, and said, "Who was it?"

"Paweł Grabiański."

Which was not the disaster it might have been, although Rudi's crew should really have been able to cope without him and Mirek. He'd thought he had them organised better than that. There should have been a shuffling of the pecking order. *Someone* should have taken charge. He realised he was going to have to yell at them, something he had once sworn he would never do in his kitchen.

"Paweł's a pretty good chef," he said lamely.

"He just looks so *sad* all the time," Max told him. "Like he's going to burst into tears."

"I've had days like that myself," Rudi said, taking the clipboard from Max's unresisting fingers. Max had only checked a couple of items from the stack of recycled plastic crates sitting in the middle of the kitchen.

"You look tired."

"I'll get everything cleared away and I'll have a nap for a couple of hours, all right?"

"You should go home and sleep properly," Max told him. "I'll call the agency for today's lunch service."

"They might send Paweł again."

Max's face showed an agony of indecision.

"I'll be all right," Rudi said. He tucked the clipboard under his armpit and went across to get himself a cup of coffee from the espresso machine he'd bullied Max into installing in the kitchen.

Max was obviously struggling not to ask about what had happened in Hindenberg. Rudi said, "I saw him."

"And how did he look?"

"It was dark; his face was in shadow." Rudi wondered how long they were going to continue the charade about Max's 'cousin.' He said, "I have to talk to Dariusz."

"And so you shall," Dariusz said, stepping out from the corridor that led into the courtyard behind Restauracja Max. "And the magic number is?"

"Fifty-seven," said Rudi.

"You're sure?" said Dariusz.

"Fifty-seven," Rudi repeated.

"You've done very well," said Dariusz, and he turned and went back down the corridor. Rudi heard the courtyard door open and close. He and Max looked at each other.

"Did he seem well?" Max asked.

Rudi poured himself a cup of coffee. "I told you; it was dark." This was obviously not sufficient for Max, so he said, "He certainly *sounded* well."

Max nodded. "Good," he said, a little awkwardly, Rudi thought. He turned away and walked towards the swing-door of the dining room. "Good."

AND THAT SEEMED to be the end of Rudi's little adventure. Max didn't mention it again, and Dariusz didn't come back to the restaurant. It was as if nothing had happened, as if he had never taken the train to Hindenberg. He cooked, he watched sous-chefs arrive in the kitchen and then depart some days later shouting about minimum wages and unsociable hours. Max shook his head sadly, and they went on with their lives.

The chilly Polish spring gradually became the lush, oppressive Polish summer. The air conditioning in the kitchen broke down and the kitchen staff began to wilt, and in some cases to faint. Kraków began to bake in the heat. The city swelled with tourists.

One busy evening in July, one of the customers asked if he could give his personal compliments to the chef, and Rudi went out into the restaurant to receive them.

The customer was a tall wafer-thin man with gelled-back hair and a bushy walrus-style moustache of the kind you didn't see very often in Central Europe these days. He was wearing an expensive German business suit, and his wife was wearing a startling off-the-shoulder backless – and very nearly frontless – purple evening dress.

Rudi sat and allowed the husband to pour him a drink and congratulate him. The wife smiled and complimented him on the meal and leaned forward to pat him on the knee and ask for his recipe for bigos, and he found that he could see down the front of her dress all the way to her pubic hair.

He looked away and saw Max and another man standing almost toe to toe in one of the darkest corners of the restaurant. They seemed to be having a very quiet, very intense conversation. He thought there was something familiar about the other man's build and body language. Then he realised that it was familiar because all he had *ever* seen of him was his build and body language.

And then Max and the other man embraced each other. Just like long-lost cousins, in fact.

SOME WEEKS AFTER that – and Rudi thought later that they had actually given him time to think about it – Dariusz came into the restaurant and asked to see him.

"I thought you ought to know that Max's cousin is very grateful to you," said the little mafioso.

"Max mentioned it," said Rudi.

Dariusz sat back and lit a cigarette and looked around the restaurant. "How would you like," he said, "to do that kind of thing for a living?"

"I'm a chef," Rudi replied. "For a living."

Dariusz inhaled on his cigarette, held the smoke in his lungs for longer than Rudi would have thought was medically advisable or physically possible, then exhaled a tenuous aromatic haze.

"How would you like to do that kind of thing as a hobby?" he asked.

"All right," said Rudi. "So long as it's a well-*paid* sort of hobby."

THE SORCERER'S APPRENTICE

1.

FABIO WAS FIFTEEN hours late coming in from London.

"Fucking English," he said when Rudi finally met him at Jan Paweł II/Balice. "They spend about a thousand years trying to decide whether or not to join the Union, and when they do they become absolute fanatics. I mean, it's *totally* offensive. Here, carry this."

Rudi took Fabio's carry-on bag, which was considerably heavier than it looked, and followed the little Swiss-Italian across the arrivals lounge.

It transpired, between the arrivals gate and the taxi rank outside, that the English were having one of their periodic paranoid episodes – drugs, terrorism, immunisation, whatever – and Fabio had been held up while they confiscated and checked his passport and travel documents.

"I mean, not allowing one *in*, I can understand that," he fumed. "But not allowing one *out*. What sort of mind thinks like that?" He looked at the motley line of cars pulled up outside the terminal and shook his head. "No, I'm not getting into any of these taxis. I was completely ripped off the last time I got a taxi from this airport. I should have flown in to Katowice, I never had any problems with the taxi drivers at Katowice. We'll take the bus into town. Follow me."

Rudi followed.

"And they put me in that *disgusting* hotel at Heathrow while I waited," Fabio told him.

EVERY STUDENT NEEDS a teacher, Dariusz had told him, and Fabio was to be his. He was short and chubby and well-dressed enough to be mugged within minutes of setting foot on any street in Western Europe. His suit was from the cutting edge of the Armani Revival and his shoes had been sewn by wizened artisans in Cordova. His luggage cost more than a flat in central Kraków. He was, Rudi thought, one of the least covert people he had ever seen. He thought it was a miracle the English authorities hadn't arrested Fabio and then just looked for a crime to charge him with, because he was almost a caricature of a Central European *biznisman*.

Fabio had a dim view of Kraków's hotels. The Cracovia wasn't good enough for him. He refused to even cross the threshold of the Europa. He claimed the head chef of the Bristol was a convicted poisoner. He wound up staying at Rudi's flat.

"Forget all that fucking idealism about Schengen," he told Rudi on his first evening, after hoovering down the meal Rudi had cooked for him. "People in this business care about two things only. Money and prestige. You get money by doing your job, and you get prestige by taking insane risks." He drank his wine in one swallow and winced. "This is horrible."

"It's a Mouton Rothschild '41," Rudi said.

"'41," said Fabio, narrowing his eyes at his glass as if it had done him a personal wrong. "What a disgusting year."

"It's a vintage year."

"Not for me it wasn't. Don't you have anything else to drink? And that steak was overdone, by the way."

THEY CALLED THEMSELVES *Les Coureurs des Bois*, and they delivered mail.

Even before Europe had blossomed with new countries, there had been a healthy courier business, some of it legal, rather more of it not. Some things were just too sensitive or important or flat-out illegal to trust to the public mail or electronic transfer. In those days, a canny courier could wangle themselves a cheap flight anywhere on Earth if they chose their assignment well.

These days, things were more complicated. Border disputes often meant that delivering mail from polity A to nation B was impossible. So people contacted *Les Coureurs*, and the mail got through. Sometimes the mail consisted of people for whom the passage from polity A to nation B might otherwise be impossibly delicate. Sometimes it was items which nation B might be narrowminded enough to consider illegal.

They were, in other words, smugglers, although when Rudi voiced this opinion Fabio pointed out that, as with so many things, the term depended very much on your point of view.

Nobody knew who they were. Conventional wisdom had it that they were a phenomenon of the times, a gradual accretion of little courier firms into an entity which had things in common with the CIA and the Post Office. You got in touch with them the way you made that awkward first contact with a drug dealer, by knowing someone who knew someone who knew someone.

Rudi thought the popular media had inflated them out of all proportion. They were just couriers, and people had been couriering stuff around Europe since at least the Middle Ages, and smuggling things for considerably longer. They were also, if Fabio was representative, appalling houseguests. Among numerous other little personality quirks, Fabio had a thing about rearranging furniture. Every evening when Rudi got back to the flat he would find the furniture in some new configuration, and Fabio standing in the middle of the living room looking at it. He'd thought at first that the plump little Coureur was practising some bizarre Swiss form of feng shui, but after a week or so he had to wonder if Fabio wasn't just the tiniest little bit deranged.

They went over and over his trip to Hindenberg, in obsessive detail. What he remembered, who he had spoken to, where he had been, what he had observed about the people he interacted with, from the border officials to the taxi driver in Breslau to the waiter who had served his breakfast at the Pension Adler the next morning.

"You kept it simple, which is good," Fabio told him. "Simple is often best, but not always. Sometimes it's necessary to make things as complicated as possible. And sometimes you just have to wing it." He took a sip from his cup and pouted. "What do you call this?"

Rudi looked at the cup. "'Coffee,'" he said.

Fabio returned his cup to its saucer. "Not where I come from, it's not."

"You've been drinking it all week."

Fabio shook his head. "I can't stand this 'continental roast.' What's that supposed to mean? 'Continental roast.'"

Rudi stood up. "I need some fresh air."

"He's very good," mused Dariusz.

"He's driving me out of my mind," said Rudi.

Dariusz lit a cigarette. "What, precisely, bothers you about him?"

"How long do you have?"

Dariusz chuckled.

Rudi sighed. They were in Pani Halina's on Senatorska. Because Rudi knew Halina's chef, and because Dariusz was who he was, they had been given one of the restaurant's private tables, away from the lunchtime crowd of students and tourists and out of work actors.

"Nothing I cook for him is any good," he said.

Dariusz snorted goodnaturedly. "I think you'll find that people do have their own tastes in food, Rudi."

"Where I come from, it's good manners not to criticise your host's cooking."

"Perhaps it's different in Switzerland." The little mafioso shrugged. "I don't know, I've never been there. Next?"

"He rearranges my furniture."

Dariusz looked at him and narrowed his eyes. Then he shrugged again. "Fabio is accustomed to a life of action, not a life cooped up in your flat. He sounds restless."

"'Restless'?"

"Look." Dariusz waved Rudi's misgivings away. "He's here to teach you. He's to be the… the Merlin to your Arthur. The Obi-Wan to your Anakin. We have to be indulgent of geniuses."

"Must we let them move our furniture about?"

"If moving furniture about is what makes them happy."

"Dariusz, there's something *wrong* with him."

Dariusz shook his head. "Indulge him, Rudi. Listen and learn."

In Rudi's opinion, whoever had set up the Coureurs had overdosed on late twentieth century espionage fiction. Coureur operational jargon, as passed on by Fabio, sounded like something from a John le Carré novel. *Legends* were fictitious identities. *Stringers* were non-Coureur personnel, or entry-level Coureurs, who did makework like scoping out locations in the field or maintaining legends. *Pianists* were hackers, *tailors* provided technical support, *cobblers* forged documents – Rudi knew *that* euphemism had been in use in espionage circles as far back as the 1930s. He thought it was ridiculous.

The business with Max's cousin had been a test, that much was obvious. As Dariusz described it, Max's cousin had already been in contact with the Coureurs, and had been presented with a menu of options for his escape from Hindenberg. All Rudi had done was relay his favoured option. Any stringer could have done it; Max's cousin, in the face of postal problems and telephone and radio jamming and interception of emails, could have sent up smoke signals. It had been, more than anything, a test of nerve, a test of how Rudi would handle the problem.

It seemed he had passed the test. And Fabio was his reward.

"Never ever undervalue a stringer," Fabio told him. "Consider a typical stringer – we shall call him Ralf. Ralf works in a delicatessen in Lausanne. He has a wife named Chantelle, some children, maybe a dog. For much of the time, he lives a normal life. He hates his boss. He fucks his wife. He plays with his children. He takes the dog for a walk."

"Maybe," said Rudi.

"You're interrupting me," Fabio warned.

"You said *maybe* a dog." After two months with Fabio, Rudi had learned to take his pleasures where he could find them. "Now you're telling me he takes his dog for a walk."

Fabio narrowed his eyes.

"I just wondered whether we should take the dog as a given now," Rudi said.

Fabio frowned.

"These things are important," said Rudi. "You must agree."

Fabio watched him a moment longer, then looked away into the distance. "But on occasion, Ralf is asked to do more *specialised* work," he continued. "He is asked to renew a passport in a false name, to get a parking ticket, to take a lease on an apartment in Geneva. These are all things which contribute to the building of a legend. And Ralf knows *all the details* of these transactions. Invaluable operational intelligence. If Ralf should fall into unkind hands, and if he should tell all he knows, the information could bring any number of Situations crashing to the ground."

It wasn't just the jargon, Rudi thought. If Fabio was representative, *Les Coureurs* really considered themselves some form of espionage agency. Cloak and dagger, night-time streets in Central Europe, one-time pads, the whole thing. He wondered if he shouldn't have another quiet chat with Dariusz.

Fabio looked levelly at him. "Now you can cook me my dinner," he said. "And then I have some homework for you. And I don't want any of that disgusting tripe stew you served last night; my insides still haven't recovered."

'HOMEWORK' TURNED OUT to be an interminable round of offices and bureaucrats. A lease signed here, a driving licence applied for there, all in different names. He was expected to buy a car, renew a passport, take a train-ride to Sosnowiec and return with the ticket stubs, open a bank account in the name of Anton Blum, telephone a man named Grudziński and complain about the waste disposal unit in a flat. All the little tracks one leaves every day without thinking about it. And at one point, footsore and really not terribly impressed with the life of a stringer, he thought he saw the point of Fabio's tale about Ralf and his maybe dog. He could conceivably ruin half a dozen different Situations. If he had the faintest idea what he was doing. And for whom. And why.

Max said, "I suppose you could just stop any time you wanted," which was really Max-speak for 'You're spending too much time as a Coureur and I'm spending too much money on agency chefs.'

"It can't last much longer," Rudi told him. "Dariusz says once Fabio's finished with me I might not be needed for another ten years."

Max snorted. "Europe must be crawling with Coureurs then."

Rudi had some vague idea that Max was, or had been at sometime in the past, involved in some way with Coureur Central, but it always seemed indelicate to ask. He said, "How many do *you* think there are, out of interest?"

Max laughed. "In my experience? You and Fabio." Rudi had brought Fabio to the restaurant the night before for a meal. Not a happy event, for anyone.

"I'm going to be busy then."

"Looks that way," Max sighed.

*   *   *

2.

MORE 'HOMEWORK.' PHONE calls, passports applied for, job interviews attended. One day he spent an entire morning in a very untidy flat in Sosnowiec. Eventually a policeman turned up and took the details of a burglary which had been reported at the flat. Rudi gave the policeman a list of missing possessions. The policeman left.

It occurred to Rudi that, while he was certainly getting a feel for the work of a stringer, Central was also getting its money's worth out of him. He had lost count of how many legends he was contributing to. He opened bank accounts. He rented an office in Zabrze. Fabio gave him a slim attaché case and told him to place it in a safety-deposit box at a bank in Katowice.

Along with homework came *tradecraft*. And it was disappointingly run-of-the-mill stuff. Dead drops, brush passes, tips on how to drop a tail, tips on how to pick one up. It was straight out of Deighton or Furst. Almost comicbook stuff. Rudi doubted that even the security services still did this kind of thing.

Using maps, Fabio made him plan jumps from half a dozen Polish cities, peppering each one with alternate dustoffs. Then Fabio demolished each jump, one by one, in a high, hectoring tone of voice, *have you learned* nothing? *Am I getting* through *to you yet?*

As time went on, Fabio began to disappear for days at a time. Rudi would wake up in the morning, and there would be a Fabio-shaped hole in his life. No complaining about the food or moving the furniture about. The first time it happened, he thought the

Coureur had simply given up on him and gone home, but a day or so later Fabio was back, making obscene comments about Poles and daring Rudi to cook him a meal he could actually enjoy. More absences followed, at irregular intervals.

They had day-trips to neighbouring towns and cities, and Rudi was required to improvise jumps off the top of his head from this office building or that police station. Then Fabio demolished each one.

"This is a lot of fun," Rudi admitted wearily on the way back from one trip, "but I have a real job to think about as well, you know."

"Of course you do," Fabio said. "And you are free to return to it at any time. And I can go somewhere else." He smiled brightly. "Perhaps there will be decent food there. What do you think?"

What Rudi was thinking, increasingly, was *fuck you, Fabio*. "I think you're going to be stuck with me for a little while longer," he said.

Fabio sighed. "Of course. I was afraid of that."

ONE NIGHT, TEN weeks after the beginning of his apprenticeship, Rudi was woken by a strange conviction that someone else was in his bedroom. He rolled over, opened his eyes, and saw Fabio standing beside the bed.

"Get dressed," said the little Coureur. "We're going on an exercise."

Rudi looked at the clock. "It's three o'clock in the morning."

"You should have gone to bed earlier, then," Fabio snapped.

Rudi, who had promised Max that he would make one of his increasingly-rare appearances at the restaurant today, said, "Can't we do it tomorrow? Or Friday? Friday would be better."

Fabio turned and headed for the door. "You want to go back to being a cook, fine," he muttered. "I'll pack and you can drive me to the airport and I can leave this stinky little town."

Rudi felt a stirring of the spirit of resistance that Pani Stasia had lit within him. He got out of bed and pulled on a pair of jeans and a T-shirt. "I'm a *chef*, you ridiculous little bastard!" he shouted.

Fabio came back to the door and looked at Rudi. The bedroom was in darkness and the little Swiss was silhouetted by the hall lights, so Rudi couldn't see his expression.

"And this is a city," Rudi told him more quietly. "Not a town."

Fabio turned away and went into the living room. "Town, city," he said. "Whatever."

THEY WALKED DOWN to the end of the street, where Fabio had the keys to a parked Lexus. He had his heavy carry-on case with him. He put it in the boot and told Rudi to drive to Częstochowa.

At Częstochowa, Fabio directed Rudi to park the Lexus outside the station. He retrieved his case, and they walked for about forty minutes, at which point Fabio stopped beside a parked Mercedes, produced a set of keys, and said, "Get in. I'll drive."

"Are we going far?" Rudi asked.

Fabio snorted. "What do *you* care, *chef*?"

They looked at each other over the roof of the car. "Maybe I can get some sleep," Rudi said.

"Maybe I'd like that better." Fabio unlocked the driver's door. "Get in."

THEY CHANGED CARS again at a deserted-looking farm outside town. This time it was a battered-looking hydrogen-cell Simca. Fabio waited for a long time before driving back to the main road, and he waited again before driving back into Częstochowa and then driving around town for another forty minutes or so. Rudi dozed off, and when he opened his eyes they were out on the open road again and he had no idea which direction they were heading in.

They drove for hours. The roads were in an appalling state, many of them laid by the conquering Germans in the 1940s and inadequately repaired ever since, kilometre after kilometre of dips and bumps and potholes. Poland had never had enough money for public works, certainly not enough for the scale of public works needed to bring the country up to the level of, say, Greater Germany, which had roads of a lascivious smoothness. Hindenberg, which had only been in existence for a decade or so, was in comparison a Western European nation.

A lot of it had to do with Poland's stubborn membership of the EU. They had waited so long to be admitted, Rudi thought, that they had decided nothing was going to dislodge them. The only way Poland was going to leave the Union was feet first, and so the country was continually being stung for subsidies and tariffs and finding itself dragged along with the EU's seeming determination to pick trade wars with anything that had a head of state.

"Poles," Fabio muttered when Rudi mentioned this in an attempt to make conversation. "Who knows?"

"A wise view, Obi-Wan," Rudi said.

Fabio glanced briefly at him. "What?"

Rudi dozed. Fabio refused to tell him where they were going, so it was pointless offering to share the driving. Towns and villages went by, pools of light in a great darkness. Half the road signs he saw were featureless pink rectangles in the Simca's headlights, the grass and asphalt beneath them spattered with pink paint.

"*Armia Różowych Pilotów*," Rudi said when Fabio complained about the pink signs.

"What the fuck's that?" Fabio did not admit to speaking much Polish, so they spoke English.

"The Army of the Pink Pilot. I thought it was just a Warsaw thing."

"Some kind of homosexual rights organisation."

Rudi laughed. The Pink Pilot was a bona fide homegrown Polish legend, occupying a territory somewhere between Sikorski and Jan Sobieski.

"It's the Palace of Culture," he said. When Fabio frowned across at him he said, "In Warsaw. The Palace of Culture. A gift from Stalin and the Workers of the Soviet Union to the Workers of Poland. One of the ugliest buildings in Europe."

Fabio snorted, as if to say that Europe was *teeming* with buildings that offended *his* aesthetic sensibilities.

It was said that the only good thing about the Palace of Culture was that it was visible from everywhere in

Warsaw. Of course, that was the worst thing about it as well, but at least it meant you could never get lost. After the Fall, there had been much debate about what to do with this offensively Stalinist monolith, and, as with most things Polish, in the end nothing much had been done.

And then one night there was the sound of engines in the sky, a miasma of paint fumes over central Warsaw, and when the city awoke the next morning it found that the Palace of Culture had been given a makeover.

Meanwhile, over on the southern edge of the city, in the middle of a field, sat a MiL helicopter retrofitted with a crop-spraying rig, from which hot-pink paint was still sizzling onto the grass, and leading from it out across the field a line of pink bootprints growing fainter and fainter as the Pink Pilot walked away into myth.

In time-honoured fashion there were angry recriminations in Parliament. There were resignations, mostly among air traffic controllers who had failed to notice the flight of the Pink Pilot.

Varsovians, on the other hand, loved the Palace's paint-job. They claimed it made the thing so fucking *obvious* that they didn't notice it any more, and when a few weeks later the Government attempted to have it cleaned there was a small riot.

This had all happened a year or so before Rudi arrived in Kraków, and he hadn't visited Warsaw yet, but he'd seen it from time to time on various items in the news, and no matter where in the city the pictures came from the Pink Palace had seemed to lean into the background like one of those obnoxiously-drunken guests at a wedding party. Rudi thought it looked uncomfortably *carnal*.

"Poles, you see?" Fabio said when Rudi had explained it to him. "You absolutely cannot fucking predict what they will do. And now there is an army of them."

"Well, nobody's saying it's the Pink Pilot painting the road signs," Rudi said. "Just some people following his example."

"And nobody's ever caught the pink fucker."

"No," Rudi admitted, "nobody's ever caught the pink fucker."

"Well there you are then," Fabio said, wagging a finger.

"Where am I then?" Rudi asked, puzzled.

"It must be him painting the road signs. Any person who is prepared to paint one building pink will almost certainly do so again."

Rudi stared at him.

Whoever the ARP were, and wherever they came from, it was obvious that they had been particularly busy on this stretch of road. Most of the signs the car passed seemed to have been painted. This might have posed problems for drivers looking for directions, but Fabio never faltered.

Eventually, the sun came up. Rudi, who had been dozing again, opened his eyes to misty dawn light and without thinking about it oriented himself north-south, east-west.

"Where are we?" he said, struggling stiffly upright.

"*I* don't know," Fabio said. "I just know where we're going."

"That's great," Rudi muttered. "Thank you, Fabio."

As it turned out, sometime in the wee small hours they had outpaced the ARP's handiwork and were back in an area of unmolested road signs. It didn't take Rudi too long to work out where they were going, and an hour or so after that they arrived in Poznań.

"You could have told me where we were going," Rudi said as they drove towards the city centre.

"I could have," Fabio agreed. "But we are fated to go through life with too little information anyway. The sooner you learn that the better."

Rudi looked at him. "Was that supposed to be a joke?"

"After two and a half months of your cooking," Fabio said, "one develops a certain wry sense of humour."

RUDI HAD NEVER been to Poznań before, but Michał, Max's maitre d', had been born in a village not too far outside the city, and on slow homesick evenings he had regaled the restaurant's captive audience of Cracovians and Silesians and Kurds and Kosovars and Estonians with tales of his home town, so Rudi knew that Poznań had a Market Square second only to Kraków's and had, for quite a long time, been a Prussian city named Posen. He knew that Mieszko I, conqueror of Silesia and Małopolska and the first historical ruler of Poland, was buried there, along with some other early kings and queens. He knew the oldest cathedral in Poland was there – and he knew some people in Kraków for whom that *still* rankled. He knew that the name of the city might have come from a person – 'Poznań's town' – or it might be a corruption of the Polish verb *poznać* – 'to recognise' or 'to get to know.' He knew it had had a lot of odd names down the years. He knew the Line ran past the city. He had never really given the place a second thought.

Fabio parked the Simca in an office carpark just outside the city centre, and they walked to a little hotel not far from the Market Square. Adjoining rooms had been reserved for them. Rudi spent roughly thirty seconds looking around his, and then collapsed full-length on the bed.

3.

AT SEVEN O'CLOCK that evening, Fabio knocked on his door to summon him to dinner in the hotel's little restaurant. A long time ago, it had been customary for the restaurant's category to be listed at the top of the menu. *Kat* 1 or *kat* 2 were the most luxurious, with *kat* 4 the cheapest – usually somewhere a tourist would be advised to avoid unless they were feeling lucky.

Two generations of Western food writers had wrought something of a change, though. Poland these days was scattered with Michelin stars and recommendations from *Les Routiers* and the AA. So it was with a rather sinking heart that Rudi saw the words *kat* 3 printed on the top of the menu. He ordered *kotlet schabowy* with *placki ziemniaczane*, in a spirit of experiment, and found to his pleasant surprise that the food was competently cooked and attractively presented. Maybe the *kat* 3 was a gimmick.

"Why don't *you* cook stuff like this?" Fabio asked, tucking enthusiastically into his *gołąbki*.

"If I knew you liked stuffed cabbage leaves, I would," Rudi told him.

Fabio gestured with his fork. "What's that?"

Rudi looked down at his plate. "Pork cutlet and a potato pancake."

"Any good?"

"Bit too much paprika in the sauce."

"I hate chefs," said Fabio, stuffing himself with *gołąbki*.

"I know."

"Twitchy little prima-donnas." Fabio tapped the table with the handle of his knife. "Any half-intelligent person can follow the directions in a cookbook and produce food at least as good as this."

"But could they do it night after night for a restaurant with seventy tables?"

Fabio sipped his wine. "It's all in the planning, right? Any fool can do it."

Rudi poked his fork into his side-salad. "Am I allowed to know what this *exercise* is all about?" he asked.

"We'll be jumping a Package out of the Line Consulate," Fabio said without pausing in his love affair with the restaurant's food. "How would you go about that?"

"I have no idea."

"Well, fortunately this is one of those exercises where all the student is required to do is watch and learn. This wine is *really* good. What is it?"

Rudi consulted the menu. "House red."

"Really? You should talk to the staff, you know, one catering worker to another. Maybe you can score us a couple of bottles to take back with us. It's better than that piss you serve me."

THE TRANSEUROPE RAIL Route was the last great civil engineering project of the European era, an unbroken rail link running from Lisbon to Chukotka in the far east of Siberia, with branches connecting all the capitals of Europe.

At least, that had been the plan. When it actually came to building the link the various national authorities involved fell to years of squabbling about finance, rolling stock, track gauges, staff uniforms. The TransEurope Rail Company became a microcosm of the increasingly fractious European Parliament, complete with votes, vetoes, lobbying, corruption and all the other things so beloved of democracies. The Company tottered on the brink of bankruptcy four times before a metre of track had been laid or a locomotive had been commissioned, and each time it came back. There were rumours of Mafia involvement, Facist involvement, Communist involvement, investigations, Commissions, inquiries, sackings, suicides, murders, kidnappings.

Eventually, and somewhat to the surprise of most observers, the Company began to lay track in Portugal. The plan had been to build the Rail Route from both ends, starting in Lisbon and Chukotka and working towards a meeting somewhere around the Ukrainian-Polish border, but unspecified problems stopped work in Siberia for an unspecified length of time which eventually became permanent.

So, year by year, the Line crept across the face of Europe, at about the same time that Europe was crumbling around it. The EU dissolved, and the Line went on. The European economy imploded, and the Line went on. The first polities came into being, and the Line went on, the Company negotiating transit rights where it passed through the new sovereign territories. It seemed indestructible. By the time it reached the Franco-German border it appeared to have picked up some bizarre kind of momentum that kept it rolling eastward through all adversity. By now, nobody knew where the money to build the Line was coming from; it arrived from a kind of braided river delta of offshore funds and companies and private investors, and even though various national branch lines were abandoned no one could quite make out how the thing didn't just quietly go bust.

After nine years, the Line reached the Ukrainian border, where it had once been meant to connect with its westward-travelling cousin. There was a brief ceremony to mark the occasion, and then the Line rolled onward, patient, steady, unstoppable. It passed through wars and border disputes and droughts and police actions, by hill and by dale and through forests and over rivers and along the shores of lakes and under mountains. It rolled through the Xian Flu. It seemed inexplicable, pointless.

The Company went through seventy-two chairmen and three full changes of voting members. It generated a bureaucracy almost as large and unwieldy as that which had once administered the

EU. Truly colossal sums of cash went missing, were found, were lost again.

The Line finally reached the Chukotka Peninsula in the middle of a blizzard of Biblical proportions. The more wry commentators suggested that the next obvious step was to start digging a tunnel towards Alaska.

Instead the Company ran a single forty-car TransEurope Express, an inaugural trip, from Portugal to Siberia and back again, for the benefit of the Press and leaders of the nations and polities the Line passed through and various inconspicuous men whose origin was never explained to anyone. Then it declared itself to be sovereign territory and granted all its workers citizenship.

Which may have been the point of the exercise all along.

IT WAS SAID that the more Line stations a nation had, the more important it was. This was nonsense, of course, but it irked Poles that, though the Line crossed their country from west to east, there was only one station. Most nations had two or three; some polities had two.

The Polish government affected not to notice what was obviously a calculated snub. Of course, when the Polish government affected not to notice something it was marked by no-confidence motions, and if that didn't make any difference it led to mass resignations. And if that didn't work the entire government would implode. The Prime Minister would attempt to resign, the Sejm would refuse to accept his resignation, things would limp along for a while, then the Communists – sorry, the Social Democrats – would win the subsequent elections. It had been going on for decades. Poles had long since stopped being surprised by the process, though it always elicited astonished articles in magazines like *Time/Stone*.

There was also a certain perceived snub in the fact that the Line's only Polish consulate wasn't even in the capital. Poznań took a lot of pride in having the consulate. The city had for centuries been the main bastion of Poland's western border, and the Paris-Berlin-Moscow rail line already ran through the city. To Poznanians, it was only sensible that the Line should visit as well, and they enthusiastically assented to the demolition of a large amount of property to allow access for a branch line.

It had so infuriated the Government that there had even been talk of Poznań seceding from the Polish Republic and becoming a polity, but at some point wiser heads had intervened and decided it was preferable for the Line to have a Consulate in a Poznań that was still Polish, the better to suck out the inevitable financial benefits for the greater good, and there had been a good deal of civic feather-smoothing done in the city by ministers from the central Government. But it had been a close-run thing, and you could still buy T-shirts and fridge magnets with an *Independent Republic Of Poznań* logo – dreamed up by an advertising company in Luxembourg – on them. Just a little reminder to Central Government of the stakes that were involved.

*   *   *

"WHAT DO YOU see?" asked Fabio.

Rudi looked about him. "Trees," he said. He pointed. "Oh, look, and a lake."

Fabio glanced at him and raised an eyebrow. "What do you see?" he asked again.

Though it was impossible to tell just by looking at him, Rudi strongly suspected that Fabio was suffering from a hangover. He'd been so taken with the wine at last night's meal that he had ordered another couple of bottles, and the last Rudi had seen him he was waddling towards the lift with one in each hand. He hadn't shown up for breakfast this morning, and a discreet inquiry with the hotel's receptionist elicited the information that the gentleman in Room 302 had left a tag on his door last night requesting a room service breakfast. Which he had barely touched.

Rudi was having lunch when Fabio finally surfaced, striding into the dining room, face glowing from a recent shave, hair combed, fresh shirt and suit and tie, shoes shined. He did not, however, sit down to eat. Instead he stood by the table and informed Rudi that they were going for a walk.

What they actually did was walk to the nearest stop and take a tram. They got off a dozen stops later, walked to a taxi rank, and hired a cab. The cab drove them a kilometre or so, then Fabio paid off the driver and they got out and caught a bus. By the time they got off the bus, at the gates to a park, Rudi was completely lost. They wandered around the park for about half an hour, and then Fabio started asking Rudi what he could see.

Rudi had pretty much had enough by now. "I was enjoying my lunch, by the way," he said.

"What do you see?" Fabio asked for the third time.

Rudi sighed and looked around again. Trees, yes. Lake, yes. People out walking. He tipped his head to one side. On the other side of the little park, between the trees, he could see the matt-grey shine of closely-woven metal mesh.

"Fence," he said.

Fabio snorted and set out towards the fence. "Come on."

The fence was about ten metres high and defined the park's boundary. In one direction it curved away out of sight; in the other it ran off, perfectly straight and apparently into infinity. Beyond it was an open space perhaps a hundred metres deep, and beyond that another fence. Looking through both sets of mesh, Rudi could only make out vague shapes, but above the second fence rose the stilt-legged forms of freight-handling machinery. A goods yard.

"The Line passes about ten kilometres south of Poznań," Fabio said quietly as they walked along the fence. "There's no way they could have brought it through the city. They'd have had to demolish the place. As it was, they had to knock down a lot of buildings for the branch. It forks off just after the Line crosses the Warta and it ends just up there –" nodding casually to where the fence curved away into the city. "What you have is two sets of tracks with a fence running up both sides. Outside that there's a cleared strip that's continually patrolled and surveilled. It's sown with sensors and, if the stories are true, with anti-personnel devices. Outside that there's another set of fences–" he gave the fence they were walking beside a slap with the flat of his palm.

"Smartwire. Passive surveillance devices. The whole thing is a little over five hundred metres across." He brushed his palms together as if to knock off any dirt from the fence, and struck off at an angle to it, Rudi trailing in his wake. "How would you get in?"

Rudi thought about it. An outer fence that would detect anyone trying to climb it or cut through it. Then a hundred-metre dash across what was basically a death-strip with no cover, only to reach yet another fence. "I wouldn't," he said. "Not unless I could turn the fence and the cameras off and I had a map of the countermeasures on the other side. And even then I wouldn't."

Fabio nodded his assent.

Rudi looked at him.

Fabio looked at where the fence curved away. "About a kilometre from here, the fences draw apart and then curve back together until they enclose a teardrop-shaped space two kilometres across at its widest point. That's where the marshalling yards and the diplomatic compound are. That's where the Line's border crossing with Poland is." He dipped a hand into a jacket pocket, withdrew it holding a little plastic card between his fingers. "And that's why your passport has a work visa for the Line."

Rudi took the card. It had his photograph on the front, but it had someone else's name. "I don't remember having this photograph taken," he said.

"Mm," said Fabio.

"Have you been photographing me without telling me?" he asked angrily.

"All you have to do is keep watch," Fabio told him. "You can surely do that?"

Rudi looked at the card again. "I look like a halfwit."

"It's a good likeness, I agree," Fabio murmured.

Rudi put the card into the breast pocket of his denim jacket. "So. When do we go in?" he said. And then he realised Fabio was carrying his heavy attaché case. He hadn't been carrying it when they left the hotel, and he hadn't been carrying it a few moments earlier when he slapped the fence. Rudi looked around, wondering which of the other people wandering around the park had delivered it to Fabio. He hadn't seen the pass, hadn't even been aware of anyone coming within five metres of them. It was all done like magic. "Oh, no," he groaned.

"MY NAME IS Rausching," said Fabio, swinging his attaché case happily as they approached the border. "You call me 'Herr Rausching.' You're my personal assistant."

"I'm not exactly dressed for it," Rudi grumbled, still annoyed.

Fabio shrugged. "It's Saturday. You were going to a football match when I called you. You were shopping with your fiancée. You were taking your *maybe* dog for a walk. Anyone asks, make something up, I don't care."

"This might work out a little better if we had some time to rehearse," said Rudi.

"You don't get a chance to rehearse for life, do you?"

"Don't we have legends?"

"Well, *I* do, certainly."

Rudi fought an urge to stop and yell at the top of his voice, which would have been noticed by all the cameras mounted around the Line's border post. "Are you *insane*?" he asked quietly.

Fabio sighed. "When you're mugged and have all your money stolen, do you get a chance to rehearse?" he asked. "When one of your loved ones falls under a tram, do you get a chance to rehearse? No. When you're in some godawful pocket nation and something goes *cosmologically* wrong with a Situation, will you have had time to rehearse? No."

"I'll at least have thought through the options beforehand."

Fabio made a little *pft* sound of disdain. "You can never think through all the options. There are just too many. You'd go out of your mind trying to accommodate them all. Sometimes the only thing you can do is wing it."

Rudi scowled. "Is this a test?"

Fabio shrugged. "Sure. Why not?" He tipped his head to one side and looked at Rudi critically. "I've told you all the stuff I know about this business. Whether I've *taught* you anything, I can't say. Probably not. But I'm going through the wire now, and I need you to come with me, and I need you to be at the top of your game, inadequate though that may be. Whether you go with me or turn round and go back to being a cook, I'm going through the wire now."

Rudi looked at the little Swiss and tried to think back to the point at which his life had ceased to make sense.

"I told you," he said finally, "I'm a *chef*."

The border post was a featureless brick cube embedded in the wire of the fence. It was simple, unadorned by national symbols, although a nest of cameras and aerials rose from its roof. There was a single door, on each side of which stood an armed Polish soldier. To one side of the building a road the width of a motorway ran up to an enormous sliding gate in the fence. More armed soldiers stood at attention at the gate. The whole thing made the border post between Poland and Hindenberg look as inviting as an ivy-decked roadside *auberge*.

A queue of people snaked up to the door of the building, but Fabio just walked up the line and waved his passport at one of the soldiers guarding the door. "Afternoon, Piotr," he said as he went past. "How's the wife? Oh, this is Rocco, my personal assistant. I wouldn't let *him* through, if I were you. *Very* dubious character, our Rocco, ha ha. Show Piotr your passport, Rocco, you halfwit."

Conscious of the eyes of the guard on him, and a tidal wave of grumbling from the queue behind him, Rudi took out his passport and held it up. He attempted, but did not quite manage, a reassuring smile, but all Piotr did was wave him through and he followed Fabio into the border post.

Fabio was halfway down the narrow corridor beyond the door. Rudi hurried to catch up and give the little Swiss a piece of his mind, but as he did Fabio turned and said heartily, "Come on, Rocco, I told you to keep up, didn't I? You think I'm paying you by the hour or something?" and Rudi realised that everything said and done in the building was being recorded, probably by instruments of obscene sensitivity.

"I'm sorry, Herr Rausching," he said humbly, trying to build himself a legend from scratch.

The room at the end of the corridor was Polish customs and immigration. A single officer of the Polish border guard sat looking bored behind a desk, but he brightened up when he saw Fabio approaching.

"Good afternoon, Herr Rausching," he said cheerily when Fabio and Rudi reached the desk.

"Good afternoon, Przemek." Fabio was all goodhumoured motion and bonhomie, like a three-card monte expert. "You're well?" Case in hand, patting his pockets to find his passport. "The family?" Case on desk, searching his pockets. "Good man, good man." Extracting his passport and handing it over. "I spoke with my friend about Agata's school the other day; we should hear something in the next week or so." Patting the case. "Do you need to look through this? Oh, by the way, meet Rocco, my personal assistant. A criminal; you only have to look at him, don't you? Ha ha. Give Przemek your passport, Rocco." Case on floor.

Rudi handed over his passport. Przemek fed them both into a reader on the desk, checked the results on a monitor, handed them back and bade them both a good day. Fabio picked up his case and beckoned Rudi to follow.

Walking down the corridor beyond the room, Rudi had to fight the urge to turn and look back and wonder whether he had imagined what he had just seen. For a moment, he wondered if he was not, in point of fact, in the presence of greatness.

The next room was the Line's customs and immigration. It was identical to the Polish one, except behind the desk in this room sat a small and very blond young man wearing a severe but very comfortable-looking black uniform.

"Lars," said Fabio. "Good afternoon." For Lars, he modulated his performance. Very little smalltalk, very little business with the case, no reference to his 'criminal' personal assistant. For Lars, as far as Rudi could discern, Fabio did the whole thing with body language. From an operational standpoint, it was a privilege to witness. How had the British ever been able to hold Fabio? Why hadn't he just walked out of their country? "Yes, hello, Gerald. How's the family? Good. I'm just going to Poland, okay? Fine. Good man. See you again sometime."

Emerging into the sunshine on the other side of the building, Rudi felt his head spin for a moment. Obviously, Fabio had passed this way many times before, scoping out the jump, pressing the flesh, gently subverting the guards, but it didn't alter the fact that he had just basically talked them both through a border on false papers and with nobody on either side of the wire examining his case. Rudi thought that, even if they hadn't had passports, Fabio would have managed to get them through anyway.

"Still there, Rocco?" Fabio asked with a little smile. "Good man. Keep up."

"Yes, Herr Rausching," said Rudi.

"This shouldn't take long, and then you can go back to your football match."

"I was shopping with my fiancée," Rudi said automatically, and then wondered where that had come from.

Fabio, though, nodded fractionally as if in approval. "You'll give my apologies to…?"

Rudi said the first name that came into his head, "Danuta," and then worried that he wouldn't be able to remember it if the subject came up in conversation again.

"Danuta," Fabio repeated. "Are you ever going to make an honest woman of her, Rocco?"

"Probably, Herr Rausching."

"And you'll invite me to the wedding? No nonsense about me being best man; I can't stand all that stuff. I'll just stand at the back and wish you well."

"Yes, Herr Rausching." At that moment, Rudi would have followed Fabio to the gates of Hell. Where Fabio would no doubt have talked his way past the Devil, and then back out again, without even getting mildly singed.

Instead, what he did was follow Fabio across a wide gravelled area to a modest three-storey stuccoed building with orange roof tiles. Beyond the building there was more fencing, and through this Rudi could see a rank of railway tracks and switching stations, and two huge turntables for turning locomotives around, and a single Line train, sleek and blue and green and thirty or forty cars long and powered, if you believed the stories, by twin fusion tokomaks, although fusion power was still an infant and basically explosive science.

Beside the front door of the white building was a modest little brass plaque. It read: *Consulate Of The Independent Trans-European Republic.* Fabio was standing at the door, looking up at a camera mounted over the lintel and blowing kisses. The door made a faint clicking noise, and Fabio saluted the camera and pushed the door open.

Inside was a modest little reception room with a blue carpet and white walls and several anonymous plants standing in earthenware planters around the edges. There was a blocky white sofa facing two blocky white armchairs across a low smoked-glass coffee table. There was a pale wooden reception desk built against the back wall, and to either side of it stairs rose to the next floor. By the time Rudi had let the door close on its springs and heard the electronic lock snap shut, Fabio was already at the desk and schmoozing the auburn-haired young woman sitting behind it.

"Hazel, my dear," he was saying in heavily-accented English – a lot more heavily-accented than his usual English, "you know it does my old man's heart good to see you."

"Herr Rausching," the girl replied. A native English-speaker, Rudi thought. She was thin and pinched-faced and wearing a neat charcoal business suit over a crisp white shirt. "Working on a Saturday?"

"Something which could easily wait until Monday, but which someone in Milan believes they must have today," Fabio said sadly. He put his hand on his heart. "Everyone in a rush. Oh, this is Rocco, by the way, my personal assistant. He may be accompanying me occasionally in future, so he'll have to be signed into the system." He took from his pocket a little plastic box containing a square of plastic about the size of a postage stamp. "All his details are on there, so you don't have to go through the tedious business of typing it all in."

Hazel regarded the flash card in its plastic box dubiously. "It's not very *regular*, Herr Rausching," she said.

"I know, I know." Fabio essayed a great Gallic shrug. "But what can we do? I've been waiting for his vetting reports to come back from Security for almost a month now so he can have permanent status, but you know how they are. Every 'i' has to be dotted, every 't' crossed, and if you miss a single dot all the paperwork has to be done again. And in the meantime, I *need* his assistance, Hazel." He struck his breast softly with his fist. "Hazel. Just this once, eh? Next week, the week after, the paperwork comes back from Security and he's legitimate. All we're doing is jumping the gun a little, that's all. And anyway, a hundred years from now, who will care?"

Hazel looked at the box again. She looked at Rudi. Rudi smiled at her. She looked at Fabio. Fabio smiled at her.

Eventually, the wave of goodwill got the better of her. She snapped the flash card out of its box and slid it into a little box on the desk. She typed for a few moments on the keyboard in front of her, read her screen, typed some more. Then she looked at them both and smiled. "All done," she said. She reached down below the desk and held up a little white badge. She clipped it to a lanyard and held it out to Rudi. "There you go, Rocco. Welcome to the family."

Rudi looked at the card. It was still warm from the printer. It had his photograph embossed on the front, a row of gold contact spots along one of the short edges, and the name 'Rocco Siffredi.' He raised an eyebrow. "Thank you," he said to Hazel.

"Good girl," Fabio told her. "I always knew you'd come through for us. Didn't I say Hazel would come through for us, Rocco?"

"You mentioned it, Herr Rausching," said Rudi.

"Well." Fabio picked up his case. "I owe you a favour, Hazel. Many thanks."

"Not at all, Herr Rausching. Happy to help."

"So. We'll see you later. Rocco? Shall we? The sooner we get this done, the sooner you can go back to Diana."

"Danuta," Rudi said, catching a gleam of wickedness in Fabio's eye.

"Danuta?" Fabio asked innocently. "I'm sorry; I could have sworn you said Diana."

Rudi shook his head. "Danuta, Herr Rausching."

"Rocco has a fiancée," Fabio stage-whispered to Hazel.

"Lucky Rocco," said Hazel. She smiled at Rudi.

"This way, Rocco," Fabio said, indicating one of the staircases. He waved goodbye to Hazel.

Halfway up the stairs, Rudi moved up close to Fabio and said very very quietly, "Rocco Siffredi was a porn star."

"Was he?" Fabio replied, just as quietly. "Oh well."

AT THE TOP of the stairs a corridor ran entirely around the first storey of the house, lined on the outside with windows and on the inside with ranks of numbered doors. Fabio led him to a door marked 73, took out a key card, and put it in the slot, and opened it.

Inside was a cosy little office with a desk and some easy chairs and another of those unidentifiable pot plants. A set of shelves supported a number of photographs of Fabio with his arm round a dumpy, wistful-looking woman in various outdoor settings. In the Alps. On a boat somewhere warm. At what appeared to be a Formula One motor racing event.

"Frau Rausching?" Rudi asked.

"Hannelore," agreed Fabio. "Bless her."

"How long have you been working here?"

Fabio looked at him for a moment, but if the office was bugged and anyone was listening, it might just be considered a legitimate question. "About eighteen months, on and off."

Rudi nodded. Well, that was interesting. At least it explained Fabio's occasional absences from Kraków.

"Anyway," said Fabio. "Make yourself comfortable here for a moment. I have to pop down the corridor and consult with one of my colleagues. I'll be back shortly." And he left the office.

Rudi stood looking at the closed door for a minute or so after Fabio's departure. He was surprised to discover that, on his first live Situation, he felt like a child brought to his father's workplace.

Fabio had spent almost a week last month barking aphorisms at him. One of these had been, 'In hostile territory, always assume you're under surveillance.' In the spirit of this, Rudi decided to behave like Rocco. Bored, a little resentful at being dragged away from Danuta (who in Rudi's imagination had short blonde hair and a magnificent bust, just in case anyone asked.) He walked around the office. He looked at the photos again. Fabio and... who? Mrs Fabio? A stringer posing for some pictures in return for what looked like a fairly eventful holiday around Europe? Hard to tell, but he doubted there was a Mrs Fabio. He doubted anyone could stand Fabio long enough to get to the altar.

He went and sat behind Fabio's desk and tried the swivel chair. He waved a hand at Fabio's monitor and it lit up with a screensaver of a scruffy-looking Persian cat. There was no point doing anything else. He didn't know Fabio's passwords. And even if he did, and if, in defiance of tradecraft, Fabio kept anything interesting on the Consulate's system, it would be encrypted, and everything else would just be part of Herr Rausching's legend. It would be worth looking at, to backfill his own legend, but the securityware would be watching, and would wonder why he was looking at it.

Rudi looked at his watch. Ten minutes since Fabio left. He got up and walked over to the easy chairs, grouped around another of those smoked-glass-topped coffee-tables. There was a scatter of Polish lifestyle magazines on the table, and he sat down and leafed through one of them, shaking his head at the recipes. He looked at his visitors' pass, hanging round his neck on its lanyard. Rocco Siffredi. He shook his head again.

Another ten minutes passed. The door opened. Rudi looked up from the magazine he was reading, expecting to see Fabio, but instead two shaven-headed men wearing identical suits were standing in the doorway. They had the neckless look of career steroid abusers, and little wireless headsets plugged into one ear.

Rudi smiled uncertainly.

* * *

THEY WERE VERY polite. They took his clothes. They put him in a cell that was a windowless concrete cube about four metres on a side, whose only features were a drain in the middle of the floor and an armoured glass bubble in the ceiling containing a light source that never went out.

Rudi sat for long periods of time on the floor. When it got too cold under his naked buttocks, he got up and paced around the cell. He lost track of time, but he didn't worry. It was all a test.

He cursed himself for not realising straight away. It was patently ridiculous that Fabio would just march him across the border without any preparation at all. Therefore it was a test. It was patently ridiculous that someone like Fabio could talk his way past the border guards. Therefore the guards had been in on it. It was patently ridiculous that Fabio could wander around the Line's Consulate unmolested. Therefore everyone had been in on it. Like the Situation with Max's cousin, it had all just been a test of nerve and character. All he had to do was sit here and wait for the test to end and he could go back to Restauracja Max.

He was still thinking that, right up to the first time the Line's security men waterboarded him.

AT SOME POINT, he was given an orange jumpsuit to wear, but he didn't understand what it was and someone had to help him put it on. Then he was helped, not ungently, down a corridor to a little room containing a table and three chairs. A casually-dressed man of indeterminate middle-age was already sitting on one of the chairs. Rudi was invited to sit on the one facing him across the table. The third chair was taken by someone large and humourless.

Rudi and the middle-aged man looked at each other across the table for a long time. Rudi's legs hurt and he couldn't stop shaking and he kept feeling moments of weightlessness.

"My name is Kaunas," the middle-aged man said eventually.

"That's not a name," Rudi said through a split lip. "That's a place."

Kaunas sat quiet again for a long time. He had a hard face and greying brown hair swept straight back from his forehead. Finally he said, "How are you being treated?"

"I'm being tortured," said Rudi. "Just look at me."

"Where is Fabio?" asked Kaunas.

"He went to consult with a colleague down the corridor," said Rudi. "What day is it?"

Kaunas looked at Rudi again for a long time without speaking. Then he looked at a corner of the ceiling and said, "We'll be making a formal diplomatic protest. He knows nothing."

The corner of the ceiling did not answer, but the large humourless person in the third chair got up and lifted Rudi to his feet. "It's a *place*," Rudi told Kaunas as he was ushered firmly out of the room.

Instead of being taken back to his cell, or any of the other rooms he'd been in, he was walked up a set of stairs and suddenly found himself in the Consulate's reception room. Hazel was still behind her desk. He smiled at her as he was walked past, but it made his lip bleed and Hazel looked away.

Outside, the sunshine hurt his eyes, but it was only for a few moments. He was helped into one of those cars with darkened windows and seats so comfortable they felt like leather clouds, and he fell asleep for a while.

He woke up as he was being helped out of the car. He was marched through a loud space, then up some steps, then down a corridor and into a room with a sliding door and a big window and seats facing each other against two of the walls. He was lifted onto one of the seats. The door slid closed. He looked out of the window, and his mind refused to process the scene when everything outside started to slide backwards. He fell asleep again.

Some time later, he woke up again and the view outside the window was different. There was a big sign right outside. It read, *Kraków*, which he thought meant something to him. Then the door slid open and someone came into the room and started to help him to his feet, but his legs hurt and they didn't work properly and he threw up what little was in his stomach and then he went away for a while.

DARIUSZ CAME TO see him in hospital. Not right away, but after a few days. After Max and the kitchen crew and some (not very many, Rudi was disappointed to discover and determined to revenge) of his acquaintances from other restaurants had visited. He arrived unannounced, outside visiting hours. Rudi, who had been dozing, opened his eyes, and there was the little mafioso, sitting beside the bed and looking as if he wanted a cigarette.

"You took your time," said Rudi.

"You have our abject apologies," said Dariusz without preamble.

"Oh," said Rudi. "Abject apologies. Oh, good."

Dariusz leaned forward fractionally. "You're angry, but–"

"Yes," said Rudi. "I am angry. I *told* you there was something wrong with Fabio, but you wouldn't listen. 'He's a genius, Rudi.' 'We must be tolerant of our geniuses, Rudi.' Fuck you, Dariusz."

Dariusz paused. Then he said, "You're angry, but I need to know what you told them."

Rudi looked at him. "What?"

Dariusz reached out and touched his arm. "I need to know what you told them."

"Fuck off, Dariusz." Rudi turned away from him.

"It's important," Dariusz continued gently. "You don't know much, but what you do know could compromise... certain things."

Rudi turned back to look at him. "I kept your name out of it, if it's any comfort. But I dropped Fabio in the shit as much as I possibly could."

Dariusz sat back and nodded, as if hearing confirmation of something. "Something terrible has happened," he said. "But it had nothing to do with the Coureurs. It was about as off-piste as it's possible to be. You must understand that."

"Must I?" Rudi struggled into a sitting position, punching the pillows down behind him. "Must I? You brought me a teacher and he almost got me killed. Must I understand that?"

"Fabio was operating outside orders," said Dariusz. "He was running his own operation. What he did wasn't sanctioned by Central. He took you into the Consulate as a patsy to gain time for his own dustoff."

A patsy. "Well, great."

Dariusz took his time asking his next question. He watched Rudi's face. He looked around the room. He looked back at Rudi. He said, "Do you still want to be a Coureur?"

"I *beg* your pardon?" howled Rudi, loud enough to bring a brace of nurses running to see what all the fuss was about. By which time, of course, Dariusz was gone.

BORDERLIGHT

1.

"SMALL NATIONS ARE like small men," said the cobbler. "Paranoid. Twitchy. Quick to anger."

"Mm," said Rudi.

"I wouldn't call them *nations* anyway," the cobbler went on. "Most of them break down after a year or so. Look at me. Don't smile." He pointed a little camera at Rudi, paused a moment to frame the shot, and took four pictures. The camera was cabled, along with a number of other little devices and anonymous boxes, into a battered-looking old Motorola phone. "Thank you. In my opinion they don't have the right to call themselves nations until they've been about for a century or so."

"Is this going to take long?" Rudi asked. "I have a train to catch."

The cobbler looked at him. "Getting in and out of the Zone is child's play," he said soberly. "Residence visas and work permits are much more difficult."

"I know," said Rudi.

"My regular pianist wasn't available; I had to hire someone out of my own pocket."

"I'm sorry," Rudi said, hoping the stand-in pianist was trustworthy.

The cobbler kept looking at him. "You're very young."

This seemed impossible to argue with. Rudi shrugged.

"Change the colour of your hair," said the cobbler. "Grow a moustache."

"I don't have time to grow a moustache."

"Well have your hair cut," the cobbler said testily. "You have time to visit a barber? Alter your appearance somehow. No one ever looks exactly like their passport photograph; it makes immigration officers suspicious if they do."

"Perhaps I could wear a hat," said Rudi.

The cobbler looked at him for a few moments longer, then shook his head sadly. He went over to the phone and started to fiddle with its little roll-up tapboard. "And of course the Zone has these paper passports," he said, looking intently at the phone's screen. He shook his head at something, poked the tapboard several times. "Silicon is so much easier."

"It's supposed to be more difficult."

The cobbler shook his head again. He rapped the phone with a knuckle. "With silicon, I can do everything in here. With paper... well, you must find the correct paper, the correct inks, the correct stamps... much more difficult."

"Right," said Rudi.

"My pianist took ten minutes to hack the Zone's immigration computer and update your legend's records. Where's the security there?"

"Right," said Rudi.

"Everyone should produce passports like this," the cobbler went on. "Any pianist can hack a silicon passport, but it takes an artist to work with paper and ink."

"Right," said Rudi.

The cobbler glanced up from the screen. "You probably believe you know everything."

"That's the first time anyone's accused me of *that*," Rudi told him.

The window of the cobbler's shop looked out over a landscape of sharply-pitched roofs broken by chimneypots and about a hundred different types of radio, television and satellite antennae. In the far distance, Rudi could see the cranes of the Gdańsk shipyards. The shipyards had gone bust sometime during the early part of the century, and the land was now occupied by trendy apartment blocks and studios for artists and those little design firms no one ever quite understands the purpose of. The cranes had been preserved, as historical monuments, although nobody could agree who was supposed to be maintaining them so they were slowly and quietly rusting away.

The cobbler's shop itself was clearly one of Central's myriad temporary spaces, rented by a stringer on a monthly basis for whatever brief occupancy circumstances dictated. A dusty boxroom right at the top of a tall brick-built rooming house, floored with lino that looked as if it dated back to the Second World War. A pile of teachests stacked over in one corner, an ancient wooden rocking-horse under the window. The cobbler's equipment could be packed into two medium-sized attaché cases and moved from place to place as circumstances demanded. The cobbler himself was as anonymous as the room. Small, slight and middle-aged, with a receding hairline and battered, slightly old-fashioned clothes.

"You speak Estonian?" he asked, reading the laptop's screen.

"I can get by," said Rudi.

The cobbler nodded. "Your Polish is very good," he said, looking at the screen again. "But you're from up the coast somewhere; I can hear your accent."

Rudi took a battered bentwood stool from a stack in the corner of the attic, set it right way up, sat down, and folded his hands in his lap.

"I know," said the cobbler. "None of my business. Everyone in the Zone speaks English, anyway." He took from his pocket a small parcel wrapped in what appeared to be chamois leather. Unwrapping it, he held up a thin little book with laurel-green covers. Its front cover was gold-stamped with an extremely stylised eagle and some writing.

"Worth more than its weight in gold," he said. "Literally. Virgin; never used. Bring it back."

"All right," said Rudi.

The cobbler opened the passport and laid a thin sheet of transparent film over one of the pages. Then he fed the whole thing into one of the little boxes connected to the phone.

"We don't get many of these," he said, and Rudi wondered if he meant virgin passports or something else. He typed a couple of commands into the tapboard and a moment later the box ejected the passport. He stripped the film away and Rudi saw that his photograph and some printing were now embossed on the page.

"Actually," he said, rooting around in one of his cases, "they've been very clever."

Rudi tried to feign interest. "Oh?"

"Not many people these days have the paraphernalia to do work like this successfully." He took from the case two stamps and two ink-pads. "I had to mix the inks myself. Specific fluorescences, magnetic particles. Very tricky."

Rudi looked at his watch.

The cobbler carefully inked the stamps and inserted the residence visa and work permits. Then he took out a gorgeous antique Sheaffer fountain pen and dated and initialled the stamps. Then, with several other lovely pens, he signed several different signatures.

"Then, of course, they have to spoil it all." He typed another couple of commands and another little box ejected a narrow length of plastic printed with a barcode. The cobbler stripped off the backing and pressed the barcode onto the final page of the passport.

Finally, he opened the passport at a number of different pages and flexed the spine back and forth. Then he closed it and bent it between his hands. Then he leaned down and rubbed both covers and the edges on the dusty floor.

"Congratulations," he said, holding the passport out to Rudi. "You're Tonu Laara."

"Thank you," Rudi said, taking the passport. "And it's pronounced *Tonu*."

The cobbler smiled. "There. I like a man who knows how to pronounce his Christian name."

2.

THE POLES BEGAN to arrive a couple of days before New Year's Eve.

First to arrive, on the 29th, were about a dozen in three cars with skis strapped to their roof-racks. They all seemed to know each other, booked into their rooms, and went straight back out onto the slopes.

Early that evening, a coach arrived bearing about thirty more, all of them loaded down with ski equipment. From his hatchway Rudi watched them at the evening meal, deriding the food and calling good-natured insults to each other.

The next day, more cars and another coach. It was a package tour organised by some firm in Upper Silesia, Jan confided.

"They stop off in town and buy up all the alcohol in the supermarket and then come up here and drink like madmen," he said.

"Why?" asked Rudi.

Jan gave a great expansive shrug as if to demonstrate that the motivations of Poles were as mysterious to him as the workings of the cosmos.

Whatever. Most of the first coachload of Poles left the hotel and strapped on their skis almost as soon as the sun came up over the far peaks the next morning. The rest stayed in their rooms and began to drink their purchases, and when the second load arrived in the early afternoon, already loudly drunk, there were some fights between the two groups.

Rudi was familiar with some of these people. The skiers were just ordinary Poles, here to have a good time on the slopes and spend a nice New Year's Eve. The drinkers were in their mid-twenties and well-dressed, young Polish entrepreneurs who had made a lot of money very quickly and wanted to take their girlfriends on a cheap, loud, boozy holiday. At dinner that evening there was a lot of shouting and some food was thrown. Later on there were more fights, discharged fire extinguishers, weeping girlfriends running screaming down the corridors with their mascara smeared in long black teary streaks.

In the kitchen, Rudi put basket after basket of dirty crockery onto the conveyor of the ancient Hobart dishwasher, walked round to the other end, and took baskets of clean crockery – heated to just short of the melting point of lead, it felt like – off. After three months handling red-hot plates and cups his fingertips had blistered and peeled and he was almost bereft of fingerprints, which he thought was an interesting effect.

"It was the same last year," Jan said morosely, perched on one of the stainless steel worktops. "Fights, alcohol poisoning. They even let fireworks off in the hotel. I had to call the police."

"But imagine the income," Rudi said, slinging another basket of coffee cups into the Hobart.

Jan shrugged. He was actually the hotel's manager,

and there were always pressing demands on his time, so that he rarely went to bed before three in the morning. But he had begun his career in the hotel trade as a humble kitchen porter – Rudi's post – and seemed to feel more at ease in the kitchens than anywhere else. He had studied at the London School of Economics and spoke very good English, which was Rudi's second language. This was fortunate because Rudi's Czech – based mainly on the language's similarities to Polish – was on the poor side of rudimentary.

"Income," said Jan as if the prospect was the most depressing he could imagine. "And for what? We only spend it repairing the damage. I wanted to ban Poles after last year, but the owners said I couldn't. You speak very good Polish, don't you?"

"Not me," Rudi said. "Not a word."

"I heard you talking to that girl Marta the other day. The one on the evening cleaning shift. It sounded like Polish you were speaking."

"You heard wrong, Jan." Operationally, Rudi wasn't keen to let anyone know where he had come from. On a practical level, he was even less keen to get roped into some situation where he was called on to try and calm down a gang of fantastically-drunk Poles, which was bound to happen if Jan thought he spoke the language with any great facility.

"Ah, maybe so." Jan heaved a sigh and looked at his watch. There was a faint, muffled thud from far overhead in the hotel, and distant shouting, audible even over the rumble of the Hobart's conveyor and the hiss of its water-jets. "Christ, they're still at it."

"They're only kids with too much money," Rudi

said, walking around to the end of the dishwasher and lifting the basket off.

"Too much money?" Jan said. "You try getting them to pay for the damage they cause. Then you'll see how much money they have." He looked at his watch again. "Time for my rounds," he said unwillingly. "You're sure you don't speak Polish?"

"I would have noticed." Rudi started to take the crockery out of the tray. He barely felt the residual heat now; the first time he'd done it he'd shrieked and flung a plate across the kitchen.

Jan shook his head. "I can't understand what brings a man like you to a place like this."

"Life is full of infinite variety," Rudi said. It had become his catchphrase since arriving in Pustevny.

Jan smiled. "Okay, Mister Estonian." He hopped down off the worktop and ran his hands down the legs of his trousers to smooth them. "You carry on throwing pots and pans into the dishwasher. I know you're running away from something."

In the beginning, Rudi had been terrified that Jan was onto him, but he had come to realise that Jan was one of the world's worst students of human nature; the manager simply suspected everybody, on the grounds that he was bound to be right some of the time.

Rudi grinned. "I like it here, Jan. I just like it here."

And really it was the truth. After months living under the cloud left by Fabio's catastrophic visit to Poznań, his life had become incredibly simple. Get up, wash dishes, go to bed. Wait for the Package to arrive and make themselves known.

The Beskid Economic Zone was not a polity as such. It was more of an autonomous national park devoted to stripping tourists of their money. It paid rent to the rump of the Czech Government for use of its land, but the rent was a fraction of the megatonnes of francs, schillings, marks, złotys, euros, sterling and dollars that cascaded into the area every year. This part of northeastern Czechoslovakia had always been a popular skiing destination for the population of neighbouring nations. Even when it began issuing visas – for a small gratuity – and imposing entry and exit taxes on top of the prices of ski-passes it remained popular. It was a big mountainous snowy machine for making money, and one of the wealthiest junk nations in Central Europe.

It was perfectly placed. The Polish border was only three-quarters of an hour away by road, Prague wasn't much further in the opposite direction, Vienna only another couple of hours or so away. The Zone was making money hand over fist, and Rudi thought that coachloads of drunken Poles were a small price to pay.

The last tray-load of cutlery washed for the night, he shut down the machine and started to go through the cleaning procedure. This involved draining the Hobart's tanks and removing the stainless steel filter-baskets and rinsing the crap out of them. It was routine and boring and somehow comforting.

As the cobbler had told him, getting into the Zone was simplicity itself. He had shown his passport, just another Zone resident coming back after a holiday, and the immigration officer had waved him through without even bothering to scan the barcode and without charging him the entry tax imposed on tourists.

No one was sure how many Coureurs were drifting around what used to be Europe. Could have been a hundred, maybe a thousand, maybe ten times that. The nature of their work made them hard to find; popular legend had it that they would find you, arriving on your doorstep one dark night when you needed them most, with their stealth-suits hidden under long black trenchcoats, fedoras tilted in best *noir* fashion to shadow the eyes. This was ludicrous, of course, as anyone could have told you if they really thought about it: anybody who went about dressed like that would deserve to be arrested.

What really happened was a lot less structured and a lot more secretive. Central liked to keep these things vague; even the Coureurs themselves didn't usually know who had brought them into a Situation. There were tangles of code words and dead drops and mobile pickups and callbox routines, none of which Rudi had yet encountered.

Fabio's departure had left him without a teacher, and Dariusz had stepped into the breach, flawlessly delivering tradecraft to him in a succession of restaurants and safe houses. Lists of word-strings to memorise, dead drops planned with the help of town plans and photographs, brush-passes to practise. It was almost like working under Pani Stasia again.

"You'll probably never need to use any of this," Dariusz told him one evening in a flat over a bar in Częstochowa. "Most Coureurs do nothing more complicated or illegal than deliver mail."

"So why do I have to remember all this stuff?" Rudi asked.

"Because one day you may need it."

"To deliver mail?"

Dariusz shrugged. "Better safe than sorry, wouldn't you say?"

"By the way," Rudi asked casually, leafing through a sheaf of Zakopane street maps, "what has happened to Fabio?"

"Fabio has retired," Dariusz said, and lit another cigarette.

"You said he was good."

"He was tired." Dariusz looked at him. "Fabio's task was to teach you the basics of the trade, but instead he chose to operate to an agenda of his own, and he was not afraid to leave you behind to face the music. Don't forget that. He had begun to wonder why he was a Coureur. Some do it for the money, some do it because it offers their lives a little harmless adventure. Fabio didn't know any longer. We should not perhaps dwell too much on the subject of Fabio. And don't ask me again." Rudi himself had begun to get confused about where precisely the little mafioso belonged in the scheme of things. He understood that on certain edges Central and the criminal underworld blurred into each other along a line of constantly-renegotiated allegiances, but he couldn't be certain if Dariusz was a criminal who liaised with Central, or a Coureur who liaised with Wesoły Ptak. He had the impression that Dariusz was no longer certain of the distinction either.

"Why do *you* do it?" he asked.

"I like to think that I am keeping alive the spirit of Schengen." Dariusz tapped his cigarette against the crystal ashtray that was doubling as a paperweight to keep all the maps from rolling up. "Everyone, and everything, has the right of free access across national borders."

"Everything? Drugs? Weapons? White slaves?"

Dariusz grinned at him. "*Particularly* drugs, weapons and white slaves."

Whatever. Rudi found himself in agreement with Dariusz. He had started out for the *harmless adventure*, but the more he saw of them the more he'd begun to think that he really *really* hated borders and all the stupid bureaucratic paraphernalia that went with them.

Rudi took each of the filters out of the machine and banged them against the side of the sink to shake loose the debris that had been trapped at the bottom. It was amazing what happened to food after it had been through the machine. It was reduced to a lumpy pinkish-grey scum that eventually built up in the trays and blocked them, hindering the recirculation of hot water. In his early days, he had found items of cutlery in the trays – and more than once a cup or a glass – but he had learned how to arrange the cutlery in its baskets so the machine's jets wouldn't blast knives and forks off the conveyor to fall into the Hobart's innards.

He had also learned that you could wedge items of crockery and cutlery between the tines of the conveyor so that the jets wouldn't knock them loose. You could do that if there were just a few items to put through and the waiters were in a hurry for more clean cutlery, which sometimes happened when the restaurant was very busy and the guests were taking their time eating their meals.

After rinsing the trays, he left them beside the sink

and went back to the machine and lifted the side panels. A cloud of hot, humid detergent-scented air billowed out. He reached inside and unhooked the spray nozzles and rinsed them in the sink as well.

Finally, he hooked a hose to the tap, took a squeegee from under the sink, and washed down the inside of the machine, which quickly grew a film of mucilaginous gunk if you didn't hose it down every day. That done, he replaced the nozzles and filters, refilled the tanks with clean water, closed the machine up, and made a last tidying-up tour of the kitchen before putting on his parka and going out into the little loading bay for a cigar.

It was very cold and incredibly clear. Rudi had lived almost all his life in cities, where only the brightest stars managed to fight their way through the orange-yellow haze of streetlight pollution. Here, though, the sky was a depthless black, full of hard, untwinkling stars, the Milky Way a magnificent cloudy ribbon.

Beyond the little road that led up to the loading bay, the mountain tipped steeply down towards the tiny little constellations of towns winking down in the valleys beneath a filmy layer of pollution. Rudi saw these lights every evening when he came out for his last cigar of the day, but he had no idea what most of the towns were called. Jan had once pointed each one out and named it for him, but Rudi had forgotten the names.

Jan had also pointed a long, bony finger out into the far misty murky distance, and said, "Poland," as if it was of great significance. Rudi had merely shrugged and thanked the Czech for showing him where everything was. There was something a little disquieting about Jan's insistence that he had something to do with Poland, and he didn't know quite what to make of it.

Up above him, someone opened a window and shouted, "Fucking Czechs! Fucking Czechs!" in Polish. Something – Rudi thought it might have been a chair – came flying down out of the night, hit the piled-up snow at the edge of the road, and bounced off down the slope.

"Happy New Year," he said, and ground the cigar out on the concrete with his toe.

RUDI'S ROOM WAS on the ground floor, off the lobby and down a side corridor lined with cupboards and tiny offices. It had the appearance of having once been a cupboard itself; there were marks on the walls where shelves might have once hung. There was a tiny little rectangular window of frosted glass high up on the back wall, and a narrow bed that was a fraction too short to sleep on comfortably. A line of clotheshooks along one wall comprised his wardrobe, and a low cupboard beside the bed held his toilet things. There was enough floor-space to move from the bed to the door without having to walk heel-to-toe, but only just. The room was always comfortably warm because it was directly over the hotel's boiler, but Rudi didn't want to be here in the summer, when it would probably be unbearable.

He grabbed a towel, soap, shampoo and a change of clothes and went down the corridor to the little staff shower-room. No matter how careful he was, he always ended the day as gunky and greasy as the machine he used, and it took a determined effort to get himself clean.

After his shower, he usually liked to have a couple of drinks in the downstairs bar before turning in for the night, but as he walked across the lobby he heard lots of shouting coming from the bar, and noticed a couple of policemen heading towards the source of the noise. He peeled off and went back to his room and sat down to read.

LATER, MARTA KNOCKED softly on the door and let herself in.

"The Poles smashed up the bar," she said, taking off her housecoat and hanging it on the hook behind the door. "The police arrested six of them." Ever since the coach parties began to arrive, she had been referring to her countrymen with a fine disdain, as if trying to distance herself from them.

Stretched out, as much as he could on the bed, Rudi looked over the top of his book and said, "Mm."

Marta undid her black uniform dress and stepped out of it, hung it with the housecoat on the hook. Underneath she was wearing tights and a worn-out black bra. She was a plump, happy girl with long mousy brown hair that she dyed auburn.

"I thought you'd be hiding in here," she said.

"We mustn't speak Polish in public any more," said Rudi. "Jan heard us the other day."

Unhooking her bra, she stopped and looked at him. "We'd never say *anything* to each other in public if we did that." She actually spoke pretty good English, but for some reason she felt embarrassed to use it. She rolled off her tights and panties and left them on the floor. "Move over."

Rudi put his book on the cupboard and squashed himself up against the wall to let Marta slide under the covers beside him. Officially, Jan frowned mightily on personal relationships between members of staff, but unofficially he tended to turn a selectively blind eye, so long as the hotel's routine wasn't unduly disturbed.

"Why can't we speak Polish?" Marta asked.

Rudi put an arm round her and sighed. "I didn't say we couldn't speak Polish. Just that we shouldn't do it in public."

"But why?"

There was no easy way to handle this. For Marta, every answer only sparked off another question; they had once spent nearly the whole night on a single question-and-answer string. Rudi had eventually forgotten what the original question had been, and in the end he had totally lost track of the conversation.

"I won't lie to you, Marta," he said.

"That's what people usually say when they're getting ready to lie," she said, snuggling her head into the curve of his neck and shoulder.

Well, that was true enough. He had to give her that. "I can't tell you why, Marta."

She shrugged.

"I can't tell you why because I don't want you to get involved in it," he said, which as it happened was the pure and simple truth.

"I don't mind," she said sleepily. "I love you."

"That's what people usually say when they're getting ready to say something really silly," he told her, but by then she was snoring gently, fast asleep. Jan worked all the maids far too hard, but the hotel was understaffed because people wanted to be with their families over Christmas and New Year.

Rudi smiled and kissed the top of Marta's head. She had never asked if he was married, if he was already in a relationship, what he was doing in the Zone. When they made love they used a condom and a viricide, and that was the entire extent of her distrust of him. She was a simple, uncomplicated soul to whom nothing really bad had ever happened, just like ninety-nine percent of the population of Europe. He wanted to tell her how quickly and reasonably innocence could go sour, but he wasn't sure how to explain it.

He hugged her, and felt himself fall away from consciousness like a scuba diver dropping out of a boat.

ON NEW YEAR'S EVE, the Poles had a disco.

Jan wanted to throw them all out of the hotel, but the owners stubbornly refused to let him. The Zone was renowned for taking anyone, anytime, no matter how disgusting their behaviour. It existed to attract tourists, and if word got about that the hotels had started to sling people out for such minor misdemeanours as gang fights in the corridors, fire extinguishers let off in the bar, and the forcible ejection of furniture from seventh-storey windows, the Zone's economy might suffer.

Here, Jan and the hotel's owners parted company in terms of philosophy. Jan wanted to run an hotel; the owners wanted to make money. In an ideal world, they would have found some kind of mutually acceptable accommodation. In the real world, Jan – and all the other hotel managers – had to suffer. It would take some unusually disgusting behaviour for a guest to be permanently barred from a Zone hotel. This made the Zone a rather raucous place much of the time, but not particularly unbearable, apart from public holidays.

The disco was part of the Poles' package. And it was a package which seemed to date from the early years after the fall of Communism. A trip to the Zone, a visit to the supermarket down in the valley, skiing for those who wanted it, and a disco and meal on New Year's Eve. There was also, Rudi had begun to realise, an extramural part of the package, one which involved violence and colossal amounts of alcohol and was entirely beyond the control of the reps who accompanied the tour.

From the hatchway between the small dining room and the kitchen, Rudi watched dinner being served. Jan's patience with the Poles, tenuous at the best of times, had finally evaporated, and he had instructed Chef to take care of the other guests in the big dining room. Then he had taken off his manager's jacket, donned an apron and a chef's hat, and set about cooking for the Poles himself.

All afternoon he had been beating cheap cuts of pork senseless with a meat hammer, dipping them in flour and egg and coating them in breadcrumbs. Coming on for his shift, Rudi found him loading

trays of breadcrumbed cutlets into the fridge ready
for the evening meal.

The Poles were all dressed up. The hardcore
troublemakers, the ones who had been picking
fights and letting off fire extinguishers and pitching
furniture out of the windows, were the best-dressed
of all, in wonderfully-cut expensive suits of soft
black fabric. Their girlfriends were wearing Paris
dresses that this year were mostly chiffon and big
lace panels. Rudi had seen people like this in Kraków,
early in the evenings, getting out of chauffeur-driven
limos outside the casinos. What they were doing
here, paying a pittance to mix with poor people,
when they could have block-booked a floor in a
Marriott anywhere in Europe, was beyond him.
He'd long ago given up trying to second-guess Poles.

In the kitchen, Jan laboured, frying the prepared
pork cutlets, slinging them still sizzling with fat onto
plates, topping each one with a fried egg, and adding
boiled potatoes and string beans. The manager's face
was shining with sweat and there was a look in his eyes
that Rudi thought was a kind of deranged gleefulness,
serving this kind of crap to the Poles. Rudi wanted to
tell him the Poles loved stuff like this; to them it was
good solid home cooking, virtually national cuisine,
and Jan was making a fool of himself.

But he didn't say anything. The evening was
going to be difficult enough without having to
field the manager's questions about Poland. As
cups and glasses and plates began to come back
through the hatch, Rudi fired up the Hobart and
began loading trays.

He didn't usually drink until he came off duty, but

because this was New Year's Eve Jan had allowed a bottle of Becherovka in the kitchen, and between courses and rushes of dirty crockery they perched on a worktop and added tonic water to the bitters to make the drink Czechs called 'concrete' and toasted each other.

"Na zdraví," Jan said, raising his glass.

"Cheers." Rudi checked his watch. Ten past eleven, and the noise in the dining room already sounded like that caused by the crowd at an important football match.

Jan drained his glass and wiped his forearm across his forehead. "I'd forgotten how much fun this was."

Rudi grinned. "How do you feel about swapping jobs?"

"What?" Jan laughed and waved his glass at the Hobart. "Go back to working on that thing? I've worked for years so I wouldn't ever have to do that again." He topped up their glasses. "I was pretty good, though."

"I'll bet."

Jan raised his glass in another toast and drained it again. "I was. Really."

Rudi looked across at four trays of cups and plates and cutlery that sat along the worktop, and nodded significantly.

"No," said Jan, following his gaze.

"Why not?"

"They're already clean. It wouldn't be the same."

Rudi shrugged. "What does it matter?"

Jan smiled a sly smile. "Fifty crowns?"

Fifty crowns was Rudi's wages for a shift, but what the hell, it was New Year's Eve. "Okay."

"Fine." Jan hopped down off the worktop. "You go first."

They split the contents of the trays equally between two baskets and Jan stood beside Rudi with his wristwatch held up in front of his face. "Ready, steady. Go!"

There was a rhythm to it, a matter of twisting at the hips, not moving your feet. Cups arranged upside down on a tray and loaded onto the spikes of the conveyor, then pick up a stack of plates and deal them one by one upright between the spikes. Rudi was very good. By the time he'd finished loading one tray of crockery into the machine the cups were coming off the other, and he had to trot round and lift them off, then take the plates off and stack them. Then back to the far end to load the next tray.

"Not so bad," said Jan, stopping his watch when Rudi had stacked the last plate. "But not good enough. Here." He handed the watch over. "Press the little silver button once to reset the stopwatch, and again to start it."

Rudi turned the watch over in his hand. "Very nice."

"From the owners," Jan said, stationing himself at the end of the Hobart. "When I was promoted to manager. Ready?"

"Oh. Right." Rudi held up the watch and put his finger on the button. "Three, two, one, go."

Jan had this technique by which he just seemed to spill an armload of plates into the machine, and that was what made the difference in the end, though they both admitted he didn't win by very much.

"Best of three?" Jan asked when the money had changed hands and their glasses were full again.

"I'm impulsive, Jan," Rudi told him. "I'm not stupid. I know when I'm beaten."

"Ah," Jan clapped him on the shoulder, "that everyone was like that."

A pile of dessert dishes had appeared in the hatchway while they had been trying to out-macho each other. "Back to work."

"You did come here from Poland, didn't you?" Jan said as he watched Rudi putting the dirty dishes in a tray.

"I can't understand this thing you've got about me and Poland, Jan. I'm Estonian, for heaven's sake. I've never said a word about Poland, you're the one who's always bringing it up."

"My cousin drives a taxi," Jan said, leaning back against the wall. "He was down at the station when you arrived. He says you got off the express from Kraków." He poured himself another drink. "And you do speak Polish, don't you?"

"No." Rudi carried the full tray over to the machine, set it on the conveyor and pressed the button to start the belt. "And even if I did, what's so wrong with that?"

Jan suddenly became very serious. "Because I hate people lying to me, even about tiny little things." He drank his drink. "The way I see it, if somebody's prepared to lie to me about tiny little things they're prepared to lie to me about great big things."

Rudi went back to the hatch and started loading another tray. "I'm really getting tired of this, Jan. Your cousin has the wrong bloke. He saw somebody who looks like me getting off that train. Shall I tell you how I know this? I know this because I didn't come here by train from Kraków. I hitched here from Vienna, and I hitched to Vienna from Paris." This happened to be true; Rudi had been very careful about his approach to the Zone. "I don't speak Polish. I've never been to Poland."

Jan listened soberly to all this, nodding. When Rudi was finished, he shrugged. "You forget my position," he said. "I take on a lot of temporary staff, sometimes people just passing through the area. Are they criminals? Are they on the run from some polity's armed forces?" He looked at Rudi and tipped his head to one side. "Surely I should know these things."

Rudi looked at Jan for a moment. Then he shook his head. "I'm a resident of the Zone, Jan. I've lived here for six years. I have a resident's passport. I can apply for citizenship next year."

Jan nodded. "Yes, and very good references you have from your last job. From your last three jobs, in fact. I contacted your last three employers, and they all spoke very highly of you. Which is what makes me suspicious."

"Your logic is impeccable, Jan. My previous employers have nothing but good words to say about me. Therefore, I must be a criminal."

"Take your girl, for example."

"What?"

"Marta, your girl. Oh, come on. Everyone in the hotel knows about you and her."

Well, if he'd learned anything while he'd been here it was that it was impossible to keep a secret in an hotel. "What about her?"

"Arrived here two days before you. Impeccable

references. Hotel Bristol, Warsaw. The Warszawa, Warsaw. The Cracovia in Kraków. Wonderful references." Jan almost looked nostalgic remembering them. "And here are you, just turning up at the back door with nothing but a rucksack and a nice smile." Jan nodded and refilled his glass, apparently not caring any longer whether or not he was drunk on duty. "Terrific references." He waved his hand, forgetting he was holding his glass, and sloshed concrete everywhere. "Just like you."

Rudi said, "Jan," and then he stopped.

When he thought about it later, he thought that Jan had actually heard it *before* it happened, which he supposed was what separated the kitchen porters of this world from the managers. They had both grown used to the increasingly raucous noise from the dining room, but Jan suddenly tipped his head to one side as if listening, and then all hell broke loose.

They went to the hatch and looked out. The dining room had been reconfigured for the disco, chairs and tables pushed against the walls. The lights had been lowered and the volume of the Poles' sound system raised, and blinking lights and flashing lasers picked out an immense brawl. Bottles and glasses were flying across the room, people were punching each other, girls were screaming, glass and furniture was breaking. As they watched, a little circular table, caught in the stop-motion of a strobing laser, clambered jerkily out of the general chaos and hung in the air for a moment before falling back.

"I knew this would happen," Jan said calmly, as if perversely happy to be proved right. "I kept saying this would happen."

Rudi looked at his watch. It read 00:02. "At least they waited until midnight."

Jan sighed. "Lock all the doors in here and close the hatch. I'll go and call the police." And he went out into the dining room. The last Rudi saw of him, he was wading through the melee towards the door.

Some of the waiting staff pushed into the kitchen before Rudi managed to get the door closed and bolted. They stood around in a little group listening to the sounds of things breaking and people screaming and fireworks being set off in the dining room. Then Rudi put his parka on, took his rucksack from its hiding place under one of the counters, and went out the back door to the loading bay.

It was a lovely night. The stars were bright and hard and unblinking, and down in the valley tiny little firework explosions burst over the towns. He watched them for a while, struck by how strange it was to see fireworks exploding from above. From the front of the hotel, he could hear shouting and the deep bass grumble of the engines of tracked police vehicles.

Behind him, a shoe scraped the cement beneath the loading bay's thin layer of crusty slush.

Rudi looked round. A small, slight figure was standing a few metres away, a suitcase in one hand. The figure took another step forward into the loading bay's lights, and Rudi saw it was a small middle-aged man, shivering in his inadequate overcoat, cheeks and nose nipped crimson by the cold. They stood and looked at each other.

"Are you the Coureur?" the little man asked finally.

Rudi sighed. Dariusz had told him it was usually pointless giving Packages word-code recognition strings. They never remembered them, he said, or forgot to use them in the excitement of the jump, or just thought they were stupid and childish, which was Rudi's personal opinion as well.

But tradecraft was tradecraft. "I'm the kitchen porter," Rudi said.

The little man's face fell until something at the back of his excited, terrified mind recognised Rudi's half of the recognition string. "Oh," he said. "Right. Er, Are you with the Air Force?"

Embarrassing. Rudi rubbed his eyes.

"Hey!" another, cheerier voice boomed. "Hey! Are you cooking here now?"

Rudi took his hand from his eyes. Crunching through the snow towards them, looking like a blond Kodiak bear in a hugely-stuffed puffa suit, was the Hungarian who had spoken to him three years ago in Max's restaurant, the one who had complimented him on his good fuck food.

"I'm washing dishes," Rudi told him, trying to radiate calm on behalf of the Package.

"That's a real shame," the Hungarian said. "Obviously you're wasted here." He reached for the Package and soft-landed one huge gloved hand on the little man's shoulder. "Stay," he rumbled goodnaturedly.

The Package ignored the command, somehow managed to shrug his way out from under the weight of the Hungarian's hand, and took off for the edge of the road, dropping his suitcase as he ran.

Rudi and the Hungarian looked at each other.

Rudi wasn't carrying a weapon, and wouldn't have used one if he was. The Hungarian smiled at him.

The Package reached the edge of the service road and jumped, disappearing down the slope in a flurry of snow and flying coat-tails. There was a shout, a thump, then silence.

"Did Max fire you?" the Hungarian inquired.

"Your Polish has improved," Rudi observed.

The Hungarian inclined his huge shaggy blond head. "I find that if you work hard and pay attention, you can learn almost anything."

Two more huge blond men appeared at the side of the road, toiling up the slope with the Package dangling between them. They lifted him over the piles of snow at the edge of the road and dragged him over to the Hungarian. The three of them proceeded to have a very brief whispered conversation, during which the Hungarian never took his eyes off Rudi, then the other two started to drag the insensible Package away along the side of the hotel.

"Now then," said the Hungarian when they had disappeared from view around the front of the hotel. "What are we going to do with you?"

"He's ours," said a voice from the back of the loading bay. Rudi scowled.

"Is that so?" asked the Hungarian.

"That's so," Marta said, coming to the edge of the loading bay and looking down at them. She was wearing jeans and a big chunky sweater and hiking boots and a down-stuffed jacket. For a moment, Rudi didn't know her. Her hair was tied back, and she had removed the makeup she customarily wore. She looked at once wide-eyed and innocent and capable and businesslike. "The Package is yours. The dishwasher is a resident of the Zone."

The Hungarian grinned and winked at Rudi to let him know what he thought of the dishwasher pantomime. "It seems you have an admirer."

Rudi looked at Marta and considered the number of ways in which he had been stupid. There were, he thought, too many to count.

The Hungarian went over and picked up the Package's suitcase. It looked like a toy dangling from his massive hand. "Maybe I'll come to Restauracja Max sometime and we can have dinner."

"Don't hurry," Rudi told him.

The Hungarian looked hurt. "Ah well," he said. He saluted Rudi, bowed to Marta, and walked away into the night.

When he had turned the corner of the building, Marta walked down the loading bay steps and stood beside Rudi. "Time to go," she said.

Rudi picked up his rucksack. All of a sudden, he felt very heavy and tired.

A SHORT WALK down the mountainside, slipping and sliding through deep powdery snow, brought them to a narrow forestry road. A car was waiting, part of Rudi's dustoff. Somehow, Marta had come across a spare set of keys. She drove.

Rudi sat and watched the tunnel of snow-laden trees advance on him in the car's headlights. The forestry road hadn't been cleared, and there were ten or twelve centimetres of snow on it. The car was moving at about five kilometres an hour. It would be easy to open the door and tumble out into the deep snow at the side of the road and make his escape, but he couldn't see the point.

"It could have worked, if it's any consolation," she said.

He looked across at her. "What?"

"It's always chaos up there on New Year's Eve," she said, squinting out at the road. "You might have made it, but they were following your man all the way."

"Who?"

She shrugged. "There's no way to be sure. They bought a certain degree of cooperation from us for a certain period of time." She glanced at him. "Don't look like that. It was an interesting plan."

He watched her for a minute or so, steering the car carefully down the gentle slope of the road. "Are you from Zone counterespionage?" he asked.

She laughed. "Now *there's* a grand title." She shook her head. "What I wonder is, was that a real fight, or did you start it?"

"I was in the kitchen the whole time," Rudi said. "Jan will vouch for me."

"Not you personally," she said. "Agents provocateurs, hired for the occasion – what do you call them?"

"Stringers. As you very well know."

"Stringers, yes. I *love* Coureur terminology. It's so quaint. What I wonder is, did you hire some *stringers* to start that riot and cover your departure?"

"Like you said," Rudi murmured. "There's always chaos up there on New Year's Eve."

They drove for another ten or fifteen minutes in silence. The slope of the road rose and fell, and finally the trees withdrew gently from either side and they were driving along a two-lane road, cleared enough for Marta to accelerate to around twenty kilometres an hour.

"Who was the Hungarian?" Rudi asked.

"He says his name's Kerenyi. But you say your name's Tonu, and I say my name's Marta." She shrugged her shoulders at this world where nobody could be certain of anyone else's real name.

"You knew I was coming," he said.

"We knew *he* was coming," she said, meaning the Package. "The Hungarians told us where he would be and when he would be there."

"And all you had to do was wait for me to turn up." He rubbed his face. "What are you going to do with me?"

She was hunched so far over the steering wheel that her face was centimetres from the windscreen. "Wait and see." The car hit a patch of ice and fishtailed for a moment. Rudi listened to Marta swearing as she fought the wheel. The prospect of sliding into the path of an oncoming truck seemed quite attractive, right then.

Finally, she got the car back under control and looked over at him, and her face was pale and a little sweaty in the light of the streetlamps.

"We're not even particularly angry with you," she said.

"No?"

"This sort of thing happens once or twice a year. Somebody's intelligence service decides to mess around with somebody else's intelligence service, and they decide to do it in the Zone." She slowed the car for a set of traffic lights, the first they'd seen since leaving the hotel. "Tourism is our only industry, and in order to exploit it properly we have to be neutral."

"It's hard to be neutral."

"No intelligence operations on our soil. If we find them, we blow them. Spoil everybody's stupid little game. Eventually everyone will get the point." She was almost shouting by this time. "I mean, why don't you all just go and play in Baku or somewhere like that and leave us alone?"

"I just go where I'm sent."

"The Nuremberg Defence," she muttered. The lights changed. She put the car into gear and they moved off.

AFTER HALF AN hour or so they arrived at the border between the Zone and the Czech Republic. Marta slowed the car long enough to wave a laminated pass at the Zone guards, but she had to stop on the Czech side of the crossing for customs and passport checks.

Rudi hadn't realised quite how warm it was in the car until he got out to allow the Czech customs man to look inside. He and Marta stood side by side watching the plump little Czech and his springer spaniel sniffer dog clamber around on the back seat. Rudi couldn't be sure which of them was having the most fun.

"It's not personal," said Marta, and each word was a distinct little balloon of fog in the cold air. "I was only doing my job."

"The Nuremberg Defence," said Rudi.

She swore softly and turned up the collar of her

jacket. "How long is this going to take?" she called in Czech, but there was no reply from inside the car and she crossed her arms and jammed her hands up into her armpits for warmth. Rudi wondered why she wasn't wearing gloves. "I'll take your passport," she said to him.

"I was told to return it."

"I don't care what you were told. It's the property of my government."

He shook his head.

She glared at him. "I could take you back to the Zone and arrest you."

"But you have no powers of arrest in the Czech Republic," he pointed out. He nodded at the little customs man. "I could claim asylum."

"He'd probably have a heart attack if you did."

"Worth a try, though."

She shook her head. "We have an extradition treaty with the Czechs. We'd have you out of here in two hours."

He looked down at her. "Two hours?"

"Maximum."

He thought about it and shook his head again. "I was told to bring it back."

"Your people will never be able to use the Tonu Laara legend again."

"Oh, I imagine there'll be somewhere it will be useful." He smiled at her. "Baku, maybe."

The customs officer said, "You can go."

Marta looked at him and drew herself up to her full height. "If that dog's pissed in my car, I'll make you wish you'd never been born," she said. "You *and* the dog."

*　　*　　*

THEY DROVE FOR another hour or so, to the crossing at Český Těšín. Marta pulled the car out of the line of traffic queuing for the border and drove around behind a row of brick buildings. Rudi looked out and shook his head. Hectares of concrete and asphalt flooded with white light, dotted with brick buildings and checkpoints, and surrounded by high fences. Home again.

"I'll walk with you," Marta said, opening her door.

Outside, the wind blew down from the mountains and across all that slushy asphalt and concrete and cut right through his parka. He shouldered his rucksack and followed Marta through the shadowless illumination between ranks of coaches whose passengers looked down at them incuriously as they passed. Across the concrete, a trucker was standing beside his twenty-wheeler and having a spirited argument with a Czech Customs officer.

"If you don't mind my saying so," he told her, "you have a very unusual way of doing things."

"We're the Zone," she said brightly. "What did you expect?"

There was a tunnel of razor-wire and high fencing that angled away from the lorry-park and led down to the border. There was a checkpoint about halfway along.

"Don't you hate this light?" Rudi asked, looking up at the lamp standards that stood every ten metres or so along the path. "It's the same all over Europe. Probably all over the world." He shook his head.

"The frontier actually runs through the middle of the town," Marta said. "On this side, it's Český Těšín. Just down there, on the other side of the wire, it's Cieszyn. Polski Cieszyn, they call it. Don't look at me like that."

"Like what?"

"As if you were going to give me that Coureur speech about Schengen and free movement across borders. You people always do that. I hate idealists."

"As ideals go, it isn't a bad one."

"You're young," she told him. "You'll change."

He smiled at her. "You're young too."

She punched him in the shoulder hard enough to hurt. "Passport."

"No."

She held out her hand.

"How am I going to get into Poland without it?"

"You can use the passport that says your name is Jan Paweł Kaminski." They stood looking into each other's eyes for a few moments. "It was stupid to hide it in your room. Poor tradecraft."

It occurred to him that he was lucky to have escaped from this Situation with his life. "I think tradecraft is the least of my problems right now."

"How many of these things have you done?" she asked.

If you included the business with Max's cousin, and whatever the hell it was that Fabio had been trying to pull off in Poznań, this had been Rudi's fourth live Situation. "A few," he said in what he hoped was a wise tone of voice.

"I think you ought to stop doing it," she told him. "You're not very good."

At this precise moment, there seemed no way to argue with that. He shrugged and headed for the checkpoint.

Rudi's Polish passport was a plastic card embossed with his photograph. The Czech border guard slipped the card into a slot and the machine read the embedded chip. Rudi put his thumb on the reader, the guard looked at his screen, then looked at Marta.

"It's the dishwasher," Rudi said. "The water's too hot. It blistered my fingerprints off."

"Let him through," Marta said, and the official looked at her one more time and handed Rudi's card back and Rudi wondered just what kind of arrangements the Zone had with the Czech Republic.

"Passport," Marta said to him as the barrier slid aside.

Rudi smiled at her and walked away.

Ten metres along the tunnel, the guard at the Polish checkpoint examined his passport and enquired whether he had anything to declare. Rudi opened his rucksack and took out the bottles of Czech rum and Czech whisky he had brought with him, just in case the Package had needed a warming drink. The Customs man pulled a face.

"They all taste the same," he said. "Christ only knows what they make them from."

"They have great beer, though," Rudi said, looking back along the tunnel. Marta was still standing at the Czech border post, a small figure in a big jacket. As he watched, she took her hand from her pocket and waved to him. In her hand was something small and green and rectangular.

"Happy New Year," the guard said.

Rudi smiled at him. "And to you." He laced up his rucksack again, slung it over his shoulder and walked away from the border.

APART FROM THE Polish street-names and shop signs, and a general air of dilapidation, there seemed very little difference between Cieszyn and its Czech counterpart. The snowy streets were busy with New Year revellers and people making their way to and from church. Rudi wandered along with them.

As he passed one church, he turned and pushed through the doors. The place was packed, and he had to stand at the back with a crowd of Poles, their feet squelching in melting slush. After a little while, Dariusz came in and stood beside him.

"They sold us to the Hungarians," Rudi said quietly.

Dariusz shrugged. "Next time, they'll sell the Hungarians to us," he murmured. "The Zoners like to think they're holier-than-thou, but they're for sale like everyone else. It all equals out, in the end."

Rudi looked at him. "They stole my passport."

Dariusz nodded. "They always do that. We'll get another one."

"The Hungarians got the Package back."

"That also happens sometimes." He reached up and clapped Rudi on the shoulder. "You're all right, though. That's the important thing."

"I'm not all right."

"I know." Dariusz looked sad. "I know. Let's go home, eh?"

It was only later, sitting in the front seat of Dariusz's Mercedes and watching the inadequately-cleared lanes of the motorway unwind towards Kraków, that Rudi put his hand in the pocket of his parka and realised that he had somehow left the hotel with Jan's watch.

LEO'S
LAST JUMP

1.

ON NOVEMBER 1, in defiance of global warming, a high pressure area swept down from Scandinavia, bearing on its close-packed isobars tiny particles of snow as hard as ground glass.

For three days, the many little states of Northern and Central Europe slowly disappeared beneath a coarse, glittering blanket. In some outlying or badly-administered areas, villages and sometimes even towns were cut off. People mostly battled to work, although in some places schools and offices were forced to close when their oil-fired boilers ran out of fuel because tankers were unable to get through to make deliveries.

At midnight on November 4, Mr Albrecht finished his shift and drove his creaky old orange tram into the new depot beside Potsdam-Stadt railway station.

For the past hour, the only other person on the tram had been a figure slumped in one of the rear seats, head leaning against the window, arms crossed over its chest, in an attitude of uncomfortable sleep.

Mr Albrecht left his driver's cab, slung his satchel over one shoulder, and walked along the grime-spattered side of the tram to the rear doors.

Inside, he stood for a few moments looking down at his only passenger. The sleeping figure was bundled up in a long padded coat, its hem wet with slush and its hood pulled up. Within the hood, Mr Albrecht could see a scarf wrapped around the lower half of his passenger's face. He reached down and took hold of one shoulder and shook gently.

"Hey, mate."

The sleeping figure stirred. "Mm?"

"As far as I'm concerned, you're welcome to stay," said Mr Albrecht. "But this tram's not going any further tonight."

The figure looked up, blinked blearily. "Where?"

"Potsdam-Stadt depot."

The eyes, which were all that Mr Albrecht could see, narrowed. "Shit. I was supposed to get off at Babelsberg. I have to get to Rosa Luxembourg Strasse."

"You'll have to get a taxi."

The passenger shook his head. "I haven't got any money for a taxi."

Mr Albrecht sighed. He put his hand in his pocket and took out a folded five-mark note. "Here." He pressed the note into his passenger's gloved hand. "You can pay me back." He gestured out into the big brightly-lit shed of the depot, the ranks of parked trams. "Just leave it at the main office and say it's for Albrecht. Everyone knows me."

The passenger mumbled thanks, took a big heavy-looking duffel bag from the floor under his seat, and got off the tram. Mr Albrecht watched him disappear by degrees into the white howl beyond the depot doors, and shook his head at the chances of finding a taxi in this weather.

It was almost one o'clock in the morning when he got back to his flat on Voltaire-Weg, overlooking the hated razor-wire border thrown up by those damned New Potsdamers to keep intruders out of their pocket kingdom, but his wife was still waiting, with the patience of long years' experience, with his evening meal on the table.

Mr Albrecht had been asked never to speak of his other work, highly infrequent though it was, but he had sworn to himself on his wedding day that his would be a marriage without secrets, so when he had finished his meal and he was drinking a coffee he told his wife about the sleeping passenger he had driven to the depot.

"What was he like?" his wife asked.

Mr Albrecht had only seen the passenger's eyes and heard his voice, but he had been driving a tram around Potsdam for twenty-three years and when you do that you see all types, and you learn some things.

"He was," he said, "very young."

IN A DOORWAY not far from the tram depot, Rudi took out the five-mark note the stringer on the tram had given him. Unfolding it, he tilted the note towards a streetlight's illumination and squinted to read the time and place pencilled in tiny letters on its margin. Then he took a stamped and addressed envelope from his pocket, sealed the note inside, and left the doorway. On his way down the street, he dropped the envelope in a post box and let the German postal service dispose of the evidence.

OLDER THAN BERLIN by two centuries, Potsdam had started life as a Slavic fishing village on the banks of the River Havel. Its name – its Slavic name at any rate, *Poztupimi* – was first recorded when its charter was signed by Otto III in the year 993 AD.

Friedrich Wilhelm built himself a summer palace near the river in 1660, and linked it to Berlin with a road lined with lime trees. Frederick the Great gave the city Sanssouci, one of the age's greatest palaces. In 1747, Bach came to play for him, and three years later he debated philosophy there with Voltaire.

Almost two centuries later, Allied bombers all but destroyed the heart of the town, and towards the end of the War Truman, Churchill, Stalin and Attlee met at the Schloss Cecilienhof and decided how postWar Germany should be parcelled out. Potsdam fell within the Soviet Sector, and in 1961 the Berlin Wall cut it off from the West, severing Friedrich Wilhelm's road to Berlin where it crossed the Havel.

Sometime later, after Potsdam had grown grimy and battered under the Communists, after *die Wende* brought a certain degree of bemused rebuilding, after the world woke up from its post-Millennium hangover, a group of anarchists squatting in a building off Hegel-Allee declared their home to be an independent nation.

In this, they were only doing what hundreds of other groups had been doing, with wildly varying degrees of success, all over the world for a number of years. They issued passports, printed their own money, raised their own taxes – these being, it was understood, lamentable and temporary but necessary measures to protect their new country from the predations of the outside world. It was meant to be a suitably obscene gesture to Authority, but to the anarchists' consternation the idea spread to a neighbouring building. And then another. And then another.

The anarchists were forced to form committees to cope with finance, food, power, water and sewerage. Periodic attacks by drunken shaven-headed youths forced them to form a Border Guard. The necessity of coordinating maintenance on their buildings required some kind of works committee. Cameramen from *Die Welt* and *Bild* and *Time/Stone Online* came, took their photos, posted their stories, and went away again. There was a moment – nobody identified it until much later – when events seemed to pause for a breath.

And then the anarchists' gesture against authority was a nation a little over two kilometres across and it was called New Potsdam.

After a week of tense negotiations with the Potsdam city council – which had failed to take the New Potsdamers seriously until much too late – the anarchists were deposed in a bloodless coup by a neo-Traditionalist faction which wanted to run the

new polity along strictly Prussian lines. Most of the
anarchists departed, muttering darkly to the Press
but privately pleased to be relieved of responsibility
for sewage and economics.

Meanwhile, Berlin – which had too many of these
pissant nations to deal with already – watched the
coup and gave New Potsdam no more than two
years before its citizens were clamouring to rejoin
Greater Germany.

Until that happened, the New Potsdamers were
still trying to consolidate the country they had,
almost by surprise, found themselves living in. All
their services still depended on Greater Germany,
including their electricity grid.

Responsibility for the supply to the western quarter
of New Potsdam ran through a featureless four-storey
building in Berlin, overlooking the Spree. There, in
a room on the third floor, was a certain computer
workstation, and at this workstation, on this
particular evening early in his shift, Wolf sat down,
pushed his spectacles up his nose with his forefinger,
and air-typed a couple of strings of commands.

The heads-up drew him a schematic of New
Potsdam's security cameras and their relevant security
stations. Wolf, in his late twenties but already with a
receding hairline that gave him a deceptively serious
look, swept the cursor to a certain closed-circuit
television monitoring station inside New Potsdam,
and double-clicked.

Almost all the buildings in New Potsdam which
depended on the Greater German grid had backup
generators, but generators cost money and they
required manpower to install them and there were

little blind spots here and there. Wolf pulled up a sub-menu and scheduled a fifteen-minute brownout for this particular New Potsdam monitoring station.

He thought this was rather elegant. A blackout would have been just as easy to program, but a reduction of eighty percent would cause the monitoring system to shut itself down just as effectively, and he could imagine how much it would annoy the New Potsdamers.

Wolf's grandfather told tales of life in East Germany that were still hair-rising despite becoming progressively more and more embroidered with each re-telling, and though Wolf didn't think of himself as being particularly political, he had inherited from the old man a distrust of borders. Traudl, his girlfriend of two months, was a kindred spirit – in fact tonight's harmless bit of mischief had been her idea.

Once the idea had been presented to him, Wolf developed megalomania. The thought of blacking New Potsdam out appealed to him, but Traudl convinced him that a certain *subtle* approach was best.

"That way," she told him one night in bed, "we can do it again and again. Nobody will know we're doing it, and the New Potsdamers' security police will go slowly crazy."

"What do you mean 'we'?" Wolf asked.

Traudl giggled and snuggled up to him. "I meant you, of course," she said.

The affected monitoring station received feeds from about sixty cameras mounted here and there around the Brandenberger Tor and some traffic intersections further south. The target had also been Traudl's idea.

Wolf closed down the sub-menus one by one, then called up a section of Berlin's grid, sat back in his chair and whistled tunelessly as his supervisor passed by.

"Any problems?" asked the supervisor.

"All quiet on the Western Front," Wolf replied with a small, smug grin.

THE WEATHER WAS a bonus.

It was the sort of night Coureurs prayed for. Fifteen centimetres of snow and seven degrees of frost on the ground and a wind-chill, unhindered all the way across North-Central Europe, driving the air temperature down to somewhere in the minus thirties, a howling gale carrying snow like airgun pellets. On nights like this, people made mistakes, got sloppy, paid more attention to their own comfort than to their job.

Rudi didn't feel the weather, here on the edge of Old Potsdam in the snow and the wind and the cold. His stealth suit's insulation was so efficient that if he was to keep it sealed for any great length of time his own body heat would eventually cook him, but its surface layers remained precisely at ambient temperature, merging him into the infra-red background. It artfully scattered radar wavelengths right down to millimetre frequencies, giving him the radar signature of a moth, and its mimetic system blended into whatever background the suit happened to be standing against, like a very badly-dressed chameleon.

All of which combined to make him indistinguishable from the shop doorway in which he was crouching to watch the brightly-lit kiosk of the checkpoint. On the other hand, if a drunk should happen along and decide to have a piss in this particular doorway, nothing would save Rudi. He was invisible to most of the commonly-deployed security devices known to man, and to the naked eye of anyone more than half a metre or so away. Closer to, he looked like the indistinct silhouette of a rag-wrapped gorilla wearing a mutilated motorcycle crash-helmet. Not the sort of thing you expect to see in an Old Potsdam shop doorway, even if you're drunk.

Just over a year since its declaration of nationhood, New Potsdam's border arrangements were still on the ad hoc side of adequate. To Rudi's eye it looked theatrical and ill-thought-out, but that was the way with new polities. The first thing they tended to do was put up defences. A sure sign of a polity approaching maturity was when the work-crews came out and started dismantling the wire. Except maybe in the more paranoid parts of the world.

There were sections of wall going up, here and there, around New Potsdam, but most of the border was still a tunnel of carbon-flood light enclosing a dense spiralling hedge of razor-wire that ran down the centre-line of streets, cutting intersections in half and brushing the corners of buildings, broken at irregular intervals by checkpoints.

The checkpoint kiosks looked as if they had been brought in from car parks, had inadequately-adapted vehicle radars and infra-red scanners and barcode readers mounted on their roofs, and then been staffed by a hurriedly-conscripted border guard. In common with many immature polities, great pains had been taken with the uniform of the Border Guard. They were the work of a Berlin theatrical costumier, and more than a little reminiscent of the uniforms of the Ruritanian officer classes in the Stewart Granger version of *The Prisoner Of Zenda*.

Rudi slipped out of the doorway, taking care to move evenly to give the suit's mimetic systems time to adjust to their background. If anyone was watching carefully they might see his footprints appear in the snow along the base of the wall, but this was not the kind of night when people watched very carefully for anything.

He ghosted along the line of buildings for ten minutes, not hurrying. He ducked through the archway of an apartment building and stood in the shadows of the courtyard to yank down the zip of his suit. Hot air fountained out around his face. When he started to feel the cold he zipped the suit up again and stepped back out into the street.

Along the base of the wall again. Up ahead, in the middle of a huge intersection, windblown snow haloed a crown of lamps atop a twenty-metre pole rising from the centre of what used to be a big roundabout. The hedge of razor-wire marched into the lamps' pool of blue-white light, straight up the slope of the traffic island in the middle, down the other side, and off into the howling darkness, cutting the roundabout in two. The wind made the wire sing eerily. Rudi sank gently down on one knee and eased the cooling mask that covered his face and ensured his breath wouldn't give him away to infra-red. It was a new mask, and it pinched.

He clicked his teeth together twice and his helmet's HUD came up, a faint blue grid and discreet columns of figures hanging in front of his eyes. He turned his head left and right, and the figures flicked up and down, giving him proximity readouts. He clicked his teeth again to call up the infra-red overlay and a number of bright patches appeared on the buildings on the other side of the border where boiler chimneys vented their hot gases or the insulation wasn't as good as it might have been. One rooftop beyond the traffic island absolutely blazed. Rudi tut-tutted soundlessly at the inefficiency.

No moving heat sources, though. Not even a car. The foam bead in his ear was scanning New Potsdam's security frequencies in thirty-second soundbites, and had played nothing more exciting all night than a crash between two drunk drivers somewhere over on the other side of the polity.

The mission clock up in the top right corner of the HUD read 01:03, just over forty minutes since he began his approach to the jumpoff. The Zulu clock, set to GMT, read 03:35, twenty-five to four in the morning local time. The fifteen-minute window of downtime he had been promised on the security cameras watching the intersection and its approaches should just have opened, but he had to take that on faith because there was just no way to tell. Rudi examined the big traffic island again, starting to feel uncomfortably warm.

In a lot of ways, this was a milk-run of a jump. All the groundwork had already been done by local stringers. All Rudi had to do was turn up, take receipt of the Package, and facilitate the dustoff. He could do this kind of thing in his sleep.

The Package was a few minutes late. This was not

unusual; once, in Seville, Rudi had waited two hours, beyond all dictates of tradecraft, before reverting to the fallback location. The Package didn't show that time. He never found out what happened. He'd stopped being curious about it. Sometimes they made it to the jumpoff, sometimes they didn't. It wasn't his problem.

And it wasn't going to happen this time. A warm ruddy glow appeared on his helmet's visor, a diffuse spot of radiant heat coming hesitantly round the slope of the traffic island. He clicked back to visible wavelengths and zoomed his camera. Snowy landscape and buildings rushed towards him, momentarily out of focus.

A bulky, white-clad figure was making its way painfully slowly around the curve of the roundabout, keeping the island's bulk between itself and the nearest border post. It was carrying what appeared to be an attaché case, and from the way the figure was moving the case looked as if it was very heavy. Rudi edged closer, until he was standing just across the road from the roundabout.

The Package reached the wire, set the case down on the slope, and started to fiddle with the barrier. Rudi couldn't make out what was happening, no matter how much zoom he put on his helmet's camera, but the wire sagged abruptly as a strand parted. And again as another strand went.

This time he saw it. The stressed wire whipped back, catching the crouching figure on the shoulder. Rudi thought he actually heard the singing note change fractionally as the wire separated. The figure made no sign of having noticed, kept working. More strands parted and sprang aside. With every one, the Package picked up its case, shuffled forward a few centimetres, then set the case down again and resumed work.

03:47 Zulu. Three minutes until the cameras came back online. The white figure was entirely enclosed by the rolls of wire, deep inside the fence, picking its way onward strand by strand. Rudi could now see thickly-gloved hands attaching a little black box to each section of wire, checking to see which one carried an alarm circuit. Whoever it was out there on the traffic island – the bulky cold-weather clothing made it impossible even to tell whether they were male or female, let alone identify them – they seemed calm and unhurried. Check the wire, detach the box, move on to the next strand, check the wire, detach the box, move on. Box in one hand, a little ceramic wire-cutter in the other. Cut the wire, take a step, start all over again. It was unusual to find a Package who was quite so professional. Rudi approved.

While he waited, he clicked back into infra-red and scanned the area again. This time, four more heat sources appeared on his visor, some way beyond the traffic island, making their way down the street towards the roundabout. Shit. Sloppy, sloppy; he should have been paying attention rather than admiring the Package's technique. Cursing himself, he stood, very slowly, and undid the velcroed flap on the front of his suit that hid his popgun.

The gun was flimsy, lightweight composite compounds and bracing wires. It had a pistol-grip and a magazine the size of a wheel of Stilton, and a five-year-old could have put their fist down the barrel.

Rudi snapped the magazine into place, thumbed the selector and stood very still, watching the four heat signatures moving towards the escaping Package.

There was sudden chatter on New Potsdam's security channel. Above the radio traffic Rudi heard shouts echoing off the surrounding buildings, whistles blowing on the freezing air, a pistol shot.

He angled the popgun at about forty-five degrees from his hip and squeezed the trigger twice. The gun ported its exhaust gases back and out in narrow jets from the propulsion chamber, supposedly countering recoil, but it hadn't been calibrated quite right and it bucked like a barracuda in his hands, throwing his aim off. The first round landed on target, sending a geyser of snow and ice and frozen earth up from the far side of the island. The second hit a building on the New Potsdam side of the fence and blew a balcony off into the street.

Everything seemed to go wrong at once. More gunshots on the other side of the wire, more shouting. Sirens eerie and tenuous on the wind.

He changed the selector position and fired twice more. The magazine made a momentary chirping sound as it spun at close to supersonic speed, stopping on the selected rounds. Fountains of stinking fluorescent smoke shot up from where the charges landed, smeared almost parallel to the snow by the wind. Instead of giving proper cover, the smoke just sort of bannered and darted, springing up in unpredictable places. Rudi tried to assign possibilities, watched them being knocked down as fast as he could think them up. This was very very bad, and it was getting worse. The whole Situation was going sour before his eyes and there was nothing he could do to stop it.

The figure on the traffic island seemed not to have noticed the chaos going off all around it. It carried on unhurriedly cutting its way strand by strand through New Potsdam's border, down the slope towards Old Potsdam.

Rudi popped another couple of smoke rounds over the wire, followed them with four white phosphorus flares that landed in a haphazard fashion on the roundabout and burned in the snow to confuse infra-red.

They didn't seem to work. Warm figures came up over the crest of the island. Others were coming out of the buildings on the other side of the frontier, confused residents wondering what was going on. Rudi heard shouting, harsh Saxon accents barking orders. The Package paused a moment. It had reached the outer twirl of wire, and for a second or two Rudi willed it on. Just a couple more strands, then run like crazy. They could still do this. He selected an explosive round, raised the popgun to his shoulder, sighted down the barrel at a car parked on the other side of the wire, and waited.

The figure bent deliberately down and grasped the handle of the briefcase. Rudi watched the arm swing back, forward. Then there was a chatter of gunfire and the white figure pitched face-forwards into the razor-wire and lay still.

But the case was still moving. Rudi watched it slide on its side under the last layer of wire, gathering speed down the slope of the island. It bounced over the kerb at the bottom without losing very much speed and shot out across the crusty snow on the road like a big square hockey puck and into Old Potsdam. It bumped to a stop at the side of the road a metre or so away from where Rudi was hiding.

He checked the figure on the island again. It wasn't moving, and border guards were picking their way through the severed wire towards it.

He dismantled the popgun, sealed it up under its flap and stepped over to the case. He picked it up, making sure that it was masked from sight by his body, and started to walk calmly away.

More shouting from the roundabout. One of the guards, his head bulbous with image-amps, was pointing. Some of the men in the wire pointed their weapons. Rudi started to run. Projectiles chewed masonry off the shopfronts and exploded windows in his wake.

AFTER AN HOUR or so of skulking from courtyard to courtyard, he seemed to have left the gunfire behind long enough to stop and collect his thoughts.

Rudi looked down. His HUD was still set to infra-red, and the briefcase was shining like a beacon.

Very slowly, he turned to put his back to the street, hiding the briefcase with his body. He removed a glove and put his bare hand against the side of the case. It was hot. Not red hot. Not drop-it-right-here-and-run-like-hell hot. But it was still hot. Which, in Rudi's experience, was a first for a piece of hand luggage.

Well, okay. At least that explained how the security men had been able to shoot at him. They were wearing thermal amps, and he was carrying the infra-red equivalent of a two-hundred-watt lightbulb. That much was straightforward.

Rudi put his glove back on, reached behind him, and tore up the flap on the pocket in the small of the suit's back. Inside was a fat package about the size of a pocket handkerchief. He found a corner and flapped it and the package opened out into a baggy white hooded poncho that started to take on the colouration of its surroundings the moment it was exposed. He wrapped the briefcase in the poncho and cradled it in his arms.

The poncho was made of the same smart material as his suit, with the same mimetic and insulating layers. He was going to have to unwrap the case periodically so it wouldn't overheat, but it should give him the chance to get away from here. Of course, he didn't know how long it would take the case to overheat...

He unwrapped a corner of the case and hot air billowed out of the poncho. He gave it a minute or so to cool a little, then wrapped it up again and started to move deliberately along the street.

ANOTHER COURTYARD. HE unwrapped the poncho and a blaze of radiant heat rose about him. The briefcase was very hot, but as he watched in infra-red its colour began to darken. He set it down and saw the snow around it start to melt and refreeze as ice. The case darkened further, dumping heat into the snow and the cold paving stones, but not enough to make him feel entirely comfortable about carrying it around.

The traffic on both New and Old Potsdam's security frequencies continued unabated in his ear, too many voices to be able to follow more than a few words of a conversation. Some German voices, some Saxon, one an incongruous and comical-sounding Bavarian. Some of the voices were shouting. The Bavarian, for all his incongruity, was giving orders in a calm, controlled tone.

What it all added up to was that they'd lost him. They had begun a line-search outward from the border, hoping to flush him out ahead of them. Dogs, thermal scanners, ultra-violet lamps. The Old Potsdam polizei seemed to be cooperating with the New Potsdam security forces, which was unexpected; Rudi's information was that the two groups existed in a state of barely-suppressed armed confrontation.

So much for *that*. They still didn't know where he was. Rudi took stock. He'd managed to make his way, in little zigs and zags, about three kilometres from the border, which was good.

Normally, at this point, his procedure would have been to stash the stealth suit for collection later, and make his own jumpoff in civilian clothes. He had several dustoffs scoped out, from a Hertz car parked near the film studios at Babelsberg to an open ticket to London from Berlin-Tegel. Normally, with the local law in such confusion, it would have been a walk in the park.

On the other hand, he didn't dare stash the briefcase. Quite apart from the fact that it had come as part of the Package and he was sworn to deliver it, one way or another, he wasn't sure if it was safe to leave it anywhere. He presumed the people who were looking for him knew it was hot and, when they got themselves organised – which couldn't be much longer now – would be wandering the city with thermal cameras, looking for somebody with warmer-than-usual luggage.

Well, this was what he was paid for, all part of the Coureur ethic. Get The Package Through. All he had to do was figure out how.

A FEW MINUTES after ten in the morning. Rudi sat in one of the little wooden shelters in the Neuer Friedhof, watching the snow veil down out of a dirty brownish-yellow sky. That was Central Europe for you: pollution wherever you went, even so long after the Fall of Communism. All that cheap *Braunkohl*, burned in industrial plants that had been a marvel of technology back in the 1950s. It was a wonder the snow itself wasn't brown or black.

He had seen black snow once, in Bulgaria, up on the Danube, which was called the Dunarea by the locals. He and his Package had dusted-off on a coal barge travelling upriver towards Austria. It had been a good jump, textbook stuff. It was good when a Situation went like that. It was unusual, because in Rudi's world everything could, and often did, go wrong, sometimes catastrophically. But when it didn't, like that time in Bulgaria, it was almost like a holiday.

And then it started to snow these big fat black flakes.

Rudi and the Package and the skipper of the barge had all gone out on deck and stood, amazed, in the middle of the sooty fall.

What Rudi couldn't figure out, for a moment, was why it was so cold and wet. It was like standing under a fall of burned paper; it should have been dry and hot. He caught a few black flakes on his palm and touched his tongue to them, tasted chemicals, and then it was obvious. Just another fucked-up legacy of the previous millennium, just industrial crap frozen out of the sky.

Rudi leaned forwards and reached under the seat. His hand found the side of the briefcase. Even through his glove he could feel the case's warmth. He sighed, running the night's fiasco over and over in his mind. He should have popped that car, given the Package the distraction they needed. He shouldn't have hesitated.

He had only brought out half of what he had been sent to protect, and that jarred with him. The briefcase, whatever it contained, had clearly been the most important thing to the Package. Did that mean the Package had considered themselves expendable, and that Rudi should do the same? Rudi wasn't sure he could do that for a briefcase. For a person, maybe, but for a briefcase?

Outside the shelter, the ivy-covered gravestones and modest little tombs of the graveyard were being given another dusting of snow. Stashing the suit in a situation like this would have been suicidal. He just had to get rid of it the best way he could. He'd dropped the suit's electronics off a bridge into the Havel, and carried the suit itself with him to the graveyard. He'd dumped it under a bush, pulled the emergency tab, and waited for the enzymes to eat the material. It was always quicker than he expected, like a time-lapse effect from a bad horror film. And then he'd come here, to think. Tradecraft dictated that he get as far away as possible in as short a time as possible, but he needed to think, to compose himself, pull down the options.

Most of his dustoffs would have to be abandoned because they involved public transport. Too easily stopped and searched. Ditto the car in Babelsberg. Ditto his plan to just walk to Berlin. Ditto the plan to hitch into Holland. Ditto ditto.

Rudi rubbed his face and reached down to touch the case again. Without it, he was just another blameless anonymous figure in the crowd, hair cut neither too long nor so short as to arouse notice, clothes carefully bought at various shops in Berlin and Magdeburg in order to blend in. With the case, he might as well be carrying a big sign saying ARREST ME. All it would take would be a policeman wearing infra-red amplifiers and he'd stand out from the crowd like someone striking a match in a darkened room.

He put a hand in his pocket and took out a set of car keys, and thought of the car in Babelsberg. He sighed and put the keys away. Then he took them out again and looked at them.

THEY HAD SET up a roadblock at the eastern end of the Glienicker Brücke. A hurried, temporary thing, not much more than a couple of policemen waving the traffic to the side of the road while another couple of policemen did a cursory search. It was almost two o'clock in the afternoon and already the light was beginning to fail, and in spite of the heater frost was forming on the inside of the hire car's windows. He drove normally, just another tourist, and when they stopped him he pulled over to the kerb and wound down the driver's window.

"Papers," said the policeman who leaned down to the open window.

Rudi took his passport and identity card from the glove compartment and handed them over. "What's going on?"

The policeman's face was scoured red with the cold and the fur collar of his jacket was turned up around his ears. "Routine," he said. "Turn off your engine."

Rudi obeyed, and the policeman took the documents over to his colleagues to confer. They huddled for a moment over a palmtop terminal, and Rudi imagined one of them cursing as he tried to enter code numbers with a gloved index finger that was too big for the palmtop's tapboard.

All four of them came back. One of them had a thermal camera hanging from a lanyard around his neck. He lifted it to his eyes and scanned it over the front of the car. Another pointed a hand-scanner at the car's registration plate to read the barcoded information.

"Hans Drucker," said the first policeman, returning to the open window.

"Yes," said Rudi. He nodded at the policeman with the camera. "What's he doing?"

"What was your business in Potsdam?"

"Visiting my sister." Rudi gave the address. There was a stringer there who would if necessary testify in court that she was his sister. There always seemed to be a stringer for every occasion. "I come here every weekend."

The cop nodded. "The registration number of this vehicle, please?"

"I can't remember," Rudi said. "I only hired it yesterday morning." He handed the Hertz documents out of the window, and the cop looked them over. Then he gave them to the cop with the scanner, who compared them with his read-out. One of the other policemen was running a mirror on a long angled rod under the car, tilting his head this way and that to look at the reflection.

"You visit your sister in a hired car?" asked the cop.

"My car broke down. Have I done anything wrong?"

"Why not take the train instead of hiring a car?" the policeman asked.

Rudi turned his own collar up against the cold surging in through the open window. "I used to until last year. I was robbed on the train going back to Berlin one night. Now I drive." This was also true. Hans Drucker – or at any rate a stringer working to maintain the legend – had reported a mugging on a late-night train just outside Uhlandstrasse Station the previous year.

"The registration number of your own vehicle?" asked the cop.

Rudi reeled it off. A blue Simca, one of Coureur Central's seemingly inexhaustible fleet of phantom vehicles, was registered to the Hans Drucker legend. The cop typed the number clumsily into his palmtop. Somebody in the queue of traffic on the bridge behind Rudi honked their horn, and the policeman straightened up and gave the driver a stare which silenced them.

"Open the bonnet, please," he said, still looking back down the line of cars.

Rudi pulled the lever that released the bonnet catch, and one of the other policemen lifted the bonnet, blocking his view through the windscreen. "What's happening?" he asked.

The cop at the window was reading the reply to his request about Drucker's car. He said, "What make and colour is your car?"

"It's a blue Simca." He didn't try to make any pally wisecracks about the car, didn't try to establish a relationship with the cop. Just kept everything neutral, a little annoyed. He could do this. He knew he could. Just good old Hans from Berlin-Pankow, returning from a visit to his sister in Potsdam. That was all. Nothing out of the ordinary. He had nothing to fear. "Is there something wrong with this car?"

The cop gave him a bored look. "I just do as I'm told, mate."

"Because if there is it's Hertz's fault. I was in a hurry, maybe I didn't check it properly before I left." A little note of panic now, a straight citizen worried he might have been caught driving an unsafe vehicle. German police were legendary for their adherence to the old EU laws on vehicle safety. They were like toys, wound up and left to run down after their owner had gone away on holiday. Nobody had ever come along with new vehicle regulations after Greater Germany left the Union.

"It looks fine to me, mate," the cop assured him. "We won't be much longer." The tone of his voice told Rudi all he needed to know about Potsdam policemen being called out on a freezing afternoon to check cars. He presumed they hadn't even been told precisely what they were looking for, which could only serve to heighten their resentment.

"The boot," said the cop.

Rudi popped the boot, and another of the cops went around the back of the car to rummage.

"So what's going on?" he asked, allowing a note of annoyance to enter his voice now he had been reassured that his car was not in breach of any regulation.

The cop looked in through the window and raised an eyebrow.

There was a long silence. Rudi sat behind the wheel, trying to behave like a law-abiding citizen, and the cop continued to jab a fat gloved finger at his palmtop.

Rudi wondered if the cops realised the irony of what was happening here. The original Glienicker Brücke was a wooden bridge built by Friedrich Wilhelm, the Great Elector, to carry the road between his summer palace and Berlin across the Havel. Centuries later, it had been one of the most famous bridges on Earth.

A student of borders, Rudi remembered seeing old news footage from the days of the Wall, when this place was one of the crossing points between West Berlin and East Germany and spy exchanges took place here. He thought of all those grainy black and white clips, the two lonely figures approaching each other from opposite ends of the bridge. It seemed to Rudi, no matter how many different exchanges he watched, that something would always happen to the way they walked as they passed each other, as they suddenly found themselves closer to homecoming than captivity. Sometimes it was impossible to tell who was going West and who was returning to the East.

The greatest irony of all, of course, was that this was not the original bridge; that had been pulled down, ostensibly because it didn't meet with EU guidelines, and this new bridge, lovely as a swan, had been built to replace it, at more or less the same time that new borders began to spring up all over Europe.

Finally the policeman at the front of the car slammed the bonnet down, and moments later the one at the back did the same to the lid of the boot.

Rudi and his policeman looked at each other. "Is that it?"

"Yes." The policeman handed Rudi's documents back. He walked away, eyes already fixed on his next victim.

Rudi wound the window back up. "The least you could do," he said quietly, switching on the ignition, "is order me to have a nice day." He put the car into gear and drove off the bridge and away along Königstrasse, towards Berlin.

IN ALEXANDERPLATZ, HE parked the car in a garage under an office building and walked a block to a public phone. He dialled a number.

"Hello?" asked a woman's voice.

"Hello," he said, "is that one seven two seven three?"

The woman sighed, as if this happened to her all the time. "No, you've got a wrong number. This is a private flat."

"Oh," said Rudi. "I'm sorry." He hung up and walked another two blocks to another phone. It was ringing as he arrived. He picked up the receiver.

"Jürgen?" asked a man's voice.

"Aunt Gertrude wasn't there," Rudi said. "But she left her knitting behind."

The voice at the other end of the line sighed. Another lost Package. "You stupid bastard." Just routine tradecraft, no offence intended. "She really wanted to talk to you."

"I know. But at least she left her knitting." Central loved this kind of cloak-and-dagger stuff.

"She did?"

"She did. And it's very good." Rudi wondered if the call was being monitored, and if there wasn't some security policeman somewhere who was having a good laugh right now, without having a clue what he was laughing at.

"Well," said the voice, "I suppose that's what she wanted."

"By the way, I heard that Uncle Otto and Uncle Manfred have set up in business together." Just to let Central know that the New Potsdam security men and Old Potsdam's Polizei appeared to be cooperating for the moment. Even after five years as a Coureur, Rudi still felt slightly embarrassed when he used communication strings; it all seemed so innocently transparent to him, he couldn't understand why the presumed listeners didn't see right through it.

"Really?" The voice at the other end sounded properly surprised. "It'll never last."

"We'll see."

"All right. I'll see you around. Will you be at work tomorrow?"

Rudi frowned. "Yes."

"Maybe I'll see you there, then."

"I expect so."

They hung up. Rudi stood in the telephone kiosk for longer than was absolutely necessary, looking at the phone.

He sighed, gathered himself, and went back to the underground garage. He drove the car out into the cold again, and down a series of side-streets until he reached a little garage, not much more than a shed with warped wooden doors.

The owner of the garage was waiting for him, alerted by a phone call from a callbox somewhere between Old Potsdam and Berlin. He was a squat, middle-aged man with a squashed boxer's nose and a network of fractured capillaries in his cheeks. He opened the doors and Rudi drove the car inside.

"You're late," the garage-owner said, closing the door.

"Potsdam police," Rudi said, getting out of the car.

The owner made a rude noise. "You've got an hour."

"Okay," said Rudi, and watched the older man leave through the judas-door.

It took him forty minutes to get the engine far enough out of the car to be able to reach underneath and wiggle the briefcase out of its hiding place, just as it had taken him about three-quarters of an hour of nitpicking concentration in a Babelsberg garage part-owned by Central to get the bloody thing in there in the first place.

He hadn't actually been sure it would work, whether the heat of the engine would mask the heat of the briefcase, whether the Polizei would spot it when they searched the car, whether the case would overheat and cause some unspecified but spectacular disaster.

He felt the case again. There were half a dozen things he could have done to check what was inside, but he didn't doubt the thing was boobytrapped against x-rays and NMR scans and millimetre-wave radar and simple old-fashioned lock-picking. He wondered if there was anyone, anywhere, apart from the Package he'd had to leave behind in New Potsdam, who knew how to open it.

He put the engine back into the car – the garage owner came back about halfway through and helped him finish up – and drove it back to the Hertz office and turned over the keys, then walked to a café not far from the Alexanderplatz S-Bahn station. He bought a coffee, sat at a table near the back, and put the briefcase down on the tiled floor beside his chair.

The café was very busy, bustling with people wrapped up against the cold. It took him five minutes to finish his espresso, and at some point during that time the briefcase vanished.

He never saw it go. One moment there, next moment lost in the crowd, another moment gone altogether. He looked down at where it had been. A scrap of paper lay pasted to the tiles by the melted snow that customers had tracked in on their boots, the writing on it already blurring and dissolving. It lasted long enough to read, then he got up to go and unobtrusively scuffed the paper to bits with his toe.

ALTHOUGH THEIR EXISTENCE was regularly denied by various Government agencies, everybody knew – or thought they knew – all about the Coureurs. There were Coureur films, Coureur novels, Coureur soaps, Coureur comics, all of varying degrees of awfulness.

What none of them mentioned, with their tales of unending derring-do, was the sheer crashing *boredom* of Coureur life. In the soaps there was a new Situation every week, whereas a Coureur might in fact go for months without a sniff of action. And the action, if it did come, was usually nothing more than Coureur Central's core business, which was the movement of documents and encoded data across Europe's continually reconfiguring borders.

In the series, the Coureurs spent an hour rescuing beautiful female scientists from polities populated by characters with sinister Latino or Slavic accents, and usually wound up in bed with the beautiful female scientists, who were properly grateful for their deliverance from actors with dodgy accents.

In the real world, Coureurs spent most of their working lives delivering mail, which at its most clandestine meant nothing more than a pickup from Dead Drop A, a short train or car or aircraft journey, a delivery at Dead Drop B, and very little scope for getting laid.

The Coureur fictions annoyed Rudi. The one thing that really annoyed him was that every week these tall, wide, handsome unreal-looking people, who couldn't submerge themselves in a crowd if their life depended on it, had a new Situation. Every week the word came from Central that someone needed rescuing, some impossible task needed accomplishing. That hardly ever happened. A Coureur would do his job, dust off, and go back to ordinary life for a month or two months or six months, or years even. You never got Situations back-to-back.

THE SLIP OF paper at the café had given the address of a post office in Grunewald, and a name.

"My name's Reinhard Gunther," he said at the counter. "There may be some poste restante mail for me."

The clerk went to check. Rudi idly scoped out the post office. *Will you be at work tomorrow* was a communication string for a crash Situation, something urgent and immediate. He had never been given it in operational circumstances. It also meant that, whether he liked it or not, he was being assigned a partner.

The clerk came back with an envelope. Rudi showed him the Gunther ID he'd had made up by a cobbler in Pankow. It was a rush job and not very high quality, but it didn't have to be. The clerk barely looked at it, handed over the envelope, and Rudi walked back out into the cold.

He had rooms in two different pensions, under different names. He took a bus to the nearest, in Charlottenburg, and made sure the door was locked before he sat on the bed and opened the envelope.

Inside was a luggage-locker keycard with a photo of Hansel and Gretel, Berlin Zoo's Siberian tigers, embossed on the front.

IT WAS SAID that if you were a criminal, a member of some tinpot political party, an agitator for a minority interest group, a drug addict, a property speculator, a forger or bootlegger of any kind, an artist, a fashion designer, a writer, underground film director, musician, or just plain crazy, Berlin was where you would eventually end up. It seemed to be the repository of all Europe's extremes. Extreme poverty and extreme wealth. Extreme greed and extreme philanthropy. Extreme good taste and extreme bad taste. Everything was here.

It was a long time since Rudi had last visited Berlin, and the place didn't seem to have improved very much in his absence. The business heart of the city, built after reunification along the no-man's-land where the Wall had been, towered over the rest of Berlin in a shining clean ribbon of modern office buildings and hotels, but everything else seemed to be falling into decay and disrepair.

The streets around Berlin-Zoo S-Bahn were lined with beggars, wrapped up in layer after layer of rags and blankets and sheets of *Berliner Zeitung*. Most of them were shivering with the cold. A few had stopped shivering and just sat there, frost on their eyelashes, waiting for the evening police patrols to pick them up and take them to the morgue. They shared the pavements with whores and pushers and pickpockets and muggers and tourists and business people, all shuffling along through the filthy slush.

Inside the station was almost as bad, despite the efforts of a trio of uniformed Polizei to move the various undesirables back out into the cold. Rudi went across the concourse to the left-luggage lockers, found the door that corresponded to the number on the key, swiped the card through the lock, and opened it.

Inside, looking out at him with a surprised expression on its face, was the severed head of a bearded man.

EVERYONE IMAGINED COUREUR Central differently. In some movies it was a clean, efficient but anonymous modern office building in some neutral Western European city. Brussels, perhaps, or London, or Strasbourg. In some novels it was hidden away under a ruined hotel block or tenement in the East, access only granted to those who knew the correct code words. In at least one network series Central was housed in one of those elegant chateaux that line the Loire, and Coureur operational decisions were taken in a tense atmosphere offset by Louis Quinze furniture and ormolu clocks.

The common misconception that everyone suffered was to take the word *Central* literally. That, and the fact that the organisation chose to call itself *Les Coureurs de Bois*, led most of the European populace to believe that Central was somewhere in France.

The truth was that Coureur Central no more needed a central headquarters than any other multinational organisation. Modern communications made it possible for a company's boardroom to be in London, its personnel department in Bonn, its PR office in Prague and its computer centre in St Lucia. In the case of Coureur Central, it was somewhat more spread-out than that.

So when the crash signal came in, it had been automatically switched between four different telephone numbers before being received by a communications centre in Padua, which rerouted it still in its encrypted state to another ground station in Dubrovnik, which bounced it off two Bell-Telecommunications European comsats and through an automated switching system on the roof of the old NatWest Tower in London before reaching an attic room in – as it happened – Paris. All of this took roughly four-fifths of a second.

Madame Lebec, the occupant of the once-elegant house in the Sixteenth Arrondissement, had only heard the discreet chime of the equipment in the attic twice before. Both those times, she did what she did now.

She calmly climbed the stairs to the attic room and locked the door behind her so that the maid, Ysabelle, would not come barging in and break her concentration.

Seating herself at one of the consoles installed around the room, she typed a short string of commands and watched the encrypted message come up on the screen. She typed another string, even shorter, and the message decrypted itself.

If Coureur Central had had a central location and organisation, Madame Lebec would have been a middle-ranking executive whose security rating stopped five or six levels below the top. Central paid her a monthly stipend for the rent of her attic and the very very occasional demand on her time. Madame Lebec thought it all rather an adventure; her great-great grandmother had been with the Resistance during the Second World War, and her diaries spoke of manning a clandestine radio transmitter, with which she sometimes communicated with London.

Madame Lebec's job wasn't nearly so hazardous, no matter how much she was inclined to romanticise it. She was breaking no law and threatening no government. All she was required to do was receive messages, decrypt them, and evaluate them.

The other two times, the messages had fallen outside her remit, and she had simply typed a code-string and passed them on to someone else and forgotten all about them. But this time she did not. She sat and calmly read the two lines of text again, identified by a number of codes as being a voice message from a public telephone.

Perhaps her heart beat a little more quickly as her mind went back to the days of the War, her great-great grandmother crouched in an attic somewhere with a pair of headphones pressed to her ears, straining to make out the faint, desperate communication of an agent in trouble somewhere out there in Occupied Europe. She read the message again, trying to decide.

She typed a line of plaintext, pressed the encryption key, and pressed another key to transmit a message that would be heard on the receiver at the other end as a disinterested man's voice, giving the Coureur a communication string instructing him to be waiting at a certain public phone in twenty minutes. Then she moved to the dedicated console on the other side of the room and made her report to her superiors.

The reply came more quickly than she had expected; within a minute or so, text began to roll across the screen. She read it, and on two occasions felt it necessary to raise an eyebrow, which was about as close as she got these days, after six children, two dead husbands and the loss of four fortunes, to expressing surprise.

2.

MADAME LEBEC'S LOVER arrived shortly before Christmas.

He was a short, handsome gentleman in his middle years, very well-dressed, and his spoken French was excellent, although those who spoke to him believed they could detect a faint English accent.

This dapper little man could be seen most often in the mornings, when he left Madame's house and went down the street, immaculately turned-out, for his daily constitutional. He left at the same time every day, and returned an hour later, usually with Madame's string shopping bag bulging with groceries.

Those few neighbours who were on speaking terms with the legendarily foul-tempered Ysabelle reported that the gentleman had turned up on the doorstep at a little after eleven o'clock one night, after Madame had instructed the maid to lock and bolt the door, and that Madame had greeted him with a hesitant but forceful hug – and Madame had never been observed to hug *anyone*, not even the occasional member of her family who visited – as if he was a long-lost but fondly-remembered *amour*.

Most of the neighbours just shrugged. If the old lady, in her autumn years, chose to take herself a lover, then good luck to her. Others were a little more nosy.

Dubois the barber, for instance, had the gentleman in his chair not two days after he arrived, for the full treatment. Haircut, shave and a trim of that already-neat goatee. Dubois was able to report – having caught a glimpse of the label while removing the napkin from around the gentleman's neck – that he wore shirts from Jermyn Street in London, and left a healthy tip.

The girl on the checkout at the supermarket told her sister that the gentleman bought instant coffee, while Madame had previously only countenanced ground. He also bought wholegrain bread, which Madame had never done – in fact, the girl told her sister, she remembered Ysabelle once telling her that Madame wouldn't have wholegrain in the house because the grains somehow always worked their way under the top plate of her false teeth. Last, but not least, the gentleman's arrival coincided with a change in the dietary requirements at *chez* Lebec from butter to salt-free margarine.

Gossip had still not subsided over the gentleman when the gentleman's nephew turned up – although the neighbourhood cynics refused to believe he was a nephew because there was no family resemblance at all. Where the gentleman was short and dark and dapper, the nephew was tall and fair and untidy. He didn't go out much, but those who saw him said he always looked tired and hunted, so he was dubbed 'the Fugitive' in neighbourhood parlance.

The Fugitive could be seen, ever so occasionally, wandering cautiously down the street, as if he wanted to keep running into doorways to hide. He came back with piles of newspapers and magazine printouts under his arm. Ysabelle confided to the girl from the supermarket that almost all these publications were German, most of them from Berlin news services.

ONE MORNING, BRADLEY knocked on the door of Rudi's room and called, "A minute of your time, old son?"

By the time Rudi was dressed, Bradley was down in the drawing room raiding Madame's brandy. Bradley seemed to drink almost continually without ever becoming drunk, but Rudi had never seen him eat.

"Come in, come in," Bradley said, recapping the decanter and turning from the side-table. "How are we feeling?"

"I'm fine," Rudi said from the door. "How are you?"

Bradley flashed his brief little grin. Bradley was one of the most charming people Rudi had ever met, but he could never recall having seen the man actually smile. Just quick grins here and there, and body language absolutely loaded with bonhomie.

"Shut the door and sit down, old chap. Got something to tell you."

Rudi closed the door and turned the key in the lock and trusted to Madame to keep the poisonous old shrew of a maid from listening outside. The maid bothered him. She ate with them in the dining room and sat there looking at him all the way through the meals. He sat in one of the overstuffed fabric-covered armchairs by the window. Bradley sipped his brandy.

"How are you feeling?" Bradley asked again. "Really. No need to cover up for me. Think of me as a doctor. Or a priest, if that suits. You can tell me anything. I won't pass it on."

Rudi sighed. The days of his debriefing, closeted with Bradley for eight hours at a time, had passed very slowly. He had gone over and over the details of the fiasco in Potsdam. He had told Bradley about finding the head in the locker at Zoo Station. He had not glossed over the fact that he had lost his mind for a while after that, before he had recovered his senses enough to call in a priority signal. He had gone over every minute of his weeks-long dustoff from Berlin, via Hamburg, Gothenburg, Helsinki and St Petersburg, looking over his shoulder every few steps. He had been as honest as he could possibly manage with the little man from Central, and Bradley had never once come close to telling him what the fucking hell was going on.

"I'm quite sick of you asking me how I'm feeling, actually," he said. They were speaking English, almost certainly Bradley's mother-tongue, though with some people it was impossible to tell.

Bradley glanced into his glass and went to sit in the other armchair. "Coureur Leo," he said nostalgically. "Dear old Leo. He was in it almost from the beginning, you know. Not quite a Founding Father, but not too far removed either."

He was talking about the head in the locker, the Coureur who had been assigned as Rudi's partner in the crash Situation. Rudi didn't want to think about Dear Old Leo, about his family or his real-life job or his real-life home.

"As I mentioned before, we were fortunate that you had the presence of mind to close the locker before you left," Bradley said. "When we received your message we were able to get a team of cleaners in."

"I wondered why there was nothing about it in the papers."

Bradley inclined his head, as if the praise was entirely due to him. "We've covered your dustoff from Berlin." He looked into his drink again, as if deciding whether or not to take another sip. He decided not to. "Textbook stuff. Very good. Can't fault it."

Rudi realised that his fingertips were digging into the arms of his chair.

"You'll appreciate," Bradley went on, "that Leo was a statistical spike. This kind of thing almost never happens."

Rudi stared at the Englishman. His gradual ascent in the Coureur hierarchy had brought with it a gradual increase in the risk associated with each Situation. In Rudi's mind it had also become associated with the contacts he had with Central. Dariusz, who had once seemed mysterious and a little scary, now seemed to have been little more than a stringer, a local talent-spotter. Bradley, in comparison, was the real thing, a direct line to

Central, a case officer. It was the first time Rudi had had this sort of contact with his employers, which only seemed to underline just how catastrophic the Potsdam and Berlin Situations had been.

"Most Coureurs spend their entire careers delivering the post," Bradley went on. He weakened and moistened his lips with brandy. "Just moving packages from Here to There. No danger. No illegality, really. Not even any discomfort, much of the time."

"Unless you're Dear Old Leo," said Rudi. All the bonhomie went out of Bradley's body language for a moment; it was astonishing to watch. For a fraction of a second, he looked about ten years older. "Could I have a drink?"

Bradley reached for the decanter and held it out. Rudi got up and poured himself a brandy. He took his glass over to the window and looked through the net curtains into the street.

"Central's an apolitical organisation," Bradley said. "That's the only way it can exist. No sides, no favourites. If it threatens governments or security, it threatens them all equally. That's the whole point. Nothing we do is against the law, strictly speaking."

"Ah," Rudi said to the street. "The law. Now that's a very grey area, Bradley, from place to place."

Bradley sat down in the chair Rudi had just vacated. He looked into the fire, thinking. He said, "What happened to Leo, that's not what Central is about. We call ourselves Coureurs because that's all we are, really. Just glorified postmen. Sometimes we facilitate the departure of someone from one place or another. What happened to Leo was a clumsy warning."

"Clumsy but extremely effective," Rudi said. "Particularly for Leo."

Bradley heaved a huge, worldbreaking sigh, refusing this time to rise to the bait.

"What was the Situation Leo and I were supposed to be taking care of?" Rudi asked.

Bradley shook his head. "Not live any longer, old lad."

"So there's no reason why you shouldn't tell me."

The Englishman appeared to be thinking about it. He took another drink of his brandy. He shook his head again. "Sorry."

"Was there a jump? Everything according to plan? Textbook dustoff?" He drained his glass in one gulp. "Fuck you, Bradley, tell me what Leo had his head cut off for!"

Bradley remained sitting, completely calm and even-humoured. "Please stop shouting, there's a good lad. You'll disturb Madame."

Rudi snorted and turned to look out of the window again.

"What happened to Leo had nothing to do with the Situation you were supposed to be handling," Bradley said. He was silent for a long time, thinking. "There was an incident in Hamburg back in October. Central and German counterintelligence tried to occupy the same space at the same time." He sipped his drink. "A number of their officers were killed."

Rudi turned and looked at him. "I beg your pardon?"

Bradley looked thoughtful. "It wasn't a Situation. Just a stringer going about her business maintaining a legend. I don't know what went wrong." He shook his head. "A bad business. Very unprofessional."

"Unprofessional," Rudi repeated dully, his imagination refusing to construct a scenario where the routine maintenance of a false identity could result in multiple deaths. "Jesus Christ, Bradley."

Bradley shrugged. "German counterintelligence take this kind of thing personally, of course. They've never been comfortable about us operating on their territory. It seems that Leo was a message."

"They could have *emailed* us."

Bradley chuckled sadly. "Well, I presume they decided an email wouldn't have quite enough emotional weight."

Rudi came back from the window, topped up his drink, and sat in the other armchair. "Is Central going to do anything about it?"

Bradley thought about it. "It's possible that negotiations will be attempted. I can't really say. It may be possible to come to some kind of accommodation."

"Did you just say *negotiations*?"

"What you must understand is that Central won't fight these people," Bradley said. "It's not what we're about. Wiser heads than ours have decided to open a line of dialogue with them."

Rudi closed his eyes.

"The alternative is that we kill one of their officers in retaliation for Leo. And they kill another Coureur. And so on and so on."

"Good lord," Rudi muttered.

"Take a holiday," Bradley went on. "You've more than earned some time off; the jump you did in Potsdam was an absolute classic and you'll be more than handsomely rewarded for it."

"I had two Situations go bad on me in the space of two days, Bradley," Rudi reminded him.

Bradley shook his head. "There was nothing you could have done in Potsdam. Your Package wanted to make their own way over the Wire; short of invading New Potsdam you couldn't have helped."

Rudi rubbed his eyes.

"You did the important thing," Bradley said. "If you weren't as good as you are, the briefcase would be in the hands of New Potsdam's security forces or Old Potsdam's City Council right now, instead of at its destination. You were absolutely professional in Potsdam and I, for one, am proud of you."

Fuck you, Rudi thought.

"And the Situation in Berlin was just taken entirely out of your hands by events."

Rudi shook his head.

"Go away for a while," Bradley told him. "Relax."

"Just leave some contact numbers, right?"

Bradley positively beamed. "Absolutely."

"Is this a roundabout way of saying that the Germans are looking for me as well?"

Bradley performed a very Gallic shrug. "Better safe than sorry, old son."

"And Leo?"

The smile dimmed until it was hardly perceptible. He sighed. "That was entirely out of your control. Not your fault. Don't think about Leo. Leo, to my eternal shame, is on my conscience."

GOOD WITH LANGUAGES

1.

ONCE UPON A time, the one thing he had wanted most in all the world was to be a chef.

He could even remember the day this obsession took root. It was the day of his eighth birthday, the day his father finally relented and installed a satellite dish. Which would make it two years to the day since his mother left them, appalled by his father's decision to uproot the family yet again by taking a job as a ranger in the Lahemaa *rahvuspark*.

Rudi's father had trained as an architect, but as far as Rudi knew he had never worked as an architect. Instead, he had embarked on a series of jobs for which he was both temperamentally and educationally unsuited. He worked on the docks in Tallinn. He worked as a guard on the railways. He retrained to be an air traffic controller. He lived in squats and anarchist colonies. He was even, family tradition had it, a politician for a short while; it would have been simple enough for Rudi to check this, but he had never bothered. True or not, what difference did it make?

In the family chronology, it was while he worked as a bus driver in Tallinn that Rudi's father had met Rudi's mother. Sometimes, when he was drunk, the old man would tell his two sons about the beautiful young woman he saw waiting every morning at the Pronski stop on Narvu maantee, just going home after her shift at the Hotell Viru, how she would fall asleep in her seat, threadbare coat covering her maid's uniform. When he was very drunk, which was increasingly often when Rudi and his brother were growing up, he would wax lyrical about her hair, which was long and fine and the colour of polished mahogany, about her skin, which was the colour of milk and without any blemish, about her eyes, which had just the merest tilt at the edges to betray the Lapp heritage which lay far far back in her genes. Neither Rudi nor his brother could remember this extraordinary beauty, although they had once discovered in the back of their father's wardrobe a series of photographs of a short, dark-haired, irritated-looking young woman in old-fashioned clothes. Surely, they reasoned, this must be some old girlfriend of their father's.

There were no photographs of the wedding – at least, none that Rudi ever saw. He had to make do with his father's stories of the hundreds of guests who came to the ceremony, the big room at the

Viru booked for the reception, his mother walking like a queen through the room she would return to after the honeymoon dressed in her cleaning clothes, pushing a floor-waxing machine.

In many ways it was a miracle that his father had got married at all, even more so that he had consented to settle down in Tallinn and stay in his bus-driving job for longer than a year. There was the wedding to pay for – his parents and her parents were dead – and the flat to pay for, and after a year or so there was Rudi's big brother Ivari, and when Ivari was a year old his father's patience snapped and he moved the family to Tartu, where he had found a job as a train driver.

Tartu was also where Rudi's father's long, uncomplicated love affair with the Baltic languages began, at the University's Song Festival. He said that he had listened to the Estonian, Latvian and Lithuanian singers at the Festival with tears running down his cheeks. Ivari, who could remember attending that particular festival even though he had only been four years old, contended that the old man had been roaring drunk the whole time.

Whatever. By the time Rudi was born, the family was living in a three-room flat in Pärnu, where the old man worked on building sites to fund his growing collection of language books. At some point during this period, Rudi came along – entirely unplanned, Ivari liked to taunt him – and the old man found himself once again nailed to the spot by a family he couldn't afford to uproot.

When he thought about it, which wasn't so often these days, Rudi wondered why his mother hadn't done something. He vaguely remembered a stoic woman, patiently enduring each family upheaval, each arbitrary change of job. Surely she could have done something, he thought. He was sorry he couldn't remember her very well; he thought she must have been a remarkable woman, to stand it for so long.

They stayed crammed in the flat in Pärnu for six and a half years, which was the longest his father had stayed in one place since he graduated, and then one fateful evening his father came home from his shift on the building site, ate his dinner, sat down in front of the television, opened the paper, and saw an advertisement for park rangers. And, Rudi presumed, the temptation had just been too much for him.

IT WAS EASIER, these days, to get out to the National Park than it had been when Rudi was growing up. In those days the country was still a little punch-drunk from its years as a Soviet satellite and money was tight and you had to drive or take a number of buses from Tallinn, or get the train to Rakvere or Tapa and then get a bus.

Nowadays there was a dedicated tram-line all the way from Tallinn to the visitor centre at Palmse. It was a two-hour journey, but at this time of the year the tram was almost empty apart from some locals on their way back from shopping trips and a couple of New Zealanders huddled together down at the front, identical in their cold-weather gear and hiking packs. Rudi sat at the back with an overnight bag stuffed under his seat, periodically wiping condensation from the window in order to look at the snowy landscape passing by outside.

He couldn't remember how long it was since he last saw this countryside. Four years. Five, maybe. He'd simply lost track. What had happened to him since then? He'd seen a lot of the Continent, moved a fair number of Packages, made a reasonably good living for himself. Cooked a lot of services at Restauracja Max. Found a severed head in a Berlin luggage locker. *That* would be a good one to drop into conversations.

He closed his eyes and leaned back in his seat. Maybe he'd been a Coureur for too long; all the Situations were starting to blur together. He couldn't remember what he had done after leaving here last time. Back to Max's kitchen, certainly, but then what? Where? Andorra? Padania? Ulster? Maybe he could ask Bradley; Central would have his records somewhere. He could tell them he wanted to write his memoirs.

Christ. He wasn't thirty yet and he felt ready for retirement.

Wet snow was settling on Palmse as the tram pulled into the terminus. On the pavement, Rudi stood for a few moments. The old manor house, with its salmon-pink walls and red slate roofs, seemed not to have changed at all. It occurred to him that it had been at least four years since he had heard another voice speak a single word of his own language.

He went around to the side entrance of the visitor centre and typed the code into the door. He smiled and shook his head; they hadn't changed the number in ten years.

The door to Ivari's office upstairs was wide open. His brother was sitting at his desk, concentrating on a document he was writing on a very large and out-of-date word processor. He was not very tall, but he was very solid, like an oak table. He was wearing his ranger's blue uniform jumpsuit, its collar open, and he was squinting at the WP's screen as he typed, two-fingered and painfully slowly, picking each letter deliberately. Rudi cleared his throat and Ivari looked up, and for a few moments neither of them spoke, although Rudi shrugged awkwardly.

"Come on in," Ivari said, turning back to the keyboard. "I've got to finish this." He waved a hand towards a corner of the room. "Have some coffee."

Rudi put his bag down by the door and went over to the coffeemaker and poured himself a mug. Ivari began typing again. Rudi wandered around the office. On the walls were framed posters advertising the park, printouts of articles about the park, photographs of Ivari with various celebrities and worthies. The photos were interesting, because in most of them Ivari was striking the same pose. In one photo he was standing beside the President and Prime Minister somewhere out in the wilds of the park, pointing at something off in the distance. In another he was standing very close to Emma Corcoran, the English actress, and pointing at something off in the distance. In a third he was with Witold Grabiański, the Polish fifteen hundred metre Olympic champion, and pointing at something off in the distance.

"What are you pointing at in all these photos?" Rudi asked.

Ivari's shoulders hunched as he applied himself to the task of typing. "Anything. Nothing. The cameramen just tell me to point into the distance and look *intrepid*." He snorted. "Intrepid. I ask you."

"What's Grabiański like?"

Ivari shrugged. "Seemed all right. I don't think we said more than five words to each other."

"What about the President?"

Ivari snorted again and kept typing, one letter at a time, squinting alternately at the screen and the keyboard.

"You've had the place painted," Rudi said, looking around the office.

Ivari nodded, choosing a key and putting his fingertip down on it. "Three years ago."

Point taken. Rudi sat down in one of the comfortable visitors' chairs and looked at his brother. Ivari had their father's bland, blond good looks, and he filled the uniform much better than the old man ever had.

"How's Frances?"

"Very well, thanks."

The last time Rudi had been here was for Ivari's wedding. He'd stayed five days, and then a vague conviction that someone, somewhere, needed his help had taken him back to what he had thought of in those days as the Real World. He had, he considered, thought of it that way until very recently. Until the door of that luggage locker in Berlin had swung open, in fact.

He got up and went to the window. The snowfall had grown heavier; he couldn't see the street for a whirl of drifting flakes.

"How's Kraków?" Ivari asked, selecting another key.

"Waist-deep in English tourists."

"I heard about the riot."

Rudi had to think about that one, then he realised that Ivari meant the England-Poland football match two years ago.

"That was over the other side of town," he said. "I don't think we had one English person in the restaurant that week."

"It looked bad on the news."

It had been bad. One policeman had died and almost seven hundred fans had been arrested, both English and Polish. Rudi had been involved in a Situation in Alsace that week, and had returned to Balice in time to see groups of English fans being escorted out of the country by riot-suited platoons of police. He'd almost forgotten about it.

"It always looks worse on the news," he said.

Ivari nodded, looked for the save key, and tapped it. The screen cleared, and he turned and looked at his brother. "Hungry?"

"Starving," Rudi agreed.

IVARI AND HIS wife lived in one of the outbuildings on the Palmse estate – once the home of the von Pahlens, a merchant family who had departed Estonia for Germany after the First World War but left behind *Palmse Mois* – the Baltic Baroque manor house itself – and the distillery which now housed an hotel, and the old stables which housed the park's visitor centre. Rudi remembered his father telling him that one of the von Pahlens – he couldn't remember which one it was – had been an astronomer, and had a crater on the Moon named after him. His father had thought that was wonderful, having a crater on the Moon named after you. Rudi recalled being less than impressed, although thinking about it now, it wasn't such a bad achievement, really. More of a lasting monument than a good meal, anyway.

When Frances saw him – as he was taking off his parka and his boots in the hallway and thus preoccupied – she shouted, "Rudi, you bastard!" She pronounced it *barstard*. Frances was large and lusty and Australian, and she favoured kaftans in a variety of hallucinatory patterns, and when she hugged Rudi to her considerable bosom he felt as though he was being crushed to death by a rather vigorous migraine.

She grasped him by the upper arms and propelled him out as far as her arms could reach – which was a distance – so she could tilt her head from side to side and look judiciously at him. "How long's it been now?" she asked in good Estonian.

"It's been a while, Frankie," he admitted in English. He tried to shrug, but her hands held his upper body motionless. "Sorry."

"You'd better be, sunshine," she said. Then she smiled the radiant smile Ivari had once admitted to Rudi had stolen his heart and she tugged him gently back to her. "It's good to see you, kid."

"Good to be here," Rudi said. He had a suspicion that Frances knew somehow about his work as a Coureur. She'd always been huggy and tactile, but after he started working for Central the quality of the hugs changed in some way he couldn't quite define, as if she was afraid for his safety. Or maybe he was imagining it.

"So," she said, finally releasing him so he could take off his other boot and search through the wooden box by the door for a pair of slippers, "how long will we be having the pleasure of you this time?"

She had never quite forgiven him for taking off after the wedding. "I'm here for the foreseeable future, actually, Frankie," he said, finally finding his favourite pair of slippers and putting them on. He stood in the hall smiling at her, flatfooted after his boots but happy. "I'm on holiday. A sabbatical, really."

Frances smiled and nodded as if she knew exactly what he was talking about. "Well, that's great, because I'm sick of cooking for these two."

Rudi felt a hitch in his chest. "Two?"

"Who's that?" called a querulous voice from the living room, and with a shuffle of slippers a little old man wearing jeans, a sweatshirt two sizes too large for him, and a baseball cap with a hologram advertisement for Aeroflot on the front came out into the hallway. He was holding a tumbler half-full of an amber liquid which was almost certainly Chivas Regal, his signature drink. "Oh," he said when he saw Rudi.

Rudi's heart sank smoothly, like a recently-serviced lift. "Hello, Toomas," he said to his father.

FRANCES ASKED RUDI to cook, and he didn't have it in his heart to refuse, so he spent ten minutes rummaging in the fridge and the freezer and came up with some rolled pork loin he could slice up thickly and beat out into escalopes, and a couple of stale bread rolls for breadcrumbs. It wasn't exactly *cordon bleu*, and it was a long way from being Estonian cuisine (and anyway, in his heart he could never have argued that Estonian cuisine had set the world alight) but he was tired and escalopes were something he could do with his mind in neutral.

"How long's he been here?" he asked as he used a meat hammer on the pork.

Frances, peeling potatoes at the sink, glanced towards the door. "The old man? Couple of days."

"Still living in Muike?"

She shook her head. "He moved to the special management zone at Aasumetsa a couple of years ago. Got himself a nice house there. Got himself a nice *hausfrau* to look after him, though I haven't met her."

From the living room, Rudi heard his father singing a Latvian folk song to Ivari. "That sounds about right," he said.

Frances looked at him. "No offence, kid, but this is stuff you should be asking him yourself."

Rudi shrugged. "We don't talk about stuff like that."

Frances put down the potato she was peeling and crossed her arms across her chest. "Well maybe you should, no?"

Rudi waved the meat hammer at her for emphasis, failed to come up with any words to go with the gesture, and went back to tenderising the slice of pork on the butcher-block chopping board in front of him.

"You must have thought there was *some* chance you'd see him while you were here," said Frances.

"Every silver lining has a cloud," Rudi muttered.

"We keep asking him to retire, but he won't," Frances said. "He loves this place. He just goes out pottering around the bogs and in the forests. Aarvo – that's the new director – says the old man should go, but he doesn't dare fire him."

"Aarvo sounds like just the kind of balless wonder Toomas always took advantage of," said Rudi.

She stopped peeling potatoes again and waved her knife at him across the kitchen. "Hey, sweetheart, don't you forget the number of years your Dad's got under his belt here."

"*My* formative years, certainly," Rudi said.

"He knows this place like the back of his hand," she said, wagging the knife some more. "They never had anyone like him here before, and when he *does* retire they'll struggle to get someone else who loves it as much as he does."

"Every Estonian loves the *rahvuspark*, Frankie," he said. "It's part of our heritage. The Poles have the same thing with Białowieża."

"Come again?"

"It's a big forest on the border between Poland and Lithuania. The last stretch of ancient forest in Europe. The Poles *love* that place, Frankie. It's got wild boar and bison and wild horses and beavers, and for all I know there are bears and magicians and little green men and Elvis and Madonna there too. It's a symbol of national pride. Same with the Park."

"Ivari says it wasn't always like that."

Rudi waved the hammer. "That was the Russians.

Fuck 'em." He looked at the piece of pork he was beating out and suddenly thought of Jan doing the same, at the hotel in the Zone. He was still wearing Jan's watch, although in the intervening years the moments when he remembered it *was* Jan's watch had grown rarer and rarer. Thinking of Jan made him think of the Hungarians, which made him think of Restauracja Max.

"Rudi?"

He looked up. "Yes?"

"You *are* okay, aren't you?" asked Frances.

"Just thinking about something." He tossed the meat hammer into the air so it flipped end over end and caught it by the handle on the way back down. It was harder than it looked; the heavy head made the thing flip eccentrically and if you weren't careful you could wind up smacking yourself on the forehead. He'd practised a lot, in various kitchens, down the years, but out of the corner of his eye he couldn't discern that Frances was particularly impressed. "Let's get this meal done."

HIS FATHER KEPT his baseball cap on through the whole meal. And he expected Ivari to keep topping up his glass with Chivas. He kept looking at Rudi as if watching an escaped convict who had burst into the house and demanded to be fed. He made a number of jokes about the Poles which, his age notwithstanding, would have got his legs broken in any bar in Kraków. To make some obscure point, he insisted on carrying on part of the dinnertable conversation in Lithuanian, a language Ivari and Frances did not speak and Rudi only had a rudimentary grasp of. He was rude about the food. Rudi didn't tell him that Fabio had long ago inoculated him against people being rude about his cooking.

Toomas had always been small and wiry, but now he seemed to be somehow *lignifying*. There was an indefinable sap-dry toughness about him these days, like a little old tree bent by decades of wind but still standing. His skin was wind-tanned and his eyes were narrow and squinty in a nest of wrinkles and the years had left him a thin, mean little mouth to grow his goatee around. Years ago, when Rudi was about ten, Toomas had told him someone had once described him as looking like 'a Baltic knight.' Rudi had been too young to know what the hell he was talking about, but now he thought the comparison wasn't far out. A Baltic knight fallen on hard times and doomed to die in penury and madness, a Hanseatic Quixote.

"So, when are you going back to Poland?" Toomas asked after Ivari had cleared up the plates and gone into the kitchen with them to make coffee.

"I don't know if I will," Rudi said. "I've been living in Berlin for the past year and a half." And he regretted it the moment the name of the city left his mouth.

"Germany," Toomas mused. The land of Estonia's ancestral overlords. The ones before the Russians. The ones who built, among other things, *Palmse Mois*. He sat and stared at Rudi from under the brim of his baseball cap. The hologram logo made it look as if an Aeroflot airliner was emerging from his forehead.

"Oh, *Paps*," Frances sighed. "Can't you just be happy Rudi's here?"

"When he's been living with the *sakslane*?" Toomas asked with an old man's insolent snap of the lips. "I think not."

"He was doing it for *work*," she said, and Rudi looked at her and tipped his head to one side, unsure whether she was just saying that to defuse an argument, or if she really knew why he'd been in Germany. Certainly, he hadn't told her.

Toomas snorted. "Given the choice, a *man* would have refused."

"Maybe he didn't get a choice."

"Excuse me?" said Rudi. "Let's not forget that I'm here too, eh?"

Toomas snorted. "Never been able to fight his own battles, anyway." He picked up his glass and waved it vaguely at Rudi. "Get me a drink, *poiss*."

"Fuck you, *vana mees*. Get your own fucking drink."

Frances glared at him and he waved a hand to say sorry.

"You two were the same at the wedding," she said wonderingly, looking at them both from her seat at the end of the table. "You were only in each other's company for five minutes before you were screaming at each other. What in God's name is *wrong* with you?"

"Nothing wrong with *me*," Rudi's father said, sitting back and folding his arms across his chest and looking smug.

"That what your girlfriend says, eh?" Rudi snapped, and saw a little of the smugness drain away.

"Rudi!" Frances said. "That's enough. You're both guests in our house and I'll never forgive either of you if you keep on behaving like this."

Rudi and Toomas continued to stare at each other for a few more moments. Without breaking eye-contact, Rudi said, "I'm sorry, Frances. That was rude of me."

Frances looked at Toomas. "*Paps*? Anything you want to say?"

Toomas pushed his chair back and got up from the table. "I have to piss." As he left the dining room, he brushed past Ivari, who was returning from the kitchen with a tray laden with a cafetiére and cups and a sugar bowl and a milk jug. "Get me a drink, *poiss*," Toomas muttered as he went by.

Ivari looked at Rudi and Frances. "So," he said when Toomas was in the bathroom and safely out of earshot. "Scores?"

Frances looked at Rudi. "Seriously. What *is* wrong with you two?"

"He's my father. I'm his son." He shrugged. "What can I say?"

"Well you can stop being so fucking *gnomic*, for one thing," she said in English.

"'Gnomic'?" said Rudi, feeling the twitch of a grin. Frances glowered at him. "And?"

"You're not even using the word properly."

"How do *you* know? You're not even a native English speaker."

"Neither are you."

Frances hurled her napkin at him; it flapped open and landed in the middle of the table, but the three of them were smiling again. She shook her head.

"I'm going to slap both of you if this carries on," she said. "And when I slap people, it hurts."

He had no trouble believing that. "You'd slap a little old man?"

"He's not a little old man," she said without thinking. "He's a demon." She stopped and looked at Ivari, who was putting the tray of coffee things on the table, and Rudi, who was grinning and pointing at her. She sighed. "Your family makes my fucking head hurt," she told her husband.

"Mine too," Ivari agreed.

"What's he doing here anyway?" asked Rudi.

Frances looked at Ivari, who said, "He had a fight with Maret. That's his–"

"Yes," said Rudi.

Ivari shrugged. "He turned up the day before yesterday with a rucksack. Said he had some business with Aarvo and he needed to stay a couple of nights. And he *did* have some business with Aarvo, give him his due."

"It's one of his default settings, Ivari," Rudi said in exasperation. "He has an appointment somewhere and then he engineers a row and storms out, but all he's doing is going to his appointment. He's been doing it all his life. Haven't you worked it out yet?"

Frances scowled at him. "Don't talk to my husband like that."

Ivari said, "Coffee?"

Rudi shrugged.

"Anyway," said Ivari, pouring coffee. "Maret phoned yesterday evening in tears. They'd had an argument and *Paps* had stormed out and she was scared he was going to do something stupid."

Rudi snorted. "Another default setting."

Ivari straightened up and gestured gently towards Rudi with the cafetiére. "You can be clever about it all you want. Some of us have to spend all our time with him."

Rudi bugged his eyes out at his brother.

"I had to go up to Aasumetsa this morning and tell Maret in person that *Paps* was fit and well and staying with us. She really cares about him. You'd like her."

"Not going to happen," Rudi warned.

Frances sighed and looked at her watch. Then she looked at Ivari. "He's done it again."

"I DON'T KNOW when he started doing this," said Ivari. "He just has too much to drink."

"Which really is something new," Rudi added.

Ivari had opened the lock on the bathroom door with a screwdriver kept handy for the purpose. They were standing in the doorway looking at Toomas, who was sitting on the toilet with his jeans and boxer-shorts around his ankles. His head was leaned against the wall and his eyes were closed and he was snoring gently.

Frances, who was standing behind them, said, "The first time, it was a little worrying. The second time, it was quaint. Now?" She shook her head. "I'm in unknown territory. I have no idea."

Rudi said, "What do you usually do in these situations?" Hoping the answer would be, 'We leave the old bastard here all night so the edge of the toilet seat cuts off his circulation and his legs die. Or he gets pneumonia, at the very least.'

"Well," Ivari admitted, "if you recorded it and posted it online, I'm sure there would be a really big audience for it."

Rudi pulled a face. "I was afraid you were going to say something like that."

Frances landed a large and goodnatured hand on their shoulders. "And that's where I leave the Sons of Toomas to work their magic. I'm shattered. 'Night, boys."

When she had gone, Ivari said, "You think anyone will do this for us when we're his age?"

"I don't plan on getting into this state in the first place," said Rudi. "You?"

Ivari shook his head. "Nah. We talked about it. First time I do this, Frances is off to find a better-behaved model."

"You believe her?"

"Do *you*?"

Rudi thought about it. "Better not get in this state, then."

"We've got *Mama's* genes as well," said Ivari. "It wouldn't happen to us."

"No," agreed Rudi. "We'd run away first."

"Did you ever find out where she went?"

Rudi shook his head. At one time, he'd really wanted to know, but by the time he was old enough to do anything about finding their mother he'd had enough of being disappointed by his parents.

"I looked," said Ivari.

Rudi looked at him. "And?"

His brother shook his head. "Better you don't know."

"Ivari," Rudi said, quite seriously, "we're standing here looking at our father sitting fast asleep on a toilet with his underwear around his ankles. How much worse can it be?"

Ivari shrugged. "Well, she went to England."

"I beg your pardon?"

Ivari nodded. "After she left us, she went to England. Place called Doncaster. After that, I don't know."

"Are you sure it was her?"

"Oh yes. These political people who keep coming here to have their photographs taken with me? They keep saying, 'Anything you want, Ivari, just name it.' They don't mean it, of course, because they think I'll ask them for money, but now and again I ask them about Mother."

"And they bother to look?"

"I've got no way of checking, of course. But, I mean, *Doncaster*. Either that's real or someone fancies themselves as a writer of fiction."

"Do we have any family in England?" Rudi asked, not because he was particularly interested but because every minute Toomas sat there unconscious with his skivvies around his ankles was another little victory over his father.

"Not that I could find out," Ivari admitted, himself not conspicuously eager to rescue Toomas. "Wasn't there somebody who went to Plymouth?"

Rudi shook his head. "He came back. Almost immediately."

"I thought so." Ivari looked at his father. "Have we waited long enough?"

"Do you have a camera?"

"I do, but is that going to make you feel any better?"

"I've had moments, these past few years, when it might have," Rudi admitted.

"Me too."

They stood there, side by side, looking at their father as he snored and snuffled on the toilet, for quite a long time without moving.

Finally, Ivari said, "Oh, sod it," and stepped forward, and Rudi stepped forward with him.

AFTERWARDS, THEY RETIRED to Ivari's study, where Ivari had a bottle of Johnny Walker Blue Label and an extractor fan powerful enough to tow a car, Frances being opposed to smoking in the house. Ivari paused in the kitchen long enough to collect two glasses and a carafe of water, then he closed the door of the study behind them, switched on the extractor, and put bottle, glasses, carafe and a small ceramic ashtray down on his desk. He took his battered Aeron chair at the desk; Rudi got the comfy armchair in the corner beside the bookshelves.

"Well," said Rudi eventually. "That went better than I expected."

"It does help, having an extra pair of hands," Ivari admitted, opening a drawer of his desk and taking out a packet of Marlboros and a Zippo. He waved the packet of cigarettes at Rudi, but Rudi shook his head and showed his brother a tin of small cigars. "Frances won't help me."

"I don't blame her," Rudi said, lighting a cigar.

Ivari poured measures of whisky into the glasses, handed one to Rudi. "Help yourself to water."

"Thanks. Where did you get Blue Label from?"

"Oh, Christ." Ivari sat back in the Aeron and crossed ankle over thigh as he took a cigarette from its packet. "You wouldn't believe the stuff some of these people bring."

"These people?"

Ivari nodded as he lit the cigarette. "The celebrities," he said in a cloud of smoke. "Grabiański. The President. They don't feel able to visit the Park without bringing gifts. Flowers. *Fruit.* Fluffy toys. Flash keys full of their native folk music. Chocolates." He picked up his glass and waggled it. "Alcohol." He took a sip. "*Much* the most useful gift of all."

Rudi added some water to his drink, sipped it, added a little more.

"We divide most of it up among ourselves," Ivari went on. "Kaisa and Jaan have a couple of kids, so they get all the fluffy animals. Mikhel's really keen on world music, so he usually gets that. The flowers go into the Manor. Brighten the place up for a while." He took a drag on his cigarette, exhaled through his nostrils. "The Americans gave us a car."

"Americans?"

"The President gave us a car. One of those little fuel-cell things. Humptys? Humbles?"

"Humboldts."

Ivari shrugged. "Fat lot of good it would have been here. A good strong wind would have blown it into the Gulf. Either that or it would have vanished forever into a bog. We gave it to a hospital in Tallinn."

"I don't remember seeing a photograph of you with the President of the United States," said Rudi.

"We weren't allowed to take any." Ivari raised his glass in mock salute. "Nobody was allowed to know he was here. Security. Officially, he never travels outside the United States because there's always a chance some crazed foreigner might blow themselves up next to him."

"Whereas in the United States that chance is just vanishingly small," Rudi added.

Ivari shook his head. "*That* was an experience, let me tell you. We never got any warning he was coming, but afterwards I thought about it and for the six months or so before he arrived we had a big spike in visitor numbers. Some Americans, but quite a few Brits too. Germans. Poles, *lots* of Poles."

"Security," said Rudi. "Scoping you out."

"That's what I thought, afterwards. And after he'd gone, three rangers who'd been working here for almost a year handed their notice in. No explanation, no reason. Just gone. Good people, too. Not easy to replace. We missed them."

"What was his security like?" Rudi asked, out of professional interest.

"There wasn't any."

"You're joking."

Ivari raised his hand. "No lie. Just him and three other people. They drove up to the Manor one morning in a people carrier, got out, wandered around a bit, came into the centre and introduced themselves. I didn't believe them. I mean, I'd seen him on the news and everything, but you see people out of context and they don't look like themselves, you know?"

"I know."

"So they showed me a whole lot of documents – and to be honest with you they could have mocked them all up with a laptop and a printer. Stuff from the Foreign Ministry. Stuff signed by the President – *our* President." Ivari shook his head again. "What a farce."

"Didn't he have any identification?"

"The President of the United States doesn't carry any." Ivari saw his brother's face and nodded. "Yes. But if you think about it, why would he need any? He's driven everywhere, so he doesn't need a driving licence. He doesn't need a passport because everywhere he goes is American territory, however temporarily. He doesn't need an identification card because, let's be frank about it, when is anyone ever going to question his identity?"

"You did."

"One of the other men with him was the American Ambassador. *He* had identification. Enough identification to choke a gorilla. Which, incidentally, the third man resembled. Big bloke with a big briefcase chained to his wrist."

"Launch codes."

"Well, yes, I figured that out. Tell me this, Rudi, what kind of world is it where the President of the United States has to go about like a thief in the night?"

Rudi shrugged. It was the world of GWOT, which had so far not shown any sign of a victory for either side. The Americans' low-key tactics were interesting, but he was willing to bet there had been backup not more than a few seconds away, had the need arisen.

"Turns out he's Estonian," Ivari said. "Well, his great-great grandfather was. Wanted to see the ancestral homeland. He had a *really* strange accent. When I asked him about it he said he was from Minneapolis."

"Oh, *him*," said Rudi.

"Him. Long streak of piss." Ivari took a drink. "Ach, he seemed all right. Asked a lot of good questions – seemed to have done his homework. Most of them don't bother. We went up to the coast and the Ambassador took our photograph with me pointing towards Finland and looking *intrepid*. Then we all shook hands and they went away. About four minutes later this *really* beautiful woman turns up with a briefcase full of documents she wants us to sign. I mean, you've never seen a woman like her, Rudi. That line in Chandler about making a bishop want to kick in a stained-glass window? That was her. Jaan was standing there with his tongue hanging out; if Kaisa had been on duty that day and not visiting her mother in Rakevere, she'd have divorced him on the spot. So all these documents were non-disclosure agreements. If we told anyone, *anyone at all*, that the President had been here…oh, I can't remember. They'd kill us and all our families and our pets and all our friends and burn our homes to the ground and salt the earth so nothing would ever grow there again. Something like that."

"You're telling *me* about it."

"He lost the next election. Fuck him." Ivari drained his glass. "Another?"

"I haven't finished mine yet."

"Anyway." Ivari poured himself another drink. "A month or so later this big container lorry drives up and the driver and his mate unload this Humbly.

Humboldt. Got me to sign for it. Gift from the President of the United States." He shrugged. "We drove it around the estate for a while, but it was no use to us, so Liisu – her brother's a surgeon – drove it to Tallinn and gave it to him for the hospital to use. I think they ferry old folks to and from day clinics with it."

"But no photographs."

"*Ah.*" Ivari gestured with his glass. "This is a good one. After he lost the election – about a year after he lost the election – I got an email. A *huge* email. From the US Embassy. All the photographs the Ambassador took of us. And a little note saying, it's okay for you to display these now and the President would be proud if you did." Ivari took a drink of Scotch. "As I said, fuck him. If he comes back now, when he's not in power, maybe I'll *display* them."

Rudi looked at his brother and tipped his head to one side. "Are you all right?"

Ivari looked at him and sighed. He ground his cigarette out in the ashtray. "*Paps.*"

"Well, yes," said Rudi.

Ivari shook his head. "He's… he wants the park to declare independence."

"I beg your pardon?"

"He wants the park to secede. Become an independent nation. A… what do you call it?"

"Polity," Rudi said, feeling numb.

Ivari made a half-hearted *gotcha* gesture. "Polity. Yes."

"You talked him out of it, though?" said Rudi. He saw the look on his brother's face and put his hands up. "Sorry. Pretend I didn't ask that."

Ivari lit another cigarette. "A park in Lithuania did it a couple of years ago, I don't remember the name."

Rudi nodded, though he couldn't remember the name either. But it included part of the great primeval forest he had been telling Frances about earlier. "It didn't last long," he said.

"Yes, well, the old man says they were a bunch of amateurs. He says he's got it all thought out."

Well, at least that would be true enough. Rudi rubbed his face. "He can't possibly make it work. He needs a big percentage of the population to agree to his proposal in the first place, before he goes anywhere with it."

"There aren't more than seven hundred people living in the park these days, Rudi," said Ivari. "Most of them are as pissed-off as he is that the Government keeps all our tourism revenue."

"And gives it back," said Rudi. "Upkeep of the Manor and the visitor centre. The tram-line. Maintenance of the roads."

Ivari shook his head. "He's right about that, at least. We only ever see a fraction of it. We get the absolute minimum that we need. We're having to cannibalise one of the Humvees just to keep the others going. The rest of it?" He shrugged.

"It wasn't always like that," said Rudi, thinking back to when he was young and they moved here for the first time. "The Government used to *hurl* cash at us. You remember President Laar? 'Estonia's most precious natural resource. We will never neglect it.'"

"Laar was a long time ago. We were just kids, Rudi. Back then *Paps* could go to the Ministry and ask for anything his black little heart desired, and they'd give it him. Not any more. Now we're a big tourist cash-cow, and most of the cash goes into someone else's pockets."

"It sounds as if the old man's got *you* convinced."

"He's got a point about the money," Ivari insisted. "When I took over from *Paps* as head ranger, we got on all right with the Government. They didn't let us bathe in asses' milk, but they granted us funds for a lot of projects. Nowadays I spend half my time in Tallinn with my cap in my hands." He poured himself another drink and looked at the glass. "Oh, sure, the President comes up here a lot. The Prime Minister, as well. Lots of ministers. And what do we get?" He knocked back the drink in one swallow. "Flowers. Fruit. Fluffy toys."

"Governments change, Ivari."

"Nah," Ivari said, pouring another drink. He held up the bottle. "You want?"

"Yes," said Rudi, taking the bottle from his brother. He topped up his drink, put the bottle on the floor by his feet, out of Ivari's reach.

"Nah," Ivari said again. "It's *institutionalised* now. *This* arsehole, he's made everyone realise just how much we can help them feather their own nests."

Rudi shook his head. "It can't work. The park can't possibly earn enough from tourism to be self-supporting."

"*Paps* is talking about getting the *Laulupidu* moved out here."

"The song festival? That's never going to happen."

Ivari looked at him. "Why not? It wasn't in Tallinn originally; it was in Tartu."

"But the Festival Grounds are there, the *Lauluväljak*. It's where the Singing Revolution happened. Nobody's going to move the festival from there."

Ivari looked sourly at him. "With *Paps*'s contacts in the folk-song community? All it takes is his pals to decide to boycott the festival and come here and have a rival one of their own." He shook his head. "Not even difficult. Those old guys *love* him, Rudi. They'd walk into hell if he asked them to. Nah." He shook his head again. "All he has to do is say the word, and the *Laulupidu* happens right here. Let Tallinn keep the *Lauluväljak* for heavy metal concerts."

One of the biggest song festivals along the Baltic. Tens of thousands of people. If they could turn it into an annual event, rather than every five years, it might generate enough revenue to make a difference. If they could build a suitable venue for it here.

Rudi said, "He has to go to the UN with the proposal. Their fact-finding study alone could last ten years."

"He's got a precedent."

Rudi felt his blood chill.

"That place in Berlin. The one with the anarchists."

"New Potsdam," Rudi said dully.

Ivari nodded. "That was a spontaneous thing. *Paps* thinks that if it happens *spontaneously* enough here, the UN will concede to it, just like they did with New Potsdam."

"The government could keep him in a UN Special Court for the rest of his life, arguing about that," Rudi said, grasping at straws.

"True. But in the interim, the UN has no power to prevent a provisional government being set up here.

We'd have to accept Peacekeepers, but let's face it, they might come in handy."

Rudi put a hand to his face and rubbed it in a horrified, circular motion, as if trying to erase his features. "The old bastard," he said, not without admiration. "He wants to hand the UN a *fait accompli* and let them sort it out."

"And by the time they *do* have it sorted out…"

"…this is a functioning country and they have no right to abolish it. They have to recognise it." Rudi blinked. "Fucking hell." It was, he thought, either the work of a genius or a madman. With his father, it was usually impossible to tell which.

"Of course, we'd have to *prove* that we were a functioning country, in the interim," said Ivari. "But *Paps* has it all costed out. He's got spreadsheets, he's got presentations, he's got the results of divinations from the entrails of chickens. God only knows *what* he has. He's bent the figures so far out of shape they don't even look like numbers any more. He's got a Constitution and a Parliament. In an emergency he's got a government that looks a lot like the Divine Right of Kings." Ivari held his hand out flat, about a metre above the floor. "He's got a stack of notes and proposals and suggestions *this* high."

"Could it work?"

"I don't know. I've seen all his paperwork. Half of it looks as though it was written by Aleister Crowley. On a costings level? We'd have a few tight years in the beginning, then we'd start to show a profit. We'd licence settlers, sell visas. Make the visas really arty so people would regard them as souvenirs. We should have a park mascot. Villem the

Bear. Everyone loves bears. Especially if we design him right." Ivari put his hand to the side of his head as though massaging away a pain.

"There aren't enough people here to defend the borders," Rudi said.

"Haven't you been *listening*?" Ivari shouted, taking his hand from his head. "The *United Nations* will do that *for* us."

Rudi raised a hand. "Okay. My mistake."

Ivari sighed. "Can I have a drink, please?"

Rudi looked at the bottle of Scotch. After a while he picked it up and passed it over. Then he sat back and lit another cigar.

"Either he's going to be the saviour of the park," Ivari said, pouring a very large measure of whisky into his glass and carefully putting the bottle down where he could get at it when he needed it again, "or he's going to destroy us." He picked up his glass and took a big drink. "And I'll be honest with you, I don't know which it's going to be."

Rudi looked at his brother, caught between a rock and a hard place. "We could always kill him," he suggested.

"You see?" Ivari gestured with his glass, slopping whisky over his hand. "I *knew* you'd take this seriously!"

Rudi sighed. "I'll talk to him."

"*That* sounds like a rash promise."

"I know."

"And it won't work anyway."

"You underestimate my powers of persuasion."

"You underestimate how stubborn *Paps* is."

Rudi shook his head. "No. No, I never did that."

* * *

THE ABSENCE OF his mother didn't bother him at the time. His father told him that she'd had to go away for a little while, and she'd be joining them in Lahemaa when they got settled. That was fine by him. There was the excitement of the move, packing stuff up, saying solemn goodbyes to his few friends at school, promising to keep in touch. Then there was the day of the move itself. Their furniture and most of their possessions had gone ahead a day or so earlier, so they were sleeping in an empty apartment, using sleeping bags and eating takeaway pizzas. Rudi didn't sleep at all the night before, too excited by the prospect of the great adventure ahead. He couldn't work out why his father wasn't excited too. Couldn't work out why he actually seemed rather sad. Ivari too.

The next morning, of course, he was exhausted. Years later, he found he couldn't actually remember leaving the apartment for the last time. Or the car journey to Lahemaa. He thought he may have slept through the whole thing, because his first concrete memory of Palmse wasn't the Manor itself, or the forests, or the Gulf. It was his father balancing precariously on the roof of the little house they shared on the estate, trying to attach a satellite dish to the chimney.

Toomas had previously never allowed television in any of the houses and flats they'd occupied, on the grounds that much of what was available on television was either unsuitable for children or just plain crap. Looking back, Rudi wondered whether the sudden appearance of television hadn't been in response to some awkward questions about when, exactly, their mother was planning to join them in Palmse. A typical bit of Toomas misdirection. Anyway, both Rudi and Ivari were excited to finally be getting a glimpse of the forbidden fruit. Ivari, if anything, was more excited than Rudi – although, again with hindsight, Rudi thought that what Ivari was chiefly excited about was the prospect of Toomas losing his footing and plunging headfirst off the roof.

That didn't happen, though, and eventually Ivari and Rudi were allowed to sit down in the living room in front of the alien invader in their life and watch the screen fill with...

The first television programme Rudi ever saw was a cookery programme. A large man speaking an unintelligible language was doing something inscrutable to a piece of meat.

"Well we're not watching *this*," said Ivari, using the remote to flick through the channels until he found one that was showing an IndyCar race.

Rudi had memorised the original channel.

He came back to it later, when everyone was out, and sat waiting to find out what the large man had been doing with the piece of meat. He had to wait quite a while, as the old programmes repeated. He watched the large man make salads and desserts and prepare vegetables and truss various cuts of meat in various unlikely ways. He had little hands and fat fingers, but he was very dexterous, particularly when he was chopping vegetables. His name was Maciej Kuroń. Rudi googled him and discovered that he was Polish, the son of a famous union leader from the

1980s and 1990s. Rudi thought that was interesting, that the son of a famous union leader – although he didn't quite understand then *why* he was so famous – would wind up cooking on television. By the time the channel repeated that first programme, it turned out that what Kuroń was cooking was actually quite mundane – something involving a joint of pork and a colossal amount of cream – but Rudi was hooked. He wrote Kuroń's dialogue down phonetically, and downloaded Polish vocabularies to try and work out what he was saying. When that didn't work, he downloaded a Polish language course and worked at it every spare minute he had. He downloaded audio files of Polish speakers, loaded them onto his tablet, listened to them all the time, and slowly individual words started to emerge from the endless stream of gibberish. And then the words started to make sense. And one day he was able to watch one of Kuroń's programmes and understand it perfectly. He was ten years old.

By then, he'd discovered a channel which showed nothing but old food programmes. Almost all of these were in English, so he started again the way he'd started with Polish, although by now he had a key in the form of the names of vegetables and cuts of meat and cooking techniques. He noted the names of the chefs and googled them. Ramsay, Oliver, Bourdain, Blumenthal, Keller, the list went on and on. He absorbed their biographies. He read their stories of life in the kitchen, found himself much taken with Bourdain. He read Bourdain's novels. He watched Ramsay's television series over and over again, all the time wondering at the rage in someone who had begun his career as a *patissiere*, but taking some of the clips out of context he detected a certain *stageiness*. He downloaded cookbooks, decoded them like Enigma transmissions.

By the age of twelve he was fluent in English, Polish and French. He could have walked into any kitchen in Germany and Italy and got by. He was starting to experiment in the kitchen himself, finally (and with some difficulty finding the proper ingredients) treating his father and Ivari to a paella one evening.

"So," he said conversationally as he served the dish to his rather surprised father, "when's *Mama* coming?"

RUDI WOKE THE next morning with a headache and a faint suspicion that he wasn't sure where he was, exactly. He opened his eyes unwillingly and looked at the bedroom and tried to jigsaw it into his memories. He lay there for a while as the bits clicked into place. Finally he groaned and clambered out of bed and availed himself of the room's en suite facilities. Then he located his bag and put on some clean clothes and went downstairs.

In the kitchen, Ivari and Frances were sitting on opposite sides of a pointed silence. Frances kept glaring. Ivari kept grimacing. Rudi walked through it and grabbed a mug from the draining board, filled it from the coffeemaker, and kept spooning sugar into it until he felt better. The remains of a loaf of rye bread sat on a board on the worktop. Rudi cut himself a slice.

"So," he said, "how are we all?"

Frances made a snorting noise and, with a final glare at Ivari, got up and stormed out.

"I detect negative waves," Rudi said. He took a bite out of the slice of bread.

Ivari looked at him and rubbed his eyes.

"What time did we go to bed?" asked Rudi.

Ivari shrugged.

"Don't blame me," Rudi said. "You're the one who brought out the whisky." He took another bite of bread, washed it down with a mouthful of coffee. "Is the old man up?"

"He's been up for hours," Ivari muttered. "He's gone up to the coast."

"You're kidding."

Ivari shook his head. "The old bastard isn't human."

Rudi leaned back against the worktop and nibbled his slice of bread. "Do you know where he went?"

"He took a Hummer and said he was going to have a look at the Gulf, that's all," Ivari said.

Rudi nodded. That at least sounded familiar. He swigged some more coffee. "Do you have any spare Hummers?"

Ivari turned to look at him. "They're all out," he said. "But a couple of the quad-bikes aren't signed out today. You're welcome to one of those."

Rudi drained his mug. "Yes, well," he said. "You could try to be a bit more supportive, *brother*," he said.

Ivari gave a great hungover shrug.

A QUAD-BIKE was basically a car without any creature comforts. Or a motorcycle without the ever-present fear of losing one's balance. Rudi had been riding them since he was fifteen years old. He checked one out of the visitor centre's garage and gunned it up the trails through the forest towards the coast.

And there, at the end of the trail, on a promontory overlooking the Gulf of Finland, stood his father, like a figurehead.

"So, boy," Toomas said in English.

"So, father," Rudi replied in kind.

Toomas took a long deep breath, held it, and let it out. "Smell that?" he asked. His English was almost accentless. "No smell like the smell of the Baltic wind. Guaranteed to cure a hangover, every time."

"You must come out here quite a lot, then," said Rudi.

Toomas looked at him and smiled. "Very good," he said. "You can do cynicism in English. Very hard to do cynicism well in a foreign language, you know." He switched to French. "How about in French?"

"In French, I find I'm more laconic than cynical," Rudi said in French.

"Of course, you're a cook," said Toomas. "You'd have to know French."

"Well, I never worked under any French chefs, but I take your point."

Toomas asked a nearly-unintelligible question in Lithuanian.

"*Paps*," Rudi said, "you know I don't speak Lithuanian."

Toomas looked taken aback. "How am I supposed to know that?"

"Because I told you last night when you were holding up your part of the conversation in Lithuanian."

"Ah. Okay." Toomas went back to English. "But you're good. You really are. You and I, we have an ear for languages. I'll bet you speak pretty good German, too."

"I've been practising a lot, recently. Some people say I sound *Berlinerische*, but I wouldn't know about that."

"You see? Ivari doesn't have it. I love him like a son, but he's hopeless with languages."

"Ivari *is* your son, father. Unless there's something else you haven't been telling us all these years."

Toomas waved it away. "A figure of speech."

"One would hope."

His father looked at him. "Why did you come back?"

"I missed you."

Toomas nodded irritably. "Okay, okay, you can do cynicism in English. I got the point. Why did you come back?"

"I needed a break," Rudi said, deploying the legend effortlessly. "I've been opening a new restaurant in Berlin and things got a bit hectic. I was starting to shout at the kitchen crew." He shrugged. "Time to take a few days off."

"Your own restaurant?"

Rudi shook his head. "My employer's. In Poland."

"A Pole is opening a restaurant in Berlin?"

"Max thought it was time to repay the favour for 1939. He's Silesian, anyway. That's sort of German."

Toomas rubbed his face. "You see, I can't understand why you wound up there when there are perfectly adequate restaurants in Estonia."

"Well, that's the important phrase, isn't it? 'Perfectly adequate.' Not 'really excellent.'"

"Will you invite me to the grand opening?"

"Would you come?"

"To Germany?" Toomas made a spitting sound.

"Well then."

Toomas looked out over the Gulf of Finland and took another deep breath. "I suppose Ivari told you."

"Told me what, father?"

Toomas looked at him. "Don't do that 'told me what, father?' You're not a good liar."

"I certainly didn't inherit *that* from you."

His father grinned. "I'll bet you thought that would make me angry, eh?"

"I'll bet it does, too. You're just a better liar than me."

The grin went away. "We're fighting for our very existence here."

"Oh, please."

"Really. It's not like things were when we first came here. Governments always loved the park, they gave us anything we wanted. They understood it's the heart of every Estonian."

Rudi snorted. "It's a very large and picturesque area of otherwise not very useful land, father."

Toomas thumped his chest. "The heart!" he cried.

Rudi looked out over the sea.

"But now we have this band of brigands in Tallinn," Toomas went on. "All they see is an opportunity to suck us dry for their own benefit."

"You're just pissed off because they won't give you everything you want, old man," Rudi said. "I know how you work."

His father shook his head. "We get a UN Heritage Grant. Or we should. I know how much that grant is, to the penny. It's been two years since we saw any of it. And it hasn't been for want of asking."

Rudi glanced at him. "You're sure?"

"Do me a favour. I trained as an accountant."

"You trained as an architect."

"And some time after that I trained as an accountant. Don't look at me like that. I know how to read a balance sheet. I asked the UN Heritage Organisation for their disbursements and they emailed them back to me the same day. I asked the Ministry about them and I still haven't heard back." Toomas hard-landed a fist in his palm. "It's graft on a colossal scale. It's a national disgrace."

"So go to court."

"In this fucking country?" Toomas yelled. He waved the prospect away. "Please, don't mention that again."

"This fucking country being the country you love so much, and everything."

Toomas drew himself up to his full height and adjusted the bill of his baseball cap. The Aeroflot logo protruded from his forehead like the horn of a mythical beast. "I know what you're thinking," he said.

"If you *really* knew what I was thinking, you'd already be running," said Rudi.

Toomas ignored him. "You're thinking this is the last act of a lonely, bitter old man, a last stab for immortality after a wasted life."

Rudi shrugged. "Crossed my mind," he admitted.

"And there's some currency in that," Toomas admitted. He spread his hands. "I mean, how much longer do I have, realistically?"

"Stop that," Rudi snapped. "Just stop it. I've been listening to that bullshit since I was eight years old and I don't have to listen to it any more."

Toomas sighed. Then he sighed again, and for a long time he didn't say anything and they stood side by side watching the Baltic lap unhurriedly at the edge of their homeland.

"I love it here," Toomas said finally, and it was as though all the bullshit had been stripped from his voice. "I spent my entire life looking for somewhere to belong, and I found it here. And we had a lot of good years after that. And then the pirates moved in. They've been nibbling away at the edges of the park for the past two years. New towns, developments, sports arenas. Nothing I say does any good, the land just gets eaten up, year after year, hectare by hectare. One day there'll be nothing but a line of hotels where we're standing now. It'll all be gone. Because greedy men came to power in Tallinn. *They* don't care about our heritage. All *they* care about is their foreign partners, the ones who are coming in to build the sports arenas and the hotels. We're just an irrelevance. Something to be swept aside in the name of *progress*."

Rudi looked about him. "You'd have to be out of your mind to build an hotel here," he said.

Toomas shook his head. "That's not you talking," he said. "That's how you feel about *me* talking."

Rudi thought about it. "Fair point," he said finally. "So this is why you want to secede."

Toomas pouted. "No one listens, boy."

"I do wish you'd stop calling me *boy*, you know?"

"No one listens, *Rudi*," Toomas said loudly. "So I'm going to take it away from them."

Rudi scratched his head. "If what you say is true and so much money's at stake here, they'll try to stop you."

"Oh, that's started already."

"Really?"

"Oh yes. We've had some vandalism in the park over the past few weeks. Nothing dreadful, certainly nothing we haven't had before from drunken lads out on a dare, but this is different. It's too careful, too well-executed. It's not about to make me stop, and *they* know that. It isn't supposed to make me stop; it's just to open a conversation with me, let me know they're ready and waiting."

Rudi looked at him. "People are going to get hurt."

"Is that supposed to deter me?"

"Well, it might make most normal people at least stop and think about what they were doing, but no, I was just stating a fact. People *are* going to get hurt if this thing goes any further."

Toomas rammed his fists into the pockets of his parka hard enough for Rudi to hear stitching break. He walked away a few steps.

"It's the *government*, Dad," said Rudi. "They can't get the Ministry to fire you because that would be too obvious, but there's a lot of other stuff they can do. You have no idea."

"Maret found child pornography on our computer," said Toomas.

Rudi regarded his father levelly.

"Oh," Toomas waved his hand irritably, "*not* mine. Planted there. Another part of the conversation."

"What did you do?"

Toomas shrugged. "Formatted the drives and then took them out and physically destroyed them."

"I hope you destroyed them thoroughly."

"I put them through a woodchipper."

"That'll do it," Rudi allowed.

Toomas glared at him. "You're enjoying this."

"It's not without its humorous side, but no, I'm not really enjoying it. That won't be the end of it, you know. There'll be some stuff in secure online storage somewhere that leads back to you, with passwords only you'd know."

"I know. They were just letting me know it's ready and waiting for them to use to discredit me, if they think they have to." Toomas sighed. "Maret... Maret said she believed me when I told her I knew nothing about it. She said she believed me when I told her it was planted there. But I saw the look in her eyes, and she wasn't sure."

"Oh." Rudi scowled and rubbed his face.

"Those motherfuckers have come between me and my partner," said Toomas. "Coming after me, I could accept that. I'm a big boy now and I know the rules of the game. But involving Maret..." He shook his head. "No. I won't stand for that."

"It might have been a move to provoke you into doing something stupid," Rudi warned. "Make you do most of their work for them."

"Why would they care about that? They have plenty of resources."

"It limits their exposure. The less they have to do, the less there is for nosey journalists to discover after it's all over."

Toomas's shoulders slumped. "So what should I do?"

"About the pornography? There's nothing you *can* do. There's no way to find it because we don't know where it is. We can't just google your name and 'child pornography' and there it'll be, sitting on a server in a cupboard in Dushanbe or Buenos Aires. You'll have to be proactive. Write to the news channels. Tell them what you found on your computer. Tell them you suspect there's another stash out there, just waiting to be 'found' to blacken your name."

"They'll deny it."

"Of course. But it makes it a little harder for them to suddenly 'find' it and make it look credible. And it gets you into the conversation." Rudi ran a hand through his hair. "Listen to me. I came out here to talk you out of this madness and I'm giving you advice instead."

"Can you and your friends help?"

Rudi felt a chill touch him. "I'm a chef, Dad. Most of my friends are chefs. We could do the catering for you."

"Frances says you're with Intelligence."

Oh, so *that* was it. He breathed a barely-detectable sigh of relief and then burst into real laughter. "No, Dad, I'm not with Intelligence. I just cook food."

Toomas's face fell. "I thought…"

"No," said Rudi, for the first time in many years feeling anything approaching sympathy for his father. "Just a cook."

Toomas grimaced. "Ach, you'd have to say that."

Rudi spread his hands in exasperation. "Just a cook," he said again. "And if I *were* with Intelligence, I'd be working for the Government and I'd be the very last person you'd want to ask for help."

"So it's true? You're a cuckoo in my nest, then?"

Rudi slapped his forehead. "Dad, *no*! I *don't* work for Intelligence. I'm a *chef*." He rubbed his eyes. "The only way to get out of this thing is to stop it."

Toomas shook his head. "Won't happen."

"Send them a message. Tell them you're prepared to compromise."

"No compromise."

"Tell them…" He searched for the words. "Tell them you'll back down if they guarantee the status of part of the park in perpetuity. Tell them you'll settle for that, they can have the rest for their hotels and arenas." He spread his arms wide. "It's a *big* park, Dad."

Toomas had not stopped shaking his head. "No. No. No. No compromise. No surrender. They don't get their filthy hands on another square millimetre of this place. They've driven a wedge between me and Maret and I'm not going to sit down and let that pass. One of us gets the entire park, the other gets nothing. That's how it will end."

"It will end with you dead," Rudi said.

Toomas abruptly stopped shaking his head. He looked at his son and then he walked back towards him until they were almost chest-to-chest. "You think I care about that, *boy*?" he snarled.

"There's going to be a catastrophe here if you carry on," Rudi snarled back. "Seriously. And it won't just involve you. It'll involve Ivari and Frances and Maret and everyone you ever cared about."

Toomas tipped his head to one side and looked at Rudi. "You think we have a chance."

Rudi glared at him. "From what Ivari told me, yes, you have a chance. *They* think you have a chance, otherwise they wouldn't be opening a *conversation* with you."

Toomas poked Rudi in the chest with a bony forefinger. "They're scared!" he shouted triumphantly. "And scared people make mistakes. We can win this, boy."

"If they *are* scared, they are very *powerful* scared people, and those are the worst kind," Rudi said. "If you keep provoking them they'll just squash you and carry on as if you never even existed."

"You think I'm afraid?"

"I think you ought to be."

Toomas looked at his son for a long time without speaking. Finally, he shook his head. "I'm not stopping now. We're having a meeting in the Conference Centre on Wednesday night. You should come."

"I'm going into Tallinn on Wednesday," Rudi said. "I don't know when I'll be back."

Toomas shrugged. "Please yourself." And he turned and walked back to the Humvee.

Rudi heard the motor start up, heard the old man bully the big vehicle into what sounded like a fifteen-point turn before driving back down the track. He waited for the sound of the engine to die away. Then he waited another couple of minutes, just watching the sea. Then he took out his phone and dialled a number.

When it was answered, he said, "I'm afraid Laurence has food poisoning and won't be able to attend this evening." Then he hung up and stood watching the sea for a long time.

*　　*　　*

IT HAD BEEN a while since he'd been to Tallinn. He didn't count flying into Ülemiste the other night and getting a cab straight to the Palmse tram. He didn't know whether to be mildly pleased or mildly irritated that nothing seemed to have changed. The city looked more or less the same as he remembered. Maybe a few more big office buildings. The harbour hadn't changed at all, and neither had the Old Town. Even the semi-drunken English stag parties were still coming here. Walking past the Hotell Viru, he spotted half a dozen young men in cold-weather clothing and colourful woolly hats stumbling singing out of the front doors of the Soviet-era edifice. He stopped across the street and watched them them go. Then he looked up at the façade of the old Intourist hotel. Legend had it that the KGB had bugged every room in the place, back when certain people thought these things mattered. He wondered if it was true; certainly someone would have checked, after the Russians left.

He took a couple of buses. Had a drink in a bar down by the harbour. Stood and watched one of the big supercats boom in from the Gulf, forty-five minutes from Helsinki to Tallinn and completely impervious to the weather. Nordic Jet Line boasted that their catamarans could sail through the eye of a hurricane, although that had not been required of them yet.

He took another couple of buses. He paused outside the Zoo, insanely large considering how relatively small the city was, but decided not to go in. He took another bus out to Kadriorg and spent an hour or so walking in the grounds of the Palace.

He took some photographs. Then he took another bus back towards the centre of town.

In the Old Town, he wandered for a while, looking in shop windows. He bought himself a couple of sweaters and a tin of small cigars. Feeling peckish, he wandered from restaurant to restaurant, checking menus, before deciding to eat at Troika.

Troika hadn't changed, either. From the vaulted cellar ceilings to the brightly-costumed staff to the menu, it was exactly the way it was the last time he'd been there, two days before he left Estonia for his long odyssey down the coast towards Restauracja Max.

He ordered *pelmeni*, and asked the girl who took his order who the chef was, these days, and when she told him he smiled and said, "And tell him I want proper *pelmeni*. Not the insipid crap he serves to the tourists."

She looked at him and smiled uncertainly. "I'm sorry?"

"Let me write it down," Rudi said, gently taking her order pad from her and scribbling a note. "And make sure he gets that. I'll know if he doesn't and I won't give you a tip."

She went away and Rudi poured himself a glass of water and lit a cigar and waited.

Five minutes later, a small, red-faced man in chef's whites came storming through the restaurant, shouting at the top of his voice in Russian. The waiting staff fled as he approached Rudi's table. Rudi stood up and the chef came right up to him and flung his arms around him.

"Sergei Fedorovich," said Rudi, returning the hug. Sergei let him go and took a step back to look at him. "You lost weight," he said critically. "You don't eat well, wherever you are."

"I'm in Poland," said Rudi.

"Pah. There you are, then." Sergei snapped his fingers at one of the waitresses, who were just coming out of hiding. "You. Stolichnaya and two glasses." He looked at Rudi again and shook his head. "You don't eat well," he said again.

They sat and Sergei raided Rudi's cigars and lit one. "So," he said. "You came back."

"I'm on holiday," said Rudi.

"You got your own restaurant yet?"

Rudi shook his head. "I'm working for someone. In Kraków. It's a good place; you should come down sometime."

Sergei sniffed. "To Poland? Those guys got long memories."

"And we don't?"

Sergei took a drag on his cigar and blew out a stream of smoke. He smoothed a hand over his thinning hair. "Things are not so bad here these days, you know?" Anti-Russian sentiment had run deep in the Estonian soul, even after the Soviets left. Estonia's small but vocal ethnic Russian community had felt somewhat embattled ever since. "I'm not saying things are perfect now, but it's better, you know?"

Rudi nodded and sat back in his chair. Troika had been the first professional kitchen he'd ever worked in, Sergei the first professional chef he'd ever worked under. He'd thought the little man was an unequal mixture of magician and ogre. Sergei had been the first chef ever to hit him. With a roasting pan.

"Now I'm going to make things awkward for you and ask why you didn't stay in touch," said the Russian.

Rudi didn't feel at all awkward; he'd rehearsed this the night before. He shrugged. "I was travelling. I was working all hours God sent. By the time I had a chance to write...well, it would have been embarrassing."

Sergei tipped his head to one side. "You're different."

Rudi laughed. "I'm a better chef now."

"I should bloody well hope so, all this time gone by." Sergei narrowed his eyes. "No, you're different. Some bad stuff happen to you."

"I'm a chef, Sergei Fedorovich. Bad stuff happens to me all the time."

"That'll be true," Sergei admitted. The waitress returned with a frost-rimed bottle of vodka and two glasses and then departed again. Sergei poured them both a drink and then held up his glass. "Fuck your mother," he said and knocked his drink back in one.

"Fuck your mother," Rudi said, and knocked back his vodka.

"Okay." Sergei refilled their glasses and then snapped his fingers at another waitress. "You. Black bread, butter, pickled cucumbers, some of that venison sausage."

Rudi held up a hand to stop her. "I'm meeting someone, Sergei. But after they're gone, I'll have a proper drink with you. I didn't want to sit here and be rude by not saying hello."

"Sure. No problem." Sergei stood and held up his glass. "Fuck your mother."

"Fuck your mother," said Rudi. They drank their drinks.

"Okay," said Sergei. "I'll go and make sure your *pelmeni* are the worst you ever tasted."

"And I've eaten some pretty bad *pelmeni*," Rudi said. "Many of them here."

"Pah," said Sergei. "I'll see you later."

A minute or so after Sergei had left, someone came over and sat in the vacated chair. "Well," said Bradley in English, "that was touching." He put his brandy glass down on the table and smiled at Rudi. "Enjoying our holiday?"

"Visiting old friends."

"Can't beat it," said Bradley.

"I need some help," said Rudi.

Bradley spread his hands. "I'm all ears, old son."

Rudi had also rehearsed this conversation last night, but now he felt as though he hadn't rehearsed quite enough. "My father's a ranger at the national park up at Lahemaa," he said.

Bradley nodded. "I know."

Rudi looked at the Coureur. Of course he knew. "He wants to turn the park into a polity."

"I know," Bradley said again. When he saw the look on Rudi's face, he said, "We haven't been keeping tabs on your family, but when you had that spot of bother in Berlin we did some checks." He held up a hand to stop Rudi's protest. "We just wanted to know who you were, what your background was. That's all."

Rudi scowled at the Englishman. "Is there anything we can do to help?"

Bradley looked nonplussed. "'We,' old son?"

"Central. Is there anything Central can do to help?"

Bradley looked around the restaurant, just starting to fill up with the lunchtime crowd of tourists. "Like what?"

"I don't know. Advice?"

Bradley sighed and picked up his brandy snifter. He looked at it and put it down again. "Operational security forbids that I tell you where I was when we got your crash signal," he said thoughtfully. "But it was quite a long way away, I've not had a very good journey, and I've spent all day following you around waiting for you to settle in order for us to have this meeting. So it would be nice if you could tell me I'm not here just because your dear *papa* has decided to set up his own country."

Rudi sat and looked at him.

Bradley shook his head and picked up his glass again. This time he drained it. "You were given that number and that string in case of dire emergency," he said, putting the glass down and twirling the stem back and forth. "Not to ask Central to help your father become a pocket Emperor."

"I–"

Bradley shook his head again. "Central does not do that," he said calmly. "Central does not facilitate in any way, shape, or form, the creation of any type of quasi-national entity. How can they? We must remain impartial, and we can't do that if we help people set up their own nations."

Rudi opened his mouth to say something. Closed it again.

"Best of luck to your father," said Bradley, "and if he's successful then we'll be happy to do business with him or anyone in his new nation. But until then, we have to stay out of it. And I advise you to stay out of it, too."

"He's going to get himself killed," Rudi said.

"That will be sad, obviously." Bradley stood. "I'm not going to apologise for Central's position on this, because it's not a position which needs apologising for. But we will not help your father, and you shouldn't have asked. And the next time you use that crash code, everyone would appreciate it if it was a genuine emergency."

"Fuck you, Bradley," said Rudi.

Bradley came over to Rudi's side of the table and leaned down close so he could speak in Rudi's ear. "And I meant it about your not becoming involved," he said quietly. "I can't force you, but I strongly recommend that you have nothing at all to do with your father's nationbuilding activities. If someone were to discover that a Coureur was involved, it would call into question the activities of all Coureurs. No one would trust us any more. You think about what that would mean."

Rudi turned his head to look at Bradley. "Have a nice trip," he said.

Bradley straightened up. "You're good at what you do," he said. "You don't think so, that's obvious from our conversations. But you *are* good. You could help a lot of people who really need your help. You can't do that if people don't trust you." He put a hand on Rudi's shoulder and squeezed gently. "Don't get involved in this business." And then he was gone.

Rudi poured another vodka and drank it. Eventually Sergei himself came out of the kitchen with a plate full of *pelmeni* and brought it to Rudi's table.

"Did your friend not turn up?" he asked, putting the plate down in front of Rudi.

"Something came up," Rudi said. "He couldn't stay."

"That's a shame."

Rudi smiled. "Yes." He picked up his knife and fork and regarded the plate of dumplings, boiled in meat broth as usual, a nod to Sergei's Siberian heritage. "Let's see if you've got any better at making these, shall we?"

NOT ENTIRELY SOBER, but not nearly as drunk as he would have liked, Rudi made it to the last tram for Palmse. In the summer they ran until almost midnight, but out of season the last tram left at eight and he had to move smartly to get to the stop in time. The whole tram was empty. He clambered into the last car, waved his phone at the reader to pay for his ticket, curled up on one of the seats, and fell asleep.

He was woken, sometime later, by someone gently shaking his shoulder and saying, "Hey, mate."

For a moment, Rudi didn't want to open his eyes, afraid that if he did he'd find himself back on the tram in Berlin on the night that everything had started to go wrong. On the other hand, he thought, while the hand kept shaking him and the voice kept saying, "Hey, mate," more and more insistently, when had things ever gone *right*? He'd had some small successes, moved some Packages in not-too-strenuous circumstances. But it was the disasters that stayed with him. Potsdam. Berlin. The Zone. The Line. He had to wonder about an organisation that retained an employee with a record like that. Were Central just being pragmatic in not wanting to lose even the most inept Coureur, or did the greater proportion of Situations actually end in catastrophe?

He opened his eyes and saw the tram driver standing beside him. "Hello," he said.

The driver straightened up. "End of the line, son," he said irritably. "If you want to go back to Tallinn tonight you'll have to walk."

Rudi looked out of the window and saw the Manor and all the other buildings of Palmse lit up. He sighed. "No, I'm home, thanks," he said.

WHILE THE TOURIST industry had always been important, for decades Palmse had earned a good living as a conference centre. Computer nerds and captains of industry and science fiction fans and lingerie executives had come to stay in the hotel and have their conventions. Office workers from up and down the Baltic coast had come for team-building weekends and paintballing sessions. When he was growing up, Rudi liked to watch these groups. One weekend, a conference of international chefs had come to the Manor, and fifteen-year-old Rudi had sneaked into every discussion and panel and demonstration he could. He'd attached himself, in the irritating way of certain adolescents, to a Russian chef named Sergei, whose permanently incandescent temper only made him more interesting. Every time Rudi saw Sergei he fell into step beside him or sat down beside him at mealtimes, and bombarded the Russian with questions. Fortunately, Sergei spoke good Estonian.

Finally, driven beyond endurance, he said, "Listen, kid. You want answers? Huh? You come to Tallinn, to my restaurant, you get all the answers you can handle, maybe more. Here." He handed Rudi a card with the name of the restaurant embossed on it. "Now will you just *fuck off* and leave me in peace, actually? Okay?"

The following weekend, it was a conference of machine-tool manufacturers from the North of England. Rudi had chores, but instead he caught the bus into Rakevere, and from there made his way to Tallinn, and by asking for directions from almost everyone he encountered he made his way to the address on the card, on Raekojaplats in the Old Town, and he pushed open the door of Troika for the first time.

"You're fucking kidding me, right?" Sergei said when he emerged from the kitchen, summoned by the rather bemused waitress to whom Rudi had shown the business card.

Rudi raised his chin. "You said there'd be answers here," he said.

Sergei – he had a magnificent head of hair, back then, swept back and leonine – looked him up and down. "You're out of your fucking mind, kid," he said, and turned to go.

"You said there'd be answers here," Rudi said loudly enough for most of the restaurant to hear. "Was that a lie just to get rid of me?"

Sergei stopped and his shoulders set in a way Rudi would become familiar with over the next few years.

"Because if there aren't any answers here," Rudi went on, "maybe I'll go to another restaurant and try and find them there."

Sergei turned back to look at him. "How old are you, kid?" he asked quietly.

Rudi mistook the quiet tone of the chef's voice for calm. It was the only time he made that mistake. "Eighteen."

Sergei tipped his head to one side.

"Sixteen," said Rudi.

Sergei pursed his lips.

"In November," said Rudi.

Sergei nodded. He snapped his fingers at the waitress Rudi had shown the card to. "You. Get his name and phone number." He looked at Rudi. "You. I'll call your parents, see if they'll let you come spend some time here, okay?"

Rudi's heart filled with joy. "Okay," he said.

"Okay. Now fuck off." And Sergei turned and went back to the kitchen.

Rudi never found out how the conversation between Toomas and Sergei went, although in later years he found himself wishing someone had made a recording. In his mind, he reconstructed it thus: Toomas was furious that Rudi had missed his weekend chores and was becoming annoyed that his son spent more time dicking about in the kitchen than doing proper men's work out in the park. Sergei was annoyed that this Estonian teenager had attached himself to him like a limpet. Both men, for their own reasons, wanted the situation to end. So Sergei had agreed to break Rudi and Toomas had agreed to let him.

The first weekend, Rudi turned up bright and early and smiling and happy, and Sergei handed him a mop and worked him almost continuously for forty hours. Every shitty kitchen job was given to him, often simultaneously. He napped in a side room, returned to Palmse with muscles and joints aching so much he could barely walk. And as he went past the visitor centre he saw his father, and he saw the look of glee on Toomas's face, and the next weekend he went back to Troika and they did it all over again. And again the next weekend. And the next. And the next. And one day he came home – not aching very much at all because the work had hardened him – and he saw the gleeful look on his father's face falter, and he knew he was going to win.

Sergei was a tougher prospect than Toomas. While Toomas started to make whining little speeches about missing Rudi around the place at weekends, Sergei kept yelling and hounding and, on one occasion, whacked him in the face with a roasting pan that hadn't been cleaned to his testingly microbiological standards.

And then one day, after almost two years of this, Rudi was preparing food.

Rudi couldn't actually remember what had led to this, but he did remember that both he and Sergei were somewhat surprised that it was happening. Sergei maybe more so. And then of course the real nightmare had begun.

ABOUT FIFTEEN YEARS ago, the Ministry had granted Palmse the funds for a new purpose-built conference centre. They even ran an international competition, which attracted entries from as far afield as New Jersey, to provide a design for the new building. In the end, though, graft or nepotism or patriotism or simple excellence had won out and a firm of architects from Tallinn had got the commission. Rudi had never understood why, but he was a chef, not an architect. His father, who *was* an architect, at least by some degree of training, had praised the Conference Centre for its "innovative use of the Baltic Tradition," but to Rudi it just looked like a huge wood and glass box adorned with fiddle-faddling Baroque decorations copied off buildings from St Petersburg to Vilnius. On the other hand, his father had once described his beef wellington – a dish of which he was very proud at the time – as "a crime against good beef," so really it was, as the English liked to say, horses for courses.

This evening, the big gingerbread box was all lit up by halogen spotlights mounted on its lawns. It looked like one of Crown Prince Rudolf's final fever-dreams, or something Ruritania might have come up with if it had ever made it into the twenty-first century. The car park was crammed with vehicles. A large percentage were hummers, the weapon of choice on Lahemaa's roads, but there were also sleek BMWs and Mercedes and battered old Land Rovers and fuel-cell-powered people carriers and five Polish-built Fiat minibuses. Rudi looked at the minibuses as he went past. They were all identical. He walked around one of them and was quite impressed by how clean it was. Its numberplate was a barcode designed to be read by automated toll-road computers, but there was also an index number which showed it was registered in Tallinn. As was the next minibus. And the next. Rudi looked at the buses. He looked at the Conference Centre. He began to run.

The Centre was built around a lecture hall designed like an open-cast mine, a stage surrounded by concentric rings of fifty ranks of seating rising steeply towards the ceiling. Around the outer edge of each ring of seating were offices and smaller conference rooms and dining rooms and performance suites and communications rooms. The whole place smelled of polished wood and new carpets and air conditioning and hot lights.

The lobby, several hectares of hardwearing carpeting and hidden lighting and modern-style furnishings and coffee-points separated from the night by floor-to-ceiling panels of smoked glass, was deserted. Rudi could hear waves of shouting rising and falling in the auditorium. He tried the doors, but they were locked. He tried the lifts, but they had been switched off. He took the stairs two at a time and finally emerged halfway up the amphitheatre into an unoccupied rank of seating.

The noise which greeted him as he burst through the doors was not unlike that made by football fans who have spent a large amount of money to watch their side play in a European Cup Final. They haven't been able to get tickets to the match itself, but they've travelled to the venue city anyway, to support their side and for the 'atmosphere.' The venue city has set aside a couple of public spaces for visiting supporters, complete with a huge screen on which they can watch the match. The fans have been drinking good-humouredly all day. The match kicks off. Then the screen breaks down. It was that sort of noise.

From where he was standing, between the seats and the row of office doors, Rudi could look down into the auditorium and see the tiny figure of his father on the stage. The auditorium had expertly-designed acoustics, and that and the PA system meant that Rudi could hear his father say, "...the beating heart of Estonia..." before his voice was overwhelmed by a cresting wave of shouting from the packed ranks of seating around and above him. Rudi could see fights breaking out in the rows below him, heard his father call out, "No, don't give them the satisfaction..." before his voice vanished into the noise again.

Rudi turned to head back for the stairs to try and find his way to the floor of the auditorium, and at that moment the door behind him opened and someone grabbed him by the shoulders and jerked him backwards.

He found himself standing in one of the office suites with three men. They were all identically dressed in black combat suits, body armour, boots and helmets. They all had machine-pistols attached to ripaway slings on their chests, automatics at their hips, combat knives strapped to their thighs, and various other bits of equipment attached to loops all over them. They closed the door and stepped between it and Rudi.

"You have to be kidding," he said.

The middle figure raised its visor, revealing a strong, middle-aged face. "Major Ash, sir," he said in English. "SAS. I'm authorised by His Majesty's Government to offer you political asylum."

"I beg your pardon?" Rudi asked.

"I'm also authorised to sedate you and extract you anyway if you turn down the offer," Ash continued. "Personally, I'd advise against that. The sedative leaves you with a terrible headache and some other side effects. You'd be wiser to come with us voluntarily."

"I don't need political asylum," said Rudi. The noise from the auditorium grew even worse. Rudi started to make for the door. "Please thank His Majesty for me, but I'm needed here." And he felt something sting the side of his face and the next thing he knew he was waking up in Finland and, as promised, he had the worst hangover in human history.

KING'S BENCH WALK

1.

THE FIRST DAY, he resolved to be uncooperative.

This turned out to be a piece of cake. Angry, tired, and suffering the after-effects of the sedative, it was all he could do to clamber out of bed, drag himself to the lavatory, allow his body to do something indescribable, and drag himself back to bed. Also, no one tried to interrogate him. Dizzy and nauseous and suffering an almost literally stunning migraine, he watched young English people approach him, inquire anxiously how he was feeling, dab at him with damp towels, and then withdraw. An older gentleman who spoke Swedish in a voice which seemed to boom in from another dimension appeared from time to time and shone a light into his eyes, which hurt beyond human imagination, and gave him injections, following which the world withdrew beyond a howling black-and-white kaleidoscope animation and he experienced periods of absence which he later thought might have been sleep.

As far as sticking to his resolution went, the first day was an outstanding success. It lasted, so far as he could tell, a little short of a million years.

ON THE MORNING of the second day, he opened his eyes and found himself lying in the most comfortable bed he had ever encountered. It was the kind of bed that a person would have to be bodily picked up and carried away from just in order to get up in the morning. But it paled in comparison to the pillows his head rested on, stuffed with down to such precisely-calibrated firmness that they could only have been the end-result of centuries of research. He was covered with crisply-laundered cotton sheets, topped by an old-fashioned quilt. He felt warm and safe and perfectly relaxed. Whatever else had happened to him, he had clearly fallen into the hands of people who took sleep seriously, and it was difficult to hate such people.

He lay there for a long while staring up at the ceiling, which was high and painted a cream colour. In the centre of the ceiling a complex floral rose executed in plaster dropped a cable from which hung a four-branched light fitting in what looked like tarnished brass. Nice. Understated. A little old-fashioned. Not fussy.

Unwillingly, because if he was to be honest with himself he would much rather have spent the rest of his life lying there with his head supported by those marvellous pillows, he sat up in the bed and looked at the room.

And it wasn't bad. Not very large, decorated in a Baltic rococo revival style he remembered from a magazine article he'd read a few years ago. Two of the walls had large windows, and between them stood the clean pale-wood lines of various pieces of furniture – wardrobes, dressing tables, chests of drawers, cabinets. The wallpaper, which only a few hours ago had seemed so outlandishly garish that he'd thought in a rare lucid moment that it had been put there specifically to drive him out of his mind, was actually a rather muted and thoroughly decent Regency stripe. The door to the en suite facilities, which yesterday had seemed as far away as Proxima Centauri, stood ajar just a few steps from the bed across the rug-covered floorboards.

From his sitting position, he saw a dressing gown draped across the foot of the bed. This seemed like an invitation, so he swung his legs out of the bed and put his feet down and they landed in a pair of slippers which had been placed in exactly the correct spot. The slippers were in the moccasin style, soft leather lined with what appeared to be sheepskin, stitched together with brightly-coloured thread, and the moment his feet hit them he never ever wanted to take them off again. He sat there for a while on the edge of the bed, wiggling his toes in the miraculous slippers. He was, he realised somewhat belatedly, wearing cotton pyjamas.

He stood up and felt a little light-headed for a moment, but it passed. He picked up the dressing gown and looked at it. It was navy blue, with a monogram on its breast pocket. After examining the monogram for some minutes, he decided it consisted of a design composed of every single letter of the alphabet, picked out in gold thread and surmounted by an heraldic animal he was unfamiliar with. He put the dressing gown on, did up its belt, put his hands in the pockets.

In hostile territory, always assume you're under surveillance. No need to skulk about, then. He walked across to the nearest window, pulled the curtain and the net curtain behind it aside, and looked out. The window looked down into the courtyard of an anonymous five-storey building. It was a big courtyard, and it was covered with a fresh fall of snow. Right in the middle someone had built a snowman, complete with a broom and a carrot for a nose. The snowman was wearing a black top hat.

Rudi craned his neck. All he could see was rows of windows in the other wings of the building, all identically net-curtained. Doors at ground level. Aerials on the roofs.

He let the curtains fall and started to explore the room. One door led to a small kitchen. Microwave, induction hob, kettle, fridge-freezer. In the fridge were bottles of water with labels in Finnish, packages of cooked sliced meat, a pack of unsmoked back bacon, a block of unsalted butter, six eggs, a litre of semi-skimmed milk, a bag of prewashed salad. In the freezer were neatly-wrapped and labelled packs of beef, pork and lamb, several bags of beef mince, a tub of chocolate Häagen Dazs. A cupboard beside the sink revealed a wire basket full of onions, carrots, potatoes. Another revealed a bin containing four different kinds of loaf. Mugs and cups and saucers. Paper packets of flour, plain and self-raising. Packages of tea and coffee and sugar. An unopened bottle of sunflower oil, an unopened bottle of olive oil. Some of those little packs of chocolate biscuits you got in hotels. Packets of stock cubes – beef, lamb, pork and vegetable. A spice rack on the wall with little jars of spices dangling from it, all their seals unbroken. Acrylic salt and pepper grinders. Pots and pans, utensils. He stood for a few moments looking at a knife-block the size of a small rucksack, from which protruded the handles of what appeared to be one of every kind of cook's knife ever made. He took one out and weighed it in his hand. Sabatier. Not the way to treat it, putting it in a block. He slid it back into its slot and checked the kitchen bin, which contained nothing but a plastic bin-liner.

Back in the main room, he stood with his hands in the pockets of the dressing gown and blew out his cheeks. He went into the bathroom, half expecting chaos and disorder, but everything was neat and clean, no sign of the terrible things his body had recently been doing there. Nicely tiled in pale blue. Toilet, bidet, washbasin, shower, all in white. Wrapped soaps and unopened bottles of shampoo, all with Finnish labels. Toothspray and brush still sealed in crinkly plastic beside the washbasin, alongside two similarly-sealed glass tumblers and a can of shaving gel and a package of plastic razors. Cupboard under the sink with spare toilet rolls on one shelf, cleaning materials on the one beneath. He looked at himself in the mirror over the washbasin and he looked not so bad, really, considering. A little pale, maybe. There was a tiny little red mark on his cheek where one of Ash's men had shot him with what he presumed was a soluble crystal of sedative. He ruffled his hair and went back into the bedroom.

Cupboards. A wardrobe containing nothing but empty hangers and a couple of those little scented cloth sachets that are supposed to deter moths. A desk with drawers containing ballpoint pens and tablets of unheaded good-quality notepaper. Opening the door of one of the cupboards revealed a state-of-the-art entertainment centre, gestural interface, onboard base of thousands of albums and movies. He waved up the main menu, looked at the options, shut it down again and put his hands in his pockets and looked around the room.

All of which, obviously, was intended to make him feel safe and calm and happy. Which it did, and not just in the obvious way. As much as anything, the room was a message. It told him the people who had abducted him were not without resources. It told him they were professional. It told him they had done their homework – they'd given him the means to do his own cooking. It told him how lucky he was not to have woken up chained to a radiator in a derelict flat in one of the many bad parts of Warsaw. It told him that if the people who had abducted him had *wanted* him to wake up chained to a radiator in a derelict flat in a bad part of Warsaw, that was where he would have woken up.

It did not, of course, tell him who the hell they were. Just *claiming* to represent the English government did not make it so.

There was a discreet knock at the door. Rudi turned at the sound, and when he didn't say anything the knock sounded again. Obviously, they knew he was up and about, but they were determined to be polite. He said, "Hello?"

He didn't hear a key turn in the lock. The door opened and a young woman wheeled a trolley covered with a grey sheet into the room. She had auburn hair tucked up in a bun and an outdoorsy flush to her cheeks. She was wearing a long fawn corduroy skirt and a white blouse clasped at the throat with a silver brooch in the shape of a little owl. She was smiling sunnily.

"Morning," she said breezily. "How are we feeling today?"

Rudi hurriedly ran through the options, loaded his English with an Estonian accent and his body language with as much outrage and confusion as he could, and said, "Who are you? Where am I? What are you doing with me?"

The woman just kept smiling and wheeled the trolley into the middle of the room, where she removed the sheet. On the top was a small soup tureen, a bowl and a spoon. On the shelf underneath were some cloth packages.

"You must be hungry, you poor thing," she said. "We thought you'd like some chicken soup."

"Who are you?" he said again. "What is this place? What do you want?"

"Oh, you don't need to worry about any of those things," she said cheerfully as she ladled soup into the bowl and carried it over to a table by one of the windows. The soup smelled wonderful, but Rudi stayed where he was.

"I don't want soup," he said. "I want to know what's going on. Why am I being kept prisoner here? Who are you?"

"You can call me Jane, if you like," she said. She turned from the table. "You should eat, you know. Keep your strength up."

"I'm not hungry," he said, although he was.

"You can cook something for yourself, of course," said Jane. "We just thought you'd prefer something made for you this morning."

Rudi took a deep breath. "Who are you?" he yelled. "What is happening?"

Jane looked so sad that Rudi immediately felt guilty for shouting at her. She looked as if she was about to burst into tears. "Look, if you don't want the soup..." Her bottom lip actually trembled.

Rudi sighed. "Yes. Yes, I want the soup. Thank you. Sorry."

Her smile brightened a little, as if someone had turned an invisible rheostat up a degree or so. "That's the way," she said, in a subdued-sounding voice.

"I want to know what's happening to me," he said more calmly.

"Of course you do. And someone will be in to tell you soon. I promise." She moved away from the table and went past him to the door, giving him a wide berth as she did so and not meeting his eyes. "There are some clean clothes on the trolley," she added. "I'll be in later to clear the soup things away." And she let herself out.

After she had gone, Rudi stood for a while where he was in the middle of the room, trying to parse what had just happened. He seemed to have been completely disarmed by a teary English girl. He wondered whether he was still drugged.

He went to the door and tried to open it, but the handle wouldn't turn, though he hadn't heard it being locked. He sighed and went over to the table, picked up the spoon, and looked at the bowl of chicken soup. It was clear and golden, with just a sheen of fat on the surface, and tiny fragments of carrot and swede and celeriac floating in it. He dipped the spoon into it and lifted it to his lips. It was the best chicken soup he had ever tasted. Possibly the best chicken soup that had ever been made. He sat down and started to eat.

THE CLOTHES TURNED out to be a beautifully-cut pair of jeans, boxer shorts, socks, a plain black T-shirt, and a light-grey fleece that zipped up the front. They were the best-fitting clothes he had ever worn, and that was starting to become irritating. A part of his mind was delirious with pleasure at all this fantastic stuff. Another part was annoyed by the thought that while he was unconscious someone must have poked and prodded and measured him in order to outfit him this well. Another part was actually quite angry, now he thought about it, to be so transparently manipulated. And even more angry to discover how easily he could be bought by a comfortable bed.

He ate the entire tureen of soup with several thick slices of rye bread. It crossed his mind, halfway through the third bowl, that the soup might be drugged, but by then it was too late and he considered the possibility of being drugged worth it just to eat this marvellous soup. When it was finished, he dressed. Then he wandered around the suite again.

At the entertainment centre, he waved up the interface again and went through the most common hacks he could remember. They would be expecting him to do this, so there was no point not bothering. None of the hacks worked. None of them confirmed his location; none of them allowed him to phone or email or SMS or tweet out. None of them allowed him to post on any bulletin board or social network.

He gave up and tried the news. There was what appeared to be local rolling news, and yes, it did appear to be in Finnish. Although there were also American, French, Italian, German, Spanish and British channels, and none of them seemed to have been assigned a priority.

He sketched a menu ring in the air in front of him, put his finger through it, pulled down, and on the screen a white infosheet dropped down with a list of options, all in English. He pointed at 'Internet' and Google came up as the homepage, along with a keyboard representation. He cocked his hands in front of him and air-typed 'Palmse.'

There were reports – not very many and mostly on Estonian news sites – of the riot at the Conference Centre. The Government were presenting it as a bunch of proto-separatist thugs smashing up the Conference Centre as an act of defiance against Tallinn. A few bloggers – citizen news gatherers, in modern coinage – were posting their suspicions that the 'proto-separatist thugs' had actually been bussed into Palmse by the Government to break up the meeting. One, who called himself *ironrabbit* –

Rudi was fairly sure it was a young man – even said he had interviewed one of the rioters, who had told him they had been paid for their efforts that evening. *Ironrabbit* hadn't posted anything since then.

As leader of the proto-separatists, his father featured quite heavily, at least in the local news stories. They all got his age wrong and one spelled his surname incorrectly. He was in hospital with serious but not life-threatening injuries. Of Ivari, not a word. Rudi checked the park's website, but the news section hadn't been updated for over a month. He googled Ivari's name. Nothing but a few pages of old photographs of his brother with various celebrities in the Park, pointing into a mythical distance and looking *intrepid*. He looked at the photographs for a while. Then he closed everything down and went and stood at one of the windows. It had started to snow again.

BY THE THIRD day, he was bored.

It was all very well shouting at young English people and demanding answers and being difficult, but the whole act just bounced right off them. They were so painfully polite that he felt bad about offending them. Some of the girls became teary. It was utterly surreal, and in the end quite pointless.

Finally, he said to Jane, who had come to the suite to inquire whether he needed anything, "All right. I am a Coureur. I would like to speak with a representative of my organisation. A man named Kaunas, if at all possible."

She didn't reply, other than with her usual pleasantries, but an hour later a response arrived, in the serene, pudgy, septuagenarian shape of a gentleman who introduced himself as Gibbon and who settled himself into one of the armchairs in Rudi's suite, unzipped one of those old-fashioned leather document folders, extracted an antique fountain pen, and blinked at him.

"I want to leave," Rudi told him when the preparations were complete.

Gibbon shook his head sadly. "I'm afraid we have information that your life is in danger," he said regretfully.

"From whom?"

Gibbon consulted the documents in the folder. "Certain factions within Greater German counterintelligence," he said, running the butt of his pen down the list. "The Estonian government. Coureur Central."

"I beg your pardon?" said Rudi, feeling a chill down his back despite knowing that this was almost certainly part of a provocation.

Gibbon raised his eyebrows and returned the butt of the pen to its previous position. "Yes." He looked calmly at Rudi. "We have rather good intelligence that your own people want to kill you. I'm afraid we don't know why."

"That's impossible," Rudi said, trying and failing to imagine something so heinous that Central would want to kill one of their own.

"It *is* rather good intelligence," Gibbon told him again.

"Where does it come from?"

Gibbon sighed and scratched his head. "Yes, well, we *always* give our sources away to complete strangers," he said with some sarcasm. He clipped his pen to the documents in the case and folded his hands across his ample belly. "The fact is, there are very few safe places for you right now, and one of them is with us."

Rudi looked at him for a few moments. "Is business so slow these days that English Intelligence is carrying out individual rescues?" he asked.

Gibbon laughed as though he found this genuinely funny. "Oh, goodness gracious me no," he said, shaking his head. "Although it's a good thought, it really is."

"So, assuming we accept this fantasy story you've just told me, you obviously want something from me."

"Presumably," agreed Gibbon, still chuckling at the idea of MI6 riding around the globe like a knight on a white charger.

"'Presumably?'"

Gibbon shifted in his chair. "May I be frank with you?"

"It would make a pleasant change, yes."

"My station was tasked with facilitating the insertion of Major Ash's team into Estonia and their extraction of yourself. We were tasked with looking after you until you'd recovered sufficiently to travel."

"Travel where?"

Gibbon looked nonplussed. "Well, London, of course."

"Where all answers will be forthcoming?"

Gibbon shrugged as if to say, *well, London, who knows?* He zipped up the folder again. "You realise I'm telling you all this as a professional courtesy," he said. "London tend to look down their noses at you

Courier chaps, but out here we hold you in rather high regard."

"Not high enough to get our name right," Rudi said, and felt cheap the moment the words were out of his mouth. Gibbon was at least treating him decently, even if everything he said was probably a lie.

Gibbon raised an eyebrow. "Aye, well," he said. "Anyway, you'll be going to London. And perhaps all answers *will* be forthcoming there. I'm just sorry we had to meet under these circumstances. I'd have welcomed a chance to chat with you about operational matters."

"Except we'd have to kill each other afterwards," said Rudi.

Gibbon chuckled. "Yes, there is that."

"It's really a very boring life."

"*Yours* doesn't seem to be."

"That isn't really my fault."

"Are you sure?"

"I was on holiday when your pet special forces men kidnapped me."

"Saved your life," Gibbon corrected gently.

"Allegedly." Although a thought sent a pulse of goosepimples up his arms.

Gibbon was either very good at reading faces, or he was telepathic. He nodded. "It would have been rather an opportune moment to bump you off, with all that chaos going on, wouldn't it?"

Rudi swallowed down a sense of fear, of forces beyond his comprehension. "It's ridiculous. What am I supposed to have done?"

Gibbon shrugged. "I'm only privy to the intelligence I just passed on to you, I'm afraid."

Rudi stared at the Englishman for a very long time, completely at a loss for words. Gibbon, for his part, sat serenely in his chair as if regarding a particularly restful countryside scene. No fuss, no hurry, not a thought in his head.

Finally Rudi said, "When do I leave?"

2.

THE JUMP WAS utterly beyond belief.

Rudi's dealings with the intelligence services of governments had been fairly limited, down the years. They were, in his experience, mostly professional, if entirely without scruple.

MI6, in contrast, appeared to be making everything up as it went along, using a joke book as its guide.

At six o'clock on the morning after his interview with Gibbon, there was a brisk knock at his door and Major Ash, looking rather avuncular in tan chinos, blue blazer, blue shirt and red-and-blue striped tie, put his head into the room.

"Ready to go, sir?" he asked cheerfully.

Rudi was still in his pyjamas and dressing gown, sitting in front of the entertainment centre, his hands poised in mid-gesture as he read through the BBC News website. "Not really, no," he said.

Ash stepped into the room and closed the door behind him. He was carrying a black nylon travel bag, which he held out. "Flight's in three hours," he said. "You might want to get dressed."

The bag contained some fairly blameless casual clothing – jeans, sweatshirt, underwear, training shoes, another zip-up fleece to go over it all. Rudi looked at it, then looked at Ash, then went into the bathroom to dress.

He had no luggage, so leaving was fairly straightforward. He actually felt a little pang when Ash led him out of the room. He'd rather liked it there.

Ash led him down a thickly-carpeted corridor and into a lift, which deposited them in a basement garage. A lovely black BMW was waiting for them. They climbed in, and it accelerated up a ramp and into the pre-dawn darkness of Helsinki's morning rush hour.

Rudi didn't know the city well enough to orient himself; he caught a glimpse of a large, imposing, official-looking building as they drove alongside the Embassy, but that was all he ever saw of its exterior, and to be honest it could have been *any* large, imposing, official-looking building. By the time he had some vague idea where he was, they were on the road to the airport.

Where, utterly appalled, he found himself queuing to go through passport and security checks along with families, old people, teenagers and a large and extremely boisterous group of university students who, from their shouted conversations, appeared to be on their way to Madrid.

In the car, Ash had provided him with an envelope containing a false passport and a printout of an eticket. The passport was the only thing Rudi could later identify as even faintly resembling tradecraft, and by then he could no longer hazard a guess what went on in the heads of the British Security Services.

The eticket was for a seat on a scheduled budget airline flight. Rudi stared at it for so long that he almost forgot to hand it over at the desk.

On the other side of the checks, Ash led him to a departure lounge Starbucks and there, mind reeling, Rudi sat for fifty minutes until their flight was called.

At one point, Ash got up and said, "Just going for a wee. Back in a sec," and walked off across the lounge in the direction of the toilets, leaving Rudi quite alone.

Was he being watched? Was it a test? All thoughts of running off had entirely deserted Rudi when he found himself going through the passport and security checks. He sat where he was and drank his coffee, enthralled by the awfulness of it all.

The flight itself was the kind of thing where you only got a seat and the attendants selling you overpriced coffee and perfumes and airline-themed knicknacks. Ash had had some sandwiches made up at the Embassy and handed one over. Rudi prised it open and saw a wafer-thin slice of meat and gelatine trapped between two doorsteps of heavily-buttered white bread. He closed it again with a pained look on his face.

"Lunch tongue," Ash said when he saw the look.

"I'll just have a coffee, please," Rudi said, handing the sandwich back.

"Well, if *you* don't want it..." Ash said, tucking in.

And a couple of hours later they were in England, landing at Stansted, *queuing up at Passport and Immigration*. When the passport officer asked him the purpose of his visit, he had to bite down an urge to say that he was starring in a very, very bad spy movie.

To Rudi's mind, the favoured way of getting a high-profile Package out of a country if you were a sovereign nation would be in a private jet under diplomatic cover, no security or customs officials at either end, car waiting on the tarmac on arrival to whisk him down the motorway to his destination. He was almost in a dream state as they took the *train* into London and then the *Underground* to Blackfriars and then *walked* along the Embankment of the Thames a short distance to a place Ash called 'The Temple.'

Which turned out not to be a temple at all, but a set of quiet, linked squares of tall terraced buildings and gardens that tilted down to the Embankment. Ash led Rudi to one of the buildings – as they entered Rudi saw a hand-lettered sign, at the top of which were the words 'Smithson's Chambers' above a list of names – in the entryway of which waited an incredibly tall and imposing-looking American man who shook his hand firmly and said, "You call me 'Red,' okay?"

And that was Rudi, stolen from Estonia by the SAS, babysat by MI6, and delivered into a Kafkaesque dream.

3.

AT WEEKENDS, THE area was deserted. You got some tourists wandering up and down Fleet Street, but it didn't start to get busy until you were past the High

Court and heading towards Trafalgar Square. On a Sunday, you could walk up out of the Mitre Court gateway onto Fleet Street, and for minutes on end you wouldn't see another living soul.

Weekdays were different. Then, Fleet Street was a main artery between Westminster and the City. A shockwave of commuters emerged from the stations at City Thameslink and Blackfriars and Farringdon and Temple and Chancery Lane between about eight and ten. Passengers on the top decks of passing buses, all bent in unison over their morning news or novel, seemed to lean forward in anticipation of the day's work. And then in the evenings it all happened in reverse. The commuters were swallowed by their stations, the bus passengers regarded their *Evening Standard*s or went back to the chapter of the novel they were reading that morning. Rudi had been watching it for almost seven weeks, and he thought he had life in London more or less summed up by now. It was *tidal*, like its river, a great flood of humanity washing in and out of the Capital. And at some point the tide had washed him in.

"Hey, there," Mr Bauer said cheerfully, passing through the living room on his way to the study. "How's our boy today?"

"I'm very well, thank you, Mr Bauer," Rudi replied in English.

Mr Bauer came to a stop in the middle of the worn Afghan rug and regarded Rudi with his hands on his hips. "Now how many times have I told you?" he asked. Rudi was about to say it must have been ten or fifteen times, but Mr Bauer went on without waiting. "It's 'Red,' son. Nobody calls me 'Mr' Bauer."

"Mr Self does," answered Rudi, and he watched Mr Bauer's eyes disconnect slightly as he tried to process the answer.

Mr Bauer was an American with the aspect of a mighty but ruined building. Well over two metres tall, and impressively broad-shouldered, he strode through the Temple like Ozymandias, his great mane of white hair blowing in the wind, dispensing hail-fellow-well-mets to his fellow barristers, whether he knew them or not. You had to get a little closer to Mr Bauer to see the pockets of his suit, which were ruined from carrying things which were never meant to be carried in the pockets of suits, to see the ruddy good-health on his cheeks resolve into spiders'-webs of broken veins, to see the scuffed and worn-down heels of his once-magnificent GJ Cleverley shoes.

Mr Bauer's eyes snapped back into focus. "But, hey," he said, wagging a finger at Rudi. "You have to call me 'Red,' okay?"

"Okay," Rudi said, laying his book aside.

Mr Bauer raised his impressive eyebrows. "We have a deal, now, don't we?"

Rudi nodded. "We have a deal," he said dutifully from his chair on the other side of the room. "Red."

"*That's* the spirit!" Mr Bauer proclaimed. "We have a deal. Yes. Now, if you'll excuse me, I have to, um…" and he turned and left the way he had come in.

Rudi sat where he was for a while. He looked at the book lying face-down on the table beside his armchair. William Shirer, *The Rise And Fall Of The Third Reich*. Mr Bauer's rooms were full of old paper books, some of them almost a century old. It was impossible, from examining the titles, to discern what Mr Bauer was actually interested in, unless he was interested in *everything*. History books rubbed shoulders with the manuals of computer operating systems long-forgotten except in certain parts of the Third World, where the obsolete discarded flotsam and jetsam of the Computer Age had come to rest in the name of Aid. Great stacks of film-star biographies, most of dispiriting thickness. Novels in such broken-spined and dog-eared profusion that it seemed impossible that one lifetime would be enough to read them all. Two cookbooks, one which seemed to be a first edition of the *River Café Cookbook*, and the other a bizarre little spiral-bound volume with a cartoon dog's face grinning on the cover beneath the words *Let's Cook With Hari Vex!* Hari Vex – if it was indeed he – appeared to be a Bernese Mountain Dog, and the recipes inside seemed to have been assembled by a chef on the verge of a catastrophic nervous breakdown.

Fortunately, for matters culinary – and much else – Mr Bauer had Mrs Gabriel, brown-haired, pigeon-chested guardian of laundry and kitchen, keeper of the keys, and the only person in Smithson's Chambers who actually knew where everything was, or could at least locate it while it was still needed or indeed vaguely relevant. She wore thick brown stockings and a hideous blue nylon housecoat over her street clothes, and flat shoes with soles composed of some substance which caused her to scuff up cracking little charges of static electricity, so that it was possible to hear her approaching across the Chambers' worn carpets like a tiny electrical storm. Rudi had invested some time in wondering about her relationship to Mr Bauer. Wife? Daughter? Mistress? Nurse? And then it had all become clear; Mrs Gabriel was Mr Bauer's housekeeper, and therefore transcended all those merely temporal descriptions. Without Mrs Gabriel, Mr Bauer would not only have been unable to function; he would have been unable to exist at all. Mrs Gabriel was a steady cook of the unadventurous English type, whose heavy food and nourishing gravies had sustained generations of public schoolboys all the way back to the days of the Great Game. It wasn't that Rudi *disliked* her food, exactly, but when she brought her steak-and-kidney pies to the table, with their ritual accompaniment of boiled potatoes, boiled carrots and boiled peas, the Limoges gravy boat carrying its velvety cargo in their wake, he felt a dark wing of depression fold around him. He would have suggested other English dishes, perhaps á la Fergus Henderson, but he suspected the first mention of roasted marrow bones would galvanise Mrs Gabriel and her fellow housekeepers into a moonlight assault on Smithson's Chambers with pitchforks and scythes and burning torches.

Beneath Mr Bauer's rooms, Smithson's Chambers went on with their everyday work, giving hope and succour to the weak, the indigent, the hopeless and the frankly criminally insane. Mr Bauer had arrived from Harvard Law almost fifty years ago, clutching his newly-minted degree, independently wealthy due to his connections with some Boston Brahmin family and determined to carry out *pro bono* work of the most hopeless kind, defending clients no barrister in the history of the Inns of Court would have been crazy enough to defend. And for quite a long time – a *very* long time, actually – he had made a success of it. He had driven England's most eminent judges to their knees in court, over and over again, leaving them bleeding and weeping for mercy while his clients walked free. He defended peers and petty thieves, blackmailers and perjurers, murderers and – once – a Traitor of the Realm, a Foreign Office clerk who had been caught passing confidential ministerial briefing papers to a contact in the Russian Embassy. He lost that one – some said deliberately, because loyalty to one's country was of paramount importance to Mr Bauer. But he won enough cases to blaze a trail through the British legal system. There was even an old biopic of him, made during one of those blink-and-you'll-miss-them windows when Hollywood was interested in courtroom dramas.

That he was a decayed colossus these days was fairly well accepted. But he was still a colossus. And that was why, when he did his hail-fellow-well-mets around the Inns, people replied to him, because even if he didn't know who they were, they knew who *he* was, once upon a time.

Rudi thought he had been kidnapped and put in the hands of lunatics.

As if the thought had summoned him, Mr Self passed through the room, probably looking for Mr Bauer. Mr Self was a cadaverous young man with sharp suits and even sharper sideburns and one of the most insincere smiles Rudi had ever seen. He deployed it the moment he saw Rudi sitting in the armchair.

"Hey, Rudi," he said, all golly-gosh bonhomie. "Got everything you need? Good. That's the way, eh? Looking for Mr Bauer, actually. Great man passed through here recently?"

"He'd prefer it if we called him 'Red,' actually," Rudi said without stirring from the chair.

"I know," said Mr Self. "Silly old sod. Can't do that." His eyebrows went up. "See where he went, did you?"

Rudi pointed, and Mr Self nodded thanks and left the room.

The past seven weeks had been a genial and thoroughly civilised learning curve for Rudi. He had learned that the Temple was actually part of London's legal heart, named after the Knights Templar, who had once had a house there. It housed two of the Capital's Inns of Court, the professional legal associations so-named because once upon a time they really had been inns, places of residence for barristers. These days the Inns were mostly barristers' offices, known as 'Chambers,' of which Smithson's Chambers, a group of about a dozen barristers led by Mr Bauer, was one.

All of this information was doled out in a laconic drawl by Mr Self, who was notionally Mr Bauer's clerk but who seemed to have a busy and full life all of his own, to judge by the little time he actually spent in the Chambers.

Rudi was mostly left to his own devices, which gave him many diverting hours in which to think back over the events of the past couple of months.

Firstly, it was all bullshit. The whole thing. The jump from Palmse, as much as he remembered it, seemed relatively professional. Indeed, it had happened more or less the way he would have done it, using the cover of the riot. It reminded him of the abortive jump in the Zone. In fact it reminded him *too much* of the abortive jump in the Zone, and for that reason he found it suspicious. Gibbon seemed to have known about the recent problems with German counterintelligence, therefore Rudi had to assume Gibbon also knew something of his operational history, and if Rudi were going to jump another Coureur and wanted to gain their confidence, he might very well use a scam which had worked for the Coureur before, appeal to their professional vanity. It was too obvious.

So that was that. Then there was Gibbon's little speech at the Embassy. Rudi couldn't guess which spy novels these people had been reading, but it was clearly not the better ones. No intelligence officer with any self-worth at all would have told him all those things, even if they were lies. Life was not like fiction. In real life, aged British espiocrats did not just suddenly emerge from the woodwork and tie up plot points for everyone.

And he had no evidence that he had actually *been* at the British Embassy. He'd been unconscious when he arrived, and he had never left his suite until the final morning. The drive to the airport had been disorienting enough to confuse him. The only thing he was actually certain of was that he had been in Helsinki. Unless whoever was behind all this had gone to the trouble of mocking up an entire airport for his benefit.

Secondly, when he finally arrived at his destination,

no one showed the least professional interest in him. Not once in seven weeks had anyone tried to debrief, interrogate or even ask him an intelligent question. Mr Self appeared to be his liaison with whomever, but all Mr Self was interested in was whether Rudi found his lodgings to his satisfaction. No one seemed particularly bothered when Rudi went for walks in the Temple and sat for hours in the gardens, looking out at the Thames and the wall of buildings on the South Bank. No one seemed to care at all.

There was still no indication of why his hosts should think that Central would want him dead, nor indeed how they had come across this information. The subject was never mentioned. His Coureur life was never mentioned. It was as if he was a favourite nephew, come over from Europe to visit his Uncle Red for a couple of months. Mr Bauer was the very image of the amiable, absentminded and indulgent uncle. Mrs Gabriel was the very image – the very archetype – of an English housekeeper. So much so she might have clambered down off the pages of a Conan Doyle novel.

That, in the end, was what decided Rudi. These people all came from Central Casting, and in his experience there was no such thing as an archetype.

After about a month observing the comings and goings at Smithson's Chambers and the other chambers on King's Bench Walk, Rudi began to see a discrepancy. You had to look carefully for it, and even then you might still reasonably convince yourself that you were imagining things, but Rudi had a Coureur's eye for surveillance, and he knew. Smithson's Chambers was a shopfront. Fewer clients were passing through its doors, fewer barristers worked there, than at the other chambers. Taken with other observations, the logical inference was that Mr Bauer was a sockpuppet. If he extended that inference, Mr Self was a troll representing, however tenuously and deniably, the people who had set up the shopfront.

Quite what the shopfront was for was another matter entirely. Just a safe house for babysitting people of... unusual provenance? Or something more? It was impossible to say with any certainty.

It was all very odd. Struck by the lack of instructions to keep his head down, Rudi decided to push the envelope one day, informing Mrs Gabriel at breakfast that he intended to do some sightseeing.

"I'll see if we can find you some maps somewhere," she replied, standing by the table with a tray of cleared-away breakfast things in her hands. "Mr Bauer collects maps like other people collect stamps or train numbers."

Sitting there, looking at his half-eaten breakfast, Rudi almost weakened and told her not to bother, but instead he said, "Thank you, Mrs Gabriel, that would be very kind of you." The very act of speaking English in London seemed to bring out an exaggerated politeness.

For tourists, Londoners still produced paper maps, and Mrs Gabriel brought a sheaf of them to Rudi a minute or so later – surely not long enough for her to consult her superiors and get their consent, certainly not long enough for them to organise a tail. Although London was by some distance the most surveilled city on the face of the Earth, and anyone who knew what they were doing would have had a tail waiting outside, twenty-four hours a day, for just this eventuality.

The maps were tattered and frayed from constant refolding, and useless in any operational sense. The street maps showed tiny cartoon representations of notable buildings and big advertisements from corporate sponsors. The Underground map simply looked *unlikely*, a multicoloured circuit diagram inviting travellers to have a go if they felt lucky.

Outside, on King's Bench Walk, he fought down an urge to stand and look at every passing clerk and barrister and tourist. Movement was the important thing.

Up through the archway and onto Fleet Street, and he stood for a few moments trying to get a sense of the place.

This was not, he felt right away, a European city. You could visit Paris or Brussels or Madrid, even St Petersburg, and know you were in Europe. London was different. London was... he couldn't quite put his finger on it. Even standing there watching the everyday workers and tourists go by, he heard snatches of conversation in half a dozen languages. London was certainly cosmopolitan. More than that, it was an immigrant city. First, waves of conquerors. The Romans. The Normans. Then waves of migrants from... well, from *everywhere*. Jews, Huguenots, Somalis, Bangladeshis, West Indians... the list went on and on. Rudi had even found, in one of Mr Bauer's books, a mad story about a group of exiles from fallen Troy who were supposed to have sailed up the Thames at some point in the far and misty past to found the city.

His phone, of course, had never been returned to him, and a replacement had not been provided. And Jan's watch had vanished somewhere along the way, which bothered him obscurely. But he judged that he had been standing there long enough for a tail to be organised by any half-competent security service, so he turned right and set off down the slope of Fleet Street towards St Paul's.

Within the first fifteen or twenty minutes he decided that, if anyone was following him, they were fantastically good at their job. He prided himself on being fairly sharp at spotting a tail, and he couldn't see anyone even vaguely suspicious. He tried four or five fairly lazy evasion routines, on the grounds that it might lead the people behind Smithson's Chambers to underestimate him, which was never a bad thing, and when he'd completed the routines there was no sign of anyone picking him up again. Fine. Fuck it.

So he just forgot about surveillance and walked, map in hand, for hours. He did a long, leisurely tour of the City, the square mile that enclosed the oldest part of London and housed some of the city's financial institutions. He walked out of the City and into the West End and theatre-spotted. Did a tour of the awesomely primal kitsch being sold on stalls in Covent Garden. Stood in Trafalgar Square and stared at Nelson's Column.

The map he was using was about six years old, pre-dating the massive terrorist truck bomb which had blown a six-metre-deep crater in Whitehall and led to the gating off of the entire street. He stood at the gates for a little while, looking down towards Westminster, then he turned away and walked down to the Embankment, crossed the road, and sat for almost an hour on a bench watching the Thames and the various working and tourist boats passing by up and down the river. London, he had decided, was a mad place, very much of itself, entirely unique. He thought he liked it. He wondered if he would be able to make a run for the Estonian Embassy, and whether they would take him in if he got there.

Finally, hunger got the better of him and he walked back along the Embankment to Temple Station, through the side gate into the Temple, and back to Smithson's Chambers, where Mrs Gabriel had prepared some doorstep sandwiches – what was it with these people and colossal hunks of white bread? – of boiled chicken and a big pot of Yorkshire Tea.

AND SO IT went on, day after day, week after week. He dutifully ate Mrs Gabriel's meals, worked his way steadily through Mr Bauer's library, went for walks. He had no money with which to access public communications; he walked in and out of internet cafés hoping to catch an unattended terminal with some credit still on it, but without success. He thought he detected a boundary when he asked for some money to buy a pass and explore the Underground network and it was refused, but nobody made a big thing about it. It wasn't even a refusal, properly speaking. He raised the subject with Mr Self one morning, just in passing, and Mr Self said he'd see about it, and it was never mentioned again. He considered repeating the request, but he'd got the point.

Anyway, Central London turned out to be surprisingly small, once you got to know it. All the important stuff was within walking distance, so long as you enjoyed walking. From the eastern edge of the City to the western end of Oxford Street was an hour and a half's easy walk, and you could make it from Euston all the way over Waterloo Bridge to the great glass and steel blocks of the South Bank in less than that. It was hardly a stretch. And as everyone fell into a routine, Mrs Gabriel even made up sandwiches and gave him a small cardboard carton of fruit juice to take with him on his wanderings. This routine, this boredom, was of course exactly what he wanted. And equally, the inhabitants of Smithson's Chambers knew this and indulged him. And he exploited them. And they let him. And so on. He was honestly curious about how long they could keep playing this peculiar little game. He suspected it could be quite a long time. The strongest impression he had formed so far about whoever was holding him was that, as well as having an unusual way of doing things, they were people of quite considerable patience.

On the other hand, he couldn't stay here for ever. Apart from anything else, despite all the exercise he was getting, Mrs Gabriel's food was putting weight on him.

As if sensing this new strain of restlessness, Mr Self began to make more frequent appearances at the Chambers. Rudi noticed him more and more about the place, talking Mr Bauer through interminable legal documents in his office, chatting lasciviously – he was a man of some lasciviousness – to Mrs Gabriel – who giggled like a teenager and thumped him on the shoulder – and all the time making sure he knew where Rudi was. Rudi found this new behaviour quite interesting, but kept up with his daily walks all the same. For the first time in weeks, he started keeping an eye out for a tail again.

One day in the first week of March, Mr Self happened to pass through the living room, where Rudi was sitting on the window seat reading a tattered biography of Brad Pitt.

"Oh," Mr Self said as if the thought had just occurred to him, "ought to have told you. Having a party day after tomorrow."

"Oh?" said Rudi.

"Big legal wigs," said Mr Self. "Judges. High Court bods. Couple of MPs too, I think."

"Sounds like fun," Rudi said, imagining a room full of English Parliamentarians and legal types solemnly ploughing their way through a three-course meal prepared by Mrs Gabriel. He assumed bread pudding would feature somewhere, or the mysterious substance known as 'Spotted Dick.' Comfort food for men of Empire.

"Wouldn't mind staying out of the way, would you?" asked Mr Self in that English way which was really an order.

"If you give me some money I could go to the theatre," Rudi suggested. "*Fiddler On The Roof* at the Savoy."

Mr Self thought about it. "Not a bad idea. I'll see if I can get you tickets."

Rudi shook his head. "It's okay. I was only joking."

Mr Self tipped his head to one side and regarded Rudi as if examining the hitherto unsuspected parameters of *joking.* "Alternatively," he said finally, "you might want to turn in early. It's going to be dreadfully boring. Very dry."

"Perhaps I could cook for you," Rudi said.

Mr Self considered this for roughly a femtosecond before shuddering. "And upset our Mrs Gabriel? Oh no, no thank you." He laughed, but there was no humour at all in his body language. "No, I think we'd best leave the *catering* to her, old son."

Rudi shrugged. "As you wish." He went back to his book – Brad and Angelina were adopting another child – but Mr Self didn't move. Rudi looked up. Mr Self was watching him. "Was there something else?"

Mr Self kept watching him. Rudi could almost hear him composing a report. *"Subject offered to cook dinner."* He shook his head. "No," he said. "No." And he left.

Rudi laid down his book and looked out of the window at barristers and solicitors and clerks and tourists and local workers going past below. He thought he and Mr Self understood each other very well by now, and expressed that understanding with an atmosphere of polite mutual distrust. Still, a *party* was interesting. And whoever was behind Smithson's Chambers would know that it was interesting. He wondered if it was a test.

THE DAY OF the party dawned wet and windy. Mrs Gabriel's breakfast – fried eggs, fried bacon, grilled tomatoes and a rather horrible Cumberland sausage – was hurried and not even up to her own less than exacting standards. The little woman hurried about the Chambers with a vacuum cleaner and a tattered cardboard box full of cloths and cleaning solutions, making a valiant and rather noteworthy attempt to bring the cluttered and dusty rooms up to a standard which would not offend legal bigwigs and Ministers of Parliament, and everywhere she went she kept having to move Rudi out of the way because he was sitting or standing just where she needed to clean or dust or hoover next, and finally this enraged her so much that she spluttered that it would please her very much indeed if he would just *go out* and leave her in peace to get the place ready, please. To which Rudi protested that it was raining. Which broke Mrs Gabriel's reserve entirely and caused her to say, in a very loud voice, "I don't care if it's cats and dogs pelting down outside, sir. I need to get this place ready!"

Unwillingly, grudgingly, Rudi put on his shoes and shrugged into his jacket, and, collecting an umbrella from the elephant's foot stand by the door, went out into the wet windy world.

Which wouldn't have fooled anyone, but that wasn't the point. The point was simply to cause nuisance. So he unfurled the umbrella and put it up and set a brisk pace up to the archway and out onto Fleet Street, imagining a surveillance team being scrambled as he turned left and stepped out towards Trafalgar Square.

It was a dreadful day, but he felt lighter of heart than he had for some weeks. He had already been more than averagely fit, and his long rambles around London had tempered him, and he put on as much of a spurt of speed as the other umbrella-bearing pedestrians allowed as he reached Trafalgar

Square and worked his way around the various street crossings to Admiralty Arch.

The vehicle gate of the arch was closed off, but the pedestrian ones remained open, fitted with scanners manned by drenched policemen. He slipped through, past the ivy-choked bulk of the Citadel, and into St James's Park.

Once in the park, he slackened his pace, wandering seemingly aimlessly. He treated it like one of Fabio's training exercises, scoping out likely locations for dead drops but not being quite as careful as he normally would. He imagined the surveillance team – and he knew they were there, they could not *not* be there, his departure from the Chambers had been too obviously stage-managed for them to ignore it – arriving flustered, catching up, seeing him looking for somewhere to stash – or collect – something. What could he be planning? What could be going on in his mind? What could he possibly be going to do later? He imagined Mr Self snorting at all this but being unable to ignore it, *just in case*. Rudi was so obviously, transparently, *taking the piss*, but how to be certain? Could it be a double-bluff...?

So he spent a leisurely hour in the park, then he picked up his pace again and walked down to Victoria, and from there onto the Embankment for a nice calm stroll back to the Temple and Smithson's Chambers, where Mr Self was waiting with a barbed glance and a flustered and busy Mrs Gabriel was waiting with a *cold collation* – a couple of cold chicken drumsticks, some thickly-sliced ham, doorsteps of white bread, salted butter, and a pot of tea – and a request to please stay out of my way for the rest of the day, please, sir. Rudi smiled. *Been a bad boy. Sent to bed without my dinner.*

On the way up to his room, carrying a tray laden with Mrs Gabriel's efforts at supper, he saw Mr Self again, and the look that passed between them was so freighted with meaning and nuance that it could have won a Nobel Prize for Literature, or at least an Oscar. It was a look, finally, of acknowledgement, of recognition. They smiled at each other. Mr Self's smile was ghastly. It made Rudi's heart lift like a dirigible.

BUT IN THE end, the day had merely been mischief, a diversion from the creeping boredom that had been gathering around him. It had been fun, in an anarchic kind of way, but now it was over and he was contemplating his *cold collation*, he felt a bit low, almost post-coital. Annoying his hosts had been terribly gratifying at the time, but it hadn't actually achieved anything.

He took up Brad Pitt again, and read while the antique streetlamps outside came on and the noises of Mrs Gabriel clattering about trying to clean up downstairs were gradually replaced by an expectant silence and a scent of roasting meat and boiling vegetables mushrooming up through the Chambers, and then, quite slowly, the increasing hubbub of a dinner party getting into gear in the rooms beneath his feet.

Rudi lay on his bed, reading by the light of the little green-tasselled bedside lamp, listening to the murmur of conversation on the floor below, judging the arrival of each course by lulls in the noise. It sounded as if quite a few bigwigs and MPs and assorted top hats had responded to Mr Bauer's invitation.

At some point between the main course and dessert, Rudi got up from the bed and went over to the door of his room. He opened the door quietly and stepped out onto the landing.

Smithson's Chambers, like the other Chambers on King's Bench Walk, occupied a building on six floors. The ground floor was where the main business of the Chambers was conducted – interviews with clients, administration and so on. The first, second and third floors were accommodation. Bedrooms, dining rooms, sitting rooms, the kitchen. The sixth floor was a chaotic space under the eaves of the roof, piled haphazardly with old furniture and dusty rolls of carpet and cardboard boxes of ancient ribbon-tied legal files.

The floor below that was a tiny maze of quiet corridors lined with closed and locked doors. Rudi had scoped it out, by degrees, in his first couple of weeks here. There were no obvious surveillance devices in the corridors, and none of the less obvious ones, and an open saunter around the fifth floor one evening had prompted no reaction from any of the other occupants of the Chambers. Which was not in and of itself any proof, of course.

Rudi walked calmly around the fifth floor, examining the locked doors. There was dust on some of them, in spite of Mrs Gabriel's best efforts, but two of them were clean and shiny, their big brass escutcheons scratched by generations of badly-aimed keys. He unlocked one with a biro and the hook broken off a coat hanger and turned the handle slowly. Nothing obvious on the frame. No wires. No contact spots, shiny or matt. He pushed the door open, stepped inside, and closed the door behind him, all in one movement.

Light came in through the windows from the lamps five floors below, picking out a room lined floor to ceiling with filing cabinets. There was a desk and a chair. A kickstool sat in a corner, for those hard-to-reach top drawers. Tiny illuminated numbers glowed on the front of all the cabinets, where combination lock keypads guarded the secrets within. No point bothering. Rudi opened the door, backed out into the corridor, locked the door again, moved on to the next one.

Inside, another desk and chair, and on the desk a computer monitor running a screensaver of two kittens playing with the cardboard insert of a roll of kitchen paper. Rudi stood with his back to the door for quite a long time, watching the kittens playing.

It occurred to him that what seemed, on the surface, to be many weeks of sitting around doing nothing had actually been a complex conversation between himself and Mr Self. And through Mr Self with the people who actually owned and ran Smithson's Chambers. He wondered how long this computer monitor had been sitting here, running its cute screensaver, waiting for him to break into the room. As a piece of entrapment, it was so transparently obvious that there seemed no harm at all in going over to the desk, sitting down, and waving the kittens away.

The computer's menu was sparse to the point of comedy. Just the operating system and three spreadsheet files. The first sheet was a list of names and long numbers. Banks and account access codes. The second sheet was filled with random-looking five-figure groups, obviously encrypted. The third sheet was a mixture of encrypted groups and sets of figures in clear-text. A list of payments?

Rudi looked at the screen. Smithson's Chambers was a black bank, a deniable source of funds for covert operations. Want to infiltrate a trade union and need some cash to set up the op? Smithson's Chambers was your one-stop shop. Need to finesse the demise (political, religious or physical) of a troublesome imam? Smithson's Chambers would dole out the money you'd need.

None of this was actually world-shaking. Intelligence – the *real* world of intelligence, not the stuff politicians were told about – ran on black money, reptile funds, cash that sloshed back and forth across continents in constant motion in case anyone happened upon it. The truly intriguing aspect of all of this was that he had been allowed to discover this fact, and discover it without being bundled off to his room. Here he was, sitting here quite comfortably, with the bank codes to access fourteen and a half million Swiss francs – as always Europe's most copper-bottomed currency – literally beneath his fingertips. It was not, he found himself admitting sadly, the actions of a national intelligence service.

On the other hand, he thought, it might, just *might*, be the actions of a national intelligence service faced with a situation so bizarre and *outré* that only a bizarre and *outré* response would suffice.

He sat there looking at the pages of numbers for a long time. Much longer than he should have done, strictly speaking. It was such an obvious *offer* that it was almost comical, but it opened up an abyss of possibility. He wasn't caught in an agony of indecision, so much as trying to think through the ramifications.

Finally he dug around in his pockets until he found a leaflet which had been thrust into his hand by a Hare Krishna in Leicester Square the previous day. He sat for another moment or two, Biro in one hand and leaflet in the other, then he started to copy out the list of bank codes.

THE NEXT COUPLE of days passed rather pleasantly. Rudi thought he detected a certain *relaxation* in the Chambers. Mr Self was less in evidence. Mrs Gabriel even smiled at him on several occasions. He sensed that they knew what he had done, and that they knew that he knew that they knew. Quite which direction the game had now taken, he couldn't tell, but it was as if he had entered into a form of unspoken contract with these people and the people who controlled them, and it pleased them.

He continued with his walks, the folded Krishna leaflet tucked inside his sock. Not wasting time but trying to gain momentum.

One brisk spring midmorning he left the Chambers, not a thought in his head, and walked down the Strand and up into Covent Garden.

The area was, as ever, crowded with tourists and workers on their lunch break. Rudi wandered among them, hands in pockets, casually scoping the place out, rather enjoying the hustle and bustle of being out among ordinary people.

Crossing the Piazza, just outside the Royal Opera House, he found himself behind two young women, office workers from their clothes, walking side by side deep in conversation. One of the women was carrying a leather shoulder bag, unwisely left unzipped, and from the opening protruded what looked very much like the top half of a purse.

Rudi lengthened his stride slightly, and as he passed the woman he watched his right hand reach out and take the purse from her bag. He thought of Mr Bauer and Mrs Gabriel and Mr Self and their invisible masters and he peeled away from the two young women as naturally as anything and wandered unhurriedly off at a tangent.

He was at Cambridge Circus before he decided to snatch a look at the purse in his hand, and the moment he did so he realised his mistake. The purse was covered with thousands of tiny stiff plastic hairs, like the hard component of velcro, and the moment Rudi had it in his hand the little hairs had tasted his DNA, decided they didn't recognise him, and the purse had armed itself.

As security measures went, it was from the cheap end, something you'd pick up on a market stall. It was meant to deter only the opportunist thief – you could circumvent it easily enough just by wearing gloves. But Rudi hadn't thought to wear gloves, and if he tried to look in the purse now it would detonate a dye capsule and he'd be left wandering around Central London with a fluorescent green face. Without breaking stride he palmed the purse into a rubbish bin and moved on.

There was no way to stop now. He was in the most surveilled city in the most surveilled nation in Europe, and undoubtedly his theft of the purse had been recorded somewhere.

He did have some small advantage, though. He knew the truth about surveillance. Ever since the dawn of GWOT the nations of the West – apart from the United States, where civil libertarians tended to carry rifles and use them on closed-circuit cameras as an expression of their freedoms – had put their faith in creating a paranoid state, one where every move of every citizen was recorded and logged and filmed and fuck you, if you've got nothing to hide you've got nothing to worry about.

Whether this had had any great influence in the course of GWOT was a moot point, but there was one thing not generally appreciated about the paranoid state. It was *incredibly* labour-intensive.

There were simply not enough people to monitor all the cameras. Every shop had one, every bus and train and theatre and public convenience, every street and road and alleyway. Computers with facial recognition and gait recognition and body language recognition could do some of the job, but they were relatively simple to fool, expensive, and times had been hard for decades. It was cheaper to get people to watch the screens. But no nation on Earth had a security service large enough, a police force big enough, to keep an eye on all those live feeds. So it was contracted out.

To private security firms all trying to undercut each other. The big stores had their own security men, but they were only interested in people going in and out of the store, not someone just passing by. So instead of a single all-seeing eye London's seemingly-impregnable surveillance map was actually a patchwork of little territories and jurisdictions, and while they all had, by law, to make their footage available to the forces of law and order, many of the control rooms were actually manned by bored, underpaid, undertrained and badly-motivated immigrants.

The woman whose purse he had stolen – and who was now at least half a mile away – would discover it was missing soon, if she hadn't already. After that... well, it was anyone's guess. She'd either shrug it off as something you had to put up with when you lived in London – her cards would be firewalled and she probably didn't carry much, if any, cash – or she'd contact the police. Around here that meant – if she didn't walk up to a patrolling bobby and report the theft on the street – visiting West End Central at Charing Cross. Someone would have to take a statement, the statement would have to be processed, investigating officers would have to be assigned. Rudi thought that, if anyone at West End Central took the theft of a purse even remotely seriously – and he had to assume for argument's sake that they did – he had an hour from stealing the purse to someone checking the cameras in the area where the theft had taken place. After that, a grab of his face would be posted on bulletin boards and its parameters circulated, and it was too much of a risk to assume that the people who had stolen him from Palmse weren't monitoring such things.

So. An hour. Actually, a little over forty-five minutes now. Rudi wandered unhurriedly along with the crowds and up onto Oxford Street, panicking inside.

With thirty minutes to go, Rudi ducked into a pub. It was dark inside, the only illumination coming from gaming tables and the impressive bar. It was also packed to the rafters with lunchtime drinkers. It obviously didn't have enough staff to adequately keep up with clearing the tables, and he snagged an abandoned half-glass of beer as camouflage and sidled through the crowds with it in his hand.

It took him almost ten minutes to do a complete circuit of the pub. There was a little group of young business types sitting at a table near the back, mildly drunk and mildly rowdy, jackets hung on the backs of their chairs, ties loosened, sleeves rolled up. Rudi paused at the table next to them long enough to dip a hand into a jacket pocket and come up with a phone, then he moved on through the crowd until he was near the door.

This was the tricky part; the phone was a new Nokia and its security measures included a little tag the owner wore on their clothing. If the phone went more than twenty metres from the tag, it would cook the bubble-memory of its SIM down to slag, rendering the handset useless. Rudi called up the phone's browser, dug the leaflet out of his sock as discreetly as possible, and started to type strings of numbers.

Five minutes later he left the phone under a chair and was out of the pub and moving again, having really gone past the point of no return. One of the strings of numbers had connected him to a secure anonymiser. Another had put him through to a bank in the Cayman Islands. Another had called up a certain account where, an itchy paranoia beginning to grow on him in recent months, he had started to bank his savings. Another string had set up a new account at the bank. And several more strings had transferred the entire contents of the black bank at Smithson's Chambers into the new account. Alarm bells would be ringing in King's Bench Walk and elsewhere.

Just before leaving the pub he had Googled the nearest shop selling phones. It turned out to be a newsagent's half a dozen doors along the street. He went in, gave the shopkeeper the code for the purchase he had made with the stolen phone in the pub, and the shopkeeper gave him a pack of ten disposable phones, each one prepaid with five hundred pounds of credit.

He used the first phone in a cheap clothing store next door to the newsagent's. Jeans, T-shirt, a new pair of trainers, a zip-up fleece, a nondescript dark blue canvas jacket. He dithered for a few moments over buying a hat, already deep into a game of doublethink with the people who would be looking for him. One of Fabio's first rules for evading surveillance was to change your appearance, but the thing most people do is buy a hat to hide their face. Knowing this, the watchers keep a special lookout for people wearing hats. The idea right now was to look just different *enough* to get out of the shop, not so different that he attracted attention. On the other hand, the people who would be looking for him knew he was trained in this kind of thing, therefore a hat would be something they wouldn't expect. On the *other* hand, they would know this and be on the lookout for someone coming out of the shop in a hat... Ah, fuck it. No hat. He added some underwear and socks, bought a canvas shoulder-bag, waved the phone at the till to pay for his purchases, and used the shop's changing room to change into his new clothes.

Back on Oxford Street, he walked for a few hundred yards and turned up a side-street, then down another one, then up another. On the corner of the next street was a camping supplies shop. He went in, bought a stout pair of hiking shoes, another fleece, and a heavy-duty waterproof jacket. He changed into the fleece and the shoes and the jacket in the shop, stuffed his previous purchases into the shoulder bag, and was out on the street again ten minutes later.

No cabs – too easily stopped and the doors had central locking. Ditto for buses.

And then something occurred to him, and he stopped there in the street, stock-still, while he thought about it. He thought about it for quite a while. So long that he turned and looked into the window of the nearest shop so he wouldn't attract attention. The shop wasn't actually a shop – it was the frontage of a little graphic design business – and he found himself engaged in a staring contest with the firm's rather puzzled secretary. It crossed a distant corner of his mind to stand there and see how long it took the secretary to become alarmed by the strange man staring through her window and call the police.

He looked around the street. No one looked especially suspicious. No more so than your average Londoner, anyway. No tells or little giveaways that someone might be less innocent than they were trying to appear. No signs that seemingly unrelated pedestrians might actually be working as a team. He felt a weight slowly lift off his shoulders. In truth, the thought of what had just occurred to him actually made him feel a little giddy. It was the final, unrecoverable step into the unknown, an act of faith in his own reasoning.

He took a deep breath and stepped forward to the edge of the pavement.

He hailed a cab, and was gone.

PART TWO

RUNNERS
IN THE WOODS

LEGEND

1.

THE ALBANIANS DOWNSTAIRS must have been out on one of their periodic shoplifting expeditions, because the bowel-rearranging concussions of one of the new Sri Lankan crush bands were shaking the furniture when the Coureur got back to the flat.

The rest of the block's inhabitants called the Albanians 'gypsies,' but the Coureur, who had spent some time among Europe's Roma population, knew better. The people downstairs were the heirs of Enver Hoxha, heirs of catastrophically-failed pyramid-investment schemes. Their parents and grandparents had crossed the Adriatic on fishing boats loaded down with indigent cargo until waves slopped over the gunwales, had evaded Italian coastguard cutters, had landed at dead of night wearing their cheap leather jackets and bootleg Levis and Reeboks and scattered into the countryside in search of a better life.

They were everywhere now, Albanian only insofar as their Polish or English or German was seasoned with a few Albanian words and phrases, their dreams with images of a lost homeland.

They were not, as far as the Coureur could ascertain, Gypsies.

He locked the door behind him and stood looking down the hallway. Coats and jackets dangled haphazardly from pegs on one wall. Halfway along, a pile of boots and training shoes was gently collapsing across the parquet. There was a smell of overcooked cabbage, burned chickpeas and cheap aerosol air-freshener. At the far end of the hall, the toilet door was wide open. The Coureur wrinkled his nose.

A moment's silence. Then a mighty concussion heralded the beginning of a new track downstairs. A tattered basketball boot rolled off the pile of footwear.

The Coureur walked down the hall and into the kitchen. Pots and pans unsteadily piled in the sink. Several meals' worth of crusted plates on the table. Cupboard doors left open. Empty milk cartons on the work-surfaces. A couple of dirty forks and a steak-knife on the lino beside the fridge. The Coureur considered looking in the fridge, but decided against it.

In the living room, all the cushions had been removed from the sofa and armchairs and roughly arranged in a pile in the middle of the room, beside a miniature Stonehenge of Eisbrau bottles, the various entertainment deck handsets lined up on the floor close to hand.

The Coureur extracted a cushion from the pile, dumped it on a chair, and flopped down, rubbing his eyes. Coming home was always the same. Lewis, his flatmate, seemed to lack the necessary genes for tidiness. The Coureur would leave for a Situation and no matter how serious or far away or downright complicated it was, when he got back exhausted, or bored, or wound-up (or, once, with a newly-stitched wound in his leg) the flat always looked as if it had been sub-let to a maniac.

He got up and went to the window, looked down into the narrow street, then across at the balconies and curtained windows of the building opposite, then at the tilted topography of roofs and terraces and air-conditioning hoods and downlink dishes. Craning his neck slightly, he could see the Underground tracks running in their cutting parallel to Farringdon Road. A Metropolitan Line train, identifiable from this distance because the Metropolitan Company still hadn't modernised its rolling stock, rattled and rolled along the cutting, from tunnel to tunnel, and was gone. A colossal amorphous murmuration of starlings surged and darted across the darkening topaz sky.

The front door opened, banged shut. "That you, Seth?" called Lewis.

The Coureur went to the living room doorway. Lewis was taking off his jacket, a great pile of yellow and white Europa Foods carrier bags slowly collapsing around his feet and allowing tins of beans and loose yams and okra to topple onto the floor.

It was a sure sign that there was nothing to eat in the entire flat; Lewis refused to enter a supermarket unless the only alternative was starvation, and he would not phone out for meals because he believed They kept lists.

"Good trip?" he asked, tossing his jacket in the general direction of the coathooks.

"Not bad."

"Great." Lewis bent down and started to lace his fingers through the tangle of shopping-bag handles. "I didn't manage to do much cleaning up."

"I noticed," said Seth.

Lewis straightened up, lifting the carriers off the floor. The bottom split out of one and about a hundred apples rolled everywhere.

"Oops," said Lewis.

LEWIS'S BELIEF-SYSTEM was a complex territory of conspiracy theories. He trusted neither the government nor the police. He refused to believe anything he saw on the news networks. One boozy night, he told Seth that at least ten percent of the passengers travelling on scheduled British Airways flights never reached their destinations.

"Documented fact," he said, nodding sagely and levering the cap off another Budvar.

"So where do they go?" asked Seth, only slightly less drunk.

Lewis leaned forward and his voice dropped to a conspiratorial whisper. "Madagascar. Colossal internment camp."

Seth thought about it. "Why?"

Lewis sat up. "I don't know," he said. He waved his bottle of beer at Seth. "But you'd better watch yourself the next time you get on a BA flight, old son. Mark my words."

Unpacking after one of Lewis's infrequent shopping expeditions was an adventure. Lewis had a theory that there was something secretly crafty about bar-codes, that They were tracking each bar-coded item and compiling vast lists for a purpose made even more sinister and terrifying by being entirely unknown.

So trips to the supermarket inevitably ended with bags and packets piled on the kitchen table, Lewis bent over them with the scissors, cutting off bar-codes, to be burned later. When Seth first saw him doing this, he had inquired whether his flatmate needed regular medication, but it had turned out that Lewis was a relative rarity: a completely sane man whose world-view was almost entirely irrational. Sometimes, thinking about it, Seth wondered if Lewis might not actually be right. And then he usually wondered what Lewis would think if he knew what his flatmate really did for a living.

IN HIS ABSENCE, their landlord, an immensely aged Malaysian whom Lewis had dubbed, for no good reason, The Grasping Bastard, had visited the flat and entrusted to Lewis the twice-yearly message of happiness and joy that was their rent increase. This in itself was not a problem. Seth was reasonably well-off, and Lewis made a truly colossal amount of money developing advertising campaigns for products from which he would one day be cutting bar-codes. However, the Grasping Bastard had been unable to predict with any great certainty when a replacement for their recently-deceased washing machine would be forthcoming.

Which meant that, at around half past nine that evening, Seth was sitting on a padded bench in the neon-lit tropical heat of the local laundrette, watching his underwear doing flickflacks in the drier. Ah, the endless romance of the Coureur's life...

He'd had a busy couple of months, four or five Situations on the run that had involved him flying off to Warsaw, Bruges, Barcelona and Nicosia, picking up sealed pouches, and flying with them to Berlin, Chicago, Dublin and Copenhagen. The last Situation had subsequently involved a train, bus and taxi ride to Narvik, a clandestine pass in a department store, and a dustoff through Helsinki. The first three Situations had been straight corporate data-transfer, routine stuff. The Narvik thing smacked of industrial espionage. Or maybe even real espionage; Central usually frowned on real espionage, preferring to leave it to nations, but in practice, at street level, it was impossible to know who you were taking a delivery from, impossible to know what was in the pouch. You made the jump, took the money, told yourself you were keeping alive the spirit of Schengen, and forgot about it.

The door opened, billowing cool air through the steamy laundrette. Seth looked up from his book. A middle-aged woman wearing biker boots, US Army desert camo trousers and a chunky black sweater was standing in the doorway, a big blue plastic carrier bag dangling from each hand. As the door closed behind her, she went over and started to walk down the line of washers, looking for a machine that wasn't being used. Seth went back to his book.

Central had its roots in the hundreds of little courier firms which had been operating in Europe before the turn of the century, moving various items of merchandise – printed material too valuable to be entrusted to the postal system, disc-encoded data too important or secret to be entrusted to the net, and so on. If Central had had a single stated objective, it would have been the eventual abolition of borders and free movement for all, and if Central had been a moderately-sized multinational, Seth would have been one of the boys in the post-room.

This suited him, more or less. Central's bread-and-butter business went on constantly, offered boundless opportunities for travel, and paid pretty well. There were strata above him in which the Packages moved by Central were people, the circumstances of their jumpoffs far more fraught and exciting, but for Seth those sorts of Situations seemed too much like hard work.

"This fucking thing doesn't work."

Seth looked up. The woman was standing by the detergent dispenser, a plastic cup in one hand and her washing-bags on the floor by her feet.

"This fucking thing doesn't work," she said again, pointing at the dispenser.

"You've got to buy a card," said Seth, nodding at the box by the dispenser. "Ten pounds."

The woman stood looking at him for a few moments as if she was thinking very hard about what he had told her. "I only want some fucking soap powder," she said finally.

"The card works the machines as well."

She narrowed her eyes at that, and Seth sighed. The last time this had happened to him, it had been aboard the bus to Narvik, when a grossly overweight Latvian had squeezed himself into the seat beside him and proceeded to try and sell him a small cardboard box which he claimed contained the mummified penis of Joseph Stalin. He didn't know why these things happened. Maybe he had the sort of bone structure which proclaimed to lunatics *here I am, talk to me*.

"Look," he said, getting up and going over to the card dispenser. "Why don't I buy you a card, eh?"

"Don't you fucking patronise me, sunshine," said the woman. "I've got washing in these bags older than you. I can buy my own fucking cards."

Seth spread his hands and stepped away from the dispenser, not quite being able to resist a half-bow at the last moment. The woman glared at him and put a £10 coin in the slot.

Seth went back to his seat and his pirouetting smalls, but it was impossible to ignore the woman as she wrestled the contents of the plastic cup of detergent into one of the empty machines – through the door, mind, not into the hopper on top – and hurled her washing in after it. Then she came back and sat beside Seth, heaved a huge sigh of relief, took an impressively abused-looking old paperback from one of the thigh pockets of her combat trousers, a pair of spectacles from the other pocket, and started to read. Seth felt his heart sink.

After they had been sitting side by side in silence for about ten minutes, Seth said, "I only just got back, you know."

The woman looked up from her book. "Beg pardon, lovely?"

"I only just got home," he said. "I'm shattered. I don't want to go back out just yet."

She looked at him and raised an eyebrow.

"The glasses," he said. "They're antiques."

"I could have inherited the frames from my granny," she said.

Seth tipped his head to one side.

She sighed. "Okay." She took the spectacles off and looked at them, a little abashed. "There's always something, isn't there? I thought this was bloody good camo, too." She beamed at him. "Well spotted, mind."

He shrugged. *I am a Coureur, witness my mad spectacle-identifying skillz.* "What have you got for me?"

"Oh, *I* dunno," she said, recovering her cheerfulness. "I just deliver 'em. Nobody tells me anything. Here." She passed him the book. "Have a read of that."

He took the book. *Atlas Shrugged*, the back cover and half the front torn off. It appeared to have spent quite a long time in a sauna as well; its pages had swollen up until it was almost twice its original thickness, which had already been considerable. "I've heard of it."

"It's shit," the stringer said, standing up. "Woman was barking mad." She turned to leave.

"What about your clothes?" Seth asked.

She turned back to him. "What?"

He nodded at the clothes in the washing machine.

"Oh, they're not mine," she said happily. "They're just props. Fuck 'em. 'Bye."

THE FLAT WAS on the top floor of a converted warehouse building on the edge of the confusing maze of little streets between Farringdon Road and the Grey's Inn Road, just south of Clerkenwell Road. Back in the '90s the whole area had experienced a spasm of conversion, but by the 2000s nobody could afford the rents so the converted blocks had been sold off, one by one, to housing associations. Artists and students and musicians moved into flats once occupied by young upwardly-mobile couples. Refugees and asylum-seekers from the newer states and polities of Europe and Africa arrived. Meetings of the Residents Association began to resemble sessions of the UN Security Council during an interpreters' strike.

Seth had come here six years ago and fallen in love with the area at first sight. He'd been a Coureur for a couple of years by then, and his life consisted of drifting across the Continent moving Packages from place to place, living in hotels and Travelodges which were all somehow identical to each other. It was a busy couple of years, but at some point he found himself sitting in an hotel room and looking about him and wondering where precisely he was. Padania? Ulster? Somewhere in the Basque country?

He decided it was a bad sign, and logged-off for a couple of months to find himself a solid base, somewhere to call his own. He came back to London, visited his father and stepmother in Hampstead, spent some time with his sister and her family in Cornwall. He saw an ad in the online edition of *Loot*, and two days later he was introducing himself to Lewis.

If Lewis had been better-off there would have been no way he would have consented to share the flat, but in spite of being rather well-paid for what he did, he was in danger of losing his lease if he didn't find someone to help him with the rent. Seth later found himself feeling a glow of professional pride at the fact that, of all the applicants for the flatshare, Lewis had felt him to be the least suspect.

Trying to look at himself objectively, Seth supposed that he represented the perfect flatmate. Neat, tidy, unobtrusive, forgiving. Away for extended periods on business. Willing to cook meals and wash up afterwards without complaint. But most important of all, pretty well-off. In this way, he convinced Lewis that he was not an Agent Of Them. Seth thought this was quite amusing, considering he really did work for what amounted to a global conspiracy.

Lewis was out again when Seth got back with his washing. Seth had never found out what his flatmate did on his evenings out. Certainly pubs featured somewhere, but which ones, and with whom, he didn't know. Sometimes he pictured upstairs rooms in dingy Fitzrovia taverns, a circle of conspiracy theorists perched anxiously on chairs arranged around the walls, pints of real ale clutched in their fists as they discussed in hushed voices the latest convoluted doings of Them. Them, of course, being a chimera of Science, the Military, the Government and anything to do with America. Lewis did have a girlfriend, a wispy presence named Angela who did makeup for advertising shoots and who sometimes drifted through the flat, naked but for a huge butterfly barrette in her hair, in search of toast and tea to take back to Lewis's bedroom. Seth had never had a meaningful conversation of any kind with her beyond answering the question, "Where's the marmalade?"

This all rather suited him. Apart from that one time with the leg wound, he had never brought his work home with him; there had never been any need to. Home was where he went when he wasn't being a Coureur, a solid hub about which to rotate a peripatetic lifestyle. He liked it here. He liked Lewis, and he even rather liked Angela, to the extent that she existed in his life at all. For all that he could never predict, from one week to the next, where work would take him, it was a settled life and he had it organised the way he liked it.

For example, all his jobs were delivered to an anonymised email account which deleted and rewrote itself twenty-eight times every day on an all-but-forgotten secure server in a basement at the Ministry of Defence. He was used to this, used to the familiar little ping on his phone as some new Situation was delivered.

He could count on the fingers of one hand the number of times a stringer had hand-delivered instructions to him.

It was also some years – not since his entry-level days as a stringer himself, in fact – since he had been asked to create a legend for someone.

He sat on the sofa and looked at the slip of paper he had extracted from between the pages of the brick-sized copy of *Atlas Shrugged*. Male. Caucasian. Light brown hair, hazel eyes. Height so and so, weight such and such. Name: Roger Curtis. And that was it. He was, in effect, being asked to build Mr Curtis from the pavement up.

Which, while undeniably interesting in an academic sort of way, was a bit pedestrian and quite a distance outside his usual briefs these days. On the other hand, it was stuff he could do without having to leave London. And the note included a URL and a set of code strings which gave him access to an operational account and a line of credit running to a little over a million euros.

That last gave him some pause. Operational funding was perfectly normal – one had to buy tickets, book hotels, sometimes hand out bribes – but the sum here was beyond his experience and it left him a little flatfooted. It was up to him who Mr Curtis was, but who wanted to be Mr Curtis for this fantastical amount of money?

The note also included a link to an online dropbox which contained a single notepad file with the words 'I used to date the Rokeby Venus.' A recognition string by which the recipient of the legend – or at least a go-between come to collect it – would make themselves known to him. This at least was perfectly standard. Everything about the job was perfectly standard. Except the money. The money stood out from the perfect standardisation like a sore thumb, and he had to ponder why whoever was wrangling this job had allowed that to slip by. A message? *This is important. Don't screw up?* Or just simple honest carelessness?

Impossible to know. A job was a job. A quick check of his account confirmed that he had already been paid for it, and paid well.

Fair enough. Seth took out his phone and created a couple of new contacts, then disguised the bank URL and code strings as phone numbers and web addresses. He memorised Mr Curtis's physical attributes. Then he ate the slip of paper and opened the copy of *Atlas Shrugged* at the first page.

After a dozen pages, he closed the book, got up, and dumped it in the kitchen bin. The stringer at the laundrette was right; it was terrible.

MR CURTIS WAS a Scot. That was the first thing he decided. Scottish independence had not been the simple, pain-free process envisaged by generations of SNP politicians, and many municipal buildings – including the record offices of a number of towns – had been torched in the Separation Riots and their documents and servers destroyed. There was an enormous black hole in Scotland's public data, and it was a simple matter to insert a nonexistent person into it. It was also a bit of a cliché, but just because something is a cliché doesn't make it untrue. Hundreds of thousands of real people had had all their personal data destroyed during the Riots too. He checked through newspaper files of the Separation, noted which record offices had been destroyed, which schools.

He took a train to Edinburgh – sat for an hour at the border post outside Berwick while Scottish

customs officers searched the carriages for drugs
and other contraband – and wandered the city for
a couple of days, getting a feel for the place. He
thought Scotland was having a bit of a rough time
these days. The tail-end of North Sea Oil which the
new state had inherited had become uneconomic to
extract some years before, tourism hadn't taken up
the slack to the degree everyone had been banking
on, and the big tech firms had fled Silicon Glen for
more stable parts of Europe. The city, even its historic
heart, was looking shabby and the locals looked grey
and thin and unhappy. A debate had already begun at
Westminster over whether to allow Scotland to rejoin
England; the consensus seemed to be a resounding
no at the moment. There were still English MPs with
long enough memories to want to punish the Scots
for leaving the United Kingdom in the first place.

Back in London, he did the hacking himself.
He wardrove around the City and the West
End, latching on to corporate hotspots whose
encryption hadn't been kept up to date, sat in
nearby libraries and coffee shops and calmly
inserted Roger Curtis's birth and education
information into the databases in Edinburgh. He
backstopped the data with fragmentary bits about
Mr Curtis's parents – both deceased now, sadly
– supposedly retrieved from riot-damaged servers
and seared filing cabinets. In hacking terms, it was
shooting fish in a barrel. Desperate for funds, the
Edinburgh government had offered the country
as a private data haven, but hadn't bothered
to upgrade its public data security for almost
a decade. He breezed through the databases,

tweaking and adjusting, and it was as if he had never been there.

University records were almost as easy. The United States was littered with the corpses of little failed colleges, particularly in the Midwest. Roger Curtis went to one of these, not far from Milwaukee. Of his classmates and tutors, a statistically-convincing number were now dead. Everyone else was scattered as far from Europe as possible, their trails becoming blurred and unreadable.

He left Mr Curtis's work history vague. A year as an itinerant citizen journalist in South America. Some volunteer work with charities in Guatemala and Chile. Then back to Britain and a succession of small temporary jobs in London with firms which had now gone bust and whose details were sparse to the point of transparency. Most recently, a flat in Balham. Seth went south of the river and rented the flat himself in Mr Curtis's name, then set about the dull minutiae of accumulating utility bills, making a slight nuisance of himself with the letting agents, getting a parking ticket in Tooting, and so on and so forth. He left as much room as possible for customisation by whoever came along later to drive Mr Curtis.

The whole thing took him about three weeks, and at the end of it he still had most of the operational funds left, which he felt professionally rather proud of. He gave the data one last tweak, left one last complaint about the drains with the letting agents, left a message in a Coureur dropbox that the legend was ready for handover, and headed to Padstow to spend the weekend with his sister.

*   *   *

AT AROUND EIGHT o'clock on Sunday night a previously-unknown wing of an almost-overlooked homegrown terrorist organisation blew up a signal junction box just outside Swindon.

The box, about the size of a shoebox, was a switch for about seventy optical cables carrying data from points and signals between London and Land's End. The explosion, achieved by drilling a hole into the switch's casing and then pouring in gunpowder obtained by opening up fireworks, was so discreet that it was only discovered the following morning when engineers located the cable break and went to repair it. At roughly the same time, a very vague and barely-literate press release claiming responsibility for the outrage began to make the rounds. Hardly anyone had ever heard of the culprits before, and no one ever heard of them again.

The signal break didn't stop trains altogether, but it caused delays for an hour or so until a workaround was sorted out, and that caused a knock-on effect which meant that the six forty-five from Padstow, due to arrive in Paddington at ten o'clock, did not actually get into Paddington until almost midnight. Seth, lugging his weekend bag down the platform with the rest of the disgruntled passengers, avoided the enormous scrum at the taxi rank, left the station altogether, and walked down to the big hotels near the bottom of the Edgware Road, where there were always taxis aplenty. He waved one cab down as it made to pull into the rank beside the Marriott, slung his bag inside, and settled back against the seat with his eyes closed.

* * *

IT WAS VERY nearly one in the morning when Seth paid off the taxi outside his building in Farringdon and dragged his bag tiredly up the stairs. Kids from the local council estate had managed to bypass the street door's lock again and they'd smashed all the lightbulbs on Seth's landing. He could feel the glass crunch under his feet as he walked along by the dim light of his phone's screen, and he made a note to tear a strip off the building's security in the morning.

Outside his door, there also seemed to be something sticky mixed up with the glass. Seth grumbled to himself and unlocked the front door and stepped inside and immediately fell over something lying on the floor in the hallway.

Swearing at the top of his voice now, Seth got up and tried the hall light switch, but it didn't seem to work so he took his phone out again and turned on its screen and by the light from that he saw Lewis lying on his back on the floor, his eyes open, a little black hole in his forehead and his face distorted as if it had been badly inflated. Under his head and shoulders was a big puddle of a dark liquid, which had run out under the door and onto the landing.

Seth's mind refused to process any of this.

Nor would it process the hunched figure lying half in and half out of Lewis's bedroom doorway, the barrette which had once been in its hair now tumbled against the skirting just outside the kitchen.

He heard glass crunch, behind him.

He turned and saw a dark figure detach itself from the shadows of the doorway opposite. By the light from his phone he saw that it was wearing tight-fitting dark clothing and carrying what appeared to be a pistol with a very long barrel. The figure raised the pistol and gestured with it and Seth raised his hands above his head. Another gesture, and Seth took a step back down the hallway as the gunman reached the doorway and raised the gun and pointed it at his head.

There was a soft coughing noise, and the top third of the dark figure's head fountained off in a pattering spray of droplets and bits of bone and tissue. For a fraction of a second, the body remained upright, then its knees unlocked and it crumpled to the floor.

Seth stayed where he was, hands above his head, face spattered with gore.

After a few moments, another figure moved into the doorway. This figure was also holding a gun.

"Anyone else?" the figure asked.

Seth shrugged.

"I didn't see anyone else about." The figure stepped into the flat and nudged the gunman's body with a toe. "Jesus Maria," he said. "What a mess." Now Seth could see him properly, he could see he was of medium height, quite unremarkable-looking. Unlike the gun he was holding, which looked like something knocked together in someone's shed from bits and pieces of garden equipment, bits of hose and short lengths of two-centimetre copper piping.

He looked at Seth. "Put your hands down," he said, and he closed the door behind him. "Is there anything in here you absolutely can't live without?"

Seth shook his head and lowered his hands.

"Okay. Get changed, wash your face and get a coat. And hurry."

Seth tipped his head to one side. "And you are…?"

His unremarkable-looking saviour looked at him. He shrugged, and that weird *improvised*-looking gun seemed to disappear into the folds of his coat.

"Call me Leo," he said.

THERE WAS A battered old Espace parked around the corner, and Leo had the key. Seth allowed himself to be put into the front passenger seat, watched himself do up the seat belt, watched through the windscreen as the early-morning streets began to unroll in front of him. He felt as if his life had suddenly become something he was watching from outside. He was faintly aware that he was trembling.

"That shouldn't have happened, and I'm sorry it did," Leo said, navigating them around the tricky one-way system and late-night pavement-diving drunks of King's Cross.

Seth turned his head to look at the unassuming young man, found that he was quite unable to speak.

Leo glanced at him, then had to perform an emergency stop as a cab launched itself from the kerb without signalling in front of them. He did not, though, hammer the flat of his hand on the middle of the steering wheel in order to sound the horn, as another driver might. He muttered a few words Seth didn't recognise, and let the cab go.

"One day," he said to himself, "I'm going to come back here and revenge myself on the fucking drivers in this town." His English was excellent, almost Received Pronunciation, but he had a faint accent Seth couldn't place.

Seth said, "I'm going to be sick."

Leo got the car stopped at the side of the road and helped Seth out and over to the mouth of an alleyway, where Seth threw up what felt like everything he had ever eaten and then knelt with his cheek pressed against the rough brickwork of a wall, sobbing while the world yawed and pitched around him.

Then he was in the car again, without remembering getting back in, and unfamiliar streets were opening up ahead of him in the streetlights and the red lights of vehicles ahead of him stretched up into a terrible unknown distance and Leo was talking again.

"I tried," he was saying. "I tried to keep you all away from the flat, but I was having to improvise and it didn't work. Your friends... I'm sorry. It didn't work."

Seth opened his mouth to say something, but all that emerged was a hopeless exhalation. He wondered if he would ever stop shaking.

"I owe you an explanation, at the very least," Leo said, but then he seemed lost for words because he didn't say anything for quite a long time. They reached a large traffic junction with a big pub in the middle of it and Seth realised they were at Archway. Leo navigated them around the junction and onto the Archway Road, up onto the long hill northward out of London towards Highgate.

"I've become involved in something... complicated," Leo said as they passed under the great iron bridge that carried Hornsey Road high above the Archway Road. "I don't know what it is, and in order to make any sense at all of it I need to get back to mainland Europe. And I need a legend."

Seth turned his head and looked at Leo.

Leo glanced at him ruefully. "I used to date the Rokeby Venus," he said. When Seth just stared at him he said, "I'm afraid this whole thing is a bit off-piste."

The first words Seth managed to say since King's Cross were, "'A *bit*'?"

"Nobody was supposed to die," Leo said angrily. "It's me they want; I didn't think they'd involve bystanders."

"*They?*"

Leo shook his head. "I don't know. Someone told me Central wants me dead, but I don't believe that. They also told me Greater German counterintelligence wants me dead, and I find that easier to believe but I have no idea why because I haven't done anything to make them angry. I just don't *know*. I need to get back to the mainland, talk to people, try and make sense of this catastrophe."

Seth made several attempts to parse all this, while they drove up through East Finchley and North Finchley, but none of the words seemed to fit together in his head. It was just noise.

He said. "Lewis. Angela."

"Your friends? I'm genuinely sorry about that. If I could have stopped that, I would have."

Seth started to fumble in his pockets for his phone. "Someone should tell Lewis's parents..."

Leo reached out and took the phone from Seth's hand, opened the driver's side window, and dropped the phone out. Seth momentarily heard the faint sound of things breaking on the road, then it was gone.

"Sorry," he said over Seth's gasp of surprise. "No phone calls."

Seth gaped at him for a few moments, and then he found himself hunched breathless against the passenger door, a pain in his jaw. There were scratches on Leo's face, and a driver behind them angrily sounding his horn.

"Please don't do that again," Leo said. "Or at least try to wait until I'm not driving."

"Who *are* you?" Seth yelled.

"I'm a Coureur," Leo replied. "And I'm in a Situation. I mean you no harm. I need your help. We need each other's help, actually, because they're coming for you now as well."

"Because of a *legend*?"

"Because it was a legend for me. I don't know; I don't understand any of it. They've already killed my brother."

Another long silence in the car. They were in Barnet before Seth said, "The Germans."

"I don't know for sure that it *is* the Germans. I was told it is, and I was involved in something... strange in Berlin a little while ago, so it's at least credible. It just doesn't make any sense."

Another long silence. The car drove through Barnet and Potters Bar and out into the Hertfordshire countryside.

Seth said, "I'm going to be sick again."

Leo slowed the car, pulled over to the side of the road. Seth threw off his seatbelt, opened his door, and leapt out. He crashed straight through a hedge into the field beyond and kept going as fast as he could.

"Don't be stupid!" he heard Leo call behind him. "You need my help. You won't last more than a few days on your own."

Seth caught his toe in a rut and fell full-length.

"Hey!" Leo called. "Where are you?"

"I'm here," Seth called back. "I think I've broken my ankle."

"IT'S ONLY A sprain," Leo said.

"Well, *that's* all right then," said Seth. They were back in the car, way out in the sleeping unlit countryside now. He had no idea where they were, but he had a sense that they might have turned east at some point. "What happened to your brother?"

For a moment he thought Leo wasn't going to answer at all. "They tried to get to me through my family," Leo said finally. "My father was seriously hurt. My brother got in the way."

"What about *my* family?"

Leo didn't say anything.

"We have to help them," Seth said.

"I know." Leo shook his head.

"So?"

"So we'll help them. First we need somewhere to rest." He glanced over. "Am I going to have to tie you up or something?"

Seth thought about it. "Help my dad and my sister first. Then we'll talk about it."

THEY WOUND UP in a Travelodge on the outskirts of Bishops Stortford. Leo booked them into a twin room, bought support strapping and painkillers for Seth's ankle from the motel's shop, and they carried their bags inside.

With the door locked behind them, Leo took a little grey box not much larger than a book of matches from one of his tote-bags and stuck it on the jamb, near the top. Then he did the same with all the windows, even though they were on the fourth floor of the motel. Then he took his overcoat off and Seth finally got a clear look at the thing he had shot the gunman with. There was a little metal bottle strapped to his belt, and reinforced hoses running from it and down his arm to a bundle of copper tubes about six inches long, mounted on a sliding rail arrangement buckled around his forearm.

Leo saw him looking at the contraption. "I was in a hurry," he said. "I got a blacksmith to put it together for me."

In Coureur terminology, a blacksmith was an armourer. A mythological figure in Seth's world. "What is it?"

Leo unstrapped the thing and put it on the table and looked sadly at it. "Flechette gun. Powered by compressed air. Lovely piece of work, at such short notice." He glanced at Seth. "Can I trust you not to fiddle about with it when my back's turned? There wasn't time to put in a safety catch."

Seth nodded.

"All right." Leo unzipped another of his bags and took out a laptop and a packet of disposable phones. "Let's see what we can do about your family, then."

It took him over an hour of picking about on various websites and anonymised chatboards and making calls – one call per phone and then discarding it. Some of the calls sounded tense, others completely obscure. Seth used the room's facilities to make them coffee and paced back and forth so much that Leo told him to sit down, which Seth answered with a heartfelt couple of expletives.

Finally, Leo sat back and closed the laptop.

"Is it okay?" Seth asked.

"We'll know in a little while. The great thing about *Les Coureurs* is that it's a completely compartmentalised organisation. Everyone's used to getting anonymous orders and carrying them out, and half the time nobody knows why they're doing what they're doing. You just have to hack into that structure and so long as you know who to talk to and you have the right recognition strings no one ever questions their instructions."

"Like me."

Leo rubbed his eyes. "You, the stringer who passed you the job order. Just doing what you were told, because why shouldn't you?" He blinked blearily at Seth. "It was such a low-level job. I honestly thought it would go without a hitch. I'm sorry." He sighed. "What a fucking mess."

"Why me?"

"Sorry? Oh. Just the luck of the draw, really. I had a list of about half a dozen people who could have done it. I didn't want to use stringers; I wanted someone with experience, someone who'd do it right."

"You should have split the job up into segments and given each one to a different person."

"Yes, more anonymous that way, I know. But the more people know about something, the more chance there is of it coming to light. I decided it was best to give it to just one person." Leo checked his watch – a cheaply-printed thing that looked as if it had come as a free gift with a pair of printed shoes. "Get some sleep. Nothing's going to happen for a couple of hours."

"You have to be kidding."

"You must be exhausted. I know I am."

"Not a chance. Tell me how my friends wound up dead and I wound up on the run. That'll keep us both awake."

So Leo – *Rudi*, apparently – told him a mad story of chefs and restaurants and catastrophic jumps and hot briefcases and heads in lockers, a riot in a national park, a fake barristers' chambers, a year of moving from place to place incognito. The story was interrupted a couple of times by calls to one or other of the disposable phones, which Rudi answered tersely. Finally – it was daylight outside now – one call came through and Rudi held the phone out to him, and when he took it and put it to his ear he heard his father's voice demanding to know what the hell was going on and why there was a strange person with a gun in his house.

"Dad," he said when he got a moment's silence. "Dad, just go with them. They're there to help you. They're going to take you somewhere safe."

"Safe? Safe from what? Take us where?"

"Just go with them, Dad, please. I'll be in touch later." Rudi was holding another phone out to him. "I've got another call. I'll be in touch." And he took the other phone and had a similar conversation with his sister.

When he'd finished and put the phones down on the stack on the table, Rudi told him, "There was someone outside your sister's house."

Seth stared at him.

"I wanted them taken alive so I could find out who sent them, but there was... um." Rudi shrugged. "Anyway, your family are on their way to safe houses right now. I'll organise something more permanent for them in a day or so. *Now* will you get some sleep?"

IT WAS MID-AFTERNOON before Seth woke up, still tired and headachey, on the bed. Rudi was nowhere to be seen, but his bags – and the custom-built flechette gun – were still there, so Seth had a quick shower, dressed in fresh clothes, and went for a wander.

He found Rudi in the motel's almost-deserted bar/restaurant, talking quietly on one of the disposable phones and staring at a sausage sandwich as if it had done him an unforgivable wrong. He ordered an Americano and a burger and sat down across from the young Coureur.

"So," he said when Rudi had finished his call.

Rudi rubbed his face. "Well, Roger Curtis is unusable, I'm afraid. He's wanted for the murder of your flatmate and his girlfriend." He shook his head. "Which is actually quite elegant, if you think about it. Someone less sophisticated would have framed you or me."

"I can get you out," Seth said.

"I beg your pardon?"

"I might not be all high and mighty and important like you, but I've got some contacts. I can get you out. But it won't be cheap."

"Nothing worth having ever is." Rudi shrugged. "I'm sensing an 'and' hanging in the air between us."

"I'm going with you."

To his credit, Rudi didn't even try to talk him out of it. He just nodded tiredly. "Yes, well, I'd taken that as a given, rather. Is it my imagination, or is there *another* 'and' here as well?"

"We have to go to Scotland."

Rudi opened his mouth to say something. Closed it again.

"It's all about jurisdiction," Seth said. "And the Acts of Union."

Rudi shook his head. "I've spent almost a year on the run trying to get out of this fucking country. Why did nobody ever tell me about this?"

"It's nuance," Seth told him. "Nitpicking stuff. Body language, really. There probably aren't more than a dozen people in the whole country who appreciate it properly, and they don't want the public to know about it because it looks bad."

They were driving across a rain-lashed landscape of moorland and forest in Northumberland. The B-road they were on was in a terrible state of repair, and the Espace's suspension kept bottoming out in potholes and ruts in the tarmac. It was half past one in the afternoon, and already the light was taking on a dim, failing, underwater quality.

"Are you trying to tell me," Rudi said, "that the border isn't *there*?"

Seth sighed. "1603," he said. "James VI of Scotland becomes James I of England. Most people think that's when England and Scotland became one country, but actually, although there was one monarch, there were still two Crowns."

"Because joining two countries together is just as complicated as splitting one up," Rudi said. He lit a small cigar, opened the driver's window a crack to let the smoke out.

"It used to be easier," Seth said. "But that was when kings wore full armour and rode into battle on great fuck-off big horses and all you had to do was kill the other side's king." He took a bag from beside his feet, rummaged around in it, and came up with an apple. He took a bite. "Anyway, they actually had three goes at unification. First was under James I. He called himself 'King of Great Britain,' and he thought unification was a shoo-in, but the English Parliament was worried that it would mean some of the powers he had as King of Scotland being imposed on England. So. Close, but no cigar.

"Second try was in 1654. Cromwell occupies Scotland during the Civil War, and afterwards he issues an edict creating a Commonwealth of England, Scotland and Ireland. Scotland gets MPs at Westminster. This of course all disappears automatically when Charles II takes to the throne, and the Scottish MPs have to go home. He tries to get unification talks going again in 1669, but it all grinds to a halt."

"Do children in this country have to memorise this stuff?" Rudi asked.

"This is just background," Seth replied. "Anyway. 1707. Queen Anne. A Treaty of Unification is ratified. And ever since then the Scots have wanted to leave."

"Ungrateful bastards."

"The Scots started to call officially for devolution around the middle of the nineteenth century, I think," Seth said. He shook his head. "After that it all just gets too fucking complicated. But the point is, when the Separation did take place twenty years ago, it happened in a hurry after a long and fractious history, and there was a lot of bad blood on both sides."

"And all of a sudden, after a little more than four hundred years, there was a border between the two countries."

"Well, there was always a border, but most of the time it was just marked with a couple of signs or some farm fencing. You drove back and forth or you got the train or you walked. Nobody stopped you. Half the time you didn't even realise you'd crossed it. But yes. All of a sudden there was a border. Something that needed defending, patrolling, surveilling."

"Which costs money."

Seth grinned. "Oh, it's *much* more complicated than that," he said.

THEY STOPPED AT a bed-and-breakfast place, a farm more or less out in the middle of nowhere. There had been no need to make a reservation; the place was so isolated and the weather was so bad that they were more or less the only vehicle to pass by that day. The owner, a tall, patrician-looking woman with a strong Scots accent, seemed overjoyed to see them and happily booked them into adjoining rooms.

Later that evening – though notionally a bed-and-breakfast, there wasn't anywhere within an hour's drive to buy lunch or dinner – they sat in the farm's little dining room, where Rudi seemed to thoroughly approve of the lamb stew and dumplings on offer, even going so far as to ask the landlady for the recipe.

"Scotland waited too long for independence," Seth said when the landlady had gone back into another part of the farmhouse to watch television with her husband. "The country was almost broke when the Separation happened, but there was no going back once it had started. There would have been a catastrophe."

"It was pretty violent anyway, from what I understand," Rudi said.

"It was in the cities, certainly. But there was no way to stop it. If the government had tried to row back there might have been civil war. It wasn't a popular government to start with." He shrugged. "And then, all of a sudden, they're trying to kickstart an independent nation with the barest of mandates and no money in the Treasury to pay for... well, for anything, pretty much. There was a police force, but no army, navy or air force. The Westminster government was unwilling to provide any help, and the EU wouldn't bail them out until Scotland became an EU member."

"Which can take a while."

"Which can take a while." Seth drank some of the landlady's husband's excellent homebrew and looked around the empty dining room. "Anyway, Holyrood finally made a deal with the Chinese. Which pissed off Westminster and Washington and Brussels and just about everyone else, but really they had no choice. Prestwick Airport is now a Chinese airbase, the Scots got enough money to survive the transition to nationhood, and the Ayrshire Coast is targeted with enough megatonnage to make it glow at night for a million years."

"And the Anglo-Scottish border is one of the most heavily-defended on Earth."

"Yes. And no."

Rudi raised an eyebrow.

"The Scottish Government has been on the edge of bankruptcy for almost the entire time the country's been independent," Seth said. "The border's less than a hundred miles long – call it about a hundred and fifty kilometres, which isn't very much – but the Scots can't afford a border defence force. They've got a volunteer force of a couple of hundred people, and for most of its length the border runs through country like..." He gestured at the outdoors with his fork. "Wild, horrid country. Even the Romans hated it up here, and they were used to being out in all weathers."

"Whereas the English...?"

"Everything. Garrisons just south of Berwick and Gretna, regular patrols, fences, sensors. Drone flights along the border – which the Scots tend to shoot down; the Chinese gave them some obsolete automated sentry guns. The thing is..." He smiled.

"The thing is...?" asked Rudi.

"The English are watching for stuff coming south. Not going in the opposite direction."

IT WAS STILL raining the next morning, and great gusts of wind and water were blowing in veils and sheets down the valley where the farm sat. Seth and Rudi came to breakfast – a very passable selection of sausage, bacon, black pudding, fried potatoes, grilled tomatoes, mushrooms, toast, fried bread, baked beans – to discover that in the night the bed-and-breakfast had acquired two more guests, a couple of young women named Annette and Lauren, who had taken shelter at the height of last night's storm.

"Couldn't see more than a couple of feet past the end of the car," Lauren told them from the adjoining table. She had a Glaswegian accent. "Just a solid wall of water. Right, Nette?"

"Right," said Annette, who was small and taciturn and sounded – from the few words she said – as if she was from down in the West Country somewhere.

"Thought we were going to have to pull over and sleep in the car, then Nette spotted a sign for this place. Right, Nette?"

Annette was examining a triangle of fried bread as if the conjunction of frying pan and bread had never occurred to her before. She looked up and nodded. "Right."

"We're off to Hawick, see my parents," Lauren said. "How about you guys?"

"Glasgow," said Seth. "We're opening a restaurant."

"Yeah? Whereabouts?"

"Down by the river. Near the SEC."

"Ach, I wish you luck with that," Lauren said.

"Thank you," said Rudi.

Lauren looked at her watch. "How's the rain?"

Seth leaned back in his chair so he could see out of the window; the glass was running with water. "Still pouring down."

"Hm. What do you reckon?" she asked Annette. "Shall we chance it?"

Annette put down her fried bread. "I can't eat this," she said. "What's wrong with you people?"

Lauren chuckled. "Nette's not been feeling well," she told them.

"I feel all right," Annette protested in a low voice. "How can you do this to bread? It's a sin."

"Okay," said Lauren, getting to her feet. "That's us away, then. Nice to meet you, guys." Annette stood up too, and looked around the dining room as if searching for more abused bread.

"Drive carefully," said Rudi.

"Yeah, you too," said Lauren. "Happy trails."

After the girls had gone, Seth looked at Rudi. "We ought to be getting on our way too, you know."

"I hope you know what you're doing," Rudi told him.

"I know what I'm doing," Seth said.

"Good."

"I'm going to Europe with you, we're going to find out who ordered that bloke to kill Lewis and Angela, and I'm going to kill *them*."

Rudi sighed. He looked down at the remains of their breakfast. "She's right, you know."

"Who?"

"That girl. Fried bread. I'll never understand what goes on in the heads of the English."

THE RAIN SEEMED to be easing up a little as they checked out and carried their luggage out to the car, but the moment they were on the road again it started bucketing down. The hills and moors and forests withdrew behind a pounding grey curtain and all the windscreen wipers did was divert the stream of water first one way, then the next.

"This is a terrible place," Rudi said from the passenger's seat, having turned the driving over to Seth for a while. "I'm never coming here again."

"Northumberland," Seth said, peering through the windscreen. "Part of the ancient kingdom of Bernicia."

"The fucking Bernicians are welcome to it. Are you *sure* you know what you're doing?"

"Yes, I am."

"Hm." Rudi crossed his arms and stared out at the lashing rain.

They drove through what seemed to be a huge area of forest, and skirted the edge of a big lake, its other shore completely lost in the rain, then out onto moorland and back into the forest again. At one point a colossal truck carrying logs emerged from the rain, lights blazing, and blew past them at such a speed that the car rocked in its wake and Seth swore and fought not to lose control of the wheel.

A few minutes later they passed a car pulled up at the side of the road, its bonnet open and two sodden, wind-lashed figures standing looking at the engine. Seth drove past a hundred yards or so, then pulled in to the side and stopped the Espace. When he saw Rudi staring at him he said, "We're Coureurs. We're supposed to help people."

"It's the two girls from the farm," Rudi said, "and they're part of the English security presence here."

"No they're not," Seth said, opening the driver's door. "The farmer and his wife are."

They took their bags from the back of the car and trudged back along the roadside to where Lauren and Annette stood waiting.

"I think it's the electrics," Lauren said, gesturing at the engine of her car.

"We're in a hurry," said Seth.

She looked at him. "Aye," she said, nodding. "Aye, everyone's always in a hurry. Get in." She turned and dropped the bonnet, then she and Annette got into the front seats and Rudi and Seth in the back. Lauren drove. The engine started first time.

"What about our car?" asked Rudi.

"Someone's following two miles behind us," said Lauren. "They'll pick it up and take it to Manchester or Newcastle and leave it with the keys in the ignition. It'll be nicked in an hour, resprayed and replated in three."

"You're not Coureurs," Rudi said.

"No," Annette said, turning in the front seat and holding out two cloth bags. "We're not. Put these over your heads."

"Why?"

Seth put his hood on. "Nobody knows how they do this," he said, his voice muffled. "They want to keep it that way."

Rudi shrugged and put the hood on.

They drove for another ten minutes or so, then made an abrupt left turn onto a jolting, uneven road, then another series of right and left turns until Seth had no idea where they were. Then all of a sudden Lauren stopped the car.

"You can take your hoodies off now, lads," she said brightly. "Welcome to Scotland."

"I'm sorry?" Rudi said, removing his hood.

Lauren said, "Welcome to Scotland," again, and pointed through the windscreen at a narrow track running away through the forest. "If you walk down there about five miles, you'll come to a road. You can get a bus into Hawick from there. After that, you can get a train anywhere you want."

"Is this some kind of joke?" Rudi asked.

"No, it's not," said Seth. He took a fat envelope from his jacket pocket and handed it to Lauren, who opened it and rifled through its contents. "Come on," he told Rudi.

They got out of the car and stood in the rain while Lauren turned the vehicle around. She lowered the driver's window and poked her head out. "Don't try and follow us," she told them. Then she rolled the window back up and drove off into the dripping, windy dimness between the trees, leaving Seth and Rudi standing in the middle of the track.

"How much did you give them?" said Rudi as the car's lights bounced away down the track.

"The rest of the operational fund," Seth said.

"The rest of the operational fund," Rudi repeated, looking around him. "Okay."

"I heard about them when I was in Edinburgh," said Seth. "There's a group running people and contraband back and forth across the border, and nobody knows how they do it."

"I hope those girls had very good bona fides," Rudi said.

Seth shouldered his bag. "Let's find out."

* * *

IT TOOK THEM almost three hours to reach the end of the track. It opened out onto a rutted, damaged B-road. A hundred yards or so further down, a transparent plastic bus shelter almost covered in sprayed graffiti stood all alone by the side of the road. They stood in the shelter, shaking rain from their clothes and looking about them.

"How did you get in touch with them?" Rudi wanted to know.

"I didn't. They contacted me." Off in the distance through the rain, Seth could see the approaching headlights of a vehicle.

"They contacted you."

"While I was in Edinburgh doing research for Roger Curtis. They wanted to know what I was up to." Seth picked up his bag. "I was impressed; I was being pretty careful."

"And on that basis you just handed over a very large amount of money to two strangers, without any evidence of their claims."

"Of course not," said Seth. The vehicle was now close enough to be identified as a bus, bouncing and bumping along the appalling road. "I asked for a demonstration and they gave me a freebie. This is how I came back across the border." The bus pulled to a stop at the shelter, its illuminated destination sign reading 'HAWICK.' "Shall we?"

A DAY IN THE LIFE
OF CAPTAIN DEATH

1.

AT DAWN, THE Revisionists rocketed Building 2.

They used RPGs and at least one aged TOW wire-guided anti-tank missile, but they must have bought the munitions at one of the anarchic car-boot sales on the outskirts of the city because most of them failed to detonate. The few that did caused little damage, and fire-suppression teams were able to cope.

Still, it was a message that Xavier and his cohorts had not yet given up. They'd been quiet for almost a month until this morning, and some of the Kapitan's advisers had begun to murmur that perhaps the opposition had seen the error of its ways. The Kapitan, who had found Xavier under a pile of rubbish behind the Anhalter station and raised him like a member of his own family, had known better.

Kapitan Todt rarely slept these days, anyway, so the attack wasn't a colossal surprise. He spent his nights moving from window to window, watching Building 4 through image-amplifying binoculars, and he'd caught the signs of movement, the figures flitting about in rooms across the Parade Ground, that presaged some kind of action. Xavier must want him to think he was getting sloppy. By the time the first rocket propelled grenade was fired, he had already brought the Grandsons – who had been on a state of red alert for over a year now anyway – to full readiness and there were no casualties and only minimal damage.

In the fitful grey light of morning, once he had satisfied himself that the attack wasn't a feint or the opening move of a full-scale assault, the Kapitan did a quick tour of the damaged areas, mostly in the centre of the building between the eighth and fifteenth floors. Broken windows. Rubble. Some fire and smoke damage. Emergency teams were already cleaning up the mess. The Kapitan nodded appreciatively, offered some quiet words of thanks and support, all smiles and calm.

Inwardly, he was furious.

Later, when his intelligence chief answered the summons to his office, the Kapitan closed the door behind them and then grabbed the man by the front of his shirt and threw him across the room.

"Intelligence failure!" he shouted. "People could have been killed! For an intelligence failure!"

The intelligence chief, whose name was Hansi,

picked himself up off the floor and wiped blood from a cut on his face. "None of our sources reported anything like this, Kapitan," he said.

"I should dangle you out of this window by your cock and let Xavier and his friends take pot-shots at you," the Kapitan snarled. The last intelligence failure had missed the Revisionists' hiring of an expert sniper from Bremen. Eight people had died before an assassination squad broke into Building 1 and killed him. The Kapitan had made Hansi lead the squad himself, and had let him live when his mission was successful. Kapitan Todt did not feel quite as well-disposed towards Hansi today.

"I give you money," he yelled. "I give you resources. And in return for that I expect to hear when they go out on a shopping spree and buy missiles!"

"Xavier himself went to buy them, Kapitan," the man blustered. "On his own. He didn't hand out the weapons until moments before the attack."

"Oh, you know all about this *now*, do you?"

Hansi took half a step backward. "It's... it's the only way it could have happened, Kapitan."

"And nobody noticed he was *missing*? Your *spies*? Your little *sneaks* on the other side of the Parade Ground?"

Hansi opened his mouth. Closed it again.

"Every time you come to me for money, you promise me that Xavier will not be able to take a shit without one of your *rats* reporting about it to you. And now apparently he can leave the Municipality at will and come back with a van stuffed with high explosives and nobody notices." The Kapitan took a step towards Hansi and Hansi took another step back. "Find out how this happened, Hansi," he said. "Find out where he got the rockets from, and then fucking get *me* some!"

After Hansi had left, the Kapitan's second-in-command, Leutnant Brandt, emerged from one of the other rooms and said, "Dangerous man."

"Incompetent man," the Kapitan said.

"You should get rid of him, before he goes across the Parade Ground."

Kapitan Todt snorted. "Xavier's welcome to him. It would probably work out in our favour." He looked out of the window – painted with one-way reflective paint ever since the sniper incident – and after a few moments he said, "You think he's getting ready to defect?"

"That sort are only ever in the fight for the rewards," said Brandt. "As soon as they start drying up they're off looking for someone else to leech onto."

"Well I'm not going to keep hurling resources at him if he gets things this badly wrong," the Kapitan said mildly. "I'd have to be an idiot to do that." He sighed. "He knows where too many bodies are buried to take the chance. Bury him with them."

"Yes, Kapitan."

"And Brandt?"

"Yes, Kapitan?"

"I'm constantly reviewing *everybody's* loyalties."

Brandt seemed to falter momentarily, searching for an answer. Finally he said "Yes, Kapitan."

BEFORE BRANDT THERE had been Mundt, and before Mundt there had been Falkenberg, and before

Falkenberg there had been Meyer, and before Meyer there had been Xavier.

Xavier. Xavier X, who encouraged people to call him 'Twenty' because of his initials and who wore under his shirt a necklace of ears reputedly cut from the heads of shopkeepers and businesspeople who had been shortsighted enough not to join in with his protection rackets.

Kapitan Todt had found the boy hiding from the Anhalter Bahnhof *polizei* one rainy night in March, ten years ago. The Grandsons – they had still not quite geared up to make the jump from football hooliganry and medium-level racism to running their own country – had attacked another gang of supporters in the station concourse. The private security police had broken the fight up and everyone had scattered, the Kapitan and his predecessor, Kolonel Aldo, finding themselves in a little-visited area of dumpsters and piles of refuse bags behind some of the station's fast food franchises.

As they crouched, panting quietly, waiting to see whether anyone had followed them, Aldo heard something moving under a nearby pile of bags. The two young men threw the bags aside, and found a filthy boy crouching under them, the neck of a broken bottle clutched in one hand and a brand new Sony microtainment centre, still in its box and somehow smuggled out through the Sony franchise centre's security procedures, at his side. What struck the Kapitan, even then, was that there was no fear at all in the boy's eyes. He would have tried to kill them both if he had to.

"Crazy little fucker," Aldo chuckled.

"We should keep him," said the Kapitan, who in those days was still known as Florian.

Aldo raised an eyebrow. "I bet he'd be handy in a fight," he allowed. "How about it, kid?" he asked the boy. "How'd you like to join the Grandsons of Gavrilo Princip?"

"Fuck off, granddad," the boy spat scornfully. But when Aldo and Florian decided the coast was clear and made to move off, he followed them back to one of their clubhouses, where the *frauen* made a fuss of him and cleaned him up and it turned out he was on the run from a state orphanage and had nowhere else to go, and by then there was never any doubt about whether he would stay with them or not.

Not a single one of them could have said who Gavrilo Princip was without recourse to Google, and if it wasn't for voice recognition software most of them wouldn't even have been able to do that because the majority were illiterate. Like Twenty – he demanded to be called Twenty, it was only some months later that they discovered the name's derivation – most of the Grandsons were either graduates of or runaways from Berlin's notoriously tough orphanage system. Even the ones who had homes and families wouldn't have called them conventional or loving. They came together out of a common love of football and a common hatred of opposing clubs and supporters. They fought with a finely-honed desperation against fans of other Berlin clubs, other German clubs, other European clubs. Italian Ultras were the best. Ultras literally refused to stop; they just kept coming, long after more rational opposition would have faded away. It was a privilege to fight Ultras.

Aldo was in Plötzensee now, eight years into a life stretch for torching a Somali community centre in Dahlem and killing fourteen people. The state had demanded the death penalty, but was contenting itself with periodically withdrawing Aldo's segregated status in jail and waiting to see how long it took the Moslem inmates to try to kill him. So far, the longest he'd survived in the general population without being attacked was fifteen minutes. The Kapitan visited, when he could. Aldo knew the prison guards would intervene in any disturbance, but even so, eight years of it were starting to take their toll. His hair had gone completely white.

Aldo was almost forty, the oldest of the Grandsons, basically a Methuselah figure. A true visionary. While Xavier was fighting his way up through the ranks, Aldo was proving his visionary credentials by meeting with the leaders of other supporters' groups, cutting deals, forging alliances. The Grandsons began to join with some of the other gangs, then to absorb them, then to overwhelm them. By the time Aldo was arrested the Grandsons of Gavrilo Princip were almost two thousand strong and they ruled their own country.

NOTWITHSTANDING TODAY'S OUTRAGE – to which he was already planning an apocalyptic response – mornings tended to be fairly quiet times. The Grandsons' fondness for industrial quantities of beer and schnapps and, quite often, substances which had not yet been legalised for human consumption, meant that mornings were, for the most part, times of introspection rather than violence. The Kapitan ruled his half of the Municipality with a fist which aspired to be fair but which was still, when all was said and done, a fist. He had his followers divided into watches, and woe betide anyone who indulged in any kind of stimulant stronger than coffee less than twelve hours before their next watch.

So when the rocket attack began this morning, all of his people were alert and compos mentis and doing their jobs to the best of their abilities, which was only as it should be, and they were still doing their jobs now, calmly and methodically. Of course, as soon as their Watch was over they would do their best to get entirely off their faces...

Kapitan Todt considered himself to be a genuine military commander. Aldo had taught him discipline and its value, and those lessons were paying off now. When the war with the Revisionists was over and the Municipality was unified again, perhaps they could relax. But not yet.

Aldo had also taught him to trust his instincts, but Aldo's advice was no help as he walked down the corridors of his kingdom with the strangest feeling that he was being followed. The small group of advisers and lieutenants walking with him seemed not to notice.

Aldo's plan to unify or absorb or simply erase all the other football gangs in Berlin had reached its apotheosis when he decided his new army needed its own country, and he set his sights on the Municipality, an old housing development a few minutes' drive from the swanky new blocks in East Kreuzberg.

The Municipality was four huge apartment blocks arranged in a square around a patch of ground the size of a football stadium. In the past, the open ground had been a park, a play area, a place for children to ride their BMX bikes and skateboards, but the development's former residents had been moved out to newer estates around the city and it was almost empty. The few anarchists and Greens who were squatting there moved out in a hell of a hurry when Aldo led his people to the Promised Land. Like Moses, however, Aldo was fated not to live in the Promised Land. Within a day or so of the Grandsons taking over the blocks and fortifying them against the authorities – who had better things to do than worry about winkling a group of teenagers out of a couple of old blocks of flats – Aldo had been lifted off the street and advised by his lawyer that he would be on trial for his life.

In his place, the Kapitan – with Twenty at his side – had set about turning the Municipality into the nation Aldo had intended it to be. And for seven years all had been well. Under the Kapitan the Grandsons branched out from protection rackets into drugs and prostitution and illegal firearms. They made sure they got on well enough with the city authorities to keep police visits to a minimum, they made a good living, their numbers swelled.

And then the Swimmer had arrived, and the civil war had begun.

ALTHOUGH IN TRUTH it had only been a war for about a week, and the bloodshed had been awful.

Xavier's followers lost more than half their people, the Kapitan roughly the same. After that everything had settled down into an armed standoff punctuated by moments of extreme violence. After a few tense moments at the beginning, the authorities had decided to keep out of it for now and negotiate some kind of accommodation with whoever survived. It was less labour-intensive, they reasoned, to let the Grandsons thin out their own ranks.

Numerous skirmishes saw the Kapitan finally in control of Buildings 1 and 2, Xavier occupying 3 and 4 and the two groups facing each other across the desolate wasteland of rusting jungle gyms and roundabouts and concrete biking ramps and skateboarding pits, occasionally shooting at each other, occasionally running infiltrations into each other's territory.

For the Kapitan, the war was nothing short of a catastrophe. He had a large and diversified criminal network to run, and for the last year or so he had had no one to run it with. Gangs from other cities, sensing opportunity, had started to move in to Berlin while the Grandsons' attention was elsewhere. Already half the Kapitan's protection rackets had fallen to Chechen incomers from Hamburg, and the drugs business had been entirely taken over by a patchwork of *mafiye* organisations from all over Greater Germany.

He sat behind his desk in his office and worked his phones and he watched the empire that Aldo had founded and he had worked so hard to consolidate drifting away like a fog, and there was nothing he could do to stop it. The Grandsons' hold on Berlin's underworld had been predicated on extreme violence and weight of numbers, and while they were locked in this face-off there was very little he could do to stop things falling apart. The moment he sent any significant numbers of people out to attend to business, Twenty and his people would over-run the Kapitan's half of the Municipality and that would be the end of that story.

The tour over, he went down to the refectory and sat alone with a cup of coffee and stared into space. Years ago, when the Municipality was built, the architects had wanted each block to be a self-contained little microcosm of society – an arcology, almost – with shops and kindergartens and communal cafés. Much of that experiment had failed quietly. The cafés had gone out of business, the kindergartens had run out of funding, the shops had closed. Residents drifted away to the new ribbon developments out in the countryside, the blocks began to fall into disrepair and disorder.

The Grandsons had reversed that. They had reopened the kindergartens, turned the cafés into spartan but passable canteens. They had even taken down the shutters on some of the shops, mainly to use them as fronts for fencing stolen goods or marketing drugs. With a potential army of almost two thousand people ready to repel any action by the authorities, the *polizei* were reluctant to intervene and start a war, so the shops flourished. Outwardly, the Municipality had come back to life in rather sprightly fashion. You just had to ignore the all pervading air of criminality.

Hearing something behind him, the Kapitan turned in his seat and looked across the refectory, but could see no one. Just ranks of empty chairs and tables.

He finished his coffee and took the cup back to the counter – discipline in all things – and went down ten flights of stairs to the building's foyer. The foyer was dimly lit by battery-powered lanterns – the great glass wall which had given a view out onto the central space of the development had been boarded up and barricaded and reinforced – and a team was stationed there at all times with a Gatling railgun in case the Revisionists tried a frontal assault. All the windows on the lower floors – up as high as the fifth floor – had been bricked up and the rooms sown with antipersonnel mines. The Kapitan presumed Twenty had ordered similar measures on the other side of the Parade Ground. He chatted with the railgun team, offered some words of encouragement, made sure they were being well-supplied with food and coffee, and moved on across the foyer to a set of stairs leading down to the basement.

The ground under the blocks was wormed with networks of utility tunnels and rooms. At one time they had all connected up, so one could move from block to block without ever seeing daylight. In the wake of the outbreak of hostilities, the Kapitan had ordered large amounts of builder's rubble to be trucked in and piled up in the tunnels leading to the Revisionists' blocks, and here too he had stationed railgun teams. As in the foyer, he spoke with each of the teams, hearing their reports – Twenty's people periodically tried to clear a way through the piles of brick and earth and concrete filling the tunnels – and here too he had the itchy sensation that he was being followed.

Finally fed up with it, he went up to the twentieth floor of Building 1 and consulted with Doktor Rock.

"It's hardly a surprise," said Doktor Rock. "You barely sleep, you don't eat properly, and your enemies are trying to kill you. A little paranoia's to be expected."

Kapitan Todt shifted uncomfortably on the chair in the doctor's consulting room – a former hairdressing salon. "Can you give me something for it?"

"Almost certainly. You probably wouldn't be able to function effectively for days afterward, though."

"Fuck you."

"And fuck you too, Kapitan." Doktor Rock was sixteen years old, his face inflamed with acne. He took out a small joint and lit it – as the only doctor in the building he was exempted from the rules about on-duty substance abuse. It was the only way he could keep going. "Alternatively, I prescribe a holiday."

The Kapitan snorted. "Malta?" The doctor was obsessed with Malta, for some reason.

The doctor inhaled on his spliff, held the smoke for longer than was probably medically advisable, and breathed out. "There are worse places."

"I should hear your report, while I'm here."

Doktor Rock sat back in his chair and put his feet up on his desk. "I'm short of everything. End of report."

The Kapitan looked levelly at the doctor.

The doctor sighed. "Field dressings," he said. "I have none left; we're tearing up T-shirts and boiling them to make them sterile. Antibiotics. Hardly any. Surgical sutures – well, let's just say that I'd rather no one needed surgery. Painkillers. Rationed. Anaesthetics. Ditto."

"Noted. What about the general health of the population?"

The doctor looked at him. "When did we last have one of these little chats?"

"Last week."

"Well, nothing much has changed since then, Kapitan." He took his feet down off the desk and leaned forward. "I expect to start seeing scurvy quite soon. It's a miracle we haven't had typhus and cholera yet, but when they start they'll go through the blocks like a fire through a dry eucalyptus forest. Pubic lice are at epidemic levels. I'm noticing a lot of nervous skin complaints, insomnia, short tempers, listlessness..." He sighed. "This has gone on too long. People are just falling ill from being cooped up in this place. Eventually we'll have cases of rickets among the children, and then, dear Kapitan, I am off."

Kapitan Todt regarded the doctor for a long while. Despite his youth, Doktor Rock was a more than competent medic. He and his team of ad hoc nurses worked tirelessly. "We need one last decisive strike," he said.

The doctor looked exasperated. "I can't treat the casualties from *any* kind of strike, Kapitan. Haven't you been listening? We've reached a point where even something as straightforward as a burst appendix will be fatal because I just won't be able to operate, or give even the basics of post-operative care. If you're planning some kind of *strike*, better make sure none of our people gets hurt." He stubbed the joint out in an old tobacco tin on the table. "And you'd better win."

*   *   *

LUNCH WAS A solitary bratwurst, eaten at his desk, with another cup of coffee. Food was running low; it was days since he had been able to spare anyone for a foraging expedition. The sausage was of poor quality. One of the kitchen staff knew some English and joked with him that they were 'down to the worst of the wurst.' The Kapitan made a mental note to move the man to a work gang.

He finished his sausage, drank his coffee, then sat up straight behind the desk and said, "I know you're there. Show yourself." It was, if anything, an act of absurd faith.

But it was rewarded. A patch of shadow in one corner of the room rippled and shimmered, and all of a sudden a figure was standing there, apparently dressed in rags and an unusual-looking motorcycle helmet. It moved its hands and from the folds of the rags emerged the muzzle of a small semiautomatic rifle.

"Not a move," said the figure quietly. "Not a sound."

The Kapitan sat where he was and prepared to die.

"Florian Grüber," the figure said. "Styling himself Kapitan Todt."

"Yes," said Kapitan Todt.

"I've been sent to help you escape from here."

The Kapitan processed this statement. Apparently he wasn't going to die just yet. He said, "If you're the chef, you're more than a year late."

The figure removed its helmet, revealing the face of a young man, his brown hair tousled. "What?"

There had been a point, a day or so into the civil war, when he had believed that he was going to lose, and the Coureurs had become a real option.

He had no qualms about this; he needed to survive, to recover and regroup, if he was to finally defeat Twenty.

The Swimmer had counselled patience. "Let me set it up for you, Florian," he said. "I know how to do this kind of thing."

And so the Swimmer had made connections and organised things, and Kapitan Todt had waited and waited, and the Coureurs didn't come but some victories did. Now, he was in a position to make off from the Municipality himself, any time he wanted. He thought he might even be able to get across the Greater German border into Switzerland, where he had family. Thoughts of daring Coureur-aided escapes had faded from his mind. And now here was one of them, standing before him.

"The Swimmer wants to talk to you," he said.

The Coureur raised his gun. "I want to know what's going on."

"The Swimmer will tell you. May I stand up?" When the Coureur made no response, the Kapitan said, "All I have to do is raise my voice and a dozen armed people will come in here and kill you."

"Not if I kill you first, you scumbag."

The Kapitan shrugged, but he stood up anyway. "You were supposed to be here more than a year ago. What happened?"

"I got sidetracked. Who's the Swimmer?"

"I'll take you to him. You might want to... disappear again first, though. I'd find it hard to explain you."

The Coureur thought about it. Then he put his helmet back on, seemed to *shrug*, and vanished into the shadows once again. "I'll be right behind you," said his voice from the corner of the room.

"Good. Follow me, please."

THERE WAS A room deep in the heart of Building 2. It had once been a community centre, a space big enough for parties and dances and the like. The Kapitan had ordered it reinforced to what some of his people privately regarded as a ridiculous degree. Deep courses of reinforced brickwork and breezeblocks had been laid inside the existing walls and on the floor. Thick plastic sheeting had been stapled over every flat surface and then sprayed with a thick, durable layer of white paint, and into this newly-white and well-nigh impregnable room they had installed the Swimmer.

He lay in the middle of the room in a glass-walled tank filled with a clear medicated gel. Almost every inch of his body was terribly burned, and the machines and devices and bottles of fluid and gas which kept him alive lined the walls, clear plastic tubes running everywhere across the floor. A bulky mask was strapped to his face, feeding some kind of oxygenated fluid into his ruined lungs.

Only Kapitan Todt and the doctor had keys to this reinforced room. The Kapitan let himself in, stepped inside to allow the invisible Coureur to enter, then closed and locked the door behind them.

"He finally turned up, Uncle," he said.

Behind him, the Coureur shimmered into visibility again and took off his helmet. A few seconds later a synthesised voice from a pair of speakers beside the tank said, "Well, you took your time about it, *cook*."

The Coureur stared at the tank. "*Fabio?*"

THE SWIMMER HAD come to the Municipality at an inauspicious time. The Kapitan had been watching Twenty closely for years, and he saw the signs. His lieutenant was schmoozing other members of the hierarchy, whispering in ears, making promises. *Anschluss*, the Kapitan's late father would have called it. Tensions between the two men had been heightening for weeks. The Kapitan was starting to believe that the only way he could possibly survive this situation was to make a bold statement, drive Xavier into the ground like a tentpeg.

And then, late one night, a large van had turned up at Building 1, and inside, accompanied by several large, silent men, was the Swimmer, encased in a kind of gel-filled transparent body-bag, clearly close to death. He had a voice-synthesising computer which he somehow controlled by eye movement, and using this he was able to make his demands.

When the Kapitan called his senior officers together to tell them of the situation, Xavier was having none of it. The Kapitan over-ruled him and made arrangements to have the Swimmer installed in Building 2, and Xavier and his co-conspirators attempted a coup.

"Twenty didn't want anything to do with this," said the Kapitan. "He said it was *espionage*. He said it would bring down on us all kinds of unwanted attention. Really, though, all he wanted was an excuse to try and take over."

The Coureur was sitting on an old kitchen stool in front of the tank, where the Swimmer could see him by using a mirror strung overhead. He seemed to be in the grip of several powerful emotions at the same time.

"What the hell happened to you?" he said.

There was a pause, while the Swimmer's eyes picked out the words. Then the speakers said, "I was *fired*." And then they made a horrible noise which the Kapitan had decided was laughter. When that died away, the Swimmer said, "I was made an example of. I wasn't supposed to survive, of course, but I'm not without resources."

The Coureur appeared to be at a loss for words.

"I won't apologise for what happened to you in Poznań," the Swimmer continued. "That would be an insult to your intelligence. There was something I needed at the Consulate, and you were a means to obtaining it."

"You utter *bastard*," said the Coureur. "They nearly killed me."

"It was a chance I needed to take. It was nothing personal."

"You set up this jump too, didn't you. Off-piste. For him." He gestured at the Kapitan.

"My sister's boy. Little Florian. She married an Austrian. A bad lot. He gave me shelter when I was in need; it was the least I could do to try and help him. Tell me, why has it taken you fifteen months to get here? I taught you better than that."

The Coureur stared at the burned man in the tank. He said, "I was in New Potsdam. I got a crash message for a new Situation. I was supposed to meet up with a partner. When I found him he'd been murdered. I went to ground and things have been going very wrong for me ever since. Is this all to do with *you*?"

"And it's taken you this long to find out what the Situation was? I really am disappointed."

"Fabio, you prick, I've been running all over Europe. I've been kidnapped. My brother's been killed. My life has been destroyed. Is this all to do with you?"

"I took three proofs from the Consulate," said the Swimmer. "Florian knows where they are. He'll give you the key. Use them as you see fit. Powerful people want these things, want to know how to use them, want to stop them being used. I place them in your hands. Now go. Take Florian with you; he's a criminal little shit with the morals of a slime mould but he's still family."

"No," said the Coureur. "No. I'm not moving from this stool until you explain this to me."

"No explanations," said the Swimmer. "You wouldn't believe me. You have to see it for yourself."

"See what? What do I have to see? Who did this to you?"

"Central wanted the proofs. They wanted to stop them falling into the wrong hands. I wouldn't tell them where they were."

"Wrong hands? Whose?"

"Yours, for one. Now go."

The Coureur glared at him, then tipped his head slightly to one side. His eyes unfocused and he seemed to be listening. Then he said, to no one in particular, "All right, we're coming out." He looked at the Kapitan. "Your little bum-boy's decided to make a move in broad daylight."

Despite himself, the Kapitan had to smile. "Fucker," he murmured.

The Coureur stood up and started to fasten the front of his stealth-suit. "What about you?" he asked the Swimmer.

Again, that awful laughing noise. "I don't have any future left. Word will get around if I turn up in any hospital in Europe and I'll have an 'accident.' Florian's people have done their best, but I'm on the edge of multiple organ failure. They can't help me much longer. Go."

The Coureur looked round the room and said, "Jesus Maria, Fabio."

"Go," said the synthesised voice. "Just go."

The Coureur seemed to come to a decision. He grabbed the Kapitan and urged him over to the door. "You. I want this key he was talking about, and I want to know where these proofs are."

"In my office."

"Right. Let's get them and get out of here."

THEY STOPPED FOR a few moments in the Kapitan's office, where he unlocked his safe and took out an envelope and handed it to the Coureur. The Coureur stowed it in a pocket of his suit and then they were out again, running down corridors full of people panicking at the Revisionist attack. The Kapitan shouted some orders, tried to calm things down as he passed, but it did no good. "He has a *tank!*" someone shouted as they went by.

Instead of going down, they went up. Up endless flights of stairs, ascending into quieter and quieter parts of the building. At one point there was an almighty *bang* and the whole building seemed to shake dust off itself and the Kapitan found himself on his hands and knees, the Coureur dragging him back to his feet and urging him on through the stinking dusty corridors.

And then they were at the top of one final flight of stairs and the Coureur was throwing open a door onto a patch of late afternoon sky and they were on the colossal flat roof of the building.

"Seth!" the Coureur shouted over the sound of small-arms fire from far below on the Parade Ground, and a patch of air alongside a pile of boxes and metal bottles shimmered and became another stealth-suited figure.

They ran over to the figure, who pulled back its hood to reveal the anxious face of a young black man. "These people are not normal," he said.

"Football fans," said the Coureur. "Don't know why they couldn't just have got themselves lives." He grabbed the Kapitan and planted him front and centre. "Get this piece of shit out of here."

The second Coureur began buckling nylon straps all over the Kapitan. Then he snapped a harness to the straps. "What are you going to do?" he asked.

"I'll meet you as arranged," said the first Coureur. "I have to collect something first."

"Right." The second Coureur opened one of the boxes on the roof at his feet and snapped several lengths of line to his stealth suit. Then he stepped right up to the Kapitan and fastened their harnesses together so that they were face to face just inches apart. He grinned. "I understand you're a right-wing racist bastard."

The building shook again, and a wall of smoke billowed up from the side closest to the Parade Ground. "You two will have plenty of time to get to know each other," said the first Coureur. "But we ought to get out of here."

"Okey dokey," said the second Coureur, and he pulled a cord and three of the boxes exploded as the balloons inside them suddenly inflated. He looked into the Kapitan's eyes and beamed. "Run, you fucker," he said quietly. And together, awkwardly, the big balloons above them tugging them up on their toes, they ran sideways towards the far edge of the roof as the first Coureur was still strapping himself into a harness.

At the very last moment a gust caught the balloons and swept them up into the sky, and for a few seconds, before their combined weight took over and began to drag the balloons in a slow arc that would eventually deposit them on the other side of the Landwehrkanal and safety, the Kapitan could see into the Parade Ground. Hundreds of people were fighting there. Hundreds more were lying on the ground, very still. And yes, Xavier did have a tank. Clever boy.

IT WAS THE same locker.

Rudi paused and looked at the number printed on the key given to him by Fabio's nephew. Thirty-eight. He tried to remember the number of the locker he had looked into the last time he was at Zoo Station, and found that he could not. But it was the same one. He knew it was. There were no coincidences any longer; he was in the hands of what was, basically, a malicious God.

You cheeky bastard, Fabio...

He was also attracting attention, standing here like an idiot. He put the card into its slot and opened the door.

He half-expected to see Leo's head, mummified and shrunken but still with that surprised expression on its face, but instead there was only Fabio's burnbox, a calfskin-covered attaché case which would incinerate its contents at the first sign of unauthorised tampering. He grabbed the handle, pulled it out of the locker, swung the door closed, and limped out across the concourse.

At every step he expected to be shot, or stabbed, or mugged, or arrested. None of those things happened.

He left the station, went down the steps to the U-Bahn, got on a train to the Hauptbahnhof, and there boarded a train for Hannover.

Twenty hours later, he was sitting in an hotel on the Channel coast, a few miles from Dieppe. He was a thousand years older. Looking at himself in the flyblown mirror in his room, he thought it was a miracle that his hair hadn't turned white.

THE MAN
FROM SIBIR

1.

THIS YEAR WHEN the season ended, Lev decided to kill
himself.

He stood on the jetty and watched the last of the
tourists being ferried back to their floating country
and he put his hand in his pocket and felt the few
drachmas and euros and dollars there and knew he
couldn't survive the winter. All of a sudden his legs
felt watery. He sat down on a bollard and looked
out over the bay and some of the younger fishermen
laughed at him. The older ones, though, the ones
who knew how quickly and completely a man's life
can fall apart, kept a grim and respectful silence.

The great white ship in the bay was simply
called *Nation*. It was a country for tourists, a

country *of* tourists, making a year-long tour of the Mediterranean and Aegean before wintering in dry-dock in Kiel. It was a nation of the aged and the wealthy from all over the world.

This year, the great vessel brought him Myrna, on a cruise to console herself over the death of her fifth husband. "Did it when Danny died as well," she told him. "And George. And Charlie." And she smiled, and Lev felt himself shrink inside. When she smiled, she reminded him of owls. Not the wise owls of legend, but the mouse-destroying birds of prey.

Myrna. Ripped and exercised to the point of mutation, barely an ounce of fat on her, like a woman made entirely of twigs and the tufts of hair left by sheep on barbed wire fences. No way to tell how old she was, but old. She had wined him and dined him and consented to let him pleasure her, but she had been unwilling to bestow any more lasting gifts upon him. Gifts, for instance, which he could sell to pay his rent.

Gods but it was hot, even though winter was howling its way along the Med. This place was no good for Russians. Too hot. Too alien. The food tasted wrong and the alcohol was terrible, although one was able to overlook that if one drank enough of it.

He had come here four years ago, island hopping until his funds ran out and he could no longer afford a ferry fare. In Greek, the island's name meant something like 'The Place Where We Forgot Where We Were,' which seemed appropriate. Lev's arrival had coincided with *Nation* dropping anchor in the bay and disgorging its population, including Penny. Penny from Pittsburgh, who had taken a shine to

Lev to the extent that when she left he was able to sell all the things she had given him and rent a single filthy room over a *taverna* in the Old Town and survive, somehow, until the next boatload of tourists came in.

Nation's next visit had brought Alice. Then Corinne. Between times, Lev scratched a living teaching English and Russian and proofreading guidebooks, although the material return for that was tiny. He began to regard *Nation* with the fervour of an eighteenth century cargo cultist.

But he supposed he had known, in his heart of hearts, that one day it would all have to end. Either the people who owned and ran *Nation* would suddenly decide to send her on a round the world cruise instead, or the ship would hit an iceberg and sink, or he would simply latch on to a woman who would take more than she gave. And so it had happened. Myrna, on her way to pastures new, glowing with memories of her Russian lover, while her Russian lover starved and was thrown out of his room and eventually just walked down to the harbour, picked up some very heavy object, and jumped into the water with it.

And why not, if he was going to be honest with himself, do it now? Why go through the inevitable pleading and begging and promising with Mr Eugenides the *taverna* owner when the result was in no doubt? He looked around the bustling quayside and spotted a small anchor lying on the stones. He wondered if he could hang on to it long enough to do the job. He wondered whether anyone would bother trying to save him.

He was actually in the process of standing to walk over to the anchor when a shadow fell across him.

"Professor Laptev?" asked a voice in Russian. "Professor Lev Semyonovitch Laptev?"

The speaker was a young man wearing jeans and a light cotton shirt, a hemp shoulder bag in one hand. He was leaning on a black cane, one of those things made of innumerable carbon leaves, thin as a little finger but capable of denting the roof of a car. He looked harmless, but Lev's heart froze like a Siberian pond in winter.

"Who are you?"

The young man smiled. "My name's Smith. I'm someone who would like to take you for a drink, perhaps even some *meze*." His Russian was flawless, but Lev could detect a Baltic accent behind it. *Smith indeed.*

"Oh?" said Lev.

The Balt spread his hands. "No strings attached. I'd just like to ask your advice. I'm prepared to pay a consulting fee, if that would suit you."

Fear and desperation fought it out in Lev's heart. Desperation forged an alliance with hunger and won a bare victory. "Very well," he said.

THEY WENT TO one of the smarter *tavernas* over on the new side of the harbour, and Lev immediately felt dirty and dishevelled and out of place. The Balt insisted on ordering a little bit of everything, and when a huge platter was deposited in the middle of their table he smiled broadly and insisted that Lev tuck in, but Lev held back even though he was ravenous.

Had they finally caught up with him? Lev knew they used people like this, *spetz* operatives, young men with hard eyes and an outer layer of normality carefully shaped over a crystal core of ideology. But this one was different. He looked tired. No, actually, now Lev thought about it, that wasn't quite right. He looked into the Balt's eyes and saw a different *kind* of tired. It was not, he realised, the tired of someone who has stayed awake for a few days, travelled a few hundred kilometres, dealt with a few mildly complicated situations. It was the tired of someone who has gone right over the ragged edge of total exhaustion – physical, mental and emotional – and then somehow has found the space to begin to recover. Not completely yet, but enough to be functional for the moment, enough to do what needs to be done. Lev recognised that look. He had seen it, not all that long ago, in his own shaving mirror. And that was the only thing that made him relax, made him believe he could survive this. If Centre *were* to send an assassin to tidy up the tiny loose end represented by Lev Semyonovitch Laptev, they would not send someone who looked as though their entire world had been carved away. This boy was not an assassin; he was something else; something much rarer, much scarier.

"Eat," the boy said. "It looks good."

Lev looked at the platter. There was almost nothing on it that he would have chosen to eat unless he was, as he was now, utterly starving. "No it doesn't."

The boy sighed. "No, it doesn't, does it. Tourist food. I could do better than this." He poured them both drinks and put the bottle back on the table and sat back and regarded Lev. "I need a pianist."

Lev shook his head and drained his glass. "I'm afraid you've come to the wrong person. You see, I'm tone-deaf."

The Balt smiled. "Not that kind of pianist, Professor Laptev. A *pianist*."

Oh, a *pianist*... "We used to call them telegraphers." Lev shrugged. "Unimaginative, I know..."

The Balt refilled Lev's glass. "A telegrapher, then. A telegrapher who is an expert in codes."

Lev grunted. "There are no more experts in codes, Mister Smith. Why do you think I'm sitting here on this filthy island instead of shining like a star in Moscow? Today there is only Kolossal, and Kolossal is unbreakable."

"I'll bet you tried, though."

Tried? Lev swallowed his drink. Oh, they'd tried all right. Kolossal was the code-world's version of mutually-assured destruction. It had sprung, fully-formed, onto the Net about five years ago, a completely foolproof unbreakable encryption system. Even if you knew how it worked, it was impossible to break out a message encrypted using Kolossal unless it was meant for you. Rumour was that it had been developed by a group of cypher-nuts in Turin, who had then decided that *everybody* should have it and proceeded to post it into public domain. Now everybody used it. Moscow, Langley, London, the multinationals. Everybody.

The Federal Security Service had run a supercomputer and thirty of Russia's elite coders at Kolossal continuously for a year to discover its secrets, and they had been none the wiser. In desperation they had tried to kidnap one of the original Turin team, but they were nowhere to be found. Spirited away by the Mafia, the story went, for whom they were developing Son of Kolossal, which would not only encrypt messages but dance the gavotte while it did it.

At the end of that year, Lev had found himself wandering naked along the banks of the Moskva with no idea who he was or what had happened to his clothes.

"It's a wonder we didn't *all* go insane," he said quietly.

Smith was looking at him with an unreadable expression on his face. Lev hoped it wasn't pity.

"It's not Kolossal," said the Balt. "But it might be just as unbreakable."

Lev blinked at him. "Anything less than Kolossal," he said, "is just not safe."

The Balt grinned suddenly and took a folded sheet of paper from an inside pocket of his jacket. He smoothed it out and handed it over, and Lev looked down at the number-groups printed on it and felt an almost sexual surge of nostalgia.

"Which language is this in?" he asked.

"Russian."

Lev snorted. "Do you have a pen?"

The Balt didn't. Finally they asked the waitress – who also didn't have a pen, but did have a rather blunt eyebrow pencil, which she deigned to lend them, all in the spirit of fun, and Lev did a frequency count on the message, jotting his figures on a napkin. The Balt poured himself another drink and sat back to watch.

*   *   *

TEN MINUTES LATER, Lev looked up and said, "Very funny."

The Balt smiled.

The message was a basic poem-key encryption, the kind of thing that had been dangerously leaky during the Second World War. The plaintext consisted of a dozen names and addresses lifted from the Moscow telephone directory. The poem... Lev spent another ten minutes doing sums... well, it was certainly *Russian* – dark birch forests, a lost love, the looming threat of winter. Pasternak? Turgenev? Lev thought it was familiar, but really it could have been almost any Russian poem; it could almost have summed up the Russian soul. It certainly summed up his. All of a sudden he felt rather sad and ashamed.

"I think you should ask someone else to do this thing for you," he mumbled, starting to stand up.

The Balt didn't move. "The last person I showed that poem to told me he'd need at least two hours and access to all kinds of tables and reference books," he said.

Lev shrugged, hardly even surprised not to have been first choice. "*Classicists*," he said.

"You decrypted it in twenty minutes with a paper napkin and an eyebrow pencil. I think you're exactly the person I've been looking for." When Lev remained standing, the Balt said, "A hundred thousand Swiss francs, in any currency you choose, in any bank account you choose, anywhere in the world. Half now, half when you're finished."

Lev sat down, eyes brimming with tears, knowing how close he was to doing it for the price of a couple of drinks. "It's been..." He sniffed and rubbed his eyes. "It's been a long time. I may not be able to help you."

"Perhaps a consulting fee, then," said the Balt. "Paid daily. Perhaps that would be fairer."

Lev nodded. "I would prefer that."

"Before we begin, I should warn you that there may be some danger."

"Danger?"

For the first time, the Balt looked fractionally uncomfortable. "I don't know how, or why, but there may be some danger. But that's my problem and I'll do my best to protect you while you work, and afterward." He blinked at Lev. "If you were to get up and leave right now, I wouldn't hold it against you."

Lev did think about it. For almost a second. He waved a hand, inheritor of the Cheka, the NKVD, the KGB, child of Enigma and Kolossal. "I no longer have anything to be afraid of," he said, and cringed inwardly. Such a *Russian* thing to say.

The Balt looked sad. "Well, let's hope this doesn't turn out to be a learning experience for you. Is there anything you will need?"

Lev looked at him, wondering how his life had suddenly taken such a turn. "I will need to retrieve my laptop from Mr Keoshgerian," he said.

LEV'S LAPTOP WAS made entirely of cloth. It looked like something from a fabric conditioner commercial. The tapboard resembled an alphanumeric embroidery sampler, and the printer/scanner/copier could have been mistaken for a brightly-coloured hand towel. All rolled up and stuffed into a small drawstring bag, it looked like one of those little cushions people buy to rest their heads on during long coach journeys. Rudi had never seen anything like it before.

"We did magic, once upon a time," Lev said with a ghost of pride. "And we never told anyone."

"How does it work?" Rudi asked, thinking about the patents involved.

Lev shrugged. "Don't know. You just plug one end into an electrical socket, the other end into an entertainment set, and it works. You can even wash it, but if the water's too hot it destroys the memory and processor threads, and then all you've got is some bits of rug. We'll need to buy cables for it. And an external hard drive. A big hard drive."

"Not a problem."

Lev ran his fingers over the woven surfaces. "I never could bear to sell it. Pawn it now and again, perhaps, but never sell it. I did think once I'd take it to one of the hardware houses, sell them the technology. But my former employers would have heard about it, and they would have sent someone to kill me. Someone like you."

Rudi looked at the little Russian. *They would have sent someone to kill me.* Lev didn't sound sad or angry, just rather matter-of-fact, like a father who has just caught the weather forecast and discovered that the family picnic is going to be rained off. And what was that *someone like you* all about?

"Do you need a drink?" he asked.

Lev shook his head. "I need to work."

Rudi didn't think that Lev needed to worry about his former employers. The last time he had been in Russia – European Russia, this was, what they were just beginning to call *Rus* back then – the local intelligence services hadn't been anything to phone home about.

RUDI HAD A room in one of the swanky hotels in the New Town, so Lev moved his few belongings – some books, an old iPod, a bag of clothes – in there, and after the formalities were over and he had some money in his pocket, Lev sat down and set up the cloth laptop. When it was ready he said, "Show me this thing that no one else can decrypt."

Rudi took from behind the sofa a heavy-looking attaché case and opened it by swiping a cardkey down its side and then typing in a long combination on the lockpad on top. He took out a rolled-up paper map and two old-looking books, one thick with battered cardboard covers, the other a thin leather-bound notebook.

"In case you need some background," he said, handing over the notebook, "the map's of the Line. Standard stuff you can buy anywhere. This," holding up the thick book, "is a 1912 railway timetable for the South of England. And I have no idea what any of it means."

Lev took the notebook and opened it. Tucked inside the cover were five sheets of paper covered with printed columns of numbers and letters. No, not printed... Lev ran his fingertip over the back of one of the sheets, felt the slight embossing of the typewriter. These sheets had been typed a very long time ago.

He laid them aside and paged through the notebook. More columns of numbers and letters, closely written in ink, in a clear, careful hand. He checked inside the front and back covers and both endpapers, but there were no pencil jottings, no idle calculations that might give a clue to the cypher being used.

"This may take a little while," he said.

Rudi shrugged and limped over to examine the room's minibar. "If it takes a while, it takes a while, Professor. I know these things mustn't be rushed."

Lev shrugged. He unrolled the laptop and scanner, plugged in the newly-purchased hard drive, and began the process of booting everything together.

2.

OF PARTICULAR INTEREST to cartographical students, Sheet 2000 – the so-called 'Millennial Sheet' – is the only surviving sheet produced by the 'Alternative Survey' begun by General H. Whitton-Whyte in 1770.

THE ALTERNATIVE SURVEY

Quite why General Whitton-Whyte undertook his own survey of the British Isles, when the same work was being carried out by the Ordnance Survey, is not known.

Indeed, much of the history of the family is shrouded in mystery. Very little remains to us of the early history of the Whitton-Whytes. In Bryce's *Great Families Of The County Of Staffordshire* (Angel and Pediment, 1887), the family merits only a footnote appended to an entry concerning the Bracewells of

Leek. In the 1888 edition of the book this footnote mentions a rumour extant in the county over a century before that the Whitton-Whytes had 'fallen upon hard times due to an illness' which forced them to sell their house, Whetstones, to the Bracewell family, and move to London. The footnote is omitted from later editions of Bryce.

In Seichais' *Cartographie Anglaises* (Spurrier, 1901), Whitton-Whyte is included mainly because of his 'eccentric system of numbering sheets,' sheets apparently being given the first number which entered the General's head on the day of publication. Some of these numbers ran to many digits (forty-seven in the case of the Birmingham sheet) and abridged numbers – so-called 'Whyte Numbers' – were later appended to the sheets for ease of cataloguing.

Of the Survey itself, details are only available of the later stages. Apocryphal stories abound of Whitton-Whyte's wild-haired figure tramping the Western Isles of Scotland or the Yorkshire Dales, theodolite in hand and – in the early days of the Survey at any rate – attended by a small army of helpers drawn from his lost estates in Staffordshire.

Clearly, it would have been impossible for one man to undertake such a survey on his own, and there are records surviving in Cumbria, Peeblesshire and Kent which suggest that the General hired local men where it was possible, while keeping a firm hand on the overall control of the project.

In many areas this contracting-out of the work may account for the friction reputed to have existed between Whitton-Whyte and the Ordnance Survey, which in a number of instances was surveying for its own maps at the same time as the General's men were surveying for his. It's said that on several occasions this friction erupted in violence.

There is a story, retold in Grey's *Maps and Mapmakers Of The British Isles* (Pitt & Sefton, 1892), relating to the theft of Ordnance Survey field drawings of Cornwall and noting – though there is no evidence that they were responsible – that Whitton-Whyte's Survey was known to be in the same area at the same time as the Ordnance men.

Comparison of publication dates, says Grey, reveals that Sheet 178923 of the Alternative Survey (Northern Cornwall) was published in less than half the time of the other sheets. However, it should be noted that, save for Sheet 2000, no records of publication dates have survived to the present day, and therefore it is impossible to authenticate Grey's thinly-veiled accusation.

In total, the Alternative Survey lasted one hundred and twenty years. In his scholarly work *Mapa i Pamięc (Map And Memory)* (Zakopane, 1920) Walerian Mazowiecki even blames the Survey for the eventual downfall of the Whitton-Whyte family.

Only one full set of the Survey was ever collected, these stored in the 'Map Room' of the Whitton-Whytes' townhouse in Islington. All but one version of Sheet 2000 – which was on loan to Mr S. J. Rolfe of the British Museum at the time – were destroyed, along with the rest of the collection, when the house burned down in July 1912, and our subsequent knowledge of its history has been gleaned from examination of surviving notes and field drawings.

* * *

SURVEY

As with so many of the other sheets of the Alternative Survey, the survey of Sheet 2000 is based on existing data. It used the Hounslow Heath baseline measured by General William Roy in 1784. Whitton-Whyte is said to have remeasured the baseline a month later, and pronounced it 'adequate.' Thereafter, this sheet, covering the area to the west of London, conforms in general to the triangulations which resulted in Ordnance Survey Sheet 7. Whether Whitton-Whyte actually made any measurements of his own beyond checking Roy's baseline is a matter of conjecture.

DRAWING AND ENGRAVING

It is believed from contemporary accounts that twelve field drawings were prepared for draughtsmen in late August 1820, when proof copies of Ordnance Survey Sheet 7 were already circulating. Whether any of these proofs fell into the hands of the Whitton-Whyte Survey is not known.

What is known is that Henry Hoskyns, who undertook the reduction of the field drawings to a form ready for engraving, made a flurry of revisions at the end of August, and was heard by his apprentice, James Summers, to exclaim that the detail of the drawings was 'as inaccurate as it is possible to be.'

This outburst, and the subsequent revisions, led to Whitton-Whyte breaking off all relations with Hoskyns – who had been involved in the draughting of virtually all the Alternative Survey sheets, man and boy. Hoskyns, his eyesight already failing, became totally blind later that year, and, unable to work, was buried in a pauper's grave when he died six years later.

It's said that, following the disagreement with Hoskyns, Whitton-Whyte himself reinstituted the original state of the map and delivered the draught in person to its engraver, Mortimer Heathcoate, charging him to 'change not one line nor one triangulation point.'

PUBLICATION HISTORY

General Whitton-Whyte never lived to see the publication of Sheet 2000. In September 1822, aged eighty, he suffered a stroke while travelling through Dorset, and died at Poole two days later. It is a testimony to the old man's stamina that, despite the difficulties of travel around England, Scotland and Wales in those days, he had managed to cover so much of the country during his life.

The Survey was not delayed by mourning, however, and Sheet 2000, now overseen by Whitton-Whyte's son, Captain John, was published as a single sheet in London on October 5, 1822, some two months after the Ordnance Survey sheet of the same area.

Comparison of the two sheets shows that Hoskyns' reservations about the accuracy of Sheet 2000 were largely unfounded, save in one area just north of Colnbrook, where the village of Stanhurst is marked. No such village appears on the OS sheet, and indeed no such village has ever existed in this location.

Quite where the inaccuracy came from is unknown, and the surviving field drawings offer no clue. It is known that, despite his advanced years, the General made many on-site surveys himself. Whether he mapped 'Stanhurst,' or whether one of his hired men made this inexplicable error, is not known. However, due to Whitton-Whyte's dispute with Henry Hoskyns, the error was allowed to stand.

1 Sheet 2000 was revised by Captain John Whitton-Whyte in 1830 and 1831, the revised state being published in 1833. This revision was undertaken to bring the sheet into line with the James Gardner printings of OS Sheet 7 between 1824 and 1840, and exhibits many of the Gardner revisions.

However, far from removing the spurious village of Stanhurst from the original state, the revision shows it as having grown in size and been joined by a neighbouring hamlet named Adam Vale, on the outskirts of Colnbrook. A contemporary account tells of Captain John taking 'a particular interest' in this portion of the map, and spending many weeks in the Windsor area, where he died of pneumonia in December 1842.

2 With the death of Captain John, his son, Lieutenant Charles Whitton-Whyte, then twenty-two years of age, found himself in charge of the Alternative Survey, overseeing new revisions and the first electrotype printings of Sheet 2000.

The first electrotype printing was published in 1849, and instead of correcting the errors in its predecessors, compounds them. Surviving field drawings show an increase of interest in the area around Windsor, and a corresponding decline of accuracy elsewhere on the sheet. The 1849 printing of Sheet 2000 therefore largely resembles the 1833 state, save in one area.

The 1849 state erases Colnbrook altogether, replacing it with an Adam Vale the size of a small town. Stanhurst's cathedral (St Anthony's) is recorded in one set of field drawings, while in another set the spurious villages of Vale, Minton and Holding have obliterated Harmondsworth.

By the revisions of 1851 and 1855, this small corner of Middlesex is all but unrecognisable. Spurious villages, hamlets and towns have sprung up seemingly overnight. West Drayton has gone, and all that marks its former position on several sets of field drawings is the legend 'Drew Marsh' and the symbol for a large pond.

From the few surviving records, it appears that the rest of the map, while perfectly accurate, was to all practical purposes ignored, being reproduced from earlier sheets or (some accounts have it) from Ordnance Survey sheets.

The quite imaginary area around Stanhurst appears to have obsessed Charles Whitton-Whyte, a reclusive man by all accounts, presiding over a family fortune mortally damaged by the cartographical endeavours of his father and grandfather. In 1846, he resigned his commission in order to devote his time to map-making.

Charles took to spending much of his time in Windsor while various family holdings fell into decline due to his neglect. At the time of the 1855 revision, he bought a small house in Datchet, and is reported to have spent many hours walking in a countryside which, according to his map, did not exist.

In 1860, aged forty, Charles met and married Jane Breakhouse of Windsor, twenty years his junior. They would spend the next twenty years trying to have children.

3 Much controversy surrounds the so-called 'Black Sheet' revision of 1863. No examples, notes or field drawings survive of this state, but from contemporary accounts it is possible to reconstruct how it must have appeared.

In this electrotype printing, Windsor is gone, as are Staines, Uxbridge and Brentford. Into the area bounded by them is inserted the 'county' of Ernshire, complete and entire with towns, villages, hamlets, roads, streams and a rail link to Paddington. The Thames cuts unchanged through the southeastern corner of Ernshire, as do other existing watercourses and physical features.

'If Mr White (sic) thinks this a joke, let him be assured that the residents of this lovely part of the nation do not consider it so,' wrote one irritated resident of West Drayton in a letter to *The Times* dated August 22 1863.

Certainly, others shared this correspondent's irritation, because on November 12, 1864, the Black Sheet became the only map in British history to be banned by order of Parliament. 'For the good of the Nation,' wrote one Minister to Whitton-Whyte later that month. Whitton-Whyte's reply has not survived.

4 The final revision of Sheet 2000, the illegal 'Natal Sheet,' was published on July 7 1890, the day of Charles's son's birth. His wife lived barely long enough to see the child and name him Edwin.

Only two examples of the Natal Sheet were ever printed, of which this is the single survivor.

On it, we can clearly see the final flowering of the Whitton-Whytes' peculiar obsession. Ernshire has consolidated itself – in Charles's mind if nowhere else.

Its county town, Stanhurst, is a bustling place roughly the size of present-day Loughborough. It has rail links to the four points of the compass, an extensive road network, a barracks in Anselmdale, farms, churches, post offices, all the amenities of a real county, even a manor house at Eveshalt.

The Parliamentary banning order notwithstanding – it was, after all, simply a revision of the banned Black Sheet – the Natal Sheet was displayed in a gallery in Islington, and seems to have engendered a curious wave of hoaxes.

All through the summer of 1890, newspapers and public institutions were bombarded with communications from the towns of Ernshire. *The Times* received letters from the inhabitants of Stanhurst and Eveshalt. Buckingham Palace received an invitation for the Queen to review the garrison at Eveshalt. A picture-postcard of St Anthony's Cathedral in Stanhurst is reported to have been delivered to the residence of the Archbishop of Canterbury, inviting him to make a pastoral visit. And a woman in Margate claimed to be having a correspondence with a young man from Adam Vale. In a fit of madness which was later to result in the sacking of one manager, the prosecution of another for fraud, and the forcible retirement to a coastal sanatorium of a third, the South Western Railway produced posters advertising day-trips to the 'historic' town of Stanhurst.

In September 1890 a special Act of Parliament was passed forbidding any member of the Whitton-Whyte family from ever publishing another map. Imprisonment was considered for Charles but rejected 'due to his infirmity.' A fine was similarly rejected due to the parlous state of the family's finances.

In the event, punitive measures proved unnecessary. The following year, Charles Whitton-Whyte left his little house in Datchet (where he insisted on living despite the fact that on his map Datchet did not exist.) He locked his front door, handed his infant son to his wife's sister, Mrs Margaret Allen, and walked away down the road.

'Of his illness there was no sign,' Mrs Allen later wrote to a cousin. 'His head was held high, his step was firm and sure, and he swung his stick with vigour as he walked away from Edwin and myself.'

Charles was never seen again.

5 Edwin Whitton-Whyte took his mother's maiden name of Breakhouse, and under his aunt's care showed no interest in cartography. Despite the shame of his father's madness he was accepted into Eton, and later went up to Oxford to study 'Greats.' In 1914 he enlisted and was sent to the Western Front, where he acquitted himself with distinction, rising to the rank of Sergeant.

Edwin kept meticulous journals, but only once did he refer to his father and to the Alternative Survey.

My father believed, he wrote, *as did my grandfather and great-grandfather, that he had discovered a county where none exists, a landscape overlooked by the very people who occupy it. My grandfather writes of maps having a power over the land, and theorises that if an imaginary landscape is mapped in great enough detail, it will eventually supplant the actual physical landscape, as a wet cloth wipes chalk from a blackboard.*

My great-grandfather, on the other hand, wrote of all possible landscapes underlying each other like the pages of a book, requiring only the production of a map of each landscape to make it real.

Whatever their motivations, my family have spent over a century exploring these theories by documenting in great detail the growth of a county called 'Ernshire,' which patently has no existence in the real world.

And yet today I received a letter purporting to be from my father! If he is still alive, he must be nearly a hundred years old, but though I have no memory of him I recognise his handwriting from his diaries and memoranda.

In his letter, he wishes me well, and says he is proud of me, though I do not know how he could be aware of my life-story, unless Aunt Peggy has been in contact with him. He claims to be living in 'Ernshire.' He begs me to visit him, and gives detailed instructions on how to get there. He says the eight-seventeen from Paddington sometimes calls at Stanhurst, and that he has 'confidantes' among the staff of the Windsor Branch of the South Western Railway who will ensure my safe passage to a county which does not exist.

Madness. This is patently a hoax, and I have despatched a letter instructing my solicitors, Messrs. Selhurst, Barley and Cainforth, to trace and prosecute the writer of this awful missive. I suspect one of my father's ex-employees, though I have also been led to believe that during the scandalous summer of my birth, a member of the South Western Railway's staff was prosecuted, in part due to the hysteria brought about by my father's maps. I have instructed Mr Barley to trace this man as a matter of the gravest urgency.

6 Edwin Breakhouse was killed leading his men 'over the top' on the Somme. Many of his personal effects were never delivered to his aunt in England, among them the letter to which he refers in his journal. All record of his contact with his solicitors was destroyed when the offices of Selhurst, Barley and Cainforth burned down in April 1918, shortly after the deaths of all three senior partners in the Staines Train Disaster of March of that year.

7 Sheet 2000 may be the last remaining example of a peculiarly English sensibility, the same sensibility which induced land-owners to build 'follies' on their estates. A folly most often took the form of a structure with no function other than the satisfaction of its builders' vanity, and Sheet 2000 could be seen as the Whitton-Whytes' folly – in both senses of the word. It remains as merely an extraordinarily-detailed scrap, a remnant of a work which occupied the lives of hundreds of people over a century and a half, and perhaps a remnant of an age now long-gone.

Students of cartography will note the painstaking detail lavished not only on the spurious area of 'Ernshire,' but on all other areas of the map. Comparison with contemporary Ordnance Survey sheets shows a certain elegance of execution absent in the OS material. Sheet 2000, for all its faults, remains gorgeously custom-made, with all the care and attention – indeed, if the word can be used to describe a map, all the poetry – that entails. It is something which we today, with our satellite-assisted, computer-drawn maps, have lost, and recalls a time when maps did exercise a power over the landscape – if only in the imagination.

8 One anecdote remains, and though its source is uncertain and there is no way to confirm it, it is in keeping with the story of Sheet 2000, and perhaps deserves to be set down here.

In the year 1926, at the age of 94, Mrs Margaret Allen was visited by a young man who claimed to be her nephew.

Sister Ruth, who ran the nursing home where Mrs Allen spent her final years, is reported to have told a friend that the old lady was extremely excited by the encounter. Sister Ruth recalled that the young man, who called himself Stephen, spoke with an indefinable rural accent, and left Mrs Allen a certain document.

Mrs Allen jealously guarded the document given to her by Stephen, and after her death it was nowhere to be found, but Sister Ruth claimed to have seen it once, and described it as 'a map.'

Sister Ruth, as far as is known, never described the map to her 'friend,' but she did mention one feature. It was marked, she said, in the bottom right-hand corner: *Whitton-Whyte and Sons. Mapmakers. Stanhurst.*

3.

"SOME KIND OF novel," Lev hazarded. "A utopian fiction."

Rudi sat with his hands clasped to the sides of his head, like a man with a horrible hangover. "This is insane," he murmured, looking down at the decrypts of the loose typewritten sheets arranged on the coffee table in front of him.

According to Lev, the code was quite arcane, a variation of something which had been developed for commercial use in England in the late eighteenth century. The cloth laptop had taken three days to crack it, but now it was happily delivering pages of cleartext at a rate of two or three a day. They were already several pages into the handwritten parts of the notebook. Columns of digits and letters were scanned into the laptop, and out came descriptions of towns, villages, hamlets, ratings of pubs and restaurants and guest houses.

"Are you sure that thing is working properly?" Rudi asked, nodding at the laptop.

"If it wasn't, you wouldn't be able to read anything at all."

Rudi picked up one of the pages of lists and looked helplessly at it. "This is..." He shook his head. "*A Gazetteer of the Towns and Villages of Ernshire*," he read.

Lev shrugged. "A fiction."

Rudi dropped the sheet of paper on the coffee table and stood up and limped over to the window.

"Do you want me to stay?" Lev asked.

Rudi looked round. "I'm sorry?"

"The laptop works itself. All you have to do is type in the groups. You don't need me any more."

Rudi shook his head. "Could this *Gazetteer* be a code itself?"

"Of course. Take such and such letters from each line and you get a message. *The Komsomol flies at night*."

"Can the laptop scan for that kind of thing?"

"Yes, but it would be quicker if you had the key."

"Which would be...?"

Lev picked up the old railway timetable and riffled its pages speculatively.

"I looked," Rudi said. "There are no marks. Nothing to suggest any of those entries is any more significant than the others. And before you ask, I did the thing of letting it fall open on its own, too. Nothing. Nothing obvious, anyway."

"Perhaps the key will turn up further on in the text itself," Lev theorised. "Although that would be quite unsecure." He added, "I don't want you to think I'm milking this job."

Rudi broke into a broad smile. "Why on Earth would I think that?"

Lev gestured at the decrypts.

Rudi shook his head. "Whatever is going on here, it's not your fault, Lev. Stay around; let's see if we can make any sense of this, okay?"

Lev nodded. "Okay."

ALTHOUGH MAKING SENSE of it was easier said than done. The Gazetteer ended, and the notebook began to yield up a history and description of a country which did not exist.

Taking as its jumping-off point the typewritten fiction which Lev had first translated, the notebook's unknown writer went on to speak of a nation he called *The Community*. The Community was the Whitton-Whytes' greatest dream, a country mapped over the top of the whole of Europe and entirely populated by Englishmen. It sounded like the setting for an enormous Agatha Christie mystery, all county towns and vicarages and manor houses. Rudi thought it was a blessing that Fabio hadn't lived to see just how worthless his great prize had been.

On the other hand...

Lev's laptop delivered three pages of decrypts a day. After the twelfth day, Rudi began to feel a vague unease, and for no reason he could have articulated and against Lev's loud protests, he booked them out of the hotel and moved them to another island.

A week later, he located the source of his unease.

One night, going through the contents of the burnbox, he took out the map of the Line again, rolled it out onto the floor of their room, weighted the corners down with ashtrays and beer bottles, and got down on hands and knees to examine it properly.

He had, he realised, been going about this the wrong way. Fabio had risked his life – had risked *both* their lives – to steal what appeared to be a perfectly standard map, one you could buy at most post offices in most countries. Fabio was eccentric and irresponsible, but he was not stupid. Therefore, it must not be a perfectly standard map. This much should have been obvious to him immediately, and probably would have been if the decrypts hadn't captured so much of his attention.

"I'm ashamed of myself," he told Lev. "The map should have been the first thing I looked at. And me a Coureur."

Lev, who was sitting on the sofa reading the day's product and drinking vodka, only grunted.

Here was the Line, and if you had any reservations about its name, here was the proof. It really was just a line, a stitch that ran across Europe, a country thousands of kilometres long but only ten kilometres across at its broadest point. Here were the towns it ran through, the marshalling yards and embassies and consulates, branch lines, maintenance depots... branch lines...

Rudi leaned down until his nose was a few centimetres from the surface of the map. The Line needed branches for shunting, and for repair crews, and to connect it to some embassies and consulates, as in Poznań, and to bring supplies in from the countries it passed through. In a lot of ways, it was less independent than it liked to pretend. Running his finger along the twin tracks of the main Line, Rudi could see dozens of branches curling off, to a depot here, a town there.

And some of them seemed to curl off into nowhere.

At the end of one branch, just before the border between Greater Germany and Poland, was a word he recognised: *Stanhurst*.

Rudi got up and picked up the previous day's decrypts. And there it was. *Stanhurst, a beguiling county town, contains one of the greatest cathedrals in the Community.*

He grabbed the railway timetable and began to page through it, and within a minute there it was. Train times from Paddington to Stanhurst.

Lev looked up from his reading. "What?"

"Pack," Rudi told him. "Pack quickly. We're leaving. It's not a novel. It's a *guidebook*."

IT WAS A guidebook to a country which did not exist.

With what Rudi later described as an act of kneejerk sarcasm, Lev instantly dubbed it *The Baedeker*. For want of any other name, its anonymous author became *Baedeker*.

The Community stretched from the Iberian peninsula to a little east of Moscow, a country of some fifteen million souls back in 1918, when the notebook had been written. It had cities and towns and a railway system, but Rudi didn't recognise any of the names of the towns and cities. It was as if Baedeker had, on a whim, invented a country, and then simply copied it onto Continental Europe. Or rather the Whitton-Whytes and their descendants, not being satisfied with creating their own English county, had simply rewritten Europe and then proceeded, very quietly, to conquer it. However they had achieved it, they had not lacked ambition. According to Baedeker, the Community had a university the size of an English county.

"No," Lev said, already more than a little annoyed at having to move for the fourth time. "No."

"What else could it be?" said Rudi.

"An invisible country? Made up of bits and pieces of other countries? Created by a family of English magicians?" Lev snorted. "It could be *anything* else."

Rudi looked at the piles of decrypts. "There's nothing here about them being magicians," he said. "They talk about landscapes containing *all possible* landscapes. That doesn't sound like magic to me."

"You've obviously had a more interesting life than I have, then," Lev said sourly, pouring himself another drink. He leaned forward and rested his elbows on his knees. "Look at me. No, look at me. Look me in the eyes. Good. Now, say after me, 'landscapes *do not* contain all possible landscapes.'"

He sat back. "You're not going to say it, are you," he muttered sourly, and drained his glass.

Rudi looked at the printout pages, the Baedeker, the railway timetable which said that back in 1912 you could have caught a train from Paddington Station to a nonexistent town somewhere to the west of London, the map of the Line that said you could still get to that same nonexistent town by going up a branch line in Germany. He tried to reassemble it in his head, but the pieces would only go together in one configuration.

This was what Fabio had stolen from the Line's consulate in Poznań. Three proofs of the existence of a parallel universe. And a map showing how to get into it.

The Community was a topological freak, a nation existing in the same place as Europe but only accessible through certain points on the map. Its capital, Władysław, occupied more or less the same space as Prague, but the way Baedecker described it, it sounded more like a mixture of Kraków, Warsaw, Paris and Geneva. Fifteen million people, back when Baedeker wrote his guidebook. How many people were there in the Community by now? What were they all doing?

Was that a secret worth protecting? Worth killing for? Rudi thought it probably was.

ONE NIGHT, WHILE they were eating dinner – something quite inedible involving squid and aubergines and a sauce made from tinned tomatoes – Rudi looked across the room and saw Fabio's burnbox sitting beside the coffee table. It occurred to him that this thing which Fabio had risked his life to safeguard had become so familiar that he hardly saw it now; it was just somewhere he stuffed the documents and decrypts and Lev's computer when they changed hotels. He still set the locks, just in case, though he had no way of knowing if the device even worked after all this time.

"What," Lev said, watching him stand up.

Rudi limped over to the burnbox and upended it over his bed. Pages and notebooks and flashcards cascaded onto the coverlet. "I just wanted to try something."

"Try what?"

Righting the burnbox, he stuffed a printout copy of yesterday's local newspaper inside, closed the lid, spun the combination, swiped the lock twice to arm the device. "I want to see what happens when this thing goes off," he said. Then he twisted the latches and pressed them outward.

What happened was Lev screaming, jumping up from the table, and diving behind the room's monumentally-ugly sofa. A few moments later he bobbed up again, shaking his head.

"Never let it be said that Lev Semyonovitch Laptev ever failed to over-react," said Rudi, who hadn't moved from beside the bed.

"Sometimes," Lev said, attempting to regain his composure without yelling, "a burnbox is designed to destroy its contents *and* the person who is trying to open it."

Rudi looked at the box. "Oh." He put his hand on the side of the briefcase, and, yes, it was warm.

Not hot, but definitely warm, the flash-heat inside leaking through the insulation.

All of which made him think nostalgically of the briefcase he had taken delivery of in Old Potsdam. He'd worried that the act of smuggling it to Berlin might have destroyed it or what was inside, but what if the Package had triggered it before slinging it under the wire? What if it had been cooking its contents the whole time? What if it had contained *maps*?

So why, in their last moments of life, had the Package slung the briefcase through the wire, if it was in the process of destroying its contents? In Rudi's world there was only one reason to do that – to get people running, to make the people who wanted the case back believe it had been delivered. And Bradley had said that the contents had got through, so either he knew the case had destroyed whatever it contained, and had been lying, or he didn't know and had been passing on a lie told to him by his superiors.

He had other things to think about. There was the steady stream of decrypts, page by page building up a picture of the Community of the nineteenth century. There were the more mundane mechanics of getting himself and Lev from hotel to hotel, from island to island.

And yet he couldn't stop thinking about Potsdam, going around and around, picking away at it.

Rudi sat for hours with the printout of the Baedeker, shuffling the pages, waiting for the *movie moment*, the moment when the hero claps his hand to his forehead and cries, *of course!* The moment when all becomes clear.

It didn't happen.

This was a Big Secret, certainly. No doubt about that. Easily worth killing both Fabio and himself. But the geometry of what had happened to him over the past ten years or so eluded him. He was certain that Potsdam fitted into that geometry, somehow, but it was impossible to say precisely *how*.

Taking the Baedeker as his guiding principle, his entire career as a Coureur took on a different aspect. There was one phrase in the book, *The Community has the most jealously guarded borders in Europe*, which altered everything. How many governments, intelligence services, espionage organisations and criminal groups knew about the Community and had tried, over the years, to gain entry? If he had learned anything from his years wandering around Europe, it was that people really hated to find places that they could not go. Thus, safecrackers broke into banks, MI6 officers passed through Checkpoint Charlie, CIA *rezidents* ran networks of stringers in Moscow and Bucharest. Oh yes, they were stealing the company payroll or gathering intelligence on the enemy. But, really, when it came down to it, they were going where others *could not go*. Rudi was aware of the sense of power, the sense of *omnicompetence*, one could derive from something like that

And the Community had defeated them. They had not been able to gain access.

Whoever they were – and he didn't rule out a committee of *apparatchiks* representing Central and every intelligence community in Europe – these were subtle men and women. Rudi thought that much of his time as a Coureur had been devoted to provocations – not to breaking into the Community directly, but to flushing them out like a beater on a grouse moor. Who are they? Where are they? What are they doing? The eternal questions of the intelligence controller.

It was possible that his first live Situation with Fabio had been a legitimate attempt to steal the map of entryways into the Community. Equally, it could have been an operation to flush out a Community operative in Poznań's Line consulate, someone who could then have been identified, arrested, interrogated, turned and fed back into the Community to report back to their new masters. It might have been a success, or it might have been a failure. Or it might genuinely have been Fabio acting on his own initiative. He would never know.

Similarly, the Situation in Potsdam (and perhaps even the one in the Zone, he had always thought there was something not quite *right* about that one) and the death of Leo had something of the stage about them, something with larger objectives than the individual players would ever be able to perceive.

This of course brought him to his present situation. Was he once again part of a provocation? Was he being run against the Community, for reasons he would never know, by people he would never meet?

It was impossible to be sure. He could, of course, elect to do nothing for the moment, and see what happened. He could try to second-guess the situation and pick the least likely course of action, but he would never be certain it wasn't the course of action he was *supposed* to take. He could throw himself into the sea and drown, but there was always the itching suspicion that someone, somewhere, would have taken that possibility into account. Unlike the espionage soaps, where there was always a way to drop a spanner into the works and somehow come out victorious, he was in the hands of planners who had seen every eventuality. They were the students of centuries of expertise, from the couriers of pre-Christian Pharaohs with secret messages tattooed on their scalps, through the agents of Francis Walsingham, through the gentleman adventurers of the Great Game, through MI6 and SOE and OSS and the Okhrana and NKVD and the CIA. They knew their stuff.

This was the basis of his epiphany on that street in London, a sense that it didn't matter *what* he did because he was part of a Plan, a Plan designed to make it seem as though he had complete free will. And he may have been right; he hadn't been arrested. Whoever They were, They wanted him to get away with the money from Smithson's Chambers, and use it for whatever ends he decided.

Oddly enough, this did not bother him as much as it might have. It was oddly liberating, knowing that whatever he did had been planned for. And so he chose to default to himself. Rudi the Coureur. Rudi, who saw a phrase like *the most jealously guarded borders in Europe*, and saw, behind those borders, people who wanted to leave.

"It sounds," he told Lev, "like a challenge."

ONE MORNING RUDI told Lev that he was going away for a couple of days. "I really shouldn't be more than forty-eight hours," he said. "If I'm gone longer than that and you don't hear from me, put everything in the burnbox and activate it. Then get out of here and drop the box in the sea." He handed Lev a slip of paper on which were printed several strings of letters and numbers, encrypted codes for private bank accounts. "Can you memorise these?"

"Are you joking?" Lev snorted. Some of the strings ran to fifty characters.

"Ah well." Rudi smiled. "You probably won't have to use them."

And he was right. For the first few hours, Lev kept coming back to the list of bank codes and wondering why he didn't get out right now, access the accounts, transfer the money, and just keep running. He never did find an answer to that question; instead, he spent the time in the room reading decrypts, eating room service meals and working his way through the minibar, and forty-eight hours after he left, almost to the minute, Rudi was back, smiling and eager to have a look at what the cloth laptop had produced for them while he was gone.

A few days later – and he wasn't fooling anyone, but Lev did appreciate the pretence of tradecraft, it was a nod from one professional to another – Rudi casually said, "I've got something for you," and handed over a passport.

Lev turned the little card over in his fingers. It belonged, according to the Cyrillic on the front, to one Maksim Fedorovich Koniev, a citizen of Novosibirsk, in the Independent Republic of Sibir. His photograph had somehow found its way onto the card, alongside what he presumed was his thumbprint, and the card's embedded chip presumably also contained other biometric data about him. He looked up.

"You don't have to *live* there," Rudi said, a little awkwardly.

"In the summer," Lev informed him, "Sibir can be a most beautiful place."

Rudi held out a shrinkwrapped disc. "There's a legend, too. I left it vague, but there's some documentary stuff in Novosibirsk and Norilsk to support it. You can leave it the way it is or do some backfilling, it's up to you. Take the bank codes; all your money's there."

So this was how it ended. Lev looked at the card again. If his former life had taught him anything, it was that we only ever see a little part of the big picture. A few lines of communication from a codenamed agent here, a list of political targets there, an impenetrable economic dossier elsewhere. What were *their* stories? At least here was a new story, a new life all ready for him to live it. "Thank you," he said, genuinely touched. The money alone would have been enough.

Rudi looked away and shrugged, and Lev thought the boy was actually embarrassed by his gratitude. "What will you do now?" he asked.

Rudi looked at him and grinned. "I'm going to shake the tree and see what falls out."

THE THIRTY CASES
OF MAJOR ZEMAN

1.

THE WAR BEGAN on a Thursday.

Petr always remembered that because Thursday was his turn to deliver the kids to school and pick them up again, and he was sitting in the car waiting outside Tereza's apartment in the morning when his phone rang.

"Boss?" said Jakub. "Put the radio on. There's been an outrage."

Jakub was a good, steady detective, but he was prone to exaggeration on occasion. Petr sighed and switched on the radio and discovered that this was not one of those occasions.

He looked out of the window and saw Tereza coming out of the building's entrance with Eliška and

Tomáš, all bundled up against the weather, schoolbags slung over their shoulders and Big Blue Cat lunchboxes clutched in their little gloved fists. His heart sank.

They crossed the road to the car and Petr lowered the window. "Sorry," he said to Tereza. "Sorry," he said to the children.

"I saw it on the news," she said. "I'll take them to school. Will you be able to collect them?"

"There's no way to tell," he said.

"I have that job interview this afternoon," she said. "You know that. It's been arranged for ages."

"Go to your interview," he told her. "I'll pick them up."

"Or you'll organise someone else to do that." She shook her head. "I'm so tired of this, Petr."

"They'll love it," he said jovially. He looked down at the kids. "How about a ride in a police car with Uncle Jakub this afternoon?" They looked uncertainly pleased.

Tereza snorted. "Uncle Jakub."

He started the engine and put the car in gear. "I'm sorry," he said again, and drove away.

THERE WAS A bar called TikTok, just off Karlovo náměstí in the Old Town, that Petr and the department had been keeping their eyes on for several months. They had some vague intelligence that a Chechen warlord calling himself Abram, having been chased from Bremen by a combination of local police and home-grown brigands, had bought himself a controlling interest in TikTok and was shaping the place to use as a beach-head in Prague.

This was obviously not an optimum outcome for anybody, but hours of surveillance and intelligence gathering had failed to confirm the rumours. Ownership of TikTok was an impossible tangle of blind trusts and offshore funds and tax avoidance schemes so complex that they were practically sentient; if Abram was in there somewhere, he was well hidden. He had also not been observed to visit his supposed new acquisition; nor had any of his known lieutenants. Petr had sent a team into the bar on the onerous mission of becoming regulars, and they reported nothing out of the ordinary, as did the young woman detective who he had sent in to get a job as a waitress. TikTok, to all intents and purposes, was utterly blameless.

"What a fucking mess," said Jakub.

For once, Petr reflected, his sergeant was erring on the side of understatement. The street was full of rubble and shattered glass and wrecked cars. Every shop window was broken, as were most of the apartment windows in the blocks above them. Huge bits of moulding and brickwork had fallen into the street.

The devastation grew worse as one looked down the street, until one's eye was drawn to the centre, the heart of destruction, the smoking pile of collapsed brick and wood and metal which had once housed the bar known as TikTok. It was as if, Petr thought, the bar had explosively vomited its innards into the street and then slumped in on itself and taken everything above and around it down as well.

Both ends of the street were full of detectives and uniformed policemen and firemen and soldiers. Further down, an Army bomb team was still sending robots into the destroyed building to check for further devices. Until they were done there was no way to allow the fire brigade or police anywhere near it and until that happened there was no way to discover just how bad the loss of life was. Preliminary reports said fifteen dead, thirty injured, but Petr knew those figures were going to rise in a hurry. The bomb had gone off just as people were going to work.

"We're presuming it was a bomb," Jakub said.

"Yes," Petr said. "Yes, we're presuming it was a bomb."

Jakub nodded. "ATG are on their way."

Petr sighed. His department's relationship with the Anti-Terrorist Group was fractious at best. "I'm surprised they aren't here already," he said, but it was a poor attempt at a joke. "Did something happen last night?"

Jakub shook his head. "Normal night, according to the boys."

Petr swallowed and asked the question that had been hanging between them ever since he got there. "Milena?"

"She's not answering her phones," Jakub said soberly. "At home or her mobiles. She'd have been starting work about now."

Petr scowled. The bombing was bad enough. Losing the young undercover detective he'd placed in the bar was a catastrophe. "Keep trying her phones," he said. "Has anyone been to her apartment?"

Jakub nodded. "Nobody there."

Petr felt sick. He took a deep breath. "All right. We can't do anything here until the Army have finished sniffing around. I want everybody out shaking snitches. I want to know how this happened without us hearing anything about it, and I want to know who's responsible."

"Yes, boss."

"And could you pick the kids up from school this afternoon?"

Jakub glanced at him, returned to looking at the wreckage of the street. "Yes, boss."

Petr made his way to a lorry parked in a nearby street. The doors of the container on its loadbed were open. Petr went up the steps and stepped inside and looked at the rows of detectives and operatives manning the consoles of the mobile control room. At the far end of the container thirty or so paper flatscreens had been pasted to the wall; they were each showing a different view of the wrecked street.

"Brabec," a voice behind him said.

Petr turned, saw Major Větrovec, his opposite number at Anti-Terrorism, standing in the control room doorway. "Miloš," he said.

"What do we have?" Větrovec was a small, round, bald man in a tight suit

"We're treating it as a bomb until told otherwise," Petr said. "All utilities have been isolated, the street's been closed off. The fire brigade can't get near the seat of the explosion until the Army are sure there are no secondary devices, and we can't go anywhere near it until the fire brigade tell us it's safe to do so."

Větrovec looked at the screens at the end of the control room and shook his head. He turned and called through the open door. "Ismail, see if you can contact the Minister. The lazy bitch should be here anyway."

"Ah, good," Petr said. "You brought Ismail."

"He's my second in command," Větrovec said. "Of course he's here."

"He stays out of my way," Petr warned. The last time he and Větrovec's dead-eyed assassin of a deputy had encountered each other professionally, they had almost wound up having a fist fight in the middle of an apartment where a terror suspect had been arrested.

"As you wish," Větrovec said as if he didn't care much either way. "I understand this bar was of interest to you?"

Petr filled him in quickly on the supposed presence of Abram in Prague, the measures he'd taken to investigate. He thought he saw Větrovec's expression soften when he told him about Milena. Větrovec was an unpleasant little bastard, but he was still a cop, of sorts, and every policeman feels the loss of one of their own.

When he'd finished, Větrovec said, "The building was of interest to us as well."

Petr smiled tightly. "Of course it was."

"Not the bar," Větrovec said, "which is why you were not on the to-know list. One of the apartments on the fifth floor. A group of Saudi students."

"Who were, in all likelihood, completely innocent."

"Who had already met with a Bulgarian mafia group and were in the process of negotiating the purchase of seven kilos of Semtex." Větrovec looked at him. "We're not amateurs, you know."

Petr gestured at the screens. "Is anyone else interested in this place who I haven't been told about? Hm? Immigration? Traffic wardens?" He was aware that he was raising his voice, but he didn't care. "Because if someone had thought to put me on your 'to-know' list I wouldn't have sent one of my detectives in there undercover!"

"Brabec," Větrovec murmured, looking around the control room at the officers who were all trying very hard not to stare at Petr. "Calm down."

"You killed her," Petr said in a dangerous voice, poking Větrovec in the chest with a forefinger. "Just as surely as if you'd blown her up yourself. Because you couldn't be bothered to share what you were doing."

"I didn't order her to go in there," Větrovec said reasonably.

Petr snarled and pushed past the ATG man and stumbled down the steps and away from the truck, chest heaving. He leaned against a wall and tried to get his breath, tried to remain in control.

His phone rang. He took it out, looked at it, put it to his ear. "Can't you deal with it?"

"I don't know, boss," said Jakub. "But you'll want to see this."

"WHO ARE THEY?"

"We don't know, boss," said Jakub. "Cleaner found them four hours ago. We'd have got the shout, but what with the..."

"We've been busy." Petr sighed. "Yes."

They were standing in a smartly-appointed apartment in Pankrác, not far from the prison. The apartment was in one of the two new blocks which the city had grudgingly, after many many years' discussion about their impact on the skyline, finally given permission for. They had filled up with young professionals – graphic designers, IT entrepreneurs, media people. Several soap opera actors lived in this block, Petr knew.

Neither of the people lying side by side in the apartment's living room was a soap opera actor. At least, he didn't recall seeing them on television. A man and a woman, they were in their middle thirties, their clothes nondescript but a little old-fashioned. Both had had their throats cut. The floor and the furniture and the walls were awash with blood.

"There hasn't been a full search yet, but so far, no ID," Jakub said. "None of the neighbours knows who they were – although one of them thinks they might have been English."

Petr groaned inwardly at the thought of having to deal with the English Embassy. "Go on."

"Well, the *really* interesting stuff's in here," Jakub said, leading the way to a small bedroom off a hallway at the rear of the apartment. "Uniformed officer who responded to the call made sure life was extinct and then went to secure the apartment, but he says he thought he heard someone moving around in here. Turns out he was imagining things – you know how jumpy you can get at a scene like this – but he took a look, and, well..."

The bedroom had been converted into a small workroom by dismantling the bed and stacking the frame and mattress against one wall. In the middle of the floor stood a couple of small trestle tables, and on the tables were boxes and tools and rolls of wire. Without touching it, Petr looked into one of the boxes. "Are these detonators?" he said.

"Yes, boss. And those bigger boxes, that's C4."

Petr straightened up and looked around the room. "A lot of these C4 boxes appear to be empty."

"Yes, boss."

They returned to the main room and stood looking at the bodies. "Oh, there was one last thing," said Jakub. He held up a little plastic evidence bag containing a cheap cigarette lighter. Printed on the side of the lighter were the words 'TikTok.'

"That's just too easy," Petr said.

"Yes, boss."

"That sort of thing only ever happens in films."

"I know, boss."

Petr sighed. "All right. When scenes-of-crime have finished and the bodies have been taken away, search this place properly for ID and anything else that looks interesting. Then, and *only then*, notify ATG."

Jakub sucked his teeth. "They won't like that."

"They can sue me."

"They probably will," Jakub noted.

PRAGUE HAD, IN general, an enviably low crime rate. Pickpocketing had been a cottage industry for decades and there were always muggings and other forms of low-level trouble in and around Sherwood, the park around the railway station, but mostly the old city had escaped the wave of crime which had engulfed other European capitals.

Following the TikTok bombing, however, a wave of murders swept the city. Organised crime figures were assassinated in their cars and in their homes. Several drug pushers were found crucified against trees in Sherwood. The Government began to take notice, which was never a good sign in Petr's world.

Two Scotland Yard detectives flew in to look at the bodies from Pankrác, failed to identify them, consented to being treated to a slap-up meal at a restaurant in the Old Town for their trouble, and flew out again without once mentioning why the job could not have been done just as easily by someone from the Embassy security staff. Petr drove them to the airport himself, watched them go through the security checks, waved bye-bye, and thought about that.

A Colonel from the Gangs Taskforce met with the heads of all of Prague's organised crime groups – this entirely off the record and as far as possible from the Press and some of the less-understanding members of Parliament – and reported back that they were as in the dark as anyone else. They all blamed each other for the killings, but when pressed could not give a single good reason why they should have taken place.

"I told them to stop, and they just shrugged their shoulders," the Colonel told Petr over a drink. "This is a territorial thing, plain and simple. You mark my words. They just won't admit it."

Except for those two bodies with their throats cut. That whole business had disappeared into the pockets of an angry Major Větrovec, but in Petr's mind's eye they stood out from all the other killings. Somehow those two murders, that room full of plastic explosive, made sense of everything else. Except they didn't.

The Press took up the story of the gang war, questions were asked in Parliament, and one day

Petr found himself sitting in the Minister's office, feeling small and overdressed in his one good suit. The Minister, a florid woman who favoured grey trouser suits and red shirts, kept him waiting while she read through something on her desktop.

"Your officers call you 'Major Zeman,'" she said without looking at him.

Petr sighed. Major Zeman had been the lead character of an infamous long-running Communist-era television series, a propaganda exercise more than anything else.

"A joke, Minister," he explained. "The star and I share a surname."

The Minister looked at him.

"Squadroom humour," he added.

The Minister said, "This is no laughing matter, Major."

"No, Minister," he agreed. "It is not."

She consulted her desktop again. "Thirty-seven fatalities. Not including the TikTok bombing. Not a laughing matter at all."

"Has someone complained that we were treating it as such?" he asked.

Another level stare. The Minister said, "The Press seems to think that the Prague police force is incompetent. Those criticisms tend to arrive on my desk, Major, not yours, and the President and Prime Minister expect me to answer to them."

"Yes, Minister."

"The Gangs Taskforce appear to believe this will burn itself out eventually."

"Do they?"

"They have something they call..." she checked

her desktop once again "...*dynamic modelling*. Are you familiar with it?"

Petr shook his head.

"Computer software," she said. "From the United States. It constructs a model of the relationships between groups. Any kind of group. Model train enthusiasts, football supporters, the fans of the latest teen pop singer, criminal gangs. It's supposed to predict the dynamics between those groups, locate periods of stability and chaos. What do you think of that?"

"I think it would probably have been more cost-effective to examine the entrails of a chicken, Minister."

A smile quirked her lips. "Dynamic modelling says that these killings will run their course and stability will return."

"Eventually we'll run out of criminals," Petr said. "Then stability will certainly return."

The Minister sighed. "Meanwhile, the latest round of budget cuts mean savings will have to be made across the board." She left unsaid the obvious, that departments which showed results would need to make the fewest savings. She took a single photo printout from a folder on her desk and showed it to him. "Do you recognise this man?"

The picture was a blurred blow-up, the face of a youngish man in half-profile. He had an ordinary-looking face, shortish brownish hair. An *ish* sort of a man, completely unremarkable. Petr shook his head.

"We believe this man is involved in the gang war somehow," the Minister said.

"Oh?" Petr stopped himself asking who *We* were. "He's been in the country several weeks now."

"This is new intelligence to me, Minster," Petr said. "May I have that photograph?"

"No." The Minister put the print back into its folder, put the folder in a desk drawer, and locked the drawer. Petr watched each of these steps with interest, wondering what exactly he was being told here. "I know you and your detectives – the whole force – are doing your best, but these killings have to stop, Major. We can't wait to see if this *dynamic modelling* is accurate or not. They have to stop now."

"I won't insult your intelligence by telling you that my officers are working as hard as they can," Petr said.

"And I won't insult yours by telling you that it's not good enough." The Minister busied herself with her desktop again. "Keep me informed, Major."

And that seemed to be the end of the interview. Petr stood. "Of course, Minister."

AND OF COURSE the pep-talk, if that's what it was, had no effect at all. The killings continued. Cars were bombed, relatives kidnapped, shops ransacked, and nothing the police did could stop it. All leave was cancelled, Army Intelligence – to the displeasure of the police – was called in. Nothing availed.

"Look on the bright side," said Jakub, "sooner or later there'll be no one left and we can live in peace."

"I told the Minister something similar," Petr said.

"How did she take that?"

"I thought she appreciated the joke."

They were sitting in a booth at The Opera, a bar whose one saving grace was that no other policemen ever used it. Jakub drank some of his beer and chuckled. He said, "There's one good–" and then the air was full of smoke and burning and Petr found he was sitting against a wall some distance from the booth and something was dripping into his eyes. He wiped it away and looked at his fingers and saw that they were slick with blood.

He looked across the bar and for a moment his brain refused to fit the images together. The interior of the Opera seemed to have shaken itself to pieces, and limping towards him through the destruction was a young man with a walking stick. He limped right up to where Petr was sitting, leaned down, and offered his hand.

"Come with me, if you want to live," he said.

"I'VE ALWAYS WANTED to say that," the young man said. "Also 'Follow that car' and 'I'm getting too old for this shit.'"

They were in an alleyway around the corner from the Opera, Petr with one arm slung over the young man's shoulders, his knees still sagging. He said, "I know you."

"You really don't," said the young man. "But I'm afraid I am the author of all your woes, Major."

"The Minister showed me a photograph of you."

The young man looked towards the mouth of the alley. Police cars and fire engines and ambulances were howling past towards the bombed-out bar. "Your Minister? The Police Minister?"

"Yes."

"What did she say about me?"

"That you'd been here a while and that you were involved in the war."

"Well, those two things are true enough. How are you feeling?"

Petr stood up straight. "Better. Where's Jakub?"

"Your colleague? He didn't make it."

Petr took a deep breath and sighed. He put his hand in his pocket, brought it out holding a pair of handcuffs, and in one move snapped one bracelet to the young man's wrist and the other to his own. "You're under arrest."

The young man looked at the handcuff on his wrist. "And you are an ungrateful bastard, Major. That little bomb back there – and it *was* a little bomb, otherwise nobody would have got out of there alive – was meant to up the ante, make things personal between the police and organised crime. It was a provocation. And I saved your life."

"You have a minute," Petr said. "Talk quickly."

"It's going to take more than a minute," the young man said. "And it's easier if I show you."

THEY WENT TO the end of the alleyway and down a connecting alley, and down another, and another, and across a street Petr didn't recognise, and down another alleyway, and all the time the young man – who called himself 'Rudi' – was talking and talking and talking. Talking about Coureurs, heads in lockers, maps, parallel worlds. And suddenly Petr had no idea where they were and all the shops looked strange and the people they saw were dressed a little oddly, a little old-fashioned, and all the shop signs were in English and they emerged from one last alleyway into a magnificent town square, all lit up and cobbled and full of promenading men and women and Petr, who had lived in Prague all his life, had never seen it before.

"We'd better not go out there," Rudi said. "We'll stick out like sore thumbs. I know somewhere we can go."

"What...?" Petr managed to say.

"Welcome to Władysław, Major," Rudi said. "And you'd better take these handcuffs off. You'll never find your way back without me, and I'm not going anywhere chained to you."

A SHORT DISTANCE from the square, Rudi knocked on the door of a handsome-looking townhouse. The knock was answered by a tall, elderly gentleman who glanced from Rudi to Petr and back a couple of times before letting them in.

"I hope you don't mind if I don't tell you this gentleman's real name," Rudi said as they made their way down a hallway. "You can call him 'John', if you want. John will have a quick look at you, clean you up."

'John' was some kind of physician, it seemed. One of the rooms on the first floor of the house was done out as a surgery. Petr sat on the examining table and let John clean and dress his wounds while Rudi kept on talking.

"Prague is the only city in Europe with paths that lead directly to the Community," he said. "I don't know why. It seemed to me, though, that existing so closely together there must have been some kind of *accommodation* between the two cities. I needed to see what that was, see how things fitted together here and in Prague."

"So you started a war?"

"There's a lot of distrust on both sides, it seems. I just gave it a nudge. Learned all kinds of useful things. What you told me about the Police Minister, for instance. That's very interesting."

"She's involved?"

"Maybe not. Maybe someone just gave her the photo and told her to show it to various interested parties. But it implies someone quite high up in Prague *is* involved." His leg was obviously giving him discomfort. He shifted in his chair while John pressed a cotton wool ball soaked in some alcohol solution against Petr's head wound. "Anyway, while everyone's attention has been wandering, I've been popping here and there, chatting to people. There's quite a useful little dissident movement here. They've let me have some very nice maps, which will come in handy."

"Who bombed TikTok?"

Rudi looked thoughtful. "The bar? The big bomb? Oh, that was them." He nodded towards the street. "Community Intelligence." He snorted. "Intelligence. They bombed the wrong bar. They were supposed to attack a bar in the next street owned by some shady Czech character. I don't know why, exactly."

"And the couple in Pankrác?"

Rudi nodded. "They planted the bomb. And were then killed – you're going to enjoy this – by colleagues of the young Arab men who were living over the bar when they blew it up." He looked thoughtful. "I suppose this means the Community is now part of GWOT. That's going to make things interesting."

"None of this helps me," Petr said.

"No," Rudi admitted. "And what I'm going to ask you to do next is not going to help you, either."

2.

IT WAS MARCH and she was thinking about taking a holiday. March was when the snow started to get patchy and rotten but it was still too cold to hike or sunbathe unless you were of a sturdy constitution. Of course, espionage was no respecter of the seasons, but early spring seemed to be the time of year when Europe's many intelligence services declared, if not a truce on the scale of the British and Germans playing football in No Man's Land during World War I, at least an informal relaxation of activities. In all her years in counterespionage, nobody had ever made trouble for her in the spring, and she had a good capable team working for her in case anything did start while she was away. Once upon a time she had stayed at her post all year round, obsessed with the thought that the moment she left something terrible would erupt. But these days she had learned to let go a little. She could spare a few days with her feet up somewhere.

That just left the decision of where to go, what to do, so she'd spent the past couple of days surfing the internet looking for something interesting. She was currently quite taken with the idea of a paragliding holiday in Wales.

Her phone rang. She said, "Yes?"

"I just had a call from Immigration," said Pavel. "They had a flag go up."

She frowned and gestured back from the paragliding site to her desktop, where flag alerts usually popped up as little red Gremlins. "I don't see anything."

"It's an old flag, from before the last system update. Immigration had it on their database but it didn't get copied over when we upgraded."

She sighed. "What's the name?"

"Tonu Laara," said Pavel. "Estonian national."

She looked through the window on the other side of her office. Beyond the glass a wall of trees dropped obliquely into a mountain valley.

She looked at the view for so long that Pavel said, "Chief?"

She blinked. "Where is he?"

"He booked into the hotel at Pustevny." He added, "The flag was tagged 'observe, do not detain,' so Immigration observed him and didn't bother to let us know until now. He's been here two days."

Yes, well. She was long overdue for a quiet chat with Major Menzel, the head of the Immigration Service. But not today. "Do we have anyone up there right now?" she asked.

"Rikki and Colin."

She rubbed her eyes. "All right. Tell them to stay in contact but not to approach. I'll go up there."

"Yes, Chief."

"And Pavel?"

"Yes, Chief?"

"It's pronounced *Tonu*," she said, getting reluctantly to her feet and bidding a silent farewell to her holiday.

HE WAS SITTING in the hotel's bar, nursing a beer and smoking a small cigar. He looked thinner than she remembered, a little more careworn. There was grey in his hair and a walking cane propped against the chair beside him, but he still looked ridiculously young. She walked right over to his table and sat down opposite him. And then they sat looking at each other. There is a peculiar intimacy between two people who have made love and then parted, only to be reunited many years later. Particularly if they spent the whole of their time together lying to each other.

"Short hair suits you," Rudi said finally.

"And you're doing *what* here, exactly?" she asked in what she hoped was a firm but not unkind tone of voice.

"Do you want a drink?" he asked.

"No thank you."

"I have a story to tell you," he said. "But first I want to claim political asylum."

She watched him without saying anything.

"And then," he said, picking up his beer, "I want to talk to the Hungarians."

THE HUNGARIANS ARRIVED on Friday, five huge men in beautifully-designed casualwear driving up in a

Peugeot hybrid 4X4 that looked as though it could tow ships up and down the Panama Canal all day. Discreet surveillance established that they were not carrying weapons beyond the odd Swiss Army knife. They checked into the hotel and headed immediately for the restaurant.

She had packed the place with her own people two hours before the meeting, but some bona fide guests had still wandered in and ordered meals, including a young black man she remembered seeing in the bar on the day Rudi made his reappearance. She walked over and sat down at his table.

"You know," she said in her sexiest voice, "I think you're really *hot*."

He looked up from his menu and said, "Excuse me, miss?" in English.

"Oh, I *love* the English," she said in English. She batted her eyelashes at him.

He sighed and laid his menu down. "Very good, miss," he said. "And I've spotted your people too. Although it would be fairer to say that I've spotted the people who *aren't* your people."

She saw Rudi coming into the restaurant. "Come on," she said. "You may as well sit in and listen to what the adults are talking about."

If Rudi was surprised to see her coming across the restaurant with Seth, he made no sign. They all sat down at the Hungarians' table and then everyone just looked at each other.

"So," said Rudi. "I have a proposition."

The leader, the one who had called himself Kerenyi, looked at him. "You've been through the mill. It shows on your face."

"I've had some interesting times."

"And not all in the kitchen."

"No. Very few of them in the kitchen. I'm going to tell you a story now and I'd prefer it if you saved any questions, comments and jokes until I'm finished. Okay?"

Kerenyi nodded.

And so Rudi told the story again, of a family of English mapmakers and a parallel Europe where dissidence was subtly and totally suppressed and nobody could leave.

"Coureur Central seems to have mixed views about the whole business," Rudi said. "On the one hand, they would *love* to get into the Community because it has no borders. You can walk from one end of it to the other and never see a border post or a customs man. Which makes it very handy. You could take a Package into the Community just outside Madrid, say, transport it all the way across Europe, and pop out again in, say, Helsinki, and nobody here would be any the wiser. Seth and I were smuggled across the border into Scotland like that. At least one dissident found her way out of the Community and set up her own little Coureur operation there.

"On the other hand, Central doesn't want anyone *else* knowing how to do it, and they're willing to kill to stop the secret getting out. And so, it seems, is everyone else who wants to know how to do it. The Line seems to be mixed up in all this somewhere, I'm not sure how yet. And in the background the Community is doing everything it can to keep its borders secure." He looked around the table. "I have some evidence that they may have been responsible for the Xian Flu."

"This is all bullshit," Kerenyi said amiably. "You had a knock on the head or something."

"They have a university. A very, very big university. It's been doing a *lot* of biological research. Some years ago their intelligence service got very worried about... something. I think maybe it was the construction of the Line, maybe they were worried they couldn't negotiate with the Line Company or something, I don't know. And whoever runs the Community sanctioned the use of biological weapons against us to stop it. That's what I'm told, anyway. And that's murder on a completely unimaginable scale, right there. Someone needs to shake these people up."

Everybody looked at everybody else. Finally Kerenyi said, "What do you want us for?"

"I'm short of manpower. I need help. I've got Seth here, and someone on the Prague police force I've managed to talk into helping, and I think our friend from the Zone might be minded to join in."

"I'm still thinking about it," she said.

He smiled. "But for what I have in mind I need more warm bodies, more backup."

Kerenyi thought about it. "What's in it for us?"

"A hundred thousand Swiss for you and each of your men, for as long as I need you," said Rudi. "And another hundred thousand for artificing."

Kerenyi betrayed no surprise. "You going to war?"

"Could be," said Rudi.

Kerenyi thought about it. "Before I answer, I have two questions."

"Sure."

"Why us?"

Rudi smiled. "Because nobody in their right minds will be expecting it. What was your other question?"

Kerenyi grinned hugely. "What do you have in mind?"

WASHING
THE BEAR

1.

Paweł woke before dawn and lay, as was his habit, in bed for several minutes, listening. He heard, far away in the depths of the forest, the snorting of a bison calling to its mate, and closer to a snuffling, sniffing noise he recognised as the old wild boar sow he had named Elżbieta, after his late wife. These were all familiar sounds, reassuring him that all was well, that it was safe to get out of bed and get on with the day.

He dressed slowly, muscles and joints stiff with the night's cold. His idiot son who lived in Berlin had sent him an electric blanket last Christmas when, as usual, he had been too busy to come himself. He had forgotten that Paweł's house had no electricity, which Paweł thought remarkable seeing as the boy had grown up there. Still, he thought cities could do that to a person. Cities made you stupid. His own father had told him that; his father's grandfather had told *him*.

Paweł slept in a pair of thermal long-johns; Damarts, sent from England by his whore of a daughter. If either of his children had had the faintest scrap of sense they would have sent a generator or one of those fancy American fuel cells Nowak had told him about. An electric blanket and thermal underwear. Amazing.

Over the thermals, Paweł pulled on a pair of quilted trousers and a thick sweater. He dragged on his boots and shuffled through into the kitchen, his breath misting faintly from his lips.

The kitchen had an astonishing smell which Paweł had stopped noticing when he was around a year old. It came from the haunches of bison meat hanging from just below the low ceiling, from the hundreds of strings of dried wild mushrooms, from thick sweat-sodden socks hung to dry beside the two-ring burner, from decades of coffee and kasza and wet woollen clothing and candles of home-made tallow and at least a dozen dogs worn out one by one over the years.

His present dog was a huge white brute, a mountain-dog from the South. He had named it Halina, after his second wife, with whom it shared some personality traits.

As he came in from the bedroom, the dog stirred in its nest of rags and ancient newspapers in the corner. It weighed almost as much as he did, and its coat was matted and filthy; it lifted its massive head and watched him with lunatic eyes.

"Not yet, you bastard," Paweł muttered, taking a crusted saucepan from the kitchen table and tossing it at the dog. "Wait, damn you."

The dog snapped its head forward with unlikely speed and caught the pan's handle in its mouth as it spun by. It dropped the pan and investigated it with a disgusting red tongue.

"Bastard," Paweł said, and pulled open the front door. The door was as warped, as Nowak liked to point out every time he came to call, as a politician, and Paweł had to put his back into the task of dragging it open. As he did so, he detected several new aches.

The privy stood fifty metres away, by the edge of the forest. Its door had rotted off years before; he pulled down his trousers, opened the trapdoor in his thermals, and sat, looking back towards the house.

The little house still looked like the fairytale hunting lodge it had been built to resemble, back in the early years of the last century when Dukes and Princes had come here to hunt the żubr and the elk and the wild boar. It was still solid, though the years had not been kind to the fabric. All the windows on the upper storey were broken; most of those on the ground floor were broken too, and had been filled in with planking that had gone silver with the years. The verandah along the front – admittedly a later addition – was rotten and unsafe and piled with rubbish. It was... well, he couldn't remember exactly *when* smoke had last emerged from the chimney; it seemed that all his life bottled gas had been preferable, and now the chimney must be choked solid with old birds' nests and muck.

He had been meaning, these past four or five years, to reopen the upper storey. He had no use for the rooms up there, particularly, since the tourist trade dried up, but he thought that perhaps some of the hunters of years gone by might have left something valuable behind, and since his imbecile children couldn't be bothered to help him out it might be time to go up the stairs and see if he could find something to sell in the village.

His bowels, like everything else, had slowed to a crawl over the years, but he didn't mind that. Sometimes he sat here for an hour or more, looking at the house and thinking. The view never changed; there was just the view of the house. Sometimes he planned what he would do with the house; sometimes he thought about cutting back another metre or so of new growth around the clearing in which it stood. He rarely acted on these meditations, but he found them calming, and they took his mind off the increasingly wayward nature of his digestive system.

This morning, for example, he considered cleaning the chimney. The living room – into which he had not ventured for three years or so – had a hearth nearly three metres across, implanted with intricate and antique ironwork and still piled with ancient ashes. He knew the chimney was a job that was beyond him, and he had no money to pay for the work, but it soothed him to think about doing it, and now he did think about it he might be able to sell the antique grate somewhere, if he ever got around to prising it out of the fireplace.

Finishing, finally, he wiped himself with a torn sheet from an old copy of *Gazeta Wyborcza*, pulled up his lower garments, and stepped out of the privy.

The house was entirely surrounded by the forest. Beyond the privy marched endless dark avenues of oak and fir, spruce and beech and alder, populated by żubr and elk and the Tarpan and beaver and wild boar. The last dark corner of Europe, Nowak called it. It straddled the border between Poland and Lithuania, but it had shifted with the demands of history ever since the concept of frontiers had come into being. It had been Polish, Lithuanian, German, Russian. Secrets had been buried here, and the lawless post-Communist years, both in Poland and across the border, had brought countless bodies to the soil under the trees. Paweł had seen it all, and very little of it had impressed him.

Back in the kitchen, he lit the two burners and set a pan of water over one. Over the other he put his frying pan and let the solidified fat melt. When it was spitting, he cut some slices from a haunch of elk venison and put them in to fry. The dog Halina stirred and raised its head; thick cords of saliva dripped from its jowls as it smelled the cooking meat.

The water was boiling; Paweł spooned ground coffee into a metal jug and a plastic bowl, and poured water into both. He let them brew; Halina was a caffeine addict and was more than usually unbearable if its coffee wasn't strong enough.

By the time the venison was cooked, the coffee was ready. He put the dog's bowl down on the floor and the evil creature slurped at it. He poured his own coffee from the jug into a cracked ceramic mug advertising Vienna's Tiergarten – another Christmas gift from his son the idiot – and stood eating the meat from the frying pan. He dropped a few scraps on the floor to satisfy the dog.

"What day is it, bastard?" he asked as he slurped coffee. The dog, as usual, had no sensible answer, only thick wet chewing sounds as it breakfasted. "I think it's a day to go into the village."

At the word 'village,' the dog stopped chewing and raised its head. When he was young, Paweł had attended school with a boy named Stanisław. Stanisław had liked to amuse himself by trapping insects and pulling off their wings and legs. He kept his crippled victims, as long as their tiny lives persisted, in a little cardboard box, and liked to show them to the girls.

Later, Stanisław had graduated to small animals, trapping and mutilating dogs and cats. By then, he had abandoned all attempts to impress the girls. Later still, the girls themselves had become his subjects. He had killed fifteen before he was arrested. Paweł had seen his eyes at the trial, and occasionally he saw something of Stanisław in Halina's eyes.

It amazed him that the dog recognised the word 'village' and showed such interest. He had never taken it to the village; he didn't dare, in case it decided to start chewing on a child. He shook his head and threw a dirty plate in the dog's direction. The dog ignored it and continued to stare at him.

"I can't take you, you bastard," Paweł told the dog angrily. "Stupid useless creature."

Halina watched him a moment longer, then seemed to perform a slight shrug and went back to its coffee, as if it had completely forgotten he was there.

* * *

PAWEŁ FOUND THAT he had forgotten quite how long it was since he had last visited the village. He thought it might have been in the late spring or early summer. On the other hand, he thought it could have been even earlier.

Whatever. Going to the shed, he found that his bicycle was almost useless. Both tyres were flat and there was rust on almost every metal surface. He couldn't remember the chain breaking, but there it was, hanging uselessly. He stood, hands in the pockets of his thick jacket, staring up at the machine hanging from the ceiling of the shed. He stood there quite a long time, trying and failing to remember when he had last used the bike. Clearly it was a while.

Never mind. He went back to the caretaker's cottage and found a stout pair of hiking boots, only faintly ghosted with mildew, under a pile of clothes. He laced them up and put on a coat and slung a rucksack over one shoulder and set off down the path that led to the track that led to the road that led to the village.

The village had about seventy inhabitants. It boasted a bar, a shop, and a garage, all of them run by the same man, and a post office run by a wan, nervous woman who had either come here or been banished here from Warsaw twenty years before. Paweł always expected her to leave, so he had never bothered to learn her name, but year after year, there she was, patiently collecting his post and waiting for him to come into the village for it.

"And how are we today, Mr Pawluk?" she prattled as he examined the pile of envelopes, parcels and packages which had accumulated at the back of the post office since he last came into the village – and he was beginning to think it had been a *very* long time since he was here last.

"*We?*" he muttered. "*We?* I'm fine, I have no idea about *you*. Nowak been about?"

"I saw Mr Nowak not ten minutes before you arrived," said the woman. "Going into the, er..." She nodded at the bar.

"Here, put this in a bag," he told her, thrusting an armful of his post at her. "I'll be back for it later." And he thumped down the steps of the post office and across the road and into the bar.

Inside, Nowak was sitting at a table, looking at a bottle of Wyborowa and two glasses. "Heard you were about," he said. "Drink?"

Paweł pulled up a chair and sat and watched Nowak fill the two glasses with vodka. They drained their glasses in silence, and Nowak refilled them.

"So," he said, taking an envelope from his jacket pocket, "a writer."

"A writer." Paweł took the envelope, inspected its contents, removed the money and pocketed it.

"He's booked the Lodge for six weeks," Nowak went on. "Says he needs the privacy or something to finish his latest novel, fuck him."

"Fuck him," Pawl agreed, and they both drained their glasses again, and once again Nowak refilled them.

"He's paying full price though," Nowak said. "The whole Lodge, not just the ground floor."

"When does he arrive?" Paweł was not a lazy man,

but he could foresee some busy days ahead getting the place tidied up. It had been a while since he had done any cleaning at all in the Lodge.

"Friday."

"What's today? Monday?"

"Wednesday."

"Fuck." Paweł emptied his glass again.

"He says he doesn't want any special treatment," said Nowak. "Says he'll cook for himself." And the two men had a laugh about that because the last person who had said they could cook for themselves at the Lodge had almost burned the place down.

Paweł was looking at the rental documents from the envelope – Nowak's business renting out the Lodge was far too ramshackle to include ereaders and tablets and palmtops. "Don't recognise the name," he said.

"Writers," Nowak said. "Fuck 'em."

"Fuck 'em," Paweł agreed, and they drank again. Paweł stood up and fastened his coat. "Better get the place ready for him, then."

Nowak poured himself another drink. "Better had."

Outside, Paweł drew himself up straight and marched across the street to the post office, where he barked orders at the woman behind the counter until she handed over his bag of post. Then he headed back into the woods, weaving only very slightly.

2.

THE TOURIST WAS very young. He had a beard, and a limp, and he affected the look of someone who had

had a hard life, but Paweł, who *had* had a hard life, knew the difference. This tourist, this *writer*, was just a boy.

He arrived early in the morning, while Paweł was sitting in the privy. He heard the sound of boots crunching twigs and leaf-litter underfoot, and when he buttoned himself up and went outside there was the boy, dressed in jeans and a black padded ski-jacket, a big olive-green canvas kitbag slung over one shoulder, leaning on a walking cane and grinning.

"Hey," said Paweł, walking towards him. "This is private property."

"I know," said the boy, smiling and holding out a hand to shake. "For the next few weeks it's *my* private property."

Paweł didn't shake hands. He thought it was a habit for city people who didn't trust each other not to be carrying weapons.

If this bothered the boy in the slightest he gave no sign. He kept smiling and stuck his hand back in his pocket and gestured with his cane at the lodge. "It's in pretty good shape," he commented.

"How did you hurt your leg?" Paweł asked.

The boy looked down at his leg, then at Paweł, and he grinned. "You know, you're one of the very few people who's ever asked me. Most folk assume I won't want to talk about it. I had a ballooning accident."

Paweł raised an eyebrow. "Ballooning."

"Slight miscalculation in weight-to-lift ratios." He leaned forward conspiratorially. "To be honest with you, I'm getting too old for all that stuff."

Paweł shrugged.

"That's when I started writing, anyway," the boy went on, starting to walk around the Lodge with Paweł in tow. "While I was in hospital." He turned and winked at Paweł. "Word to the wise, Mr Pawluk. Anyone who tells you those bone-knitting devices don't hurt? They're a liar. Here, have a watch." And he cheerfully produced from his pocket a complicated plastic box-thing containing one of the ugliest watches Paweł had ever seen, a chunky garish thing with a fat plastic bracelet.

"Go on, try it on," the boy urged, and Paweł put it on, and the boy smiled. "There," he said in a satisfied voice. "Don't take it off, though. Good luck charm."

So Paweł wore the watch during the days and weeks of the boy's occupancy of the Lodge. He hated it and was determined to sell it the moment the boy left, but he made sure the boy knew he was wearing it.

Not that he saw much of him. Sometimes he saw the boy out for walks in the woods near the Lodge, but mostly he stayed indoors – writing, Paweł presumed. Once or twice he walked past one of the unboarded windows of the Lodge on his way to do some chore or other, and he caught sight of the boy inside, using one of those computers where you typed in the air instead of on a keyboard and your arms got sore after fifteen minutes. There seemed to be quite a lot of computer equipment in the room with the boy, actually. Lots of things with screens and lights and cables. A lot more than Paweł remembered him bringing with him.

On the other hand, Paweł told himself as he got ready for bed one night, they'd had guests who were much, much worse. He remembered a party of Belgian businessmen who... well, it had put him off ever visiting Belgium. And then the six Maltese who never said a word to him, and possibly even to each other. They were spooky beyond belief.

He was too old, too slow. As he tried to turn a pair of strong, beefy arms wrapped around his waist and lifted him off his feet, waltzed him around until he was facing in the opposite direction, then a shadow lunged out of nowhere and stuck a length of gaffer tape over his mouth and before he had time to do anything about it a huge hand had grabbed both his wrists, pinning them together while someone else wrapped more gaffer tape around them. Three. Were there three of them? Or only two? It couldn't be just one person; there were too many hands. He hadn't even had time to try to shout.

Two. There were at least two. One carried his upper body; the other one held his feet immobile, and in this way he was carried through the cottage, past the body of Halina, lying on the kitchen floor with her throat cut, and out into the moonlight.

Where the boy was already kneeling, his clothes torn and his face bloody, hands clasped behind his head. Paweł was dumped beside him, forced to his knees, and he felt the cold muzzle of a weapon brush the back of his neck. "Teach you to steal from *us*," said a voice behind him.

The boy said something in a language Paweł did not recognise, and all of a sudden the clearing seemed to be full of bees and hot, sticky rain and the sounds of large things falling to the ground, and when it was over and he opened his eyes he saw five large black-clad men lying around the clearing, apparently chewed to death by something with millions of tiny teeth.

The boy turned to look at him, covered in blood, and unbelievably he was smiling. "You okay?" he asked cheerfully.

Paweł wiped blood off his own face and nodded mutely.

"Good." The boy got to his feet and helped Paweł up, removed the tape around his wrists, and looked around the clearing. The wall of the Lodge nearest to them looked as if someone had attacked it with a huge cheese grater. "Better reload, just in case." He limped up the steps into the Lodge, came back a few moments later with an aluminium stepladder and a couple of towels. He tossed one of the towels to Paweł, carried the ladder over to a tree at the edge of the clearing, and climbed awkwardly up as Paweł wiped gore off himself.

"Magic," said the boy, reaching up into the branches of the tree to pluck something... invisible... "Magic guns."

The sentry guns were matt spheres the size of grapefruit, and until the boy started to take them down from the trees they were completely invisible. Where his fingers touched them, irregular patches of mottled flesh-pink spread until, by the time he had finished reloading and resetting them, they were the colour of his hands.

There were more than forty of them, spread in a ragged ring around the Lodge, and the boy visited them all. As he replaced each one it began to disappear again, taking on the colours of its surroundings.

"I'm glad you wore your watch," he told Paweł as he replaced the final device. "The guns are programmed to fire on my command at anyone who isn't wearing one, but you could still have caught a couple of rounds if you hadn't stayed still."

Paweł said nothing.

The boy led the way back to the Lodge. In the dining room every piece of computer equipment had been smashed beyond repair. The boy stood in the doorway looking at it all.

"You'd better go," Paweł told him. "Those five will have friends. They'll be looking for you."

The boy shook his head. "I'm not worried about that."

"Well, don't you think you ought to be?"

"They're just hired muscle. I'll be long gone before any backup arrives." He sighed. "On the other hand, you're right. Their friends will want revenge, just to save face. You should go, too."

"Me?" Paweł laughed. "I'm not going anywhere."

The boy tipped his head to one side.

"There's most of an SS rifle division out there," Paweł told him, gesturing beyond the windows to the forest. "Came here in 1942 looking for Jewish resistance fighters. Only three of them ever came out, and my father said they were all insane. No one ever found the bodies. You think I'm afraid of the *mafia*?"

The boy smiled. "I'll leave you the guns, just in case." He looked around the room. "You can have all the other stuff as well. Even the broken things can be sold for spares."

"They said you'd stolen something from them."

"Not true. I found something that someone else wanted. I'm going to do something with it. They hired the mafia to stop me. Or maybe not. Maybe it was someone else. I'm still filling in the blanks."

"Who is this 'they'?"

"Well, that's the thing. I don't know for certain. There are a number of possibilities. Lots of people, apparently. And possibly some people are in the background, helping me. I don't know." He beamed at Paweł. "Exciting, no?"

"Was it valuable, this thing you found?"

The boy thought about it. "You couldn't go into a bank or a moneychanger's or a pawnshop and get money for it."

Not worth anything, then. Paweł lost interest in the subject. "You should go now," he said, thinking of the components in the smashed computers. He could get them to Nowak by this evening, and be back here the next morning with a big wad of cash. Maybe he could buy himself a new sleeping bag.

THEY TOOK SHOVELS from the Lodge's outhouse and went back into the clearing to bury the bodies. The boy searched the dead men, removed shredded wallets and lacerated phones, dropped them all in a plastic bag. They buried Halina too. It was slow, dirty, backbreaking labour but the boy did more than his share of the work, despite the obvious discomfort from his leg. It was almost dawn before they'd finished. Paweł leaned on his shovel and looked around the clearing, which looked exactly like someone had buried a number of bodies in it.

"There's a phrase the Stasi used to use," the boy said. "Something about washing a bear."

"Washing the bear without getting wet," Paweł said. Then he scowled.

The boy grinned. "Why, Mr Pawluk. Who would ever have guessed you'd be familiar with a Stasi saying?"

Paweł had a sudden sense that the boy knew everything about him, including the time he'd spent in Berlin in his youth, a couple of years before the Fall. "It means to carry out a dangerous task without exposing one's self to risk," he said. He said it without shame. He had done nothing to feel ashamed about during those last heady days of the Berlin Wall; he'd told himself that often enough to accept it as fact.

The boy nodded. "Indeed it does."

Paweł looked about the clearing. "But you seem to be exposing yourself to a *certain* amount of risk."

The boy leaned down until their faces were just inches apart and looked him in the eye. In that moment, Paweł thought he saw a high triumphant gleam of madness on the boy's face. "This," he said, "is not really *risk* at all. This is just a bunch of hired thugs. The particular bear I'm trying to wash entails a whole different order of risk."

Paweł raised an eyebrow. "Is it worth it?"

The boy smiled. "Shall we see?" he said.

Paweł was about to reply when he heard voices coming from the track that led deeper into the forest. Looking in that direction, he saw dim lights bobbing along. For a moment he thought the thugs' friends had arrived, but as the voices came closer he heard their accents and relaxed. It was just the English.

"Well," said the boy, brushing dirt and twigs and leaf-litter off his clothes. "We're hardly in a state to receive guests, but I don't think they'll mind too much, considering. Would you like to meet them?"

There were four of them, three men and a woman. They were carrying torches and they had rucksacks on their backs and hiking boots on their feet. The men were all in their late fifties or early sixties; the woman was younger, perhaps forty. They were all dressed in that irritatingly old-fashioned way the English dressed; tweeds, shirts and ties. The woman was wearing tweed trousers and jacket over a big chunky fishing sweater. They all looked terrified.

"It's all right," the boy told them in English. "You're out now; you've got nothing to worry about."

One of the men stepped forward hesitantly and put out his hand. "You have no idea how long we've waited for this," he said in that English accent Paweł's son had once described as 'mummerset,' a kind of ham actor's version of a West Country accent. It just sounded like English to Paweł.

"I know," said the boy.

All of a sudden a patch of forest seemed to shimmer into life, like the monster in that Schwarzenegger movie Paweł had seen once, and a figure wearing a sort of all-over suit of grey rags stepped into the clearing. It pulled back the hood of its suit, revealing the face of a young black man. Just behind him two more figures phased into existence, huge blond men carrying automatic weapons.

"Problems?" asked the young man, looking at

the churned-up earth where Paweł and the boy had buried the thugs.

"Nothing we didn't expect," the boy told him. "You?"

The young man shook his head while looking suspiciously at Paweł. "The map's accurate; they were waiting for me at the dustoff. All we had to do was walk back."

The boy nodded and Paweł thought he saw a huge weight lift off his shoulders. "All right, then. Take everyone inside and get them cleaned up. There's a change of clothes for everybody. Excuse the mess."

"Is this going to happen every time we do this?" asked the young man.

"No," said the boy. "Sometimes it might be really dangerous."

The young man snorted and went to chivvy the English, who were standing huddled nervously together, into the lodge. One of the big blond men said, "This is a lot of bloodshed for what was supposed to be a routine job."

The boy shrugged. "I think we've flushed out another player." He tossed the big man the bag containing the wallets and phones. "They'll have transport somewhere nearby; search it and then get rid of it. Then see if you can find out who they were and who they were working for."

The big man held up the plastic bag and squinted at the contents. "Shouldn't be hard; if they were carrying ID they weren't professionals."

The boy nodded. "That's what I thought. Anyway, I want to be out of here in half an hour. Send someone out to sweep for backup and I'll meet you all back at the rendezvous point in two days."

"Okay." And the two men pulled up their hoods and disappeared again. For such large men, they moved almost soundlessly across the forest floor; Paweł could barely hear them leave.

When they'd gone, the boy said, "So, how long have you known about them?"

"The English?" said Paweł. He shrugged. "All my life."

"Do you know where they've come from?"

Paweł shrugged again. "I'm a gamekeeper."

"Apart from the Berlin Years."

"I'm a gamekeeper," he said again. "My father was a gamekeeper, and his father. We go where we want to in the forest. Sometimes we meet English gamekeepers."

The boy looked into the woods. "Well, it's forest on both sides of the border," he said, half to himself. "I suppose sometimes it can be hard to know which side you're on." He looked at Paweł.

For quite a long time, they stood looking at each other. There seemed, Paweł thought, no point in denying it. "They say you can have these," he said finally, nodding at the Lodge. "Try and take any more out, and you'll be stopped."

"And this message is from...?"

"Does it matter?"

"From the same people who sent the mafia boys?"

"No. That was someone else. I don't know who and I don't know why." Paweł watched the boy thinking about this. "You seem to have many more enemies than friends."

"That is hard to argue with," the boy agreed. He looked at Paweł and said, "How old are you, by the way?"

Which was such an unusual question, considering the situation, that Paweł didn't even think of lying. "I'm almost ninety," he said.

"You're ninety-eight," said the boy. "And you don't look a day over sixty. Life in the forest seems to agree with you."

Paweł scowled.

"You know," the boy went on, "about eighteen months ago I met a man who swore blind that time passes more slowly on the other side of the border. I thought that was bullshit. How can time pass more slowly in one place than in another? But maybe he was right. Maybe you've spent quite a lot of time over there. Hm?"

Paweł glared at him.

The boy nodded. "Thought so. Now *that* would be a secret worth killing to protect." He rubbed his face. "Okay, Mr Pawluk. We'll be leaving soon and you can go back to keeping an eye on the paths. The next time you see whoever it is you work for, tell them this isn't over."

"You *will* be stopped," warned Paweł. "Come on; you got four out. That's a victory in itself. Isn't that enough?"

"*Enough?*" said the boy. "Mr Pawluk, in the past ten years I have been chased around Europe, kidnapped, beaten up, shot at and lied to by virtually everyone I've trusted." He turned, picked up his shovel and started to carry it back towards the Lodge. Paweł thought he suddenly looked exhausted. "A lot of people have died," he went on without looking round. "Including my brother. All because someone, somewhere, wants to stop *these people* going where they want." He paused and gestured at the Lodge with the shovel. "Or because someone else wants to know how to get into the Community. Or because someone else wants to stop people finding out about the Community. I honestly don't know any more and I'm sick of it. I'm sick of being ridden around like an old pony." He looked at the shovel for a moment as if only now realising it was in his hand, then he threw it into the undergrowth and went tiredly up the steps to the front door of the Lodge.

"Tell your friends I haven't even started yet," he said, and he went inside.

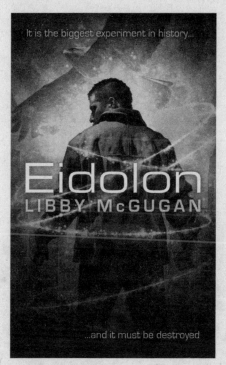

It is the biggest experiment in history...

Eidolon
LIBBY McGUGAN

...and it must be destroyed

When physicist Robert Strong — newly unemployed and single — is offered a hundred thousand pounds for a week's work, he's understandably sceptical. But Victor Amos, head of the mysterious Observation Research Board, has compelling proof that the next round of experiments at CERN's Large Hadron Collider poses a real threat to the whole world. And he needs Robert to sabotage it.

Robert's life is falling apart. His work at the Dark Matter Research Laboratory in Middlesbrough was taken away from him; his girlfriend, struggling to cope with the loss of her sister, has left. He returns home to Scotland, seeking sanctuary and rest, and instead starts to question his own sanity as the dead begin appearing to him, in dreams and in waking. Accepting Amos's offer, Robert flies to Geneva, but as he infiltrates CERN, everything he once understood about reality and science, about the boundary between life and death, changes forever.

Mixing science, philosophy and espionage, Libby McGugan's stunning debut is a thriller like no other.

'A real feat of the imagination, this is a really
exceptional book, unlike anything I've ever read before.'
Chris Beckett
Arthur C. Clarke Award winner

TONY BALLANTYNE
DREAM LONDON

UK ISBN: 978-1-78108-173-0 • US ISBN: 978-1-78108-174-7 • £7.99/$7.99 CAN $9.99

Captain Jim Wedderburn has looks, style and courage. He's adored by women, respected by
men and feared by his enemies. He's the man to find out who has twisted London into this
strange new world. But in Dream London the city changes a little every night and the people
change a little every day. The towers are growing taller, the parks have hidden themselves
away and the streets form themselves into strange new patterns. There are people sailing in
from new lands down the river, new criminals emerging in the East End and a path spiraling
down to another world.

Everyone is changing, no one is who they seem to be.